Wanted

Caren Gallimore

Heart Ally Books, LLC
Camano Island, Washington

Wanted

Cover Art by Fran Armstrong

Published by:

Heart Ally Books, LLC
heartallybooks.com
26910 92nd Ave NW C5-406
Stanwood, WA 98292

Published on Camano Island, WA, USA

ISBN-13: 978-1-63107-085-3 (paperback)

ISBN-13: 978-1-63107-086-0 (epub)

10 9 8 7 6 5 4 3 2 1

Contents

Dedication

To my family. You are the story of my life. I love you all.

Dear Reader

T hank you for purchasing my book.

Saddle up and get ready to ride with Cailyn Daniels through the Colorado mountains of 1885. But don't come unarmed. Caitlyn is an excellent shot with her Winchester rifle, but she's on a mission to rescue her fourteen-month-old son.

Luckily, neither you nor Caitlyn will be alone on this treacherous journey. Since Dakota Cabe, the rugged, handsome outlaw and father of her son, joins the pursuit just in time.

I love my characters, hope you will too, and I thank them for doing most of the writing.

Chapter 1

April 1885
Bisweak, Colorado

Caitlyn Daniels stepped across the wooden sidewalk, trying to avoid the loose planks and thick tobacco deposits that splattered the walk. She was thankful she had worn her usual riding skirt rather than an elaborate dress. She glanced up. The town's women were huddled together in a deep foray with Mrs. Clark, who led the gathering. Caitlyn checked for a detour. No doubt, Mrs. Clark would have another critical remark in store for her. It's why Caitlyn dreaded these annoying, but necessary trips to town.

She lifted her chin with dignity and stepped off the weathered board-walk to cross the street. The sharp whistles of cowboys and the protest-ing lowing of a cattle drive moving into town stopped her. Damn. She couldn't pass in time unless she ran, which, of course, would not be ladylike. Another reason why Mrs. Clark would declare her dresses not fit to purchase. After all, shouldn't dressmakers wear their designs instead of everyday riding attire? She had better things to do than promenade around in layers of fabric, despite her love for creating them.

The boisterous whoops and hollers of men rose above the thick dust squall rolling into town. She notched her chin up higher and strode back to where the women huddled.

The cattlemen drove the herd into town with the exuberance of men thankful to see the end of a rough and tedious roundup.

All, except for one.

She raised her hand, shielding her eyes from the setting sun to assess the man. He rode apart from the others. Trail boss? No. He had separated from the group and headed in the women's direction. A self-chosen loner, now the job was done. Or was he like her, an outcast?

His horse, a feisty Mustang, would have been too much for most men, but the stranger rode the horse as though the two were one beast. The man held the reins in one hand while his other hand dangled at his side near his pistol. It wasn't a hostile gesture, but one of caution. She tilted her head and examined him further. A large, dusty Stetson covered most of his face, keeping his long dark hair out of his eyes and tucked into his well-worn duster. A weary gray bandanna was tied around his neck, his bearing erect and primed as if he expected calamity to strike. He wasn't old, maybe a year or two older than she, but he appeared seasoned. Hard worked muscles showed through the strains in his shirt and the fit of his pants, and every bit as intimidating as a prairie fire out of control.

"A womanizer, that one." Mrs. Clark's tone sounded like a chicken gossiping in the hen house. She adjusted her ample bosom and peered through her smudged spectacles.

"Lordy. Not a woman in town will be safe with that one running loose," Miss Bee replied. She approached the group, her tawny eyes fixed on the lone stranger.

"I wouldn't mind." Mary Ann, the schoolteacher, sighed and dabbed the perspiration from her neck with a handkerchief.

"Watch your tongue, Mary Ann." Mrs. Clark nodded in Caitlyn's direction.

"Indeed. Bad sort of man. I wouldn't dare wander outside with the likes of him roaming the streets," Mary Ann said with a faint smile on her lips. Still dotting the moisture from her cleavage, she tilted her head, her gaze trailing after the stranger.

"More likely, he won't be safe roaming the streets," Miss Bee stated and winked at Mary Ann when Mrs. Clark wasn't looking.

The women giggled and cast awkward glimpses at Caitlyn. She nodded a quick greeting to the ladies, her lips sealed, lest she say something she would later regret.

She had accepted their opinion of her a long time ago when she and her father first moved to this town. The Wild Filly, they had named her because she could ride and shoot better than most men. She didn't care.

The stranger was an unusual man, not like the ones who moseyed around town. She had better manners than to stare like the women next to her, but damn, she couldn't help herself. He was so out of the ordinary, so different, more heavily armed than the other men were, but the weapons fit him as if they were a part of his anatomy. She squinted at him as he advanced toward them. He didn't strike her as a womanizer, not that she knew what that entailed.

Nevertheless, she didn't think of herself as a prude, especially at the age of twenty. Mrs. Clark's son, Pete, was a womanizer. A blubbering idiot who slobbered all over a woman's hand, if a woman was stupid enough to offer her hand to him, which she never did, poor manners or not. No, she couldn't picture this cowboy going to the fuss of it all.

The stranger rode abreast of the women. He pushed his Stetson back and assessed each one like livestock up for auction. One by one, each woman glanced away, discomforted by his bold appraisal.

Then his frosty gray eyes fastened on Caitlyn. His eyes so penetrating and harsh, she shivered despite the afternoon's steamy heat. Nevertheless, she didn't lower her gaze, which would have been ladylike. Why should she? He had disrespected them. Instead, she straightened her shoulders and gave him her most contemptuous glare.

He not only held her glare but also continued his scrutiny of her, shifting in his saddle to do so. In response, she adjusted her stance, set her jaw, and placed both hands on her hips in bold defiance.

"Caitlyn Daniels." Mrs. Clark's voice went a tad lower than the sound of thunder. "Good Lord, act like a lady for once in your life."

Caitlyn ignored the old biddy. She had been mistaken. This self-confident, insolent cowboy was like any other ill-witted bore of a man. Judging a woman by sight and finding her inadequate. Her quick disappointment in him stung. She shrugged off the unusual feeling. Better to make it clear to the man she was not the fainting filly in distress like these other women. But she wasn't prepared for the warm, enticing, intimate smile he bestowed upon her as if he had seen her in less than her undergarments. She dropped her glare then snapped her gaze back up, annoyed at his easy conquest of her. Complete amusement sparkled in his eyes.

"Why you damn, cocky son of a b—"

The sharp snap of Mrs. Clark's fan popping into action stopped Caitlyn.

"This, my dear..." the fan batted the air close to Caitlyn's nose, "...is the reason why I told your father you would never find yourself a husband. You shame the very essence of femininity. Look at me; I'm speaking to you, girl."

The sharp edge of Mrs. Clark's fan forced Caitlyn to face the older woman.

"Look at you." Mrs. Clark dropped the fan to the top of Caitlyn's chest.

She had to take a step back to avoid an intended whack to her riding vest.

"Running around in this tasteless garb." The woman ran a critical eye over Caitlyn's fresh, but well-worn riding attire. "Why don't you wear a dress for heaven's sakes?" The fan lifted the faded green vest to reveal a revolver tucked into her riding skirt. "Riding a horse like a man and carrying a gun. It's up to a man to protect you. What is wrong with you?" She flapped her fan up and down in a display of disapproval.

Caitlyn leaned away from the fan each time it was used to make a point.

"Attracting men with your pretty ways, and then making them appear like fools once they're smitten with you. You'll be a spinster unless you change your ways and start acting like a lady. I'm thankful my Peter saw through your charms."

The last sentence, she spat rather than spoke. Ah, so her slight to Peter had not gone unnoticed.

"You are a disgrace. Why, if your mother still lived—"

"With all due respect, Mrs. Clark, please leave my mother out of this."

"Someone needs to take her place and rectify the mess you've made of yourself. Your father doesn't seem to care."

There were only two delicate places in Caitlyn's heart, and Mrs. Clark had managed to hit both.

Caitlyn turned away. Across the street, the lone cowboy dismounted at Ruby's Saloon, the pleasure house of ill repute. When he opened the door, hearty laughter and the banging of an off-key piano rushed out the door. The bristling of her back startled Caitlyn, and she laughed at her sudden possessiveness of a mere stranger, and a cocky stranger at that. As expected, he wasn't the kind of man who would fuss around courting a woman.

Still, she couldn't shake the warm, tantalizing sensation of his smile that even Mrs. Clark's dressing down hadn't extinguished. She concentrated on the saloon's rickety door and the piano's faint melody drifting through the air. Something unfamiliar rumbled in her heart.

Holding her gloved hands out in front of her, she regarded her attire. Her riding gear clean, the gun essential. A pistol was easy to carry, unlike toting around a man. She owned dresses. For heaven's sake, she made them. She even owned a sidesaddle for her horse, but Lord, it would take her all day to get to town and back in a ruffled dress on a sidesaddle.

Mrs. Clark had been right—she was an odd one compared to other women.

Caitlyn tilted her head, amazed at her train of thoughts. When she glanced about, she found herself alone on the walkway. The women had discreetly retreated.

Fine with her. She was better off alone.

~ * ~

Two weeks later, Caitlyn prepared to make another dreaded excursion into town. She examined her small wardrobe and selected one of her few dresses.

"This is pure vanity." She held the vivid coral dress under her chin and rolled her eyes at her image in the mirror. Batting her eyelashes for effect, she laughed. "No, now you look silly."

A sigh slipped through her lips. "Though, talking to oneself may be worse."

She tossed the dress onto the bed. No point fighting herself. Her riding attire was practical for going into town, but perhaps a smaller revolver. A derringer? She snorted. It was unlikely she could hit a barn with that useless gun unless she were within two feet of the building.

Peering out the window, she spotted her father hard at work preparing the land for a new crop. Practical. Her mother had taught her proper etiquette, but her father had taught her to be practical.

Picking up her revolver, she tucked the gun into the back of her riding skirt. Easy to reach and not obtrusive. She gave herself another quick assessment in the mirror and nodded. It would do. She'd wasted enough time. The sooner she got to town, the quicker she'd be back to help with chores.

The ride into town she took at a comfortable clip, enjoying the fresh air against her face. Entering the town limits, she slowed to an unhurried pace, riding with both reins held high, just like a lady.

"Oh, bother." Mrs. Clark's opinion of her wasn't something she could change.

Caitlyn leaned over the withers of her horse and moved her foot from the stirrup to examine the old saddle cinch. It should have been fixed long before now.

"I'm sorry, Star." She patted her horse and slowed even more as she entered the town limits and headed for the blacksmith shop. Then a thought struck her. For all she knew, she might be riding home bareback. A rush of giggles shot through her. Mrs. Clark's hair would stand on end if she barreled out of town without a saddle. Caitlyn pressed a hand to her chest to stop another giggle, but was unsuccessful.

"I hope I'm not your source of amusement."

A man's deep voice and unexpected appearance caused her to jerk and almost kick Star into a bolt. Her cheeks heated.

The strange cattleman from the roundup had caught her unaware and laughing.

"Sir, I can assure you that you are not in the least bit funny." She straightened her posture and drew back her shoulders. Now she wished she had worn a dress and sat in a sidesaddle. Well, perhaps not a sidesaddle since the cinch was the primary reason for her trip.

"My apologies, ma'am. Good day." He tipped his large Stetson. His cool, steel gray eyes fastened on hers, but a flicker of warmth sparked.

"Good day to you, sir." Adjusting to a more ladylike stance, she assumed an aristocratic air. The end of her gun pinched her in the fanny, and she winced. She urged Star forward, then realized she had passed her intended destination, the blacksmith shop. Her shoulders drooped.

Her obliviousness to her surroundings disturbed her. It was the man. He had distracted her with his-his...damn, it was the man himself. She brought Star to a halt and backed up.

She dipped her chin to the man leaning against the stable wall, his gaze still upon her, she added, "I was coming to the livery today."

He smiled and pushed against the wall to stand straighter.

She flicked a spot of dust from her collar and waited.

"I see."

"Actually, I had a late start." *Why on earth do I need to explain myself to this man?*

"That can work against you."

Oh, for the love of God, Caitlyn, do not say another word to him. "My saddle strap needs to be replaced." With a slap, she placed one gloved hand across her mouth in case it continued to talk without her brain engaged.

His gaze broke from hers and traveled down to the saddle strap. "You're lucky you made it this far." He lifted his head and assessed her with a warm familiarity.

Shifting in her saddle, she inspected the thin, worn leather. Indeed, it had been luck.

"Yes, but there were other things more pressing to tend to." She dusted at an invisible spot on her saddle horn.

"Your safety should be the most pressing," he said.

She had nothing to offer back. It was as clear to her as it had been to Mrs. Clark; she didn't have a feminine bone in her body. "Oh, well, thank you. I think." Why didn't he move out of the way?

"I'm helping Sam today, while I wait for another roundup."

"Sam?"

"Yes, the blacksmith."

"Of course." Sam. "Well then, I guess you're the man I'm wanting." Did she just say that? She stared straight at him and fought the heat smoldering at her collarbone.

"Yes, ma'am. I am." He smiled, his eyes sparkling with a mischievous inner fire. He stepped forward, took the reins from her hands, and then walked her horse into the barn. "Name's Dakota Cabe."

"Caitlyn Daniels."

He paused, gave her another quick inspection, and resumed his lead.

She might as well be naked in the saddle, but she nodded.

Entering the livery, she started to dismount, but the leather strap gave way. She struggled to free herself from the bootstrap and keep her horse under control, but without the reins, she couldn't.

"I got you," Cabe replied.

He did, both Caitlyn and her saddle.

For a moment, she couldn't react. Cabe's strength alarmed and disoriented her. She'd never been this close to a man before, or this helpless to extract herself from an unexpected situation. His arm tightened around her waist, and he plucked her free from the startled horse.

"Shhh—easy girl," he whispered to her mare. Removing a knife from his boot, he cut the remaining strap.

Star calmed immediately, and Caitlyn removed herself from the seat and his grip.

"Thank you, Mr. Cabe." She adjusted her vest back into place to cover her gun.

"Of course, Miss... Or is it Mrs. Daniels?"

"Miss."

"When will you be back for your horse and saddle?" Placing the seat on the wall of the stall, he faced her.

"I'll need my horse before dark, and my saddle too, if that gives you enough time. If not, I'll come back tomorrow for my saddle."

"Do you live far from town?"

A moment passed, and she wondered at his question but didn't answer.

He held her scrutiny. "Only wondering how'd you get home if I didn't finish the saddle."

"By horseback, Mr. Cabe." Was the man dense?

"Without a saddle?"

Ah, so he wondered what kind of woman rides without a saddle. Mrs. Clark would have a quick response. Caitlyn took in a deep breath and let it out. It was pointless to pretend to be the lady she wasn't.

"Yes. Bareback." She raised her chin, waiting for his disapproval.

He smiled. "I thought so. I'll have it ready." He untied the small purse she had secured around her saddle horn and handed it to her.

She started to leave and peeked back at him. He was still smiling.

The day's heat settled in, so she hurried to the mercantile store. She had a small amount of money to spend, but she needed more fabric. If she had one womanly skill she was adept at, it was needlework. Her work didn't bring in much money, but it brought in some. Moreover, she enjoyed creating dresses, even though she wasn't inclined to wear them.

Before entering the mercantile, she glanced back at the livery barn one last time. Dakota Cabe was hard at work, shirtless, his bandanna tied around his head keeping his long, tousled dark-brown hair in check. He looked up, and she dashed into the store.

"Can I help you, Miss Daniels?"

She twirled around. One thin hand rose above the counter and waved at her, and then Raymond Clark's head popped up.

"Raymond. I didn't see you."

"Sorry, I was putting the cash drawer underneath the counter."

"It's been a good day, then?"

"One of the best we've had. Pa's going to be real pleased when he comes back in this afternoon. I hope Aunt Beatrice will be too."

Caitlyn doubted anything would please Mrs. Clark, but she kept her thoughts to herself. "That's wonderful. So, your pa and aunt are letting you mind the store alone?"

"Pa wasn't feeling well this morning, and Aunt Bea went to the bank; she'll be back soon. But yes, I work alone now and again."

She smiled at the lad, who beamed with pride.

"Were you interested in some fabric today? We got a new shipment in yesterday." Raymond trotted around the counter and motioned for her to follow him to the back. At fourteen, he was lanky and still trying to control his long limbs. As if in response to her observations, he bumped the first roll of material onto its side.

"Sorry, Miss Daniels." He bent, righted the roll of fabric, and then knocked over the next bolt. A rush of bright red touched his neck and raced up his face.

"I think I see the print I want, Raymond." The front chime tinkled.

She scanned the entrance and frowned. Two motley men had entered the store. They were unkempt and, by their behavior, drunk.

"Raymond, wait—" she whispered.

Too late. Raymond was already greeting them. "Can I help you, gentlemen?"

"You sure can, boy." The larger man smirked at his companion, then shoved Raymond toward the counter. "Your money box will be good."

Raymond appeared neither shocked nor scared. "I'll do no such thing, sir."

Closing her eyes, she prayed. Please, Raymond, give them the box.

The two men stared at one another in amused astonishment.

"A bit young to be telling your elders what to do," the taller man said, then drew his gun and backhanded Raymond.

He lost his footing and knocked into both display cabinets before careening into the flour bin.

"Stop." She hadn't meant to speak out, but she couldn't stand there and do nothing.

Easing out her handgun, she cocked it in the folds of her riding skirt. She aimed at the man who had assaulted Raymond and stepped out from the fabric section.

"Miss Daniels. Go back." Raymond lurched to his feet like a ghost and tried to get between her and the men.

The other gunman aimed at Raymond's head, and she fired her pistol. The gun flew from his hand.

His companion drew and cocked his own gun and pointed the barrel at Raymond. "I'll kill the stupid boy."

She re-aimed her gun at him, disregarding the sudden flash of motion outside the store.

"Damn bitch. Kyle, she shot my hand."

His companion took stock of his hand. "Quit whining and get your gun."

Her mistake for not aiming to kill.

"And grab the money box. Someone's bound to have heard the shot and gone after the sheriff." He headed for the counter.

Raymond squinted in Caitlyn's direction. She started to shake her head when the door banged open, and Cabe stepped in. His eyes were a glacial gray. He held one gun on Kyle and the second one on Kyle's companion.

Small beads of sweat trickled down his chest to his low-riding gun belt, and for a moment, she lost her focus. "Hello, Miss Daniels."

"Mr. Cabe." She refocused on the man in her sights.

"Shopping?"

"I was."

"Until you were distracted?"

"One could say that."

He glanced at Kyle, and his bleeding right hand then did a quick assessment of her. Heat slid through her. "You all right?"

"I am."

"I can handle this until the sheriff comes if you would like to continue your shopping."

She smiled but didn't lower her gun.

The door burst open again, and Mrs. Clark entered. "Good Lord." She blinked her eyes in a furious display of displeasure at the chaos in her store. The men, the guns, and then her nephew, covered in flour. She removed her fan with astonishing speed, then whacked the nearest target to her. Dakota Cabe.

In rapid sequence, Kyle shot wild in Dakota's direction, Caitlyn shot Kyle, Dakota shot Kyle's companion, and Mrs. Clark collapsed.

Caitlyn shoved her pistol back behind her and hurried to Mrs. Clark's side. "Mrs. Clark?" No response.

Caitlyn did a quick perusal and breathed a sigh of relief. The old biddy hadn't been shot. Snatching the fan from the woman's hand, she circulated the air around her. Loosening the woman's collar, she noticed the sudden crowd forming outside the mercantile. Sheriff Metcalf and his deputies rushed inside.

Metcalf motioned his deputies to cover both sides. "Hell's fire. Has Mrs. Clark been shot?"

"No, she fainted," Caitlyn said.

"What the hell happened?"

Mrs. Clark roused and locked eyes with Caitlyn. "I should have known you would be in the middle of this." Mrs. Clark struggled to her feet. "Raymond?"

"I'm all right, Aunt Bea."

"Well, thank the heavens. Sheriff arrest that naked man." Mrs. Clark shrugged out of Caitlyn's hold and pointed at Dakota.

Immediately, he turned both pistols around and held them out to the sheriff. "Sorry, ma'am, I would have thrown my shirt back on, but I heard gunfire."

"Who are you?" The sheriff took his guns.

One deputy came alongside the sheriff. "Both men dead, Sheriff."

"Well, don't stand there. Get those men out of here and find out who they were." The sheriff redirected his attention to Dakota. "Answer the question."

"Dakota Cabe. Came in with the cattle crew. I'm working with Sam until I ride out."

"I don't like new faces. Never have," the sheriff said.

Watching the men as the deputies dragged them out, Dakota nodded. "Can't say I blame you."

"Sheriff," Caitlyn interjected. "If not for Mr. Cabe, Raymond and I would be dead now."

The sheriff's gaze slid from her face to Dakota's. "You know anything about these two men?"

"No, but I'm familiar with their kind."

"Meaning?"

"There's more than two. I suspect you're in for more trouble." Dakota turned to Mrs. Clark. "But I wouldn't let that be common knowledge."

Caitlyn observed the two men with interest.

"You staying in the stables?" the sheriff asked.

"Until the next roundup."

"Anything I need to know about you?"

"Nothing of interest."

Sheriff Metcalf's shoulders relaxed. "Normal policy is to hold a man's gun for twenty-four hours after a shooting, but I reckon if there's more out there, we might need an extra gun. Don't make me regret this."

Dakota took back his guns.

"You might want to have the doc take a look." The sheriff nodded at Dakota's bicep and then headed for the door.

"Sheriff." Mrs. Clark threw her hands on her hips. "What about my store?"

"Woman, two men are dead. I think you can handle your store." The door slammed behind him.

Caitlyn came up to Cabe. "Let me look at your arm."

He assessed his arm. "It's just a nick. If you're all right, I'll head back to the livery."

"I can show you where the doctor is."

"No need. I've had worse."

She stared at him, not doubting that one bit. "Regardless, let me put a stitch or two in your arm. I'm good with a needle. In fact, I insist, unless you are afraid I'll ruin your reputation."

He chuckled.

"Caitlyn Daniels!"

She winced at Mrs. Clark's shrill voice.

"Have you no decency?"

"Aunt Bea, Miss Daniels kept me from getting killed." Raymond wiped the flour from his eyes.

Mrs. Clark's lips thinned as she pressed them together, but she didn't speak.

"Your saddle will be ready when you are." Dakota turned to Mrs. Clark. "Ma'am."

Quietly, Caitlyn made her way back to the fabrics and picked out the materials she needed, along with a needle and thread.

Mrs. Clark calculated the amount, and Caitlyn paid without comment.

Making a few more stops before dusk, she then hurried to the livery. She slipped inside when she was sure Mrs. Clark was nowhere nearby.

"Mr. Cabe?" She peered into the dark interior.

"It's ready."

"Oh, good Lord!" Grabbing the railing next to her, she hiccupped with fear. "I didn't see you there."

From the shadows behind her, Dakota stepped out. He wore a faded blue shirt, which accentuated his tanned skin and gray eyes. He placed his hand over hers on the railing in reassurance. "I'm sorry. I didn't mean to spook you."

She shifted her weight and withdrew her hand from under his. "I am hardly spooked, Mr. Cabe, but you do seem to materialize out of nowhere." She took a settling breath. "I brought a needle and thread."

"It isn't necessary."

"Now who's spooked?"

A slight grin lined his lips. He pushed several saddles to the side and dusted off a spot for her to sit, and then kneeled in front of her.

"Can you unbutton your shirt? It wouldn't do to stitch your shirt to you."

"All right." Once he'd unbuttoned his shirt, he tugged the fabric down below the wound. "Has Mrs. Clark recovered?"

Caitlyn smiled. "Yes. At least, until my next abomination..." She paused and fixed her eyes up at the rafters with a sigh. "Which I suppose would be now."

She sighed. *What am I doing? I don't know this man, and here I am practically insisting he disrobe in front of me.* She crinkled her nose and sat up straighter. Opening her purse, she retrieved the ointment she kept for her horse and dabbed some on his wound.

Threading her needle, she began her task. "This will take at least seven stitches. If you're still in town, I can remove them, or... Of course, you can remove them yourself."

No doubt, he had done that before, too. She knotted the thread and examined her work. The scar would be minimal. Two dots of fresh blood trickled onto his shoulder. She frowned and brushed his long hair to the side to examine his neck. "Did you know you have a cut on the back of your neck?"

"I suspected."

"But how—" She pressed her lips together to halt a smirk, then rose to her feet. "You said my saddle was ready?"

"It is. I'll saddle your horse."

"Thank you, Mr. Cabe, but I'm capable of saddling my own horse. How much do I owe you?"

"No offense, Miss Daniels, I didn't mean to imply you couldn't, but I'd lose my job here if Sam came in and saw a lady saddling her own horse."

"Oh."

"And you'll have to settle with Sam. I only do the work."

Nodding, she waited patiently while he saddled Star, then she mounted and headed home. As soon as she passed from view, she urged her horse into a full gallop. The wind snatched at her hair and jiggled it loose. She laughed. *Ole Mrs. Clark had assaulted the ferocious Dakota Cabe.*

~ * ~

After dinner and dishes, Caitlyn headed for the creek to get water for coffee. She loved this time of day. The chores done, and it was time to settle in for the night, just her and her pa over a cup of coffee.

She squatted next to the creek and dipped the pot into the stream. The slow plodding sound of a horse jolted her to attention. A solitary traveler this time of night? Maybe, but they would come by road, not hover out on the ridge. Nestling her pot in the creek so the water wouldn't carry it away, she crept back into the seclusion of the pines. She waited, adjusting her position to follow the horse and rider.

Even in the dark, she would know the large Stetson and feisty horse. Dakota Cabe. He couldn't see her, but she could see him. Though he didn't appear to be hiding, he wasn't coming for a visit either.

Horse and rider paused on the ridge above the house. She wanted to push back the pine branches to get a better view, but no doubt, his quick eye would catch the movement.

She considered his profile.

He was armed for war and far too casual about it. Caitlyn rolled her eyes. Far too casual? She snorted at the thought, yet there wasn't a better description. He had two pistols, two rifles, an ammunition belt slung across his chest, and the glint of a knife in the side of his boot. The man was dressed to kill, not to round up cattle.

So why wasn't she alarmed? If she had any sense, she would be. He wasn't a simple cowboy waiting for the next roundup. He was a dangerous man. The vision of Mrs. Clark striking him with her fan came to mind, and Caitlyn had to bite her lower lip to stop the smile.

He hadn't come to hurt her or her father. There was no sense of danger in his presence. She tilted her head at the thought. Nevertheless, he had told the sheriff that the two thugs in the goods store might not be the only ones.

As if he sensed he was being watched, he turned in her direction. She pressed her lips together and cast her gaze to the ground, waiting and afraid to inhale. Surely, he couldn't see her in the shadowy woods. She could barely make out her own fingers. The seconds ticked off, and she held her breath, keeping her gaze on a small, insignificant patch of black space before her.

He moved his horse a few steps toward her, and she closed her eyes. Abruptly, he drew back on the reins and rode off.

She stepped out from the pine cover and watched him ride away. Why had he come? Several notions came to mind, and none of them displeased her.

Chapter 2

A week passed, and every night Dakota Cabe made his mysterious visits. He never varied his approach, so she was alarmed when she spotted his horse, but not the man. She leaned out from the security of the trees. What could have happened?

"You always hide in the pines?"

She went for her revolver, but lost her balance in her precarious perch and landed on her hands and knees instead. "Good God, what's wrong with you?" She cursed.

He extended his hand out to her, and she slapped it away. She burned with annoyance and embarrassment. "Me hiding? At least, I don't spy on people." Scrambling to her feet, she glared up at him, tilting her chin in indignation. She gave him a quick once-over. "You're barely dressed this evening."

"Excuse me?" One eyebrow lifted in question.

She dipped her chin at his attire. "Only one gun?"

He gave her a crooked smile. "I thought I would visit your father. Perhaps have a cup of coffee."

She frowned. "My father?"

"Yes. Isn't that who you sit with on the front porch?"

"Why?" She hadn't expected this.

"Are you always this suspicious?"

"It tends to pay off in the long run." She dusted off her knees.

He smiled at her. "Yes, I guess it does. But I'm here to warn him."

"About what?"

"Nine men are camped on the north side of your land." He scanned the space over her head as if they were behind her.

"I haven't seen any squatters."

"That's why I'm here."

It was ridiculous to stand in the pine trees arguing with him.

"All right then, come for a cup of coffee." She tried to keep the irritation out of her voice, but it irked her that Dakota Cabe had come to tell her father something she should have known.

Her father met them a few steps from the front porch, his rifle in his hand. "Caitlyn? Do we have a visitor?" His tone was relaxed, but firm and to the point.

"Yes, Pa. He is the man who fixed my saddle. He's working for Sam."

Dakota moved past her and held out his hand. "Dakota Cabe, sir."

She gritted her teeth at her lack of manners.

Her father gripped his hand and shook it. "Jim Daniels. Working for Sam, are you?"

"Yes, sir. Until the next roundup."

"I see," commented her pa as he inspected Dakota with more than idle curiosity. "Care for a cup of coffee?"

"Much obliged, sir."

She swept past the two men and dashed inside. "Please have a seat, Mr. Cabe."

Chairs scraped on the porch as she set about making the coffee. When she reappeared, the two men were chatting. Relief swept over her, but she didn't know why.

"So, to what do I owe this visit?"

Sitting next to her father, she waited for the men's description camping on their land.

"Nine men are camped on the north side of your property."

As Dakota relaxed, her father grew tense. "I take it these aren't typical squatters."

"No, sir. These aren't family men. I'm confident they are part of a gang that came into town last week and tried to hold up the mercantile store." Dakota nodded in Caitlyn's direction.

She grimaced. "I'm sorry, Pa. I didn't see the need to tell you."

"Tell me? Were you there? Was that the day you went into town? Why am I just hearing about it, Caitlyn?"

She glanced from her father to Cabe. "I didn't want to worry you. It's not like I was involved."

At Dakota's slight grin, she shot him a hot glare.

"Well, sir, thank you for the coffee. I'll head back to town now." He started to rise.

"Just a moment, Mr. Cabe. How did you know they were camping on my land?"

Caitlyn smirked and waited for his response.

"I come this way to ride. Happened to see the men and thought you should be warned."

"Much obliged to you, Mr. Cabe."

Humph. Just like that, her father accepted his bland excuse for riding over their land. Wait! What was she thinking? What had she wanted him to say?

Standing, her father reached out his hand in farewell. "Something tells me running cattle isn't your main work."

Her gaze flew to her father, then to Dakota.

Dakota shook her father's hand with a firm grip. "It's what I do now, sir. Ma'am." He touched the brim of his hat and offered a slight smile to Caitlyn before heading to his horse.

They watched him ride off, then her father turned to her. "Anything else you've forgotten to tell me?"

There was no reason to blush, and she was infuriated at herself when she did. "No, Pa."

"Well, I'll go into town tomorrow and tell Sheriff Metcalf what that young man said. I want you to stay close to the house while I'm gone."

~ * ~

It wasn't in her character to stay home and rely on a stranger's word. As soon as she finished the chores and her father left for town, she saddled her mare and headed for the north side. Yes, she had promised her father she would stay close to home, but their land was their home. All of it. Besides, she'd be back before her father returned.

She took the back trail and circled northwest. A longer route, but it gave her the most concealment. So far, no sign of men camping, but if they were in hiding, she wouldn't see them.

She was five miles out when Dakota Cabe came riding hard toward her. Her back bristled. Why was he here?

"What are you doing out here?" he demanded when he rode up beside her.

"Excuse me?" She bit her lip and the quick retort.

"I saw your father in town talking to the sheriff. He seemed to think you were safe at home." He grunted, scanning the terrain. "I figured differently."

Dismounting, she glared at him. "Why is this any of your business?"

He dismounted as well. "You have no common sense, do you?"

His remark stung her, but she didn't let it show. "Common sense? This is my land and my home. For the life of me, I can't figure out why you're here, or why any of this concerns you."

"I told your father about the men, and he had the sense to go to the sheriff. You, however, are foolish enough to ride out here alone. What were you planning? Single-handedly confronting a pack of men?" He threw his hat to the ground in disgust. "Like I said, no common sense."

Walking away from the confines of the forest, she tried to control her flaring temper. She twirled around to address him, but he was right on her heels. "I am no fool. I didn't intend to confront them. I merely wanted to see the situation for myself."

"I told you the situation. You should be at home. Not out here."

"You told me about the situation. It's my place to decide what to do."

"Your father decided. He went to the sheriff. The sheriff will handle this."

Unbelievable. She shook her head. Who does this man think he is? Then an awful thought occurred to her. "Are you one of them?"

He glared at her as if her head had swiveled from front to back. "Hell no."

"Then why the interest?" She squinted past him at her horse standing in the trees a fair distance away. A shiver shot up her spine. Dismounting had been foolish. Perhaps indeed, she didn't have any common sense.

"Damn it, woman. Get down."

His hand came down hard on her shoulder, and she fell to her knees. She struggled to loosen his grasp and retrieve her pistol. "Get off me."

His eyes were wide and chilled as he stared at her in the growing darkness. "Don't be a fool. Those nine men you're so eager to check out are heading this way. Be still."

Try as she might, she couldn't dislodge his solid grip on her shoulder. "Then they are headed for my home. This isn't your affair."

"You have no idea what you are about to confront."

"Get off of me, or I'll shoot you."

He seemed surprised she had freed her revolver, but she had it pushed hard into his side.

"Are you that stupid?" he asked.

She slapped him when he loosened his grip on her.

"Good God, what is wrong with you, woman?"

His words bit into her, and she flinched but held his stern glare.

"Fine. I was trying to protect you."

"I don't need a man to keep me safe." Fear crawled up her spine.

Indeed, the nine men were coming down the main trail toward them. Rough-looking men and well-armed. So far, they hadn't seen them or their horses. What had she planned? She had intended to locate the men and assess their intentions, but she hadn't expected men like them. She felt foolish. He had been right. She had no idea what she might confront.

Dropping her gun from his side, she waited for his direction. He held a finger to his lips and motioned her back into the trees. With caution, they slipped back to the horses. Relieved, she sighed when she was within reach of her mount.

"You do know how to shoot a rifle, I hope," he asked, jerking his rifle free from the side of his horse and handing it to her.

"Yes. Of course."

Motioning for her to lie on the ground, he removed his ammunition belt and another rifle. He stepped to the other side of the horses, crept several yards away, then laid down.

The men were almost past them when her horse whinnied. One man stopped, stared at the trees, and motioned to the others. Soon, all the men were staring in their direction.

"Damn." Dakota sighted in the first man. "I sure hope you know how to hit with some degree of accuracy."

Biting her lower lip, she hoped the same of him.

The men charged them at a full gallop, guns drawn. Caitlyn barely had time to cock the rifle before the first shot whizzed past her. Continuing to fire, the men drew down on them. Her aim was loose and merely knocked the first man from his saddle instead of striking him in the chest. Her second and third shots were deadly accurate.

Dakota shot four men, and then the remaining two were full upon them. Drawing her pistol, she scooted back on her fanny, both hands firm on her revolver. The first man hesitated and then pointed his gun at her head. She pulled the trigger, and down he went. She dashed to her feet, wild with adrenaline and fear. A man's fist caught her on the left side of her neck and spun her into the dirt face first. She rolled over and shot the man in his stomach at the same time Dakota's bullet entered his forehead.

Dakota barreled in her direction and yanked her to her feet. "Get on your horse and ride out."

"But—"

"Git."

She staggered to her horse and heaved herself into the saddle. The reins were loose in her hands when the man who had tumbled from his horse jerked her back down. She dropped to the ground with a jolt that rattled her teeth and knocked the gun from her hand.

Rolling under her horse, she watched as Dakota pulled out his boot knife and sank it to the hilt in the man's throat. He withdrew the blade, and the man dropped to his knees and fell forward.

The sight stunned her.

"You all right?"

Unable to speak, she gaped at him. When he offered her his hand, she grasped it and embraced him. "I'm sorry. You were right. I shouldn't have come out here. Those men didn't think twice about shooting us."

His arms circled her. The heat of his gun pressed hot into her back. She relaxed and breathed more easily. His embrace was powerful, secure, and comforting, and she sank into him with relief.

"I need to get my father and the sheriff." Shame blanketed her.

Perhaps, if she hadn't ridden out here, the men would still be alive. Then again, maybe they would have butchered them in their sleep. Before this happened, she had been so sure of herself, and now she was scared, anxious, and full of self-doubt.

"I'll tell your father and the sheriff. I don't want you to say anything, especially the fact that you were here."

She rested her cheek against his broad shoulder. He stroked his hand along the back of her head, comforting her in a way she hadn't been since she was a child. She stared at the dead men, suspended in disbelief.

"Come on." Draping his arm around her shoulder, he led her to the horses, blocking her view of the dead men. He gathered both reins and walked them away from the carnage.

"What about those men?"

"I'll ride into town and let the sheriff know to send his deputies out to collect them. Chances are there's a reward, so he'll have plenty of help." He stopped and swept his thumb across her cheek and brushed her hair back out of her eyes. "You'll be all right." He contemplated the terrain beyond them. His eyes were sad and weary.

She struggled to regain her courage. "But I got you involved when you didn't need to be."

"I was involved the day I saw you in town." He set his jaw. "Can you make it back to your home?"

"Would you ride with me?" The men were dead. There was nothing to fear, and yet she was afraid.

Dakota rode back with her, waited until she put her horse up for the night, and she was safe in the house before riding off.

Late that night, when her father returned home, he had much to tell her. It became chaos in town after Dakota Cabe killed the notorious Forester gang.

"All nine outlaws dead by one man. Cabe must be a crack shot or an outlaw himself," her father said, taking the soup she offered him and settling in at the table. "And he wouldn't take any reward money, either."

A retort came quickly, but she clamped her lips shut. Anything she said would make the situation worse. She needed to think this over and talk to Dakota before she said anything.

"Sheriff's interested too. Makes you wonder what Mr. Cabe was doing out there in the first place."

"He told you he rides out there."

"In the exact location as those men? Seems a bit foolhardy, given that he warned us about them. No. Don't sound right to me. He was out there for a reason." He slurped the remaining soup.

Caitlyn chewed at her lower lip to keep her tongue under control. She had created this whole mess, and she had to make it right. However, telling her father the truth might put Dakota in a worse light. "I'm going to bed, Pa."

"I'm sorry I got back so late."

"That's all right. I'm tired." In truth, the last thing she wanted to discuss was the shootings and the horrible aftermath.

"Goodnight, dear. Oh, and Caitlyn?"

"Yes, Pa?"

"I don't want you near Cabe. I made it clear to him that he's no longer welcome. He understood. Wanted to make that clear to you as well."

Fury raced up her spine and made her head swirl. She stood ramrod straight in the doorway.

"Caitlyn? Is that clear?"

She let out the breath she held. "I'm going to bed. We can talk tomorrow."

Sleep evaded her. Every time she closed her eyes, the Forester men charged her. She repeatedly shot them, but they kept coming after her. She squeezed her eyes at the memory of Dakota telling her she had no common sense, and, sure enough, he had been right.

She rose, securing a shawl around her shoulders, put her boots back on, then headed for the door. At the door, she hesitated, returned for her pistol, then walked to the creek.

The faint moon gave her enough light to find her way to the water.

Sitting, she took off her boots, raised her nightdress to her knees, and nestled her feet in the chilled creek. Paradise. Here, she could close her eyes and not see the Forester gang. She could skip back a day, be at peace with herself, and not know the misery of having chosen poorly. Leaning back on the moss-covered ground, she pulled her feet from the creek and fell asleep.

The brisk morning air jolted her awake. For a moment, she was disoriented, then she remembered the horrific shootout with the Forester gang. She dashed to her feet and headed for the house.

Breakfast sat on the table, and the coffee prepared before her pa rose.

"I'm going back to town today." He leaned back in his chair and sipped on his coffee.

"Why?" He only went to town once a week, but now two days in a row?

"I want to see what the sheriff found out about the killings last night."

"Are you forgetting those men were criminals, camped on our land and intending us harm?"

"Doesn't explain Cabe being there."

She shook her head. "You should be grateful to the man."

Her father squinted at her and finished his coffee. "What's gotten into you, Caitie?"

"Nothing. I have chores to do." Which was the truth. She hurried to the barn and, with vigor, raked the hay into the stalls.

A few hours later, a horse approached. Her father had left for town, so it wouldn't be him. She peeked out from the barn. Dakota Cabe. Her cheeks flushed hot, and her heart ramped up a notch as she walked out to meet him. He wore a faded denim shirt, chaps, and his usual duster. Not as intimidating as when she first met him, but still well-armed.

"Miss Daniels." He tipped his hat to her.

"Please call me Caitlyn or Caitie."

He dismounted and closed the distance between them. With care, he pulled down the bandana from around her neck. The purplish green bruise she spotted this morning had to look wicked. Luckily, her father hadn't noticed.

"You all right?" he asked.

"Yes. I am."

He eyed her sharply as if he didn't believe her. "Most women wouldn't be."

"Most women have more sense than I."

"Whoa." He touched her cheek. "This is a different side of you." He stepped closer.

"I'm going to tell my father the truth when he gets home," she said. "You were only involved because of my foolishness."

Dakota sighed. "Look at me." When she didn't, he cupped her chin in his hand and lifted her face. "I don't want you to say anything to your father or the sheriff. As far as they know, I was alone."

"I can't. It isn't right. It's a lie. You wouldn't have gone out there if not for me. Now the sheriff is curious how you could have shot all nine men by yourself. Even my father is suspicious."

"Well, that's a different story. Now my ego is at stake. I had no idea they thought me so incapable."

A slight grin started at the corners of her mouth, which she soon discouraged. Her hands cupped around his, and she considered his gray eyes. They were far warmer than the day they'd met.

"You're an excellent shot, by the way." His eyes smiled. "But I'm sure that doesn't help you feel better."

"No. It doesn't."

"Those men would have killed you and your father in the middle of the night and thought nothing of it. The sheriff doesn't have the men to form a posse to go after them, so they could have killed other homesteaders. I'm just sorry you're in the middle." He paused and stared past her at the cabin. "You know your pa doesn't want me here."

She straightened her shoulders. "It's not up to him who I see, but I have to tell my pa and the sheriff my part in all of this since I created the whole mess."

"No."

"Why not?"

"For several reasons." He dropped his hands to his side and glanced back at his horse. "One, your name would be in all the newspapers. You'd be a walking target for fellow outlaws as well as your father. Two, it would be hard to explain why the two of us were out there together. So please leave it be."

"But Mr.—

"After what we've been through, call me Dakota."

His deep granite gray eyes were not as unfriendly and unemotional as she first thought. Not at all, in fact, they were enticing. Something was happening between them, but she wasn't sure what it was. She leaned into him, and he didn't step away. His hands cupped her arms and brought her to him.

His kiss was powerful, intense, and yet gentle. Caitlyn moved without thinking and enfolded her arms around his waist. His hands slipped up her arms and circled her shoulders. Nestled in his embrace, her breath caught in her chest. What was she feeling? Completeness. A part of her that she hadn't known was missing was suddenly filled. The wild emotions careening through her couldn't be harnessed or controlled, stunning her.

Pushing away from him, she stared at him boldly. "Would you ride with me?"

"Sure. I won't even offer to saddle your horse for you."

She smiled.

They headed for the trail she loved best. Riding gave her the perspective she needed, but it didn't change anything. Was this some sort of love? It had come without warning, but how could that even be possible?

She didn't even know him. The horrific shootout was still too vivid in her mind, but the man riding alongside her made the vision fade. It was more than a thin veneer of infatuation, more than intimacy born from the violence that they had experienced, or rather, she had experienced. He most likely was quite familiar with violence.

She regarded him in a new light. He fixed his eyes on her and smiled. He was all man, yet his eyes twinkled with the mischief of a boy. She smiled back and glanced at the cliffs beyond. Her cliffs. She nodded in that direction, and he nudged his horse into a run, while she followed close behind.

They dismounted at the cliffs. Walking to the edge, she sat and motioned for Dakota to sit beside her. "You're a wanted man, aren't you?"

He lifted an eyebrow, then gazed out over the ravine.

"Tell me."

He frowned. "Why?"

"I want to understand."

His eyes examined the sky. "It's not a pretty story."

"I wasn't expecting one."

He took her hand in his. "My folks were killed when I was twelve." He scanned the river below. "I went after the man who ordered it done, then I killed him." Taking a deep breath, he cast a brief look at her. "There's a longer version, but that about sums it up."

"The scars on your back?" Caitlin asked, thinking about the faded white streaks she had seen when she'd stitched his arm.

"I jumped through a window trying to escape from the man's house."

"You were twelve, just a boy."

"Old enough to kill a man—" He drew her hand into his lap and turned it over as if he could read her story from her palms. "And old enough to hang."

"Oh my God." Her mouth dropped open.

"I told you it wasn't a pretty story." He raked his hair back and glanced at her. "I should have ridden back out of town the same day I rode in."

"No." She squeezed his hand. "I'm glad you didn't. Like you said, those men would have killed my pa and me." The contrast in their entwined hands awed her. His were much larger than hers. Both were riveted with calluses, but his were rough with scars that she could only imagine their source. "Tell me the longer version."

"Which one?" He chuckled. "You do know there are several."

"Yours. The real one."

"I had a lawyer who tried to help me. Judd Williams, a friend of my father's, but there wasn't much he could do. I left and ended up living with other outlaws. Hooked up with a man named John Wakefield and his crew." Dakota grimaced. "I killed once for what I thought was justice, I wasn't about to kill for profit, so I cut out on my own. In time, the law stopped searching for me, so I started working regular jobs rounding up cattle," he smiled at her, "and stumbling upon beautiful women."

Glancing up into the sky, she startled at the rush of emotions soaring through her. Leaning into him, she slid her arm around his waist. She took in a deep breath, loving the smell of him—a mix of leather and pure strength.

He kissed her neck and pulled her closer, then pushed away. "We need to head back, Caitie. Your father wouldn't want you here with me, and I respect his wishes."

She stopped him from rising.

"Thank you for telling me." She brought her lips to his. Was she too forward? It didn't matter; she couldn't stop. Moreover, he seemed unable to as well.

He leaned backward, and she followed, kissing him without hesitation. She ached for his touch, for the comfort she would find in his arms.

Shifting slightly beneath her, he placed his hands on either side of her face, brushing back her hair. "We have to go back. It's almost dusk." He cupped her hair behind her ears.

"I suppose." She withdrew with disappointment.

At the river, she headed for home and him to town. Luckily, she arrived home before her father and didn't need to explain her unfinished chores. She got back to work and had dinner ready when her father walked in.

~ * ~

Caitlyn hated to deceive her father, and the conflict in her heart over the two men in her life grew each day.

Dakota insisted that her father be told. To continue to deceive the man, he wouldn't do. She agreed, but not yet. For a bit longer, she wanted it to be only the two of them. Dakota was more honorable than any man she knew. Would her father see him the same? She studied the ridge, waiting for him. The stable was swept clean, and fresh hay brought in. All the chores completed. If she chose, she could tell her father that the man she loved, she was forbidden to see. She regarded the distance from the house to the ridge, and then saddled her horse and headed out.

She met Dakota on the ridge and rode the land with him. Never had she been so at peace with herself. She peeked at the reason. His gaze was on her, twinkling in the setting sun.

"Race you to the river. Winner takes all," she challenged him. She nudged her mount, and off she flew.

Once in a full gallop, she took a quick glance behind her. Dakota was gaining on her. His massive horse sucked in the evening air and snorted it back out. They were a magnificent sight, and her heart pounded in time with the thundering hooves. His horse was much faster than hers, but she wouldn't give up. She rode as though racing with the devil himself.

He overtook her and her mare with a boisterous whoop. His horse splashed across the shallow water, and he quickly reined back. As soon as he released the reins, his horse pranced back into the river.

"You sure do take a race seriously, don't you?" Caitlyn laughed.

"The stakes were too high not to."

"How's that?" Her horse plodded through the shallow waters.

He brought his horse up in front of hers and blocked her path. "Well, you did say winner takes all."

Her cheeks flushed hot, the subtle meaning of his words apparent in his dark, brooding eyes. His boyish smile vanished in the wake of a man's desire. She licked her lips in anticipation. Her knees weakened, and she thanked the Lord she still sat in her saddle. She prodded her horse to the riverbank.

"Unless I took the meaning too literally." His eyes smiled at her, giving her a graceful retreat.

For a second, she hesitated. "No, you didn't."

With a broad smile, he slid from his saddle and let the reins drop to the ground. He moved toward her.

"The horses—"

"They'll be fine." He took one of her reins and tied it to his saddle horn. "He won't go far, and as long as she's tied to him, she won't either."

Caitlyn smiled at the similarity between herself and her horse. She barely breathed as she watched Dakota lead the horses a short distance away. Despite her attempts to hide her nervousness from him, his sharp eyes took notice.

Standing at the side of her horse, he squinted up at her in the day's fading light. Desire lay unconcealed in his eyes as well as compassion and tenderness, as if her apprehension of the unknown only endeared her more to him.

He extended his hands and placed them on either side of her waist. The air whooshed out of her as she lay her hands timidly on his massive shoulders. Without effort, he eased her from the saddle. His hands sizzled with heat as if burning his brand upon her. She slid slowly and leisurely down the expanse of his chest, creating sparks of desire deep within her.

Her feet barely touched the ground, and his hands continued to burn his signature deeper and deeper.

She didn't realize she held her breath until his questioning eyes met hers.

"Are you afraid, Caitie?" Lifting her chin with his finger.

He had killed men, but so had she. His viciousness with a knife, she had witnessed. The women in town whispered he was a womanizer, and as she suspected, he was indeed an outlaw. But afraid?

"No." She knew the man within, and she knew from this moment forward she would never feel safe without him. How could she? She had, indeed, fallen in love.

Their lovemaking was wild and tender. Caitlyn hadn't known what to expect, but his tenderness had been a cherished surprise. How could a man so rough be so gentle?

She fell asleep and woke to a sky studded with stars. He sat a few feet away, dressed, fully armed, and watching her. "Lay here with me, Dakota."

Standing, he walked over to her and, as commanded, lay beside her. She kissed him, then pointed to the star-studded sky. "They'll always be there, you know."

He nodded.

"When we aren't together—"

"I'm not leaving. I'll talk to your father, then we'll—"

She laid a finger against his lips. "Shhhh." Before it was too late, she had to tell him she loved him. The crushing sense of mayhem headed their way, and she could no longer ignore it.

"Just remember," she examined the stars, "no matter where we are, we'll always see the same stars." She squeezed his hand with conviction. "I love you, Dakota. I always will, and if you leave..." She held his hand tighter, not allowing him to interrupt. "I'll understand." Smiling slightly, she added, "At least, I'll try to."

Tears burned her eyes, and she was thankful he couldn't see them. She stopped the sudden hitch in her voice and added. "Don't talk to my father yet. I want to hold onto this." She brought his hand to her lips. "Just you and me, no one else, not yet, please?"

Dakota rose on one elbow and touched her cheek. "Girl, it won't be easy, but I don't plan on backing down for anyone. I love you. Trust me, all right? I'm not leaving."

~ * ~

The routine became more than familiar. She depended on it, and she depended on Dakota Cabe. Every night she waited outside of the barn, staring at the ridge beyond the pines, searching for him. Was that a good sign or a bad one? Last time she depended on someone, she had been more than hurt; she'd been devastated. She fingered her mother's pendant on her vest, longing for her presence.

"Caitlyn."

Her father's command jolted her out of her reverie, and she headed toward the house.

She stopped when she saw the sheriff. "What's wrong?" She stared at her father and then at Sheriff Metcalf.

"It has to do with Dakota Cabe. Have you been keeping company with him?" the sheriff asked.

Her heart slammed in her chest. "Has something happened to him?" She directed her question to the sheriff.

The man simply stared at her father.

"I asked you a question," she demanded.

"He's not dead if that's what you're asking, not yet anyway. I've got men searching for him, so have you seen him?" the sheriff pressed.

"Why are you asking? What's going on? Is Dakota all right?" She realized her mistake immediately.

"Caitlyn." Her father stared at her as if he didn't know her.

"He's a wanted man." The sheriff took off his hat and eyed her father as if he expected her to swoon at the news.

"For what?"

"Caitlyn, he's a wanted man—an outlaw. We've entertained him in our home. What difference does it make what he's wanted for?" her father demanded.

"You're right, it doesn't."

"He's wanted for murder," the sheriff said. "I looked him up after he killed the Forester gang. I missed it the first time. Seems a lawyer, Judd Williams, tried to get him amnesty, but he failed. There's a reward if you want to help find him."

"Are you serious?" She glanced from her father to the sheriff. "He defended me against the Forester gang. What would you have preferred, Sheriff? That those men rape and kill me?"

Her father's eyes widened in amazement. "You were there?"

"Yes. I was." She glared at the sheriff and held his eye. "And furthermore, Dakota didn't shoot all nine men, either."

"Caitlyn." Her father was beyond shocked. He was hurt.

"Why were you out there alone with Cabe?" the sheriff asked.

"Why didn't you tell me this sooner?" her father added.

She couldn't meet his eyes; she didn't have the heart. "Dakota didn't want me to, and now I can see why." Pressing her lips together, she realized this was merely the beginning.

"You haven't helped matters at all. Jim, did you know any of this?" the sheriff asked.

Her father shot a bewildered look from his daughter to the sheriff.

"No, he did not," Caitlyn said. "I went out there alone to assess the situation and got in over my head."

"Doesn't change the fact Mr. Cabe is a wanted man with a hefty bounty on his head, and now, Caitlyn, you are involved."

"My daughter had nothing to do with this, Sheriff." Her pa created a barrier between her and the sheriff.

"I'll do my best to keep her name out of this, Jim, but unless Cabe leaves before I find him, this will be the biggest news in town and then some. Needless to say, it won't look good. I'll be on my way. I just wanted to warn you about the kind of man he is, Caitlyn." The sheriff nodded in her direction, remounted his horse, and then rode away.

She stared at his retreating form, then eyed her father sharply. "Since when do we judge a man on hearsay?"

"Good Lord, Caitlyn, have you taken leave of your senses? That was the sheriff. Mr. Cabe is a wanted man. I forbid you even to entertain any notions of Cabe."

"That's not for you to decide."

The bewildered expression on her father's face wounded her.

"You've taken this too far, Caitie. You'd best forget you ever met the man."

"Pa, I'm so sorry, but I'm in love with Dakota. If he has to leave, I'll leave with him. I love you dearly." She touched his sleeve. "I never meant to hurt you. Never, but I can't change who I am or who I love. Please understand."

Jim Daniels walked back into the cabin.

~ * ~

Cabe was doing it all wrong, but he hadn't come across the right way in the short amount of time he had. There hadn't been time to think it through, though he suspected it wouldn't have mattered. He'd never planned on someone like Caitlyn Daniels, and now she was in trouble with the law. It would only get worse.

Reining his mare in, he approached the ridge and hunched over the saddle horn, trying to find a way to make it work. He couldn't. The day was long past. Would she still be waiting for him?

Yes. Her small form silhouetted on the ridge, dark against the fading sky. Dismounting, he approached her.

"Caitie." He reached for her arm, but she remained erect as though preparing for battle.

"Dakota." Her voice was tight, as if she were speaking to a stranger.

"I have to leave." Removing his hat, he took her hand in his and pulled her closer to him, but still, she hesitated.

"The sheriff told me."

She had all the facts.

"I'm sorry, Cat."

"There's nothing to apologize for unless you intend to leave without me."

"I can't take you where I'm going." He studied Caitlyn's soft green eyes. She was prepared to leave with him. "You have no idea what or where I'll—"

She stopped him in mid-sentence. "I love you, Dakota. If you love me, take me with you." Drawing his face to hers, she locked eyes with him. "I'm willing to confront whatever I must to be with you."

"I'm an outlaw." He stood to his full height.

"Tell me something I don't know."

He glanced down the ridge at the warmly lit cabin below. "You have no idea what it's like. It's no life for a woman." He shook his head in misery. "I never should have let it get this far. I'm sorry."

"You made me a promise."

"God, Caitlyn. I'm trying to do right by you. If I leave now, no one will know we were involved." He motioned to her home. "This is what you have."

"I can see what I have, and what I want." She remained in front of him.

Straightening his shoulders, he placed his hat back on his head. "I'm not taking you on the run, living like a criminal. I've made the decision. I won't change my mind." The shimmer in Caitlyn's eyes wounded him more than any gunfight did. "I'm leaving. It's for the best." He pulled free from her. He had to be firm. He had to do the right thing.

She lifted her chin and stared at the terrain beyond him. "Then go. I'll be better off alone than with a man who can't claim what's his."

"You aren't alone, Caitlyn." He contemplated her homestead, then the stars above. They were so bright tonight. Too bright.

"Then you are the fool, not I." She shifted away from him, then strode with dignity back to her horse and remounted. She paused for a few minutes before she rode down the ridge.

He waited there for what seemed like hours until she entered the light of her home. Dismounting outside of the barn, she walked her mare inside. How could he take her from this to a life on the run? It wouldn't be right. So why did he feel he was making the biggest mistake of his life to leave without her?

The light in the house went out, and the light in the barn lit. Her father went to bed, and the daughter tended the horses. What was he missing? What was he giving up that he couldn't reclaim? No, he was doing the right thing. But it felt so wrong. He had become an unpredictable, unreliable, and undependable man, everything he despised in a man's character.

Mounting his horse, he took a last look about. He had nothing to offer the woman. Here, she had a working farm and a father who adored her. Here she had a life. With him, she had nothing.

He slapped the reins—time to go. The decision was made.

Chapter 3

Two years later

"Yo, Cabe. Dakota Cabe." A man's voice carried over the still mountain.

Dakota rolled his shoulders to loosen the knot forming at the base of his neck. The fool didn't have the sense to sneak into his mountain hideaway like the others.

Tossing his coffee into the bucket, he took his fur coat off the rack and shrugged into it. After tucking his handgun in the back of his pants, he picked up his rifle.

Slipping out the back door, he trekked up the hill behind his cabin and worked his way around to the front, keeping to the shadowy areas under the pines. He cast a brief look at the distant mountains still capped with snow and then peered below where a feathery smoke line indicated a camp of men. The air was as numbing as ice. The man approaching his cabin resembled more of a five-foot, overstuffed turkey than any kind of bounty hunter, but appearances had deceived him in the past. He frowned at the men making camp for the night. It didn't make sense to send in only one man.

He crept through the underbrush to get a closer view of his uninvited guest, grateful the sun was to his back, but fur concealed the man's face. The stranger didn't pose a physical threat, and that concerned Dakota even more.

He snuck up behind the man, but the traveler seemed oblivious to his presence, blinded by some mission—a mission to get himself killed.

The ground was too damn cold to dig a grave, so Dakota grabbed the man by his multiple collars and spun him around, then brought his handgun up against the man's temple. The ominous click of the hammer echoed in the stillness.

"You made a mistake coming here, stranger," Dakota spoke in a low, harsh voice. He'd be damned if he would bother with a grave; he'd shove the man backward and let his crew do the deed.

"It's me, Dakota." The man raised shaky hands. "Judd, Judd Williams."

Judd Williams? The lawyer from years past. He yanked the hat from Judd's head, his gun still resting at his temple. Rumpled gray hair fell loose in a static mess, making the man appear more fearful. With exaggerated slowness, Judd turned and faced the open end of Dakota's pistol, his eyes wide.

"Hell, Judd. What are you doing up in these parts?" Lowering his gun, Dakota uncocked the weapon. He rubbed the stiffness from his neck and relaxed his shoulders, relieved that no graves needed digging.

Judd had enough gear on him for a lengthy expedition.

"You all right, Judd? Didn't mean to scare the hell out of you." He patted Judd's cheek and shoved the gun back into the waist of his pants. "I wasn't expecting company, leastwise, not friendly company. You dressed for the mountains, didn't ya? No wonder I didn't recognize you." He chuckled, glancing again at the attorney's substantial outer garments. "What's with the men camping down below?"

"Guides I hired to help me find this place. They won't come any further."

He read Judd's weary eyes, burdened by more than outer gear. "Come inside. You're frozen. You can tell me what brought you here." He slapped the lawyer on the back and hiked toward his cabin.

Judd followed several steps behind.

Dakota trudged more slowly to the cabin than necessary. The confinement of four walls and the prospect of bad news didn't appeal to him. He inspected the forest surrounding his home. Demons he confronted out in the open, he didn't invite them inside. Only one reason Judd, a retired lawyer, would make such a treacherous trip.

Dakota peered back at Judd. Despite the man's substantial garments, hypothermia was setting in. Hurrying through the last few steps, he pushed the door open and motioned Judd inside.

He stepped inside, and Dakota scanned the remote terrain. Clouds moved in from the west, snow or rain. It was always a mixed bag this time of year. He took in the pile of wood he had cut for the year. His legs were stiffer than wood, and he couldn't take a full breath without his chest constricting, but it wasn't because of the cold.

He stepped inside and shut the door behind him. "You hungry?"

"No, not really," Shivering, Judd rubbed his arms.

Removing his outer coat, Dakota strode across the room and hung the garment on a nail on the wall. After he placed his gun on the ledge above his coat, he faced the wall, then turned back to Judd. "Whiskey?"

Nodding, Judd took a seat at the table, then cupped his hands around his mouth and blew warm air into them.

Bringing a jug and two shot glasses to the lone table, Dakota filled one for Judd, slid the glass across the table, then filled one for himself. After he downed the whiskey, he poured himself another one.

Setting the bottle on the table, he sat, his gaze settling hard onto Judd's face. "You'd best tell me why you're here. I don't expect you brought good news."

Judd inhaled and downed his whiskey. Glancing back at Dakota, he paused and wrinkled his brow. "It's about Caitlyn Daniels."

Caitlyn? Why would he come concerning her? Did she ask him to come? No, she would have come herself. If Judd could find him, so could Caitlyn.

"I received information. Truth is, I've been following her, or at least trying to." The lawyer stopped as if expecting Dakota to object to his meddling.

"Get to the point." He stood and loomed over Judd.

"She's in trouble."

"What kind of trouble?"

"John Wakefield kidnapped her."

Wakefield? Dakota staggered away, ran both hands through his hair, then leaned backward.

Judd glanced up. "He's holding her in exchange for the bounty on your head."

"Where's her pa?" Dakota dropped both hands to his side and stepped forward.

"Dead. Wakefield killed him."

"Damn." He kicked a chair across the room and ground his jaw. He kneaded his forehead in frustration. Think, damn it. Think. His thoughts ricocheted like misspent rifle cartridges.

Refilling his glass, Judd picked it up and set it down again. "I guess Wakefield still has a vendetta against you. I figure he found out about Miss Daniels and thought this might lure you back into the gang. I reckon he knew someone would come tell you he had Caitlyn and your son."

Dakota stared at Judd. "What?" He gripped the table with both hands. Hoping he'd heard wrong. Leaning closer to Judd, he ground out, "What did you say?"

"Wakefield is holding her hostage in a canyon somewhere north of Silverwater." Judd pushed his glass around. "Would have been here sooner, but I'm no mountain man."

"A son?" Dakota could barely say the word.

"You didn't know?" The words were more of a statement than a question. Judd inhaled deeply. "I'm sorry, Dakota. I should have been more tactful. I—"

"Stop. Don't say another word." God damn it. Placing both hands over his ears, Dakota squeezed until it hurt, and he could think again. He'd braced himself for bad news, but not news on Caitlin and certainly not on a son he knew nothing about.

Judd pushed his glass back and forth and said nothing.

Dakota stumbled to the fireplace, his legs not obeying his commands. The world had tilted, and he couldn't find stable ground. Numbness encased him, like a sucker punch to the soul. Grabbing for the mantel, he calculated the time he'd been gone. How long had it been? The boy had to be 14 months old.

His mind churned, plotting out the scenario. Caitlyn had been carrying his child when he left. He hadn't known. Why hadn't he even suspected? A deep, sick fear encased him, the kind that didn't go away on its own. It would have to be chiseled out. Now, both Caitlyn and her baby were the hostages of John Wakefield.

"Dakota?" Judd spoke over his whiskey cup.

Pushing away from the mantel, Dakota stalked around the room, trapped in a self-condemnation he couldn't escape. He swept up his glass and heaved the whiskey into the fire. The fire hissed and crackled. "A son?" There was no emotion in his voice, only a baritone of lost words.

"Yes, you have a son. I guess she wouldn't have told you." Judd sighed as if he preferred the bitter frigid storm approaching than to being inside Dakota's cabin.

"She should have told me, Judd. I had a right to know." He walked back and forth across the room then leaned against the mantle. God, he was not only gut-punched but set on fire as well.

Judd waited a few steps behind him. "I've known you for years, Dakota. You probably thought you were doing the right thing. You decided on the best course of action, and that's what you did."

"Damn Judd." He spun around. "You make it sound so damned easy, like I couldn't wait to cut out. You think I said to hell with her and headed out to save my own skin? What kind of man do you think I am? You have no idea what it's like for a woman on the run. You can't even imagine the hell-holes she would be forced to enter." He stared at Judd, inviting a confrontation, even if only a verbal one.

"I didn't say you cut out on her. I'm trying to point out that your decision might not have changed, even if you had known." Judd frowned.

Thinking, Dakota shook his head. "I thought I did the right thing. I never considered she might be with child." Straightening his shoulders, he twisted his neck from side-to-side to make room for a new situation he hadn't counted on. "Hell, I thought she'd be safer without me."

Judd waited, his lifted eyebrows the only acknowledgment to Dakota's rant.

"Safer? Damn, what was I thinking?" He gripped the mantle, wanting to rip the stone from its structure. The sharp rock cut into his fingers and left blood on the rock.

"There's no way you could have known this would happen. If I could have cleared your name years ago..." Judd rubbed his forehead as if hoping to find a new plan.

Grunting, Dakota strode back to the table. "You did the best you could with what you had to work with. We both know that."

"I must have missed something." Judd ran his hands down his pants. "I still hope to get you amnesty." Settling his arms on the table in a triangle as if strategizing, he sighed and his mouth twisted into a grim line.

"Hell, Judd, you're a lawyer, not God." Sitting, Dakota poured Judd another shot of whiskey. "I'll leave at daylight."

"I'm sorry, Dakota. Honestly, I am." Judd dropped his chin into the palm of his hand and let out a long breath.

"It's nobody's fault but my own."

~ * ~

Before dawn, Dakota shook Judd awake. "I'm leaving."

He stared at Dakota his eyes wide, his eyebrows raised.

"Something wrong?"

Shaking his head, Judd pushed himself onto his elbows. "No. You look different."

Dakota regarded his apparel. It had been a long time since he strapped on a gun belt. The rough and weary belt felt looser but held his revolvers as always. He couldn't say why he shaved or why he slicked back his hair and tied it at the base of his neck.

"Yeah, well, whatever the occasion calls for, I reckon." He shrugged into a long dark duster and threw a rifle over his shoulder. He slid his hunting knife into his boot and grabbed another pistol then placed it in the back of his trousers. At the door, he stopped to pick up a second rifle. "You reckon you can find your way back down the mountain?"

"I do." Judd studied Dakota's face, then dropped his chin. "I didn't know if I made the right call coming up here bringing men."

"You did the right thing, Judd. Thank you. No one else would have gone to the trouble." He nodded at the table. "I left you some breakfast. If you don't mind, put out the fire when you leave and toss what you don't eat. I won't be back."

"Dakota?"

He faced Judd. The lawyer hadn't aged well. Deep furrowed lines arched across his forehead. He wore his concern like a topcoat. "Yeah?"

"Watch your back; it could all be a trap."

Opening the door, Dakota stepped out into the stillness of fresh snow. He planned on killing John Wakefield...unless Caitlyn did it first.

Chapter 4

Caitlyn woke up disoriented. Groping across the bed, her hands searched for her boy. "Joshua?"

Harsh reality slapped her into awareness. Her boy wasn't there. She was alone in the hotel room. She lifted her cheek from the old quilt. At least it was morning. Thank God. Another night like the last six would be the end of her.

Nightmares had beset her as soon as her eyes closed each night. Now her mind, as well as her body, was exhausted. The days of hard riding with no more than an hour or two of rest at night, never sleeping, had taken their toll.

Forcing herself to her feet, she stumbled to the washbasin and attempted to brush the wrinkles from her blouse—a pointless venture.

The water in the basin was cold to the touch. Leaning into the washstand, Caitlyn dropped her face into her hands and gave way to her emotions in a way she hadn't since being a child.

Minutes clicked by. Spent and disgusted with herself, she lengthened the tired muscles in her back, examined her face in the mirror, and laughed. Trails of dust ran in rivers down her face, only changing course to follow the last of her tears. Her eyes, puffy and red, did not convey the self-confidence she needed. Her young son was kidnapped and possibly dead by John Wakefield. The thought made her want to lie down and die.

Narrowing her eyes, she glared at herself. Good Lord, Caitlyn, get some backbone!

With the bar of soap lying on the rim of the basin, she scrubbed away every last trail of dust and despair. In furious self-contempt, she undressed, tossed the soiled riding vest and wrinkled blouse onto the bed, then returned to the basin to splash the chilly water across her chest and back. No time for a bath. When she got Joshua back, there would be time for the simple luxuries of life, all the things she'd taken for granted.

Toweling off, she reviewed her reflection in the mirror. She had changed. Not from the hasty splash bath, but from the unexpected course her life had taken. Somewhere between Dakota's leaving and Joshua's kidnapping, she had become a bitter woman.

Dakota. The thought of him pained her. Would there ever be a time she could think of the man and not ache for him? Would the day ever come when his memory would be only that, a memory? His love had completed her. He had filled all the empty places within her—places she didn't even know existed until he had vacated them.

She examined her reflection in the mirror. The misery of the past year and a half had chiseled its mark upon her features.

"Damn you, Caitlyn," she muttered to her reflection. "He's gone. Get over it." Placing her hands on her back, she straightened, stretching tired and cramped muscles.

No time for self-pity. Joshua needed her, and she was all he had. She had to be strong. Fresh tears gathered in her eyes at the thought of her dead father. It had happened so fast, so unexpectedly. She dropped her chin, set her jaw, then squeezed her eyes tight.

Dragging her saddlebags to the bed, she flipped them open. She needed fresh garments before she headed back out to find someone who knew Devil's Canyon's location. Tilting her head, she tensed at the anxious voices drifting up to her from the road outside. Holding a blouse to her chest, she hurried to the window and scanned the street.

In the distance, entering the town limits rode a lone man. That was of little interest, except that this man was more than reasonably armed. She counted the numerous exposed weapons and guessed at those that weren't. A desperado, no doubt, but why come to Silverwater? He wouldn't go unnoticed. The town had lost its glimmer and appeal a long time ago. Nothing existed here except trouble, and by her calculations, more was riding in.

Squinting, she drew closer to the window and considered the rider. She blocked out the frightened women's exclamations beneath her window and narrowed her focus. Something was oddly familiar. She pressed her cheek against the cool windowpane. No, it couldn't be. He was gone. Oh, he was somewhere, of course, but not here. He wouldn't be here.

Still, the way the man and horse rode as one—the slant of the hat; the way he scanned the town, kept her riveted to the window and dried her throat.

The old and weathered duster convinced her. The way the coat molded around the man portrayed the power of the only man it could be. She lurched back as his eyes skimmed across her window. Her heart jolted, and her breath hitched. Dakota.

~ * ~

Dakota Cabe cantered into town and then stopped to assess for dangers. Pushing his hat back, he waited for the dry, powdery dust his horse had stirred up to settle back down.

It had been years since he'd been to Silverwater, and nothing had changed. It was the same dull, unfriendly town it had been back then. The wooden sidewalks and false storefronts showed a rapid decline. The town now had an unsavory reputation, much like his own. Grimacing, he brushed the dust from his hat and pulled his bandana up to wipe the dirt from his face. He nudged his horse forward, prepared to greet the town of Silverwater.

He scrutinized the store windows and doors. The mercantile remained open, and people milled outside to inspect him. Loosening his shoulders, he sat back in the saddle and tried to make himself as non-threatening as possible. The multiple weapons he wore, he couldn't help, but he could prevent pissing off a fool.

"Looks like trouble's riding in," a tall, lean, and well-dressed man commented, leaning up against the mercantile's porch column.

"Maybe he's riding through, and he'll be gone by morning," his companion offered.

"Maybe so. Either way, I'm gonna give him a wide berth." The tall man leaned back, yanking up his suspenders, and gave Dakota a thoughtful examination. "Don't appear he's too fond of being here. I wonder what brought him in."

A third man stepped out of the mercantile and joined the other two. Unsteady on his feet with a whiskey bottle in hand, "Shit, Sam. I ain't afraid of no damn stranger, and I ain't gonna give no outsider a wide berth." The cowhand slapped a dusty hat across his aged chaps.

"I wouldn't be after any more trouble, if I were you, Jimmy. Reckon you found yourself more than you could handle last night." Sam winked with a thin smile, assessing Jimmy's swollen, purplish eye.

"Well, you ain't me, are you, Sam?"

"Nope, and damn glad I'm not, too," Sam said, though Jimmy had reentered the mercantile.

Dakota heard the same conversation in every town. Only the faces changed. Noting the cowhand's face, he dismissed the others.

Glancing down the dusty, well-rutted street, he spotted the saloon and prodded his spent horse toward the building. He needed information, and the local watering hole was the best place to get it. Bartenders ended up knowing everything in and around town. He noticed the livery and the hotel where he would likely find a meal, but both would have to wait.

The sun sank leisurely behind the tall store buildings and cast long, lonely, shadowy trails across his path. The murmuring of voices outside the hotel died out behind him, and the festive saloon sounds drifted to him from between the swinging half doors.

Several horses stood tethered to the saloon's post. Tied to one horse was a mule loaded with various furs and traps. The animals were old but well kept.

Dakota dismounted at the saloon and hitched his horse alongside them. Shrill laughter and drunken singing floated into the night air, drowning out the creak of his boots trudging up the plank steps to the swinging doors.

When he pushed inside, the cackling and the piano playing came to an abrupt halt. The only sound in the room was the squeaking of the doors, as they swung back and forth behind him. He tipped up his hat, allowing his vision to adapt, before continuing to the bar. The music resumed as if on command.

Men sat at the various tables playing cards and drinking. Four were younger and drunker than the other occupants and would be quick to make sparks. One man with a black patch over his right eye appeared to be the group's leader. He held Dakota's glare until Dakota passed him and stood at the bar.

Most of the men were well armed. Only one, a trapper, acknowledged Dakota's presence. The man's white beard traveled down his chest and ended at his waist with a streak of yellow at its tips. The trapper's face was weathered and wrinkled from the sun. Dakota guessed he was somewhere in his sixties. Crow's feet lined the corner of each eye and hinted at self-contained humor. The trapper appeared old and decrepit, but catching the sparkle in his sapphire blue eyes, Dakota judged him far from inept.

Glancing around for the barkeeper, Dakota found a crude drawing of himself tacked to the far wall, along with several other wanted posters. Luckily, he'd taken the time to shave since he showed little resemblance to the man in the picture. He grinned at the posted $3,000 reward; he was finally worth something.

"Have a drink, son, and rest yerself." The trapper's speech was slow and halting, as if unaccustomed to using words. The older man pushed a bottle and an empty glass toward Dakota before shuffling back to one side.

Nodding his thanks, he laid his rifle on the counter and then poured himself a shot of whiskey from the trapper's bottle. "Much obliged, mister." The liquor flowed hot and soothing down his dry, scratchy throat.

"Nice piece ye got there." The old trapper nodded at Dakota's well-kept Winchester.

"It suffices." He took another swig of the whiskey.

"Reckon so, but I'm still partial to them here older ladies." The trapper chuckled, patting his aged Winchester resting at his side.

Dakota glanced around again for the absent bartender, then inspected the man's rifle. For all appearances, the gun might have been the one he'd carried seventeen years ago. "My pa used to have one," he said. "It gets the job done."

"Yes, it does." The trapper patted his rifle again, then grinned at Dakota. "But I reckon our quarry runs in different woods." After taking a long drink of the liquor, he had a coughing fit. He pounded his chest twice before he could speak again. "Best be moving on. Got to unload my furs and head back out."

Dakota nodded. "I noticed them outside. They seem like fine pieces to me. They ought to bring you a good price."

Pushing away from the bar, the trapper took his rifle with him and nodded at the half-empty bottle. "Have the rest, boy. I'm heading out. Don't want to get too drunk and fall off my horse."

Lifting his glass in thanks, he gave a slight smile. The older man ambled to the door, tugging up his loose-fitting drawers, then stopped short when the young man with the eye patch stood and blocked his path.

With a grim chuckle, the trapper folded back his long coat and revealed a long, shiny gutting knife. "This one works just as well on sassy boys as it does on them there beavers I got outside." The old man's faded blue eyes shimmered with a mad glint.

The one-eyed youth stepped aside.

The trapper lumbered out the swinging doors, and Dakota stifled a chuckle. Shifting back to the bar, he took another swig from the bottle, enjoying the fiery liquid shooting briskly through his veins. The liquor chased the chill from his bones and revived his spirits. The bartender came around the corner carrying a crate of alcohol with him, and Dakota motioned for him.

"Want another bottle, mister?"

"No thanks, this will do." He nodded to the trapper's bottle. "But I am looking to buy some information."

"Two bits, and I can answer most questions." The bartender resumed stocking his liquor cabinet.

"You know a John Wakefield?"

The bartender turned back around. "Don't know many around these parts who don't. He a friend of yours?" From the tone of his voice, he wasn't himself.

"No." Dakota paused. Now he had everyone's attention, something he'd hoped to avoid. He lowered his voice, forcing the bartender to lean closer. "You know how many men run with him?"

"A dozen or so. The number varies along with the faces."

"Oh?" Dakota lifted an eyebrow.

"Dangerous occupation. Wakefield's men keep getting killed." The bartender paused and scrutinized him. "Wakefield has a short temper."

"He been through here of late?"

"Nope." Stepping back, he returned to his liquor inventory. The rest of the saloon had lost interest in their conversation.

The bartender retrieved another box of liquor and continued to stock. "There's word he kidnapped a woman and her son, and now he's holding them hostage in Devil's Canyon. Appears he's waiting for someone." After stocking the shelves and wiping the counter clean, he turned to study Dakota for a moment, leaning over the bar. In a soft voice, he added, "I know who you are, Mr. Cabe. And that fact don't matter none to me, but I don't want no trouble in here. I've worked too hard and too long to start over now. If you don't mind, I'll ask you to leave after you're finished." He nodded to the trapper's bottle and added, "No offense meant."

"None taken." Dakota didn't blame the man. Trouble did have a way of keeping company with him. Pouring a final shot, he mulled over the information the bartender had given him. It confirmed what he knew, but hell, how he'd been hoping it wouldn't.

He went over in his mind what he already knew since Judd Williams tracked him down in the Colorado Mountains a mere three days prior.

God, he had a son. He still couldn't wrap his mind around the thought. A son. He hadn't known. How could he not? Had she started to show before he left? Had he been so hell-bent on leaving, he'd been blind to the obvious?

He shouldn't have left. He should have stayed and faced whatever the law handed out. God. At least, he should have married her. Damn. He shoved away the whiskey bottle and gritted his teeth, acknowledging the same fact he always did when he traveled down this well-worn trail. Caitlyn would have gone down with him. The law didn't make exceptions for women consorting with alleged criminals, and being married to a presumed killer wouldn't have fared her any better.

He contemplated the picture of himself on the wanted poster. He would have married her. Lord knew he wanted to, but everything had gone so wrong, so fast. The townsfolk would believe he fooled her as he did them. They would think he hadn't cared for her. He'd used her, taken what he wanted, and left her to deal with the consequences. The man in the poster resembled that kind of man. Maybe he was that man, after all.

So lost in self-incrimination, he barely heard the saloon doors swing open, and two faint steps enter, then stop. He chastised himself for allowing his mind to wander when he might very well be walking into a trap. Hadn't Judd mentioned the possibility? He was a fool and probably soon to be a dead fool. Exhaustion had set in, though that was a poor excuse. Dakota ran his fingers down along the thick three-day stubble on his face. Shaving had been a waste of time.

The saloon was still as death. Seconds ticked into eternity. He waited for the inevitable booming voice to tell him to face his challenger, and yet no sound, only eerie silence. No chairs pushed back in, dreaded anticipation of gunfire—no whispers for someone to call the sheriff. Something was definitely not true to course. With ancient calm, he laid his hand on his new Winchester rifle, brought the gun to his side, then slowly swung around.

The fading sunlight streamed through the door slats, giving only a vague description of the intruder, but it was enough. He'd memorized every part of her long ago. He stared at the shadowy figure, trying to convince himself it was nothing more than a mirage. For the briefest of moments, he stood entranced like a schoolboy eyeing up a piece of candy in a store window, but common logic kicked back in.

She was no mirage. It was Caitlyn.

~ * ~

Caitlyn's eyes adjusted to the dim lighting. Canvassing the men in the bar quickly, she assessed each's mans potential threat before settling her attention on Dakota. His icy gray eyes were skeptical, showing little recognition. In fact, his stare seemed to pass right through her as if she wasn't even there.

A low appreciative whistle at her side broke the stillness like a rock against ice. The one-eyed man rose and sauntered in her direction, his attention riveted on her and nothing else.

"Well, well, take a gander at who came in for a drink with the boys." Chuckling, he winked over his shoulder at his cohorts. "And all by her lonesome." He stopped in front of her and grasped a strand of her hair with grubby fingers.

Dakota tossed several coins onto the bar and headed toward them.

Caitlyn jerked out of the one-eyed man's touch, but he seized her with a rough hold around her waist and yanked her to him. Too much liquor rendered him unsteady, and he teetered against her.

"Lookie here, Bill." The man inhaled deeply. "Ain't she a beaut? A real lady too."

"Ain't no lady comes in here." Bill clucked, still reclining at the corner table.

"Damn it." Twisting in the man's arms, she shoved her knee hard into his groin.

He stumbled backward, gasping and clutching at his crotch. The rest of his gang war-whooped, pushed back their chairs, and charged forward with anticipation of the easy bait.

Dakota's rifle butt caught the first man across the cheek and sent him sprawling to the floor. Instantaneously, Dakota drew, cocked, and pointed his revolver at the next man's face. The young man's hand rested on the top of his gun, still encased in its holster. Stone silent, a few feet back stood the third man.

"Being stupid ain't worth dying for," Dakota said. Menace darkened his eyes.

Uncertainty and humiliation burned brightly within the man's eyes, but he took a cautious step back.

Dakota briefly contemplated the one-eyed man, still immobilized by Caitlyn's self-defense, then rested his gaze on her. His piercing, indecipherable, unsympathetic gaze bored into hers as if his only joy in life would be to grip her delicate neck and choke the life out of her. For a second choice, he grabbed her elbow in a hard pinch, spun her around on her heels, then thrust her back out the saloon doors. Following closely behind her, he kept his gun leveled at the men in the saloon.

Neither his pace nor his hold slackened as he strode down the wooden walkway. His long coat slapped rhythmically against his worn boots, his spurs clicked savagely on the sidewalk. His gaze remained fixed forward, partially hidden beneath the large brim of his Stetson, and skimmed from window to door with the same careful inspection she'd noted he gave the town when he first arrived. Several people noticed them, but none appeared willing to come to her assistance.

They glided off the walkway and down the rickety steps into a dusty side alley. The sheer force of his vexation propelled them both forward. Halfway down the alley, Dakota thrust her into a small, board-ed-up doorway and blocked the only means of escape with his body.

"What the hell were you doing? You could have been killed."

The violence in his voice startled her more than the iron grip on her shoulders. When she didn't respond, he jostled her to attention. Instantly, she drew back and slapped him with all her might. Any other time, his momentarily stunned response would have pleased her. Now it made her ill.

He dropped his hands and backed up. It gave her no pleasure to see the hardened outlaw stand without defense.

"Caitlyn."

She considered him. A mixture of relief and confusion danced across his face. It would be only seconds before his calm composure fell back in place, so she waited without responding.

"What the hell is going on? Judd said John Wakefield kidnapped you."

"He never had me. He kidnapped a friend who was at the house while I was in town. No one knows he has the wrong woman, and that's the way I want to keep it."

"I don't understand."

"It's nice to see you again, too, Dakota."

The slight intake of air and the grimace of his lips gave her further reassurance that the man still hadn't found his footing. It had given her so much pleasure in the past, but no longer.

He regarded the alley in both directions.

The day had faded into a muggy, damp evening. A trickle of sweat ran down the back of her lace blouse. Numbly, she removed her gloves and busied herself with them. No one was in their vicinity. She knew that, and so did he.

He touched her gloves, and she released them. Unconsciously, she set her teeth and stared at the small patch of dry dirt that lay between them. While he had been gathering his footing, she slowly, but surely, had lost hers. She couldn't meet his eyes without crying. So she retreated into herself, willing herself not to feel, willing herself to be as cold as the nights she had spent at a window waiting for him to return. As cold as the realization when she knew he wasn't coming back.

Tucking her gloves into his vest pocket, he took both of her hands in his.

"Caitie?"

She straightened her back and continued to stare at the ground between them.

~ * ~

Her hands were small in his. More than anything, Dakota wanted to examine them, to hold them to his cheek and feel the blood pulsing through her delicate veins. He wanted the reassurance that she was real.

In his world, he never touched her again. In his dreams, she lay slaughtered, abused, and destroyed. He would arrive in time to watch her and his young son take their last breath. He had no mental picture of his son, only the horrifying sense of his death. With Caitlyn, the image materialized all too clearly. Her beautiful hair spewed out around her, soaking up her blood, her eyes staring, searching into the night. Searching for him? God, the nightmare never played out any differently.

In his terror, he always rode in half-falling from his horse, but still too late. The blood saturated his hands despite his wild attempt to stop the flow. His frantic attempts to push back the life rolling out of her without mercy mocked him. Even the sound of his voice screaming for another chance wouldn't wake him, then the brief outline of death next to her, his son—their son.

The sight of the knife in his hand as he removed it from her body ended the nightmare. The horrific realization that he had killed her, the reason why he could never get there in time.

The hands he held pulsed, warm and alive. The memory of the nightmare receded, and he pressed her hands to his chest and curled his arms around her.

John Wakefield didn't have her. She was in his arms, and she melted into him as if nothing had changed between them. For the briefest of moments, they were as they had once been, two made into one. However, the image left before it had a chance to hold. The soft, warm body he held grew tense, and though she didn't step away, her body spoke clearly enough.

He dropped his arms to her waist, and his fingers brushed over the steel butt of a gun tucked into the back of her riding skirt. So, she hadn't walked blind into the saloon. He withdrew her pistol and stepped back with it in his hand. Why had he assumed she came into the saloon without taking precautions?

He knew her better. "Why didn't you use your gun?"

Caitlyn grabbed the gun from his hand and tucked it back into the band of her riding skirt. "It appeared you could handle the situation without my assistance." A rapid change of emotions scurried across her face: fear, self-doubt, and finally emptiness—an emptiness filled with grief, despair, and a barely contained fury.

"You are all right, aren't you, Cat?" Touching her chilled cheek, he grasped her chin in his palm and tilted her face upward.

"Yes," she said, extricating herself from his hold.

Her voice chilled as ice, her posture ramrod-straight, but her eyes, sparkling with tears, betrayed her.

He dropped his hands to his side and took another step back to give her the space she requested, yet didn't appear to want. "Caitlyn?"

She refused to meet his eyes.

A small crowd formed at the end of the alley.

"Do you have a room in town?" he asked.

"Yes. At the hotel."

"Let's go." Without waiting for a reply, he took her arm and led her back the way they had come.

The crowd fell back, giving them an open path. Curious eyes watched, but no one challenged him, regardless of what his intentions might be for her.

Neither spoke to the other as they crossed the wheel-rutted road and made their way to the hotel. The fresh evening breeze tugged at the flaps of Dakota's coat, billowing them out on either side. His boots chewed at the dry ground, sending puffs of dust up behind him, while her feet scurried to keep up with his long gait.

They quickly climbed the few stairs to the hotel. The clicking sound of his boots announced their arrival as they entered the Rosebud's large stained-glass doors. The desk clerk glanced up. Caitlyn and Dakota headed for the stairs to the rooms.

"Ah... Sir, excuse me. Do you have a room here?"

Dakota evaluated the elderly clerk and grumbled, "Yes, hers."

"Yes, sir..." The clerk blushed, glancing from Caitlyn to Dakota. "Do you?"

He gave the clerk a penetrating stare, and the clerk returned to his paperwork.

Taking Caitlyn's arm, Dakota led her up the stairs. At the top, he released her elbow and waited while she went to the appropriate door and unlocked it. He glanced over his shoulder and entered the room, and she slipped in behind him, closing the door. Crossing the room's interior in two quick strides, he checked the small adjoining chamber before stepping to the window. Moving the frayed curtain to the side, he looked below. Most of the people were dispersing and heading home. One or two men loitered outside. They were too drunk to pose a threat.

Reassured, he shifted his attention back to the room. He retrieved a match from his coat pocket and lit a lamp sitting on the bedside table. The wick flickered, then caught fire, casting a warm, golden glow across the room.

A decently furnished room, and probably at one time cost a good penny for a night's stay, but the faded and thin mahogany red velvet showed its age. The white lace dollies were yellow and brittle. Two wooden chests of drawers sat on either side of the room, sagging in their middles as if life in this town proved too much even for them to bear. The rugs, though clean, faded with age.

A soft stir at the door reminded him that Caitlyn still waited. He glanced at her and followed her gaze to the bed. Her saddlebags lay half-emptied on the faded quilt. A change of clothes, intimate apparel, and yesterday's clothing made a disgruntled heap half in, half out of her bags. Walking to the bed, he brushed one hand across her garments before glancing back at her.

"Someone been in here?" his voice matter-of-fact as if he addressed a stranger.

"No, I left them that way."

"Must have been in a hurry." The glib remark meant to break the growing tension in the room had the opposite effect.

"Well, the way you ride in and out of towns, Dakota, I didn't think it prudent to waste any time."

He caught the heavy sarcasm in her words, but the quick grimace of her lips said more. Everything had changed, and so had they.

"You're exhausted. Sit down, Caitlyn, then you can tell me every-thing." His head spun with fatigue and the need to know what hap-pened, but she held the heavier burden. Where was the boy?

He waited until she sat. Her olive-green riding vest and skirt were fresh, but neither could hide the weariness of the woman who wore them. Her white cotton blouse with the crisp lace collar fastened tight to the last button. Did she think it made her appear unap-proachable? Formidable? He squinted, trying to imagine her as such. How could someone so small, despite the packaging, be anything but defenseless? He regarded the slim-cut skirt and dark leather boots, taking in the feminine shape he well remembered.

Too late, he realized he was examining her as he had the room, so he focused his eyes on her face, but he couldn't stop his inspection. Her hair was longer. Earlier, it was tied back with a strip of rawhide, but now it lay tousled and wild about her face.

He loved her beyond reason, and he reckoned with a sigh he always would. He had managed to control most things in his life, but his love for her had never been one. She was unique, like an exquisite artifact from some unknown distant land. It was a strange, unmatched combination of beauty, strength, determination, and yet fragility. Delicate and fragile.

A short chuckle slipped through his lips. Fragile was not a word Caitlyn would take as a compliment.

"Do I amuse you?" Her eyes didn't show the pain he'd glimpsed a moment before. Her expression was now like his, unreadable.

"Of course not. Caitlyn, I..." He stumbled over words. "I'm sorry," he added, then wondered what for.

She had that effect on him—always managing to keep him slightly off balance. It used to fascinate him. No one ever had that impact on him. Most people were too predictable, yet tonight he longed for both his feet to be firmly planted on solid ground.

Leaning back on the bed, she lifted her skirt hem to her thigh and tugged at the rawhide strap that bound a second pistol to her. Dakota grimaced at his condescending assumption. She hadn't walked into the saloon without any forethought of protecting herself. She would have done fine without him, which she apparently had for the last two years.

Wearily, he crossed to the bed and slumped down next to her. He felt out of place, as if he was intruding on a private matter that didn't concern him, but it most certainly involved him. Caitlyn was here and safe, but what about the boy?

"Caitlyn, where's Joshua? That's his name, isn't it?"

Her head snapped up. "You knew?" She dropped her leg ungracefully to the floor and lowered her head. "John Wakefield has him."

The defeated tone in the words hit Dakota like a bullet through his heart. His chest constricted in anguish, and yet what else had he expected her to say? What words could he possibly say that wouldn't be less than adequate? He was tired, his thinking slow, made even slower by the complexity of the situation.

The room grew dim, the air cool. Pushing off from the bed, he adjusted the lamp up, attempting to dispel the despondency settling into the room with them.

~ * ~

Caitlyn watched Dakota bend over to turn up the lamp's wick. She examined the width of his shoulders and his well-tailored form, the subtle and not-so-subtle changes.

His thick sable hair was longer. His once clean-shaven face possessed a new coarse beard, and his demeanor had become a bit rougher, perhaps a bit colder. Nonetheless, one thing remained the same in that he was solid, sure, levelheaded, and precisely what she needed.

Sitting back next to her, he draped an arm around her shoulders. The rich, comforting scent of leather and man encased her in a cloak of protection. She leaned her head against his shoulder and closed her eyes, relaxing into the hollow his arm provided, utterly spent.

"Why didn't you tell me you were carrying my child?" His words were soft, hesitant.

Leaning into his shoulder, she took a deep breath. "It didn't matter. You were leaving."

"How can you say that, Caitlyn?"

"Are you saying you would have stayed then?"

The pause lasted too long as she waited for him to reply. Composed self-preservation drifted back into her. "I didn't think so," she said, drawing away.

"I don't know. I would have done what was best. You should have sent word to me."

The cloak of betrayal draped back over her. "Oh? And where, pray tell, should I have sent word?" Lord, why did she bait him? This wasn't like her, or was it? She didn't know anymore.

"You could have found me."

"I thought by your leaving, that was the last thing you wanted."

"You know why I left." He spoke so quietly she almost didn't hear him.

"Yes, I do." Her voice was equally soft, yet sharp as a needle. "You left so I wouldn't be subjected to the perils of your life." She set her jaw and stared at him. "My father's dead, and a man who has a score to settle with you kidnapped my son. It all worked out well, didn't it?"

Her point, although well-placed, didn't compel an answer, and she didn't expect one.

He rubbed his brow. "Tell me what happened."

Standing, she faced the chest of drawers and examined the yellowed lace doily with her fingertips. "Friday before last, I went into town to get supplies. A neighbor, Elizabeth Cookman, came to stay with Joshua since Pa was working the fields."

"What kind of woman is Mrs. Cookman?" Dakota interrupted.

Caitlyn returned to the bed and perched next to him. He would want more than a brief description. "She's a young widow. She and her husband were from Boston. They came out west, invested in mining, and made a good living. Unfortunately, she lost her husband in a mining explosion a year ago, and, as a result, she sold the mine. They never had children, and she alluded to the fact that they couldn't. I believe she became attached to Joshua because of that."

"How did she end up staying with Joshua? Your idea or hers?"

"Hers, but I know where you're headed, Dakota, and I assure you she's not involved. She's a genteel lady, accustomed to cultivated people. I doubt she's ever heard of the likes of John Wakefield, let alone ever shared company with someone like him."

She paused for a deep inhale, then exhaled and continued, "When I rode back, it was dark. The first thing I noticed was the absence of a fire. At first, I thought they had gone for a walk and lost track of time, but when I entered...tables were upended, dishes broken, and two windows shot out." She moved away and bit her lower lip. "I found Pa in the side yard, his rifle in hand. I tried—" Her voice broke. "There was nothing I could do for him."

Dakota's expression darkened.

"This note was pinned to the wall with a knife." She unfolded a piece of paper from her vest pocket and handed the note to him.

Taking the paper from her, he read the crudely written words:

Cabe, got your woman and boy. Hope they're worth the bounty on your head. Don't take too long. They ain't got it. Devil's Canyon. Come alone. John Wakefield.

Dakota rolled the paper into a tight, angry ball.

"Apparently, they thought Elizabeth was me," Caitlyn added.

"You sure she wasn't part of this?" he asked.

"I'm sure." However, her words, even to her own ears, had an edge of uncertainty.

"What aren't you saying?"

Studying her hands, she weighed her following words before speaking. "She's odd. Not odd in a bad way," she added. "Just odd. The last year has been difficult for her. She never got over the death of her husband. She wanted children more than anything." She pictured Elizabeth conspiring with a man like John Wakefield. "No, she's not a part of this, Dakota. This is between you and Wakefield."

She waited for Dakota's reaction. He nodded, but she had seen that expression before. He didn't trust anyone.

"Anyway, I rode back into town and told the sheriff. I asked him not to tell anyone that Wakefield had taken the wrong woman, because I didn't want Wakefield to know the truth, and then I headed out after them. I thought if I rode hard enough, I could catch up, but I didn't. I had no idea where Devil's Canyon was."

"It's not a place most men know about, let alone a woman," Dakota said in a soft tone. "How did you know to come to Silverwater?"

"The second day out, I ran into an old trapper. He'd heard of Devil's Canyon and said it was near Silverwater, but wouldn't tell me anything more. He mumbled it was no place for a woman."

"It's not."

She ignored his remark. "Why are you in Silverwater?"

"Same reason."

"How did you know?"

"An old friend, Judd Williams, tracked me down through the Gilly pass and told me, though he didn't have all the facts."

"How did he know?"

"Judd's been keeping an eye on you." Dakota paused, as if he waited for a flare of temper.

"That's about a five-day ride from here."

"Three if you push."

She hesitated, then stretched out her hand in a peace offering. "I'm glad you're here, Dakota."

He took her hand in his much larger one and squeezed it. "I'll make this right, Caitlyn. I will get Joshua back. I promise you."

She smiled. Dakota Cabe didn't promise what he couldn't deliver.

"I'll light another lamp." Rising from the bed, he strode to the lamp by the window. Flicking a match from his pocket, he touched it to the wick. Immediately, the corner of the room brightened with additional light, and he adjusted it down to a soft glow.

Standing by the coat rack, he shrugged out of his duster and hung it and his hat over it. Returning to Caitlyn, he offered her his hand and drew her into his arms. Gently, he brushed a lock of her hair out of her eyes and tucked it behind her ear. She leaned into him, and his strength enfolded her in an embrace she never wanted to escape. The strange bitterness within began to melt and fade away. The strain in her shoulders loosened, and she clasped her arms around his waist. He was the man she loved, a man she would love until the day she died. He renewed her courage and changed her desperation into hope.

Leaning back, he swept a finger across her cheek in a soft caress before slipping his finger under her chin. He lifted her gaze to meet his. "I've missed you, Caitie. You know I love—" He stopped, took a step back out of her embrace, and all connectivity between them ended.

"I'll leave at dawn, and I will bring Joshua back." The warmth of his eyes cooled to gray ice.

Agitation overwhelmed her. She twisted her chin from his hand and pushed away. "And you want me to do what? Wait here and twiddle my thumbs? I thought you knew me, Dakota." She strode furiously across the room, struggling not to lose the fragile rein she held over her emotions. "I'm going with you."

"Don't be a fool, woman," he shot back. "You don't know Wakefield as I do. I can't take care of you and get Joshua back at the same time." He dropped his head and held out his hand, "Damn Cat, I didn't mean—"

Spinning on her heels, painful indignation snapped her frail emotional control.

"Take care of me? You must be joking. Take care of me?" she repeated in an unnaturally high voice. "Is that what you did when you rode out of town and never looked back?" Her heartbeat was in a furious tempo of pain while her emotions raced out of control. "Every day I waited for you, hoping and praying you'd come back. But you didn't. All I had for sorry consolation were your glib words of how better off I'd be without you. How much safer I'd be." Her eyes stung with tears of remembered heartache.

"You didn't even stick around long enough to find out you had a son. So, don't you dare mention taking care of me. I took care of myself, and when Joshua came along, I took care of him." She gripped the edge of the chest of drawers for support.

Springing like a mountain cat onto its prey, Dakota knocked the coat rack to the floor. "Damn you, Caitlyn." He turned on her with his own fury. "I loved you. It nearly destroyed me when I left, but I did what I thought was best. God damn it! I only wanted to protect you."

His words were biting and unsympathetic as he swallowed up the distance between them and pointed his finger at her like a weapon. "And as for my son, woman, you're shooting from the hip, and you damn well know it." He stared at her without compassion. "You could have told me."

He raked his hair back away from his face in disbelief. "You should have told me." His face mere inches from hers, his tone was low, sharp, and deadly as he said, "I had the right to know." Staring at her another moment, his anger dissipated, his strength depleted. "You've grown cold, Caitie. Do you hate me that much?"

"No," she whispered, but said nothing more.

Anguish showed plainly in his eyes, but she couldn't take back her words any more than rewrite the past. Walking to the window, she drew the curtain to the side to view the street below. It was late, a few people stirred, but all she saw was the damage both their choices had created.

"I'm going with you, Dakota. It's not open for discussion." Her voice flat, steady, and unemotional. "I can either ride with you or follow along behind."

"All right, Caitlyn. We'll leave at first light." Dakota sat on the bed.

Stepping away from the window, she watched him shrug out of his vest, undo his suspenders, and unbutton his shirt. He lifted his shirt off one shoulder. Coarse black hair peeked out from beneath his undergarments. Corded muscles strained against the faded ribbed cotton. She wet her lips and tried to focus on something other than him, but he still had the same effect on her as he did the first day she saw him.

Reaching over his head, he grabbed the back of his undershirt and pulled it off. The well-remembered scars across his back, now only faint white lines, blinked back at her. His toned muscles flexed as he rose and removed his gun belt. Her nerves stretched taut as he leaned over the bed and hung his guns on the bedpost nearest the door. She sighed with visible relief. Where he placed his firearms marked where he slept.

Perhaps sensing her scrutiny, he glanced back at her. "If we're going to get an early start, we best get some shut-eye."

Nodding, she unbuttoned her vest, then her blouse, and eased out of them, then bent to remove her riding skirt. Standing in her camisole, she peered back in time to see Dakota blow out the bedside lamp and slip between the sheets. He still wore his long drawers.

Returning to the window, she peeked out. Several young men in the street stared up at her well-illuminated figure. She blew out the lamp, hurried to the bed, and then slid beneath the sheets next to him.

His back formed a solid wall between them, making it clear any further discussions wouldn't be necessary. She stretched a tentative hand to his shoulder. Warm and smooth, but no response. He was sound asleep.

Releasing a grunt, she flopped onto her back. After an hour of useless contemplation, exhaustion, and his soft, steady breathing, she too fell asleep.

Chapter 5

Pink, purplish rays of light splashed through the open window and across Caitlyn's sleeping figure. Evidently, she had tossed and turned all night as the bed sheets were twisted around her, revealing more than Dakota needed to see. He could leave now without her. She didn't know the location of Devil's Canyon, and she would be safe here. He snorted. Nope, she'd follow along behind. Taking his gaze from her body, he walked to the far corner.

"Time to get up, unless you plan to sleep all day." He buckled on his gun belt.

Slapping off the bed covers, she threw her legs to the side of the bed, snatched her blouse and skirt to her, and then stood defiantly. "I'll be dressed before you finish putting on your artillery."

He studied her as she dressed; she was the most stubborn woman he'd ever run across. He didn't want her to come; hell, he wanted to protect the woman, not bring her to the wolves' den.

Getting into Devil's Canyon without getting his head blown off would be tough. The bounty on his head was good whether he was alive or strapped dead across his horse. He knew which option Wakefield would prefer. What would happen to Caitlyn if he were killed? She would be alone in Devil's Canyon with a bunch of ruthless outlaws. He wanted Caitlyn safe, but she wouldn't be Caitlyn if she didn't insist on coming—damn, obstinate woman.

A reluctant grin touched his lips. Her damn, infuriating pigheadedness was what caught his eye in the first place.

She slapped her gloves across his back. "Well, are you with me or not?"

He gave her a subtle smile. "I'm with you, Caitlyn. I'm most definitely with you."

~ * ~

It was late morning, the sun high in the vivid turquoise sky, before they slowed their pace and walked their horses. The landscape had changed considerably in the few hours since they'd left town.

The wide-open dust bowl gave way to rocky ground, and then to spectacular mountains. For the last half hour, they'd traveled through a mountain pass, which grew narrower and rockier as they proceeded. It was a place of beauty and hidden danger.

Caitlyn nudged her horse, leaning over her mare's shoulders as she patted its neck.

"If we keep a steady pace, we should reach the canyon by nightfall, though it gets pretty rough from here on in. We need to rest the horses soon." Dakota twisted in the saddle as if remembering. "There's a creek up around the next bend where we can stop. Come on, Caitie."

His horse responded, and Caitlyn snapped her head up. She stared at the mare, and then at him.

"Caitie?" Her voice was incredulous. "You named your horse Caitie?"

He smothered a chuckle. "Well, yes, I did," he answered, but didn't look at her. "Why?"

"It's my name. Why would you give your horse my name?"

"I don't know. Like the name, I reckon." Leaning close to the horse's head, he spoke softly, "Probably because she's hard to handle and stubborn as an ole' mule."

"I heard that."

"I said she's spirited and warm-hearted."

"Uh huh."

They rode several more yards, the rock walls closing in on both sides. A small avalanche of rocks startled Caitlyn, and she glanced up at the rocky incline. To her right, small stones came crumbling down. Alarmed, she turned to see if Dakota had noticed. He had.

With two fingers, he motioned for her to move closer to the wall and out of sight.

Caitlyn nudged her horse to the side and slid out of her saddle, pulling her rifle free. She observed Dakota, reading his eyes, unable to see up the incline from her vantage point.

He stayed in his saddle and kept his focus trained on the steep bank above her head.

In a flash of motion, he drew his rifle from its sheath, laid the gun across his arm, aimed, and fired. The gun blast startled her despite having watched him pull the trigger. She gripped her rifle tighter. Dakota's concentration traveled down the rocky incline following something she still didn't see, but heard as it softly hit the ground.

He grinned. "Relax, Caitie, just dinner."

Relieved, she repacked her rifle and stepped out from under the rock ledge. Dismounting, he picked up the rabbit and tied it to the side of his saddle. "We'll stop up there."

Her gaze followed the length of his rifle as he pointed beyond a curve in the trail.

"We'd best eat while we have a chance.

With a nod, she followed him around the bend. The trail opened into a vast basin between the mountains. A creek, a short distance away, babbled cheerfully through the quiet surroundings.

When they stopped, she flipped open her saddlebags and took out the few necessities she always carried, such as eating utensils, a tin pot, a single cup, and a small pouch of coffee. Underneath those were Joshua's things. Touching them briefly, she reclosed the bag and gazed over the back of her mare at the mountain range in the distance.

Somewhere out there in Devil's Canyon was Joshua. An innocent baby. Her breath caught in her chest. John Wakefield, a man with no morals, a reputed killer, held her baby. Her eyes burned with unshed tears, and fear rode her back like a burr under a saddle.

She pinched the skin between her eyes and tried to block out the pain and the tears. Good God, she couldn't let her emotions get the best of her now. Picking up the cooking utensils and coffee, she turned to find Dakota watching her.

She froze, transfixed like a mouse under the scrutiny of a hawk. Brushing a strand of hair out of her face, she managed the pretense of a smile, then started toward him. "I'll make us some coffee if you fetch the water."

He stood, his legs in a rigid, wide stance.

When he didn't move, she answered his questioning eyes. "I'm all right—really."

He pushed up the rim of his Stetson higher for a better view, then broke his stance. "Then I'll go get the water. I'll take the horses with me to the creek and let them drink." Taking the tin pot from her hand, he added, "Watch your back, Caitie."

Dakota led both horses down the grassy bank to the creek, his long coat slapping rhythmically against his boots. He never ceased to amaze her. He had such a distinctive walk, between his boots, spurs, and riding coat, yet she never could hear his approach.

Scouting about, she gathered a small bundle of sticks to start a campfire. The flames gobbled at the dry wood, dancing wildly as they licked the dry air. Satisfied, she sat back on her heels and waited for him, listening to the quiet sounds of the area.

In a short while, he returned and tied both horses to a nearby scrub oak and set about constructing a makeshift spit for the rabbit he'd cleaned at the creek. "Hungry?" he asked, "Hungry?"

"Getting so. How long before we start again?"

He gauged the sun. "About an hour. I don't want to get to the canyon before dusk. We'll be less visible then."

She spooned some coffee into the tin pot and stirred it.

"We didn't finish talking last night, Caitlyn, so I want you to tell me everything that's happened since I've been gone."

Nestling the coffeepot into the fire, she sighed. Where would she begin? A week ago? When John Wakefield kidnapped their son and killed her father, and she set out after them? Or two years ago, when Dakota rode out of her life and never came back?

She glanced at him, and his warmth charmed her as it had years ago. His presence melted some of the hopelessness of the situation and restored the possibility that all might be right again.

The rabbit cooked quickly. Removing it from the fire, Dakota cut the sizzling meat into chunks with his hunting knife. Caitlyn removed the tin pot from the fire with her handkerchief and poured the steamy, hot black liquid into the lone tin cup. The robust and hearty aroma was invigorating. Taking a sip, she offered the cup to him.

"Thanks." He took the offering and her hand into his and sipped the hot liquid, winking at her. "You still know how to make a mean pot of coffee, Caitie." He released her hand but held her gaze.

His features were tough but warm, much of the boy still buried within the man. She contemplated his face. What about him intimidated others? His unshaved face gave off an aggressive appearance along with his high, well-defined cheekbones and rugged chin line, but that wasn't it. His lips? No, despite being firmly set and without expression, they were soft and full...enticing, actually.

She evaluated his eyes, a bluish-gray to granite, depending on the light and circumstance. One moment, they could warm a woman like a kindled fire on a heatless winter night, and in another turn, a man's blood stone cold. Right now, his eyes warmed several shades, and for the briefest of seconds, he offered a part of himself he'd never shown her before. It was a part of him no one else would ever see.

She wondered if the darkness she saw underneath his rough façade was the fear of losing the only innocence in his life: Joshua. She couldn't prevent the hitch in her breathing. Looking away, she busied herself with the coffeepot.

"Should we pack up?" More a statement than a question, but she needed something to break the morose spell. She glanced back at him, but he hadn't moved.

He sat quietly by the fire, his elbows resting on his knees. "Tell me about Joshua, Caitlyn. What's he like?"

The question caught her by surprise. She knew her son as well as she knew the father. However, an apt description of the son for the father eluded her. She closed her eyes, unable to keep the smile at bay.

"He's fourteen months old, strong-boned, and strong-willed." She laughed. "Pig-headed is more like it." Her smile spread. "His hair is so soft, like a newborn fawn, and black, black as coal. Lord, it's as wild as it can be. Taking a brush to it is an event in itself." She tossed her head, remembering the impossible task. "His eyes are green, like mine, but darker and so deep I can lose myself in them." Her son's eyes always gave her pause. "When he laughs, his eyes laugh too."

They wouldn't be laughing now, though, would they? She snapped her eyes open to stop her sudden train of thought. Spotting an unfamiliar wildflower on the ground in front of her, she picked it up and twirled it between her fingers. The picture of Joshua was so clear—his smile, his hearty laugh, his total lack of fear, but also the quiet, unfathomable side of him.

Dropping the flower, she looked up at his father. "He's just like you, Dakota."

Dakota sat for a moment before handing her back the cup of coffee. "Thank you, Caitlyn."

Standing, he picked up a stick and then knelt back beside her. "This is how Devil's Canyon lies out." He made a large oblong circle in the dirt with the twig. "As far as I know, there is only one way in on this side of the canyon. There is an exit on the other side, and a few trails cutting out to the sides, but they aren't easy to access. You'd have to be inside Devil's Canyon to find them.

"The entrance is narrow with cliffs on either side. If we can get through here…" He indicated the canyon's entrance. "…it opens out to a large basin, which narrows again on the other end. There is a place on the far side the Indians named Flat Rock, which overlooks the entire canyon. It's an ideal location for us, but too far in for us to reach." He made a small circle inside the larger oblong shape to depict Flat Rock. Pointing again to the narrow canyon entrance, he continued. "This is where they'll be waiting for me. There's no other way in and no protection from the canyon walls."

He leaned back on his heels. "It's also where you'll come in. Since they assume they already have you, they won't be expecting you." He smiled grimly. "We'll split up before we get to the canyon's mouth. I'll ride in and draw their fire, then you slip in behind me. You'll have to play it as you see it. They're after me, not you, so I'm hoping they won't chase after you. That is, if they see you. God damn it." He threw the stick to the ground. "This is insane."

She glanced from his drawing to the man. He rarely lost his temper, at least he never showed it if he did. "Dakota?" She reached out to touch him.

"No." He backed away. "We aren't doing this."

Confused, she hesitated for a moment and then asked, "What do you mean?"

His behavior was out of character for him, but then again, two years had passed. Her heart sank. Why had she thought he wouldn't change? She had.

"Caitlyn."

His touch on her shoulder snapped her from her thoughts.

"I'm going into Wakefield's camp alone, and you'll stay here. There's no argument. That's the plan. Got it?" He pulled her to her feet with more force than necessary.

Pah. He hadn't changed one damn bit. She jerked loose her sleeve. "You're right, Dakota. There is no argument. It's been discussed and settled." Twirling about, she marched over to her gear. Yanking her rifle free, she faced him. "Am I not a better shot than most men?" She waited for the only reply he could offer.

He leaned back on one leg, jutted his chin out in aggravation, and crossed his arms.

She cocked the rifle. "Well?"

"What the hell are you doing?" he demanded.

Not checking for accuracy, she shot a stone a mere three inches from his right foot. Only the toe of his boot flinched. Cocking her rifle again, she briefly aimed and fired. His Stetson whizzed from his head and landed four feet behind him.

"Damn it, Caitlyn. Not my hat." His gloved hand palmed across his left ear, and he turned to fetch his Stetson. "So that's your damn point? Render me deaf and ruin a perfectly good Stetson?" Shaking his head, he dusted off his cherished hat, mumbling profanity.

"The point is...you'd be minus your leg and head if I chose."

He started toward her. "Fine. You're an expert shot. Better than most men. Now give me the damn rifle."

Instead, she cocked the weapon for a third time and pointed at his chest. He stopped a few feet short of her. They both knew he could take the rifle from her without her taking the shot, but would he?

"Come on, Caitie, you aren't serious." Meeting her glare for glare, he still hesitated. "You're wasting ammunition, you know."

"He's my son, Dakota. Two guns are always better than one, and now you're wasting our son's time."

He had options, but he didn't take them. Setting his teeth, he ground them slightly, then took a step back. Squatting, he grunted, then picked up the stick and, releasing a weary sigh, pointed back to the map in the dirt.

"If I'm lucky, I'll meet you here." The stick dug into the dirt, marking an alcove inside the canyon. Dakota rose again, his brows drawn together in thought. "I'll be less of a headache for them if I'm dead." He shrugged. "Bounty's good either way, so you best get past quick as you can. If my luck goes bad, I'll be able to hold them off only for so long." His words were cold, impersonal, and matter-of-fact.

"Dakota, I wouldn't leave you—"

His fierce expression pinned her in mid-sentence. "Don't waste time mourning me if I get a bullet to the head, Caitlyn. Get to Joshua and your friend, and then get out through the back. I doubt they'll leave a guard behind. There isn't anywhere for a woman and child to go in the canyon. Besides, they want me, not womenfolk." His caustic stare warned her there was no need for further discussion.

His blunt words chilled Caitlyn.

~ * ~

Dakota had been sharp with Caitlyn, but she needed to know the odds.

Years earlier, he had ridden through Devil's Canyon. A moody, menacing place, it was the perfect spot for the men who held his son. The odds of getting in were slim. Getting back out? He grunted with weariness. He needed to live long enough to draw the outlaws away from the entrance so Caitlyn could slip through and get Joshua.

The dream of settling down with Caitlyn flittered through his mind. It now had substance and form. He could picture the cabin nestled in the pine trees and a creek full of mountain trout. He could even see himself teaching Joshua what a boy needed to know to become a man. So vivid. So real. So simple. Is this what Red Wolf, his Indian friend, meant when he said a man sees his dreams clearly before he dies? Death was the easy part. Death no longer awed him. He had faced it too many times for it to hold any novelty for him now. What scared the hell out of him was what would happen to Caitlyn and his son if he died.

In the past, when the world had proven too cruel even for him, her image would come to mind. Her fiery, green, defiant eyes would taunt him, daring him to be less than she thought him to be. As long as he envisioned her face, he'd come through for her. God willing, he would this time too.

He turned and held out his hand. "Ready?"

An unbreakable bond passed between them as she placed her hand in his. His calloused hand closed around her much smaller one, and he pulled her into his embrace.

"We'll make it, Caitlyn, all of us." Bending, he pressed his lips against hers, lingering for a moment before drawing back.

She stroked his whiskers with familiarity and ran one slim finger across his lips. "I know we will."

Handing her up onto her horse, he checked her saddle straps and cinched them tighter. He double-checked both her guns and handed her one of his knives. Taking the knife, she pushed it down into her boot and took a deep breath.

He returned to the campfire and doused the embers with the remaining coffee. The smoldering ashes and makeshift map were extinguished with dirt. Retrieving both the tin cup and coffee pot, he replaced them in her saddlebag. "We don't want to forget these. I'll want a cup of your coffee in the morning."

Caitlyn gave a weak smile. "As long as you fetch the water."

"Yes, ma'am." Tipping his hat to her, he proceeded to his horse.

He checked his own guns, the chambers clicking loudly in the late afternoon's stillness. Nimbly, he threw himself upon his horse, and his horse pranced in anticipation.

Drawing back on the reins, he nodded to Caitlyn. "Let's head out."

~ * ~

Time passed quickly now that the day's heat was behind them. The rocky terrain turned gentler, and the air grew cooler. Caitlyn wiped sweat from her brow while the sun sank low behind the mountains, leaving long shadows across their path. The timing was as hoped, enough light to enter the canyon, but not enough to turn them into easy targets.

A quarter of a mile from the entrance of Devil's Canyon, Dakota reined up short and dismounted. "This is where I go on alone. You hold up here until you hear gunfire, then come and come on fast. Don't stop for anything, and I mean anything. You understand me, Caitlyn?"

His meaning was clear. If he went down, she needed to ride on. She understood.

Untying his canteen from his saddle, he walked over to her. Taking a slow swallow, he handed the container up to her. When she reached for it, a blast shattered the quiet air, and the canteen spun from her hand.

With the speed and strength of a mountain lion, he jerked her and her rifle free from her saddle. The sudden whack across the mare's rump from his rifle sent the horse bolting from danger. Bullets peppered the ground around them. He headed for the nearest haven available—a small dugout several yards away.

She couldn't breathe. His tight grip around her waist squeezed all the air from her lungs, and her feet dangled inches from the ground as he lunged for safety. Cold rock pressed into her back before he released her, and she dropped to the ground with a jolt that rattled her teeth.

He glanced at her. "Sorry."

Scrambling to her feet, she caught the rifle he tossed her.

"At least two men halfway up the embankment," he shouted over the gunfire, "and probably one or two behind us on the trail. They must have followed us from town. Damn it."

Caitlyn squinted at the rocky embankment to her right, where he had indicated. Nothing yet.

Whipping free the rifle he wore across his back, he pointed the barrel toward a gap in the rock, which hinted at another embankment. "I'm gonna circle around and clear the trail behind us, so we don't get boxed in. Cover me, Cat."

Bullets chipped at the rocky wall on either side. She dipped her chin then repositioned herself within the circle of hard granite. Lying down her rifle, she drew both her revolvers and nodded again before letting off a volley of bullets against the embankment.

He sprang from the dugout and to the gap in the far wall.

After reloading both revolvers, she then retrieved her rifle. Bullets dug into the rock surrounding her. The deep report of Dakota's Winchester grew fainter in the distance.

Fixing her gaze on the bank above her, she waited for the men to make their move. As if in compliance, a flicker of steel flashed in the fading daylight. She aimed and fired. A dark form toppled down the rocky bank and came to rest several yards in front of her. One less threat.

Scanning the wall, she watched, listening to the ensuing gunfire in the distance. She hated waiting, always had. Untying her hat, she tossed it out of the dugout. A volley of bullets ripped through it, pitching it up into the wind. The glint of a man's gun caught her eye. She sighted him in and fired. Her shot was deadly accurate, and he too tumbled down the embankment.

If her count of volleys had been correct, one man remained. Patiently, she held back until she spotted him trying to reposition. She sighted him in, but he changed course at the last moment, and her bullet whizzed harmlessly past him. Dropping to his knees, he fired in her direction.

"Damn." The bullet came so close she could feel the air part.

To prevent being trapped, she needed to move. Scrambling to her feet, she dashed out of the enclosed area. Exiting the dugout, she stood in the cool evening breeze and sighted in the man. She squeezed the trigger a bare second before his bullet chewed into her upper arm. Wincing in pain, she spun to the ground. Stunned, yet keeping her concentration on the bank above, she sighed with relief when the man pitched over the bank's side. Three men were now dead at the base of the rocky embankment.

She examined her damaged arm. The wound wasn't severe, but it hurt like an angry hornet's sting. Ripping a long strip of fabric from her undergarments, she tied the wound as tight as possible.

Picking her rifle up, she got to her feet. The area in front was clear, as was the trail leading away from it—no sound of gunfire in the distance. Cold fear shot through her.

She cocked her rifle and whirled. In her sights, above the dugout emerged two men. Their guns were already trained on her. Both were filthy, a good indication of their time on the run.

The man on the right was tall and lean, his hair a messy reddish-blond, his skin rough and scaly from the harsh sun and wind. A scar from his forehead to his left cheek stood out prominently. He smiled menacingly at her, exposing a gap where several teeth once resided.

Bracing herself for whatever might transpire, she forced a calm exterior. Straightening her shoulders, she contemplated the other man whose appearance was of no improvement. A swarthy man whose greasy black hair fell to his shoulders might have been handsome under cleaner circumstances. However, the leering smirk he bestowed upon her extinguished the thought.

She could take out one man, but eliminating both? Not likely. She'd bluff her way along until Dakota returned. As long as she had her rifle, she was safe.

A gun cocked a short distance behind her. Her stomach churned.

"I wouldn't try it, lady. You might be good, but ain't nobody that good."

The man dismounted with the squeak of leather and started to approach. The last thing she wanted to do was to turn her back on the two men in front of her, but the man advancing from behind gave her no choice. Keeping her rifle chest level, she turned.

There were, in fact, two men, one on foot, the other seated heavily on his horse. These men, as well, had their guns drawn and aimed at her.

Tilting her head back, she scrutinized the man approaching on foot.

Tall, broad-shouldered, with short, choppy blond hair cut haphazardly around his ears. His eyes were light, piercing blue. A deep scar to the side of his left eye gave his face a malicious appearance and hinted at an inner mean streak. Kin to the man behind her?

Sweat pooled around her neck and trickled down her blouse, the one sign of fear she couldn't conceal. Just as quickly, the cool evening breeze whisked them away.

The man appeared to be the leader, whether he appeared more educated or perhaps cleaner, she wasn't sure.

"Lady, I ain't playing games. Drop your gun, or I'll drop you right here, right now."

How could she give up her one means of defense, her only barrier between herself and these men? Dakota couldn't be far—unless—Dakota was dead, and he wasn't coming back. The thumping of her heart was so loud she was surprised the men didn't notice.

"Drop the gun or die, lady. Your choice."

With reluctance, she un-cocked her gun and lowered it. At least, she still had her knife.

"Well, well, ain't she a sight for sore eyes."

She glanced up at the man on horseback. His appearance both shocked and repulsed her. If the men behind her were unscrupulous, then this man had to be the keeper of hell.

Grossly overweight, his body spilled profusely over the saddle. Tobacco juice, like dried coffee stains, ran in streams from the corner of his deformed mouth to his chin and dripped from there to his chest. A long, ugly scar ran from his lips to the top of his ear, distorting the entire left side of his face. His heavily hooded eyes hinted at a recent drinking spree.

"What's wrong, girl?" Using the sleeve of his shirt, he rubbed his lips, smearing the tobacco juice across his face. His gaze roamed over her with blatant lust. "My good looks take your breath away?" He sneered at her.

She said nothing.

"So, whatcha doing, missy? Squirrel hunting?" He nodded at the three dead men. "Mighty big squirrel." His laughter, harsh and unpleasant, echoed through the canyon. "Pretty good shot, though, ain't she, John?"

Caitlyn's gaze flew to the man who had closed the distance between them. The infamous John Wakefield?

Wakefield jerked the rifle from her hands, his stare devoid of emotion or feeling. "Who the hell are you, and what are you doing here, lady?"

She held his glare, but clamped her mouth shut.

Unexpectedly, his hand shot out and caught her across the cheek. The force of his slap turned her feet into the dirt and spun her off balance. Her hands shot out to break her fall. Connecting briefly with the ground, she scooped up a handful of dirt and swept it up into his eyes. He wiped madly at them.

"A real minx, ain't she, John? I think she needs some taming." The obese man smirked.

Rubbing at his irritated eyes, John grabbed her wrist and slammed her to him. "I'll tame the bitch."

Another rider came up from the canyon with her and Dakota's horses.

"Hey, John. Lookie here. She's got two horses." A young boy, no more than fifteen, trotted up, guiding the horses behind him. Blind admiration for John shone bright in the young boy's eyes. He glanced at Caitlyn before turning his attention back to John. "Look at this one, John. Ain't she a beaut?"

The boy slid off his horse to lead Dakota's closer. John dropped her arms and walked to the boy. He scrutinized the horse, then flipped open the saddlebags. He did the same with Caitlyn's horse, removing a few of her personal items. He stopped short of Joshua's things, and she sighed with relief.

She glanced at the two men on the ledge; their guns still pointed at her.

"Don't think about running, lady," said the fat man. "I ain't ashamed to shoot a woman in the back." Tobacco juice still dripped from his mouth.

He reminded her of a rabid animal.

"I think the lady's lonely. She needs attention." The fat man grinned, licking his lips. His foot touched the ground, and John turned and aimed his gun at him.

"Get back on your damn horse, Todd. This ain't the time."

Stunned silence ensued.

"Hell, John, what's got you so riled? You never been opposed to funning before," Todd demanded.

"Take a good gander at the damn horse, you stupid fool. Does she seem like a pack horse to you?" John pointed to Dakota's horse, stating the obvious. His eyes flared with contempt at Todd.

"How you know it ain't her horse?" He glared back.

"Because I found these in the other saddlebag." John flung a few of her undergarments to the ground. "And Todd," he snarled, "if she were traveling alone, she wouldn't need two saddles, now would she?" Turning away in disgust, he walked back to Caitlyn. "Where do you figure in on all this, lady? That's Cabe's horse, isn't it? Where is he?"

She stared at him, not uttering a word. They hadn't killed Dakota. He was still alive.

"Woman, I'm talking to you." His exasperation reaching a boiling point, he gripped her jaw. "What are you doing with Dakota Cabe?"

Her determination turned stone cold.

"Cabe? Is it Dakota Cabe's horse, John?" the boy exclaimed, a new interest sparking toward her. "Do you figure he cut out, John?"

"Thinking like that, boy, will dig you an early grave," John answered the youth, but kept his gaze fixed on her. "He's around here somewheres. You can bet on it."

The boy wasn't the only one scanning the rocky terrain.

John leaned closer to Caitlyn, his expression deadly serious. "You'll talk, woman. Trust me. You'll talk."

Chapter 6

Dakota stared down the long barrel of his Winchester rifle at the men surrounding Caitlyn, John Wakefield in his sights. His finger twitched against the trigger in harmony with the beating of his heart. Seconds sped past, while thoughts churned through his mind.

No, too risky.

"Damn." He rested on his heels and let the rifle butt drop to the ground beside him. Frustrated, he knocked his hat back onto his shoulders and wiped the perspiration from his face with the sleeve of his coat. He glared up into the sky, then to Caitlyn and the men.

There were five, including Wakefield and a young boy. Dakota could take out two men before anyone reacted, maybe three.

There wasn't time to give her an opening, but then again, maybe not. She'd taken a bullet in the arm, and all the men had their guns trained on her. Damn it to hell and back; he couldn't take the chance.

Shit. He blamed himself for this latest mess. He'd been too preoccupied with the men holding Joshua and not enough to the possible bounty hunters trailing along behind.

Three of the four men he shot, he recognized from town. One was the one-eyed man from the saloon. The fourth man, whom he couldn't identify, held a wanted poster of him in his pocket.

A fifth man jumped him from behind, and Dakota ended up in a fighting match with a man who might have been a descendant of Hercules. By the time he wrestled out of the man's grasp and made it back to Caitlyn, Wakefield's men had surrounded her.

The night air grew still and colder. The sun's last rays had fallen from the canyon walls, leaving the moon to make its lonely trek across the sky. Should he give it his best shot and try to free Caitlyn? If luck went south, Joshua would become an orphan.

Hell, what if the men at the base camp had orders to kill their captives by a particular time if Wakefield didn't return? Where was the base camp? Dakota had been operating on assumptions. He had to wait.

His gut ripped in two. How could he sit and do nothing? A lesser woman wouldn't have a chance. He snorted in disgust. What difference did that make? He didn't love any other woman. Dropping his head back onto his shoulders, he forced himself to block out useless thoughts.

"Think, damn it." He glanced back at the men below.

They appeared to be as indecisive as he. Did they know who Caitlyn was? He dropped his chin to his chest. No, if they had, they would have flushed him out by now.

He calculated her ramrod statue. God, the woman, had guts. She wasn't offering any information. If their fidgeting was any indication, Wakefield and his men were leery of the situation. They would be stupid to try anything here. Dakota set his jaw, hoping his best move at this point was to do nothing.

Now on foot, Flat Rock was a possibility. Before, the horses, extra gear, and the two of them made it impossible. Now he could go around the canyon's rim and reach Flat Rock by morning. Using his rifle, he pushed off from the bank and adjusted his hat back down low on his head.

"You hang tight, Caitie." He touched his gloved fist to his lips and held it out to her. He focused on Wakefield and extended his index finger and thumb. "And you, you son of a bitch." The gesture gave him a little satisfaction when he pulled the imaginary trigger on Wakefield. Yup, one bullet between the eyes.

~ * ~

It rattled Caitlyn to her core. She was alone with a bunch of ruthless men. She tried to swallow down her fear, but it rose up like bile in her throat.

"You're a mere slip of a woman, but hell if I'm gonna take any chances." Wakefield tied her hands in front of her and then attached a long rope from her hands to his saddle horn.

She shied away from him, and he chuckled at her apprehension. Clasping her sweaty hands together, she steeled herself not to let her fear show. A man like Wakefield would feast on her terror like crows on a carcass. Dakota wasn't dead, and no doubt he had a plan. She would be ready when the time came.

"Let's move out, boys." Wakefield motioned to his men and yanked on the rope attached to her.

She almost lost her footing but righted herself and then stumbled into a half-jog. Wakefield's men followed, the young boy bringing up the rear with the new horses.

The toil of trying to keep pace with a horse soon exhausted her. The air blew crisp and refreshing on her flushed face, but it did nothing to restore her worn-out body. The rawhide had cut into soft flesh around her wrists. Blood oozed out around the bindings, irritating her skin and making them itch incessantly.

Bringing her hands to her chest, she hoped to loosen the strips of leather, but John's horse lurched forward in the dark, and she stumbled and fell. He glanced back at her when the slack in the rope went out. He smiled as she struggled to regain her feet, only to fall back again when he prodded his horse into a trot.

She had no choice but to roll over and let her back take the brunt of the hard earth. Her leather vest slid along the ground, snagging on the rough terrain, and she rocked from side to side to keep it from wearing through. The light fabric of her blouse would be no barrier from the unforgiving ground.

John jerked his horse to stop. Shifting in his saddle, he stared at her, and the other men followed suit and waited. "Get up."

She scowled at him with hatred, her body coated in dirt and mud. He quirked a brow as if surprised. She vowed again not to show any fear.

"I said get up."

Pushing herself onto her elbows and knees, she heaved herself to her feet. Unsteady, she tried to suck in a deep breath, but her lungs shuddered with the effort. Her lips tasted salt and dirt.

"I've grown tired of our game, so you best tell me what your connection is with Cabe." He waited for an answer.

None came.

"You can talk, can't you, woman?"

She stared at him while taking in gulps of air.

He considered the canyon. "You can walk the whole damn way. It makes no difference to me.

She glanced at her mare standing a short distance from her, then at the young boy. He gave her a look of respect and admiration. Why, because she wasn't dead yet, or because she rode in with Dakota Cabe? The boy was deluded. How did he end up with the likes of Wakefield? Could his story be anything like Dakota's? She raised her arms to wipe the dusty sweat from her eyes, surprised to see both arms bleeding. Her sleeves were tattered strips of fabric.

How had Dakota tolerated men like Wakefield? To have ridden and lived with outlaws like these men. She glanced back at the boy, who stared open-mouthed at Wakefield, hanging onto each word as if they were golden nuggets to cash in at a future date. Her stomach churned.

"Cabe's left you, lady. You might as well change your loyalties." Sliding off his horse, Wakefield sauntered toward her, lowering his voice as he approached. "In case you haven't noticed, these men haven't been with a woman for a long time. They could be rough on a mite thing like you. I'd be different. All you have to do is tell me about Cabe."

He curled a strand of her hair under his nose and inhaled. "Damn, I haven't smelled anything as sweet as you in a long, long time." Stepping closer, he whispered into her ear, "I don't know what arrangements you came under, but I'm sure they ain't what you thought—Cabe's like my men. Use a woman for a while, get their fill, then move on. You may want to think about warming up a bit. It might save you a hell of a lot of grief in the long run."

Some of the men weren't much older than the gape-mouthed boy. She moved her gaze away from the lad and stared at the disgusting pig of a man inches from her face. Wakefield's filth and sweat nauseated her, yet he thought she would choose him over the worst life could offer. Leaning back her head, she spat full in his face.

The force of his hand against her cheek spun her into blessed darkness.

~ * ~

Dakota made his way along the canyon's ridge, his muscles taut as he navigated the treacherous edge. The sight of Caitlyn forced to walk behind Wakefield's horse ignited a fury in Dakota that propelled him onward. He ground his teeth and pounded the ground as he climbed higher along the canyon ridge. The plan he'd been contemplating for the last hour seemed pure foolishness, considering he was up here, and she was down there. Damn! Once he reached Flat Rock, his plan might seem more feasible.

Stopping, he removed his rifle and long duster and glanced up at the steep incline yet to climb. Perspiration ran down his neck in tiny streams. His chest shuddered with each breath he took. Undoing his bandana, he wiped his face and stuffed the cloth into the back of his pants. He draped his coat over his shoulders, slung his rifle across his back, and plodded on.

Shadows from the few pine trees that dotted the canyon rim grew longer as he dogged on toward Flat Rock. The poorly lit, rough terrain hindered his progress, and he had no idea how far he'd traveled. His pace slowed as night nestled in. A careless step in the dark would send him plunging over the side and into the canyon below. He continued to climb using the stars to light his way, but nothing resembled Flat Rock.

It had been years since he'd passed through Devil's Canyon, a posse in close pursuit. A fellow outlaw pointed out Flat Rock, or he wouldn't have seen the outcropping.

The trees became more numerous and blocked out the sparse light the moon and stars offered. Discouraged, he paused, his sense of footing gone. The last thing he needed, other than falling to his death, would be to knock rocks down the canyon wall, giving away his position. He had no choice but to stop for the night.

Frustration swelled within him. When Dakota was climbing, his mind stayed preoccupied with not careening off the edge. Now his fear for Caitlyn consumed him. Leaning against a tree, he squinted at his surroundings and waited for his ragged breathing to regulate. The ridge was a shade lighter than the blackness of the canyon beyond, and somewhere out there was Caitlyn.

He crept to the edge and knelt, glancing over the murky span of darkness. He searched the area, but nothing resembled a camp: no fire, no sign of life, nothing.

The night's air blew bitterly as it whipped along the canyon's edge. Rubbing his hands together, he puffed warm air into them. Standing, he put his coat back on and stepped away from the rim. Picking out a patch of ground, he settled for the night. The stars above him were so brilliant they seemed close enough to touch. He scooted back to find the most comfortable position on the rocky ground, then bundled the bottom of his coat around his legs and laid his rifle across his chest. Taking a last glimpse at the stars above, he covered his eyes with his hat and gave in to exhaustion.

~ * ~

Caitlyn woke with dry grit in her mouth. She wanted to lick her lips, but lacked any moisture to do so. It was night, and she lay with her cheek against the hard ground. She couldn't move her bound arms or legs, the rest of her body painfully stiff.

A few embers burned nearby. Squinting, she waited for her vision to adjust. Numerous dark forms lay sprawled out in a circle around the dying fire. Everyone slept except for one lone guard several yards away. Todd.

She strained to see through the dark. A shadowy form resembling a tent caused her heart to race. Were Joshua and Elizabeth in there?

Caitlyn longed to sit up and get a better view, but she didn't want to draw Todd's attention.

Her head throbbed, and she closed her eyes to press out the pain. After a couple of minutes, she reopened them, but the throbbing remained. The chilled rocky ground seeped into her bones, chilling her. She swallowed hard to keep from shivering. The fire had gone out, leaving only the remaining light from the thousands of stars littering the sky above. Dakota was up there somewhere; she knew it in her heart.

She scrutinized the canyon's edge. Something nagged at her. Why did she assume he would be on the rim instead of behind them on the trail? She shuffled through her mind. Flat Rock. Slowly, his words returned to her.

There's a place on the far side of the canyon, the Indians once named Flat Rock. It overlooks the entire canyon. An ideal location, but too far in for us to reach.

Yet, that was before all this happened.

She considered everything he'd told her. Flat Rock was on the rim toward the back of the canyon. If her navigation were correct, Flat Rock reached beyond and above their camp. Large boulders and a natural outcropping of rock made it nearly invisible from the canyon floor—perfect concealment for the Indians in their fight against the white man.

The legend spoke of Indians using it as the best trap. While white men tried to go through the narrow pass into what the Indians considered sacred ground, the Indians would roll large boulders off Flat Rock and crush the men below. The canyon was so narrow at both ends that escape was impossible.

If the enemy had scattered into the canyon or set up camp farther in, the Indians would take the trail from Flat Rock and slit their throats while they slept. The white men never suspected danger.

Dakota said Devil's Canyon was the best spot for outlaws to hold out since the area proved impossible for anyone else to enter without detection. Wakefield had the perfect setup, unless, of course, he knew little of Flat Rock and nothing of Dakota Cabe.

However, Dakota was one man, not part of a war party. To kill all the men by himself was a ridiculous notion, and rolling boulders down from Flat Rock would kill them all. What could she be doing? She sighed—nothing until they untied her.

When that time came, she needed to free Elizabeth and Joshua and escape to the trail to Flat Rock. Her head throbbed. Should she try to escape alone, and then come back together with Dakota as originally planned?

No. Caitlyn wouldn't leave Joshua, not while she was this close to him. Her eyelids fluttered. She was tired, exhausted, actually. She arched her eyebrows, but even that didn't keep her eyes open.

~ * ~

Dakota woke with a start, his back stiff and cold from the unforgiving ground. Sliding one finger under the rim of his hat, he surveyed his surroundings. The sun had yet to make its appearance, although a few of its tentative rays reached the canyon rim. He glanced to either side of him for the small animals scurrying away.

Using his rifle as a crutch, he pushed off from the ground, walked to the canyon's edge, and glanced down. The abyss remained steeped in darkness. He turned away, took two steps, then stopped short. There to his left in the distance lay Flat Rock. No doubt. Appropriately named, the morning sun illuminated the sizeable flat outcropping of rock only a hundred feet below him and twice the distance away.

He shouldered his rifle and backtracked a short distance. Moving away from the canyon's rim, he searched for a way through the brush growing thick along the rock's edge.

At last, he found an old path and made his way to his destination. The closer he came to Flat Rock, the sparser the trees and brush. When he moved above the outcropping, he found it accessible only by a precarious path of rock and gravel.

"Well, here it goes," he muttered, removing his coat and rifle before descending. Keeping his back to the incline, he lowered himself down the slope. He splayed his arms out along the side of him and tried to maintain as much contact with the ground as he could.

About twenty feet from his destination, the earth broke apart under his boots. He grabbed at the dirt on either side of him, but only succeeded in breaking loose more ground. His body bounced down the slope, his buttocks and hands taking most of the battering.

His legs rammed into the rim of rocks surrounding the overlook. "Ah, shit." The sudden stop to his swift descent pitched his upper torso over the stones, and with a poorly executed somersault, he landed with full impact onto Flat Rock.

"A damn Indian, you're not." He grunted after he caught his breath. Lying on his back, he stared at the sky above. "You don't know what you're missing, Caitlyn."

With effort, he rolled to his feet and stretched his back, relieved that nothing appeared to be broken. He turned and studied the abandoned Indian lookout, impressed with the handiwork the Indians had bestowed on it. The strategically placed boulders formed an impregnable barrier against any threat. Large logs still sat where they once propelled the boulders down into the canyon below. Indian carvings across the stones attested to the various battle scenes between the Indian and the white man.

He focused on the carvings to the spectacular view this new location offered him. Everything rumored about Flat Rock was true. The entire canyon was visible from here. He scanned the rim he had traveled, stopping at the spot where he spent the night. Eerily quiet except for the fresh morning breeze whistling through the canyon.

Glancing down, he realized why Flat Rock proved so tricky to spot from below. The various outcroppings of rock along the canyon wall appeared smooth from this position, but when he rode through the Canyon years ago, he saw only a mass of jagged, inaccessible rock.

He noted the worn, overgrown path leading down to the canyon. It was hard to imagine so few knew of this legendary landmark. The hatred between the white man and the Indian led most people to believe that anything to do with Indians was best forgotten. It would be a costly mistake for Wakefield.

Dakota's gaze wandered across the canyon floor, searching for what he had sought last night. There in a small crook of the canyon, invisible to all except someone on Flat Rock, lay Wakefield's camp. The fire had died out overnight, and the young boy was rebuilding it. Searching the area around the campfire, Dakota considered each dark image until he found Caitlyn. His pulse quickened.

Both her hands and feet tied, she sat up against a rock. He almost smiled, wondering what she had done to provoke the men into securing her so tightly. Surely six—no, another man stayed by the tent—seven men weren't afraid of one woman, but nothing amused him about Caitlyn being with John Wakefield and his hired guns.

Wakefield had picked the right location. Towering rock formations walled the camp on either side, making the site invisible and impenetrable. The camp even had a small canyon behind it, in case they needed to retreat, but they weren't superstitious since the camp sat nestled in the exact spot where men were once crushed to death in their sleep. Unfortunately, that fact didn't help Dakota in this instance. The trail leading to the camp might be a different story.

No sign of Joshua or Caitlyn's friend, Elizabeth. They were probably in the tent, which sat several yards from the campfire. Wakefield's men were not out searching for him. Why should they? They had what Dakota wanted, and they knew he would come back.

His consternation peaked when John Wakefield approached Caitlyn with a long knife. Leaning precariously over the edge of Flat Rock, Dakota watched as Wakefield stopped above her. Dakota's nerves strung tight, waiting. Wakefield cut her hands and feet free, then jerked her up.

She remained motionless. He took a step away, grasped the tin coffee pot next to the fire and a bag of ground chicory, then thrust both into her hands. He pointed to a large jug of water before walking over to Todd. The two men soon got into a heated debate, but both kept a watchful eye on her.

She stared at the men with absolute contempt, and Dakota feared she might throw the pot at them, but after a moment she turned and moved with a stiff gait toward the water jug.

He squinted against the morning sun, trying to decipher the meaning of her unusual gait. When she turned toward the fire, the reason was apparent. Mud adhered to her backside and her riding pants, and her vest ripped. Even the sleeves of her blouse shredded. That son of a bitch, Wakefield, had dragged her behind his horse.

He gripped the rock ledge until his knuckles turned white. "That, Wakefield, you worthless piece of shit, will cost you dearly." His gaze remained riveted on Caitlyn as she rinsed the pot twice, then refilled it with fresh water. She stopped and held still as if she knew he was watching.

Chapter 7

C aitlyn longed to peek behind her and up the canyon wall, but she didn't dare.

Instead, she walked back to the roaring fire, holding her head high with the dignity that would have charmed the knickers off Mrs. Clark.

Placing the pot next to the flames, Caitlyn held her chilled hands close to the fire. Breathing evenly, she whispered, "Thank you, Lord."

At first light, Joshua's soft whimpering flowed from the tent. If only she could go to him and throw her arms around him. Two men joined Todd and John. She glanced up but shielded her eyes when she realized they were talking about her.

"I ain't never seen no woman tracker before."

"Well, you ain't seen England either, but it's there."

"She's not a tracker." John glanced from the men to Caitlyn.

"How do you know?" asked Todd.

"Cabe's one of the best trackers in these parts. He'd hardly need a woman to point the way for him." John watched her while she busied herself at the fire.

"Mighty lonely patch of territory between here and Silverwater. Maybe she got lost or sumptin' and he was helping her out," the young boy suggested.

Todd laughed. "She might be no tracker, but she don't appear to be a gal who'd lose her way. Besides, she strikes me as a woman with a purpose. She's here for a reason."

"Well, if you're so damn smart, Todd, why don't you put your pea-sized brain to it and surprise us all." An older man snorted.

"Well." Todd spit out a long stream of tobacco. "Maybe she's kin with Cabe."

"A sister?"

"Nah. I was thinking more like a fellow outlaw." Todd lifted an eyebrow, waiting for confirmation.

"Her? She sure don't appear like no outlaw to me," another man replied.

"What'd you expect, Ricky? A snaggled-toothed old woman? Damn, you need to read a newspaper instead of those stupid dime novels you're always toting. There's quite a few women on the run these days. You saw the way she used the rifle. She ain't all fluff, and I, for one, ain't gonna turn my back to her as long as I care to be using these lungs of mine."

"What you figure, John?" the boy asked, obviously not satisfied with Todd's assumption.

Caitlyn sensed his gaze on her.

"I'm not sure." He paused. "Thought at first Cabe brought her to trade. Out here, a man needs a woman almost as much as he needs a good horse and rifle, though maybe he was of the mind to trade her for his own woman and son."

"You don't think that no more, John?"

She snuck a glance at the men.

He grinned, glancing at the tent, then at her. "Nope."

"How come?"

"Because, kid, would you trade a woman like her..." John nodded in Caitlyn's direction, "...for a woman like her?" He jerked his head toward the tent. "Son or no son, a man's got his pride."

The men roared with laughter.

Gazing at the tent, he mainly added to himself, "she sure ain't the kind of woman I would have paired with Cabe."

"Maybe he came here to beg us to keep her," Todd said and snickered.

"Hell, I wouldn't blame him," the older man added.

The sun rose quickly, throwing its golden rays into the canyon. The pungent aroma of chicory coffee drifted throughout the camp, bringing the scattered men back to the campfire.

Caitlyn judged each man while she filled his cup. John was right about them not having a woman for some time if their leering stares were any indication. Much to her relief, no one said or did anything.

The youngest, other than the boy, was Pete. He wasn't more than twenty, but his rough lifestyle had aged him. His hair, a coarse, wavy brown, was chopped off even with his chin. He took his coffee back to his bedroll, and when John wasn't paying any attention, he poured a healthy shot of whiskey into his cup. Pete seemed to be a man whose moods changed with the bottle. Not as tall as John, perhaps only five foot ten, but more muscular than his leader, he possessed the demeanor of a man who enjoyed a good fight. John would have a challenge on his hands if he weren't careful. Pete tipped his hat to her when she refilled his cup, not a cordial greeting, but a mocking one.

The next oldest, Jimmy, was tall and slender like John, with the same facial features, except for the long, ugly scar she noticed yesterday. In full daylight, it appeared even more vicious. She wondered if they might be brothers. He was a quiet man, though she didn't underestimate him. His real character showed in his hard, mean eyes. He wasn't an instigator but a follower, and he would back John 100 percent.

Hoss, part-Mexican, appeared to be around 35. His dark hair fell to his shoulders, but today he tied it back in a ponytail, exposing raw features that at one time might have been handsome. He kept to himself as if he despised the company he kept. John held a stern glare on him when he came up for coffee a second time.

"I ain't no animal, John. I can wait." Hoss tossed over his shoulder at John.

But an animal of prey was precisely what he resembled.

Tipping his hat to her, he whispered in a raspy voice, "You and me are gonna have one hell of a time as soon as Cabe's history."

She turned away from him in disgust. John did indeed have the worst working for him. The situation was bound to get uglier before it was over.

Not much mattered to these men. All they laid claim to was fast money and a short life. They weren't afraid to die, and that made them all the more dangerous. None of them had anything to lose.

The oldest, Sam, was a small, squirrelly fellow who appeared close to fifty. He sat a short distance from the others. She sipped the hot coffee and eyed him over her cup. He was engrossed in egging Pete into a fight with Jimmy. He was an instigator, though John paid him no mind. The older man had a haunting laugh and thoroughly enjoyed any disparity within the group. At first, she had considered him a harmless old man, who had seen better days, but now she saw him quite differently.

She glanced at John, who had drawn Todd away from the others. She tried to block out the other men's voices to hear what the two were saying, but she only caught snatches of their conversation.

"He's around somewheres. He ain't the type to leave without his woman and boy, despite what we think of her."

"I say we go get him." Tobacco juice splattered on the ground next to John.

"And that's why, Todd, you'll always be working for me instead of for yourself. You don't think. You go off half-cocked, and Cabe will be the one pulling your trigger." John rubbed his chin and then glanced around. "Believe me, the way I've got this whole thing figured, Cabe will never know what hit him."

"What you got planned?"

"Oh, a bit of a surprise. We've got Cabe's boy, so I don't think we need the momma." John glanced at the tent with a smile. "Besides, she's getting on my nerves, the mousy little thing. It's time we show Cabe we don't fool around. I'm sure he's close enough to see what I mean." John crossed his arms with a smug grin on his face.

"What about her?" Todd glanced in Caitlyn's direction.

She focused on the ground.

Wakefield smiled. "Don't worry. I'll take care of her."

At his command, she made two additional pots of coffee. Each time, she lingered near the tent in hopes of hearing her son, but she didn't. The need to know he was all right drove her to obsession.

After the men had had their fill, she started to toss out the remaining coffee.

"On second thought, lady, fill my cup again. We don't need to go anywhere...yet."

She turned to face John but froze at a sound behind her. She glanced back at Elizabeth stepping out of the tent. The other woman moved cautiously toward the fire but stopped dead at the sight of Caitlyn. The color drained from Elizabeth's face. Caitlyn shook her head slightly and focused on the tin pot in her hands. Elizabeth hesitated, confused and flustered. Nervously, she smoothed out her skirt to regain her composure before heading to the fire.

"May... May I have some coffee?" Her voice quivered with fear as she approached John and Todd. She kept her head down and fingered the collar of her dress.

"I don't give a damn. You'll have to ask Miss High and Mighty." He motioned to Caitlyn with the sweep of his hand.

Elizabcth hesitated.

"Well, go on, girl. She ain't gonna bite 'cha. And remember, if your brat wakes up, I don't want to hear or see him. You high-tail your ass back in there if he makes a peep. You understand?"

"I-I...yes."

John grunted. "Damn woman, afraid of her own shadow."

She nodded and walked back toward Caitlyn, who turned her back, picked up an empty cup, and then filled it with coffee. When she didn't turn, Elizabeth stepped to the side of her and waited.

Caitlyn offered her the cup, but didn't release it. Holding the cup between them, she whispered, "Wakefield has something planned. I don't know what, but it bodes ill for both of us." She considered John, who now talked with Jimmy. "We must escape soon. It's the only chance we have."

Elizabeth's eyes turned into white saucers of fear.

She ignored the woman's fear and continued, "Dakota is somewhere nearby, probably toward the back of the canyon, so we'll head that way."

Elizabeth turned as if she expected him to be standing there.

"Elizabeth," Caitlyn whispered. "When you hear any commotion tonight, you take Joshua, and you run toward the back. Do you understand?"

She stared at her in stunned fear.

"Elizabeth, listen." Caitlyn's tone was low, but harsh as she said, "You take Joshua, Dakota will be there."

She surprised herself. Up to that moment, she had no idea what to do. She prayed she was doing the right thing and that Dakota would be there.

Elizabeth's face registered no comprehension.

"Do you understand?" She wiggled Elizabeth's hand, and hot coffee spilled on both their hands.

"Caitlyn, I...can't... I... Wakefield's men—"

"You have to." Caitlyn squeezed her hand hard. "We have to get out tonight." She released Elizabeth's hand when footsteps came up behind them.

"What are you two talking about?" John jerked Caitlyn around.

Elizabeth glanced from him to Caitlyn in stark terror.

"I told her the coffee is lukewarm and to put her cup next to the fire," Caitlyn offered.

"Well, I'll be. Miss High and Mighty speaks." Turning around, he scrutinized his men. "Did you hear that, men? She can talk." He took her elbow in his hand and squeezed it.

His iron grip made her arm throb with pain.

"Now that we know you have a tongue, I think we ought to discuss your interesting relationship with Cabe and where he might be."

Elizabeth dropped her cup of coffee and stared at Caitlyn. He glanced at Elizabeth, laughing.

"Sorry, ma'am," he replied. "I guess this might be quite a shock to your delicate ears. To find out your man's been stepping out with another woman. And a healthy specimen of one, too, I might add. I'd let you have the first crack at him when we find him, but I doubt you'll be around."

The men laughed.

John pulled Caitlyn a few feet away from Elizabeth. "Well now, lady, what gives between you and Cabe?"

She met John's words with silence.

"Not this again. You haven't clammed up after a few words, have you?" He threw the remaining coffee from his cup into the fire. Turning back toward her, he refilled his cup with the pot in her hand. "I admire your backbone, but it's become tiresome, and you don't want to provoke me. I can be brutal if necessary."

She stared at him, and he sighed.

"Todd. You and Sam scout up ahead, and you and Billy..." John pointed to a stocky man Caitlyn hadn't seen before. "...take two men with you and check the trail behind us. I don't want any surprises from Cabe. Don't go far, though. Cabe will pick us off one at a time if he can."

John glanced back at her and Elizabeth. "Jimmy, Pete, and I will stay here and keep the ladies company. Oh. And in case Cabe's watching—" He shot his hand out and slapped Elizabeth's cheek, taking both women by surprise, "I'll give him a taste of what's to come."

~ * ~

Dakota watched Elizabeth fall to the ground, and Caitlyn's attempt to cushion the other woman's fall.

"We'll see how tough you are when it's just you and me, John," Dakota growled. The man was putting on a show, the meaning not lost on him. This was the beginning.

He understood men like John Wakefield. It wasn't money he wanted; it was a game. The other men were bad enough, like mad dogs once they tasted blood. They would kill if someone got in their way of gain. Wakefield was different. The money came second to the cat-and-mouse game. It made him more dangerous because killing would be part of the game, and only he would know the rules.

Dakota had to get the women and his son out tonight.

He crawled back up the rocky incline. His boots dug into the loose ground as he grasped at the sparse brush. The trail the Indians used was the most appealing way down to the canyon floor, but it was also too close to the camp. One slip and they would pick him off like a can perched on a fence. He needed to go back farther on the rim and make his descent into the canyon from there. Once below, he'd backtrack to the corral and take out the lone guard he had spotted there.

Five men saddled up and rode out. Two he hadn't seen. How many more might there be?

As of yet, no one attempted to ride his spirited mount. She lingered in the corral with the other horses. He needed to saddle her and two others before scattering the rest, then he'd somehow signal Caitlyn and let her know he was coming. Once they got onto the horses, they had a chance. Getting into the camp and the corral would be the tricky part.

Stopping at the top, he searched for the trail he had spotted the previous day. He followed it along the rim, going up farther and deviating away from the edge to get around the wild brush that grew too thick to penetrate. As the rocky grade became too steep, he climbed.

His thoughts tangled in his mind, tripping over one another. He needed a distraction, something to draw the men away from camp. Should he scatter the horses into the canyon? No. The men would run right straight into him as they chased the animals. No, he needed to draw the men in the other direction.

He could stampede the horses through the camp and out the other side. The tent sat safely out of harm's way.

Pausing, he took off his coat, wiped his forehead with the sleeve of his shirt, then draped his duster over his shoulders. The plan was doable, a bit hopeful perhaps, but achievable. He nodded when nothing better came to mind and started climbing again.

An hour passed, then two. The sun beat down without mercy. Sweat poured into his eyes. Unknotting his bandana from his neck, he tied it around his head, his coat in one hand and his rifle in the other. In this unforgiving land, he needed one as much as he needed the other.

Each new sound resonated in his ears, though he doubted anyone else would be up here.

Another hour passed, and he came to the trail's end. What appeared to be nothing more than a fissure in the ground turned out to be another way down into the canyon, although barely accessible. Damn, and to think he worried one of Wakefield's men would blow his head off. They could save their damn ammunition. He'd likely break his own neck.

The view from this point didn't reveal as much as Flat Rock, but it showed the horses, as well as another trail he had missed. It would have been more accessible, but he didn't have the time to backtrack.

He focused on the back of the canyon. He'd never been back this far. On his previous visit, the lawmen giving chase had turned around before the campsite, not risking an outlaw ambush. After a couple of days, he and the other men exited the same way they entered. The canyon had a back door and several side exits if a man was lucky enough to find them. Hoping for the best, he started his descent.

At times, he strapped his rifle to his back and descended on all fours, his feet sliding as they had the day before, though this time he didn't lose his footing. He couldn't afford to.

Drawing close to the canyon floor, he paused to assess the situation. Five men gathered in what appeared to be an aggressive drinking party, all in good humor. Dakota suspected they hadn't bothered searching for him at all, but instead, being a lazy breed, decided to hole up outside of camp and drink the hours away.

"Go ahead and drink up, boys. The drunker you are, the slower you are, and that's dandy with me." He positioned himself as inconspicuously as possible within a crevice to rest. Glancing up at the sky, he calculated the time. It had taken him longer than anticipated, and nightfall was rapidly approaching. He rubbed his face to dislodge the tight mask of grit and sweat.

Overhead, a bald eagle circled several times before making its descent on some unsuspecting prey, a kindred spirit equally as trapped. The waiting drained him. His right leg had fallen asleep, and jostling it proved unsuccessful.

After a while, the men mounted and rode the short distance to the corral, where they dismounted, unsaddled their horses, and then tossed their gear into a pile before walking to camp.

Dakota removed a strip of beef jerky from his pocket and chewed on it. The number of horses confirmed eight men total. At least, he knew the odds now. Unless he grimaced, they had additional horses on the other side of camp. In that case, he was a dead man.

When the day eased into the night, he moved himself from his position. Stretching stiff limbs, he descended the rest of the way, using his rifle as a cane. At last, he reached the canyon floor, donned his coat, and stood in the open air.

Running a hand over the stubble on his chin, he glanced back the way he had come and searched the ridge for Flat Rock. Eventually, he found it. Drawing an imaginary line from Flat Rock to where he believed Wakefield's camp to be, he estimated how far he'd need to travel. The camp was so well hidden that he couldn't miscalculate. As he lingered there, the day's last sunrays melted away, and the usual canyon breeze started up its lonely trek.

He made his way to the horses. The light from a cigarette illuminated the guard's position and held the man's face in a soft halo. Falling back into the shadows, Dakota waited for several minutes as the lookout paced back and forth. When the man stopped and leaned against a tree to light another cigarette, Dakota crept in, picking up a rock as he went. The guard drew hard on the cigarette, as though willing it to burn smoothly.

Dakota tossed the rock off to the side, and when the guard swung toward the sound, he caught him on the side of his head with the butt of his rifle. The cigarette dangled loosely in the man's mouth, and he dropped to the ground. Dakota took his gun and tucked it into the front of his pants.

Cupping his hands around his mouth, he gave a long, deep hooting sound. He waited a few minutes, then called again. Moving to the nervous horses, he calmed them. In haste, he saddled his horse and cinched the saddle. John Wakefield walked a dead man's trail.

~ * ~

Caitlyn understood the expression 'sitting on pins and needles'. For hours, she listened to the men, hoping to decipher Wakefield's plan. What could she be doing? What type of escape would be the most realistic?

Not that she could do anything before nightfall. She'd also listened for Joshua's voice, reassured each time she heard his familiar giggle. Elizabeth faithfully kept him in the tent, coming out only once during his nap to eat and get water.

John taunted Caitlyn several times during the day but gave up when she wouldn't respond. Other than that, the hours passed without incident, and relief settled over her when the men came back without Dakota. Her relief soon turned to apprehension when she realized the men were drunk.

After a brief discussion with John, they grew excited like men soon to partake of a feast. Whatever John planned, it was now in motion.

She sat by the night's fire with the men grouped around her. She had put the evening's pot of coffee in the campfire, and the water now gurgled and hissed from the heat. She weighed each moment, expecting an opportunity to present itself, but none came.

Soon, she would have to do something. In a short while, they would tie her hands and feet. Impending doom washed over her. The men showed too much eagerness. John's plan was unfolding, and Elizabeth would be at the brunt of it. They had to escape.

Caitlyn sized up each man as she had earlier. She knew who was quick to the trigger and who wasn't. Folding her arms across her chest, she tried to warm herself in the chilly canyon breeze. What was John's weakness?

Then she heard the soft call of an owl.

Her ears tingled. An ordinary owl, yet it had the lonesome sound of one in search of its mate.

Wakefield paid it no mind. "Todd, get Cabe's woman out here."

Rubbing his hands together, Todd rose to his feet, a delighted sneer dancing across his face. Oh, Lord, it had begun.

"Woman, get me some coffee."

Caitlyn peered over at John and tried to show no regard for Elizabeth's predicament. Coming to her feet, Caitlyn grabbed an empty cup and then the coffeepot with her glove. She poured the steaming liquid and then walked toward John.

"Here's your coffee." She smiled, offering the cup to him.

"It's about time you started to thaw, woman," he snarled, reaching for the cup.

Bending closer, she threw the hot pot of coffee into his face.

Wakefield rocked backward, rubbing his eyes and cursing at the top of his lungs.

Swift as a fox, she swooped forward and pulled his gun out of his holster, then stepped away from him. Pulling back the hammer, she pointed the revolver at Wakefield's heart as he leaped to his feet.

"You crazy bitch. I'll kill you." He sputtered, glaring at her with blood-shot eyes. A bright red burn danced across his face. He lunged for the gun, but she darted backward. His men scrambled up from their positions, guns drawn.

She raised the gun barrel to aim between his eyes. "Go ahead and shoot, boys, but I'm taking him with me."

He dropped his hand to his side, patting the air for the men to lower their guns. "You made a big mistake, woman." His look was cruel and brutal. "How do you expect to get out of this alive?"

"If I were you…" she glared back, "…I'd be more concerned about my own destiny." She prayed Elizabeth and Joshua had escaped, though she couldn't take her attention off Wakefield to check.

She stepped around the fire and away from him, her aim never wavered from its target. The campfire light made the men's faces more ghoulish than they appeared by day. John stepped with her as if they were in a demonic waltz. She wanted to shoot him, but he was the barrier between her and the pack of animals now circling her.

Licking her lips, she maneuvered toward the back of the canyon. Her arms ached with a rigid tension that traveled down her shoulder and into her arms and fingers. If Elizabeth had gathered Joshua when she heard the commotion, she would be well out of the way by now.

Joshua's frightened cry in the distance reverberated through the canyon and startled Caitlyn. Her hand flinched only once, but it was enough. Leaping forward, John grasped her hand as the gun discharged, nicking him in the shoulder. He balled up his fist and struck her.

She briefly connected with the ground, then scurried to her feet. Her head spun with pain. Bolting clear from Wakefield, she managed to get a couple of yards between them before he reacted. Her breath came hard and sharp as her feet flew across the ground. If she could reach the darkness of the canyon, Dakota would be there, and she'd have a chance. He could pick Wakefield's men off one at a time until she got a gun. She propelled herself forward, running with all the strength and speed her body had to offer, but John's heavy footsteps rushed up behind her.

He grabbed Caitlyn's hair and wrenched her back. She battled to regain her balance, but his grip was too powerful and too determined. Stumbling, she twisted under the weight of his attack and hit the ground face first with him tumbling on top of her. She fought for her life, striking out with everything she had. Repeatedly, she thrust her elbow up into his face to loosen his hold on her, but his wild anger prevailed.

Up ahead, Elizabeth stopped and peeked back at her. Caitlyn willed them to keep moving. Joshua squirmed in Elizabeth's arms and shrieked, his hands stretched back toward her.

To Caitlyn's relief, Elizabeth turned and fled into the night.

The terrified expression on her son's face gave Caitlyn an added boost of strength, and she threw back her head into John's wounded shoulder, loosening his hold. She took advantage of his relaxed grip and rolled herself out from underneath him, but he regained his hold.

Clamping his hands around her neck, he squeezed until she gagged. Her hands clawed at him, but his rage made him impervious to the pain. His eyes glazed with triumph as she weakened. The veins in his neck expanded into dark roads of pulsating blood, and his face was one savage mass of hatred until her world went black.

Chapter 8

Dakota had Caitlyn's saddle in hand when the gunshot rang out, and the sound of running feet headed his way. Crouching low behind the scrub bushes, he waited. When Elizabeth started to pass him, he threw out his arm and caught her around the waist, careful not to disengage her from the bundle she carried.

Her eyes were white marbles of terror. She pushed away from him and tried to kick him, but her feet tangled in her skirts.

"I'm Dakota. Be still," he whispered in her ear when she continued to fight him. He waited a moment until he was sure she believed him, then released her and examined the trail toward the camp. "Where's Caitlyn?" He turned back to the woman.

Angry voices drifted out to them from the camp.

"The woman's gone, so's the kid."

"Fan out. She ain't gonna git far."

"Don't let her get to the horses."

"Where the hell's Billy?"

"He's standing guard at the horses. She ain't gonna git past him."

Dakota pulled Elizabeth and Joshua toward the only horse saddled and waiting—his. She needed a gentler horse, but the time to saddle one was gone, and he doubted she was capable of riding bareback, especially with a child.

Elizabeth stumbled to his horse, her long skirts impeding her progress. He took Joshua from her arms. "Mount up."

"What?"

"Get on the horse."

Gathering her skirts in one hand, she put her foot in the stirrup and threw her leg unceremoniously over the horse's back. Dakota handed Joshua to her.

"Ride out," he ordered, about to slap the spirited horse on the rump, then reconsidered. The woman would have enough trouble handling the horse without making it bolt.

She stared back at him. "I can't." She searched the area around her. "I don't know which way to go. I can't go alone."

"Damn it, woman, we don't have a choice. Go in the same direction you were running. As soon as I get Caitlyn, we'll catch up. Now ride out."

"No. I can't go out there. Not alone," she cried, scanning the surrounding darkness. She dropped the reins and hugged Joshua to her chest.

"Lady." Dakota placed the reins into her hands. "We don't have time to argue. Now git." He glanced toward the camp, then back at her.

Tears sprang into her eyes. "I can't do this. Oh God. God." Her voice rose to hysteria. "Don't let Wakefield and his men get me."

"Damn it, woman, calm down." He clasped a hand over her thigh and tried to refocus her on Joshua and the reins in her hands. "You're safe. Caitlyn and I will be right behind you."

"No, no, she's not coming. We have to go. Don't leave me," she wailed into the night.

The woman was unraveling. Moving her foot from the stirrup, he put his into it and heaved himself up onto the horse. Holding Joshua with one arm, he shook Elizabeth with the other, then grabbed her chin and brought her face close to his. "Get a hold of yourself, woman, or we're all dead. And what the hell did you mean, Caitlyn's not coming?"

Elizabeth's eyes resembled blue marbles devoid of life. The look of the dead. He'd seen it before. Was she shot? Before he could check for a wound, her eyes blinked, and life came back into them. She grabbed Joshua, and Dakota dropped back to the ground.

"I misspoke," she said, her voice monotone. "Caitlyn took one of the horses they keep in the box canyon. She rode out the main entrance. I saw her. They're after me, not her." She paused. "They still think I'm Caitlyn. They have nothing to gain by going after her. They want me."

He hesitated. "No." Something was wrong. "I've got to make sure she got out. You'll have to ride out alone. We'll catch up."

"I can't do it, not with him." She nodded to Joshua. "If they catch us, they'll kill us. For God's sake," she screamed at him. "Caitlyn's gone."

Her change of tone startled Joshua into a hearty wail.

Wakefield's men burst through the night toward them. Gunfire chewed up the ground around Dakota's horse and made the choice for him. Hoisting his body up behind Elizabeth, he yanked the reins from her and kicked his heels into the horse's sides. Turning slightly on the horse, he let off several volleys of gunfire back at Wakefield's men, and Joshua started to scream. She struggled to hold onto the saddle horn and Joshua, as Dakota prodded the horse into a gallop.

Slapping the reins, he forced the massive beast down a path neither one could make out in the dark. The horse stumbled across the rough ground. Grasping the reins in one hand, he wrapped his other arm around Elizabeth and Joshua. His eyes searched the canyon walls for a place to hide. He'd gained some distance while the men were saddling up, but trying to outrun Wakefield's men with three on one horse wasn't possible.

The moonlight illuminated the left bank, so Dakota concentrated his attention there. Within minutes, a large crevice in the rock wall appeared, and he turned the horse toward it. The moon, now behind them, cast its milky white light across their backs and the rocky crevice. The canyon wall approached at a fiery pace.

Joshua's frightened wail turned into soft whimpers. The constant rough motion of the horse soothed him in a way nothing else could. Elizabeth hugged the horse's shoulders with her knees, her skirts billowing out on either side. Tightening her arms around Joshua, she left the task of managing the horse and their balance on it to Dakota.

The wild pace of the horse slowly dissolved his anger toward her. He sighed with disgust. It wasn't the woman's fault. She wouldn't even be in this God-forsaken canyon if not for him. By her appearance, he guessed she was accustomed to money and the comforts it bought. For her to ride off with a small boy into the unknown was akin to asking a field mouse to attack a rattler.

If not for Joshua, he'd leave the woman in the nearest cavern, go back, and make sure Caitlyn did make it out, but Elizabeth Cookman soon proved incapable of even riding a horse. His arm ached with the effort of keeping her and his son in the saddle, plus trying to control the skittish horse across the indecipherable ground. Joshua's unpredictable cries would seal their fates. Moreover, it appeared that Wakefield's men were chasing after Elizabeth, not Caitlyn.

Stopping his thoughts, he slowed the horse to a walk. Relaxing his grip on Elizabeth, he leaned to the side to examine the ground. It was pure insanity to push a horse across terrain like this, and both he and the mare knew it, but they needed more distance from the men who followed. The lonely canyon would carry a child's cry well into the night.

He inspected the crevice before them, then glanced back into the inky blackness. He couldn't see their pursuers, but he could sense them. He nudged the horse into a controlled run.

Elizabeth's long blonde hair fell loose from the bun at the nape of her neck and floated up into the soft canyon breeze to tickle Dakota's chin. He pulled his head to the side to free the long strands from his unshaven face, but they held fast. In aggravation, he brought his hand to his chin and brushed her hair from his face, then cursed when more of her hair reattached itself.

~ * ~

Startled at the crude words, Elizabeth twisted in the saddle. The look that met hers was menacing. The sinister black glare of Dakota Cabe whispered of barely restrained violence within the man. An icy shiver of fear traveled down her spine. How far away did the real danger lie? Stiffening, she drew Joshua to her chest.

She tried to focus on the canyon's moonlit walls, but Dakota's dark face remained in her thoughts. She'd caught a glimpse of long, dark, wavy hair falling just below his shoulders. He had several days' growth of beard on his tanned, weathered face. Perhaps that was what made him so intimidating.

She tightened her grip on Joshua, as much to comfort herself as the boy. She'd never known people like Wakefield's men, but she could draw some logic. Uncouth, obtuse men with no future, they lived day to day; the only thing in their future was an early grave.

Dakota Cabe, however, was indefinable. A violent man, no doubt, but of a different caliber than Wakefield and his men, and she had nothing in her repertoire of previous acquaintances to judge him by.

She longed to see if Wakefield's gang still pursued them, but the man seated too close behind her seemed content with his pace. Furthermore, she had no desire to risk another in-depth involvement with his eyes. His first scrutiny of her made her feel as significant as day old coffee, but something else existed in his expression. Hatred? Seething anger? She couldn't be sure. It seemed directed at her, but she hadn't done anything wrong. If anything, the man should be grateful to her.

They entered a crevice; one she hadn't noticed until they were in it. The walls on either side closed in behind them, making them invisible to the pursuers, or so she hoped. She adjusted her position to relieve a cramp in her leg, aware of the warm arm encircling her and Joshua. Twice his arm had brushed up against her breast, and she'd nearly leaped from the saddle. Where his demeanor remained unfriendly and impersonal, hers was anything but. Their proximity unnerved her, but did not affect him.

She blinked in confusion. What was she thinking? Her life was in peril, and she was upset because she had no effect on a wanted man. How revolting. Taking a deep breath, she reprimanded herself to be concerned with more pressing matters. Outlaws were chasing them.

Again, she tried to dislodge the cramp settling into her thigh. Turning in the saddle, she opened her mouth to ask the man to stop for a spell so she could rest, but the words froze in her throat. His eyes resembled cold, dark steel, devoid of emotion. It was as if the man existed, but not his soul.

"We'll camp here for the night."

His voice in the still night and the sudden halt of the horse jarred her into awareness, and she shut her mouth.

Sliding off the horse, Dakota glanced behind them at the black canyon. "Hand me, my boy," He reached up to take Joshua from her arms.

She had no choice but to give the child to him. Dakota scrutinized his son's small face. Tightly closed eyes with tiny ruby lips slightly parted, his body limp. His eyebrows raised. He passed a finger under Joshua's nose and exhaled. The child slept without caring about where he was or with whom.

He examined the boy for a long time, scrutinizing his small features with disbelief and utter fascination. "He's so small."

The man's awe and gentleness surprised Elizabeth. "He's actually quite large for his age, Mr. Cabe, and heavy," she said, waiting for Dakota Cabe to assist her from the horse.

"He sure doesn't seem that big to me." Taking a blanket from his bedroll, he walked away, leaving Elizabeth still seated in the saddle.

Without speaking, she waited while Dakota fashioned the blanket into a small basket. With gentleness, he laid his son in it and then sat to watch him sleep.

She couldn't take her gaze off the man. Such a contrast, no matter how she viewed him. His duality drew her like a moth to a candle. He lived as a wanted outlaw, brutal as the land and the men who had kidnapped her, and yet he possessed a gentleness. She suffered acute disappointment when she found herself impressed with the man.

As though reading her thoughts, he turned and faced her. His sharp, handsome features startled her anew.

"Well, are you gonna get off that horse or sleep on it?"

His glib words broke the spell over her like thin glass beneath a rock.

"There'll be no fire," he continued in a matter-of-fact tone. Standing, he eyed the canyon behind them. "Too risky. Bundle up the best you can."

Striding to his horse, he removed his rifle from the saddle sheath and returned to Joshua without even a nod in her direction.

Dismay swept over her. The brute either had no manners or preferred to mock them. Anger mounting, she slid awkwardly from the horse and hobbled on numb legs toward him.

With his rifle, he pointed to a spot next to Joshua. "Sleep next to the boy and don't be getting up during the night or I'm liable to shoot you." Again, using his rifle, he indicated a thick cover of brush. "Do you need to relieve yourself?"

Horrified he would suggest such a thing, she shook her head, aware that indeed nature called her.

Seemingly not convinced, his gray eyes studied her. "If you have to go tonight, wake me first."

This time, she nodded. She'd die first. Without another exchange, she lay down on the ground beside Joshua. She was thankful the boy had eaten before this wild event had taken place, but it would be a different story in the morning. She rolled to her side, trying to find a soft patch, but the rocky ground bit into her tender flesh as she peered into the growing darkness. The dark always frightened her, and tonight was no exception.

Dakota removed his coat and knelt beside her. The scent of his unrefined masculinity scared and excited her, and she held her breath. "Do you know how to use a rifle?"

"No."

He draped his coat over her. "I figured," he muttered and walked away, taking both rifles with him.

~ * ~

Caitlyn woke with a searing headache, her throat dry and raw. The damp earth seeped into her back and legs. Her arms lay useless across her chest, and she had to wiggle her fingers to find her hands, which were resting on either side of her neck. Her hands and feet were untied, though her body was too weak and her mind too foggy to take advantage of the fact. Gingerly, she touched her neck, still feeling John's death grip.

Finally opening heavy eyelids, she waited for her sight to adjust to the darkness. Small beams of moonlight touched the earth. In agony, she turned her head. A few logs glowed red in the campfire, one lone man on guard. Where were the other men? As if in answer to her thoughts, voices broke through the quiet night.

"Well?" John asked.

"Can't find no sign of her and the kid, John. She vanished into the canyon," Pete said.

"She didn't vanish, damn it. Cabe's got her. That silly woman wouldn't know if the sun set in the west or the east unless someone pointed it out to her. Hell, she never would have found her way out of camp if not for the other damn woman. I should have shot her when I saw her."

"Whatcha gonna to do with her now?" Jimmy asked.

"Have a nice long talk with her as soon as she comes around. She'll talk this time, even if I have to beat the hell out of her."

Two other riders approached from the opposite direction.

"Find anything, Todd?" John asked.

"Nah. We followed some tracks from the corral, but they faded out. Can't see a damn thing in this canyon. We'll find them in the morning. They're holed up somewhere. We would have caught up with them if they'd headed straight for the back of the canyon."

"First light won't be for another hour."

The men drew close to Caitlyn. A stream of tobacco juice hit the ground inches from her nose, and she snapped her eyes shut.

"He ain't gonna get far on one horse."

"Do you think he'll come back for her, John?" the young boy asked.

"No. Cabe's got what he wanted. We'll have to go after him now. She come around yet, Sam?"

"Nope. Still out cold," Sam said somewhere behind her.

"Well, tie her up anyway. I don't want any more of her damn surprises."

Sam grabbed her arm and flipped her onto her stomach. Her face scraped across the ground. He showed incredible strength for a man of his age. He jerked both her arms behind her, bringing a fresh jolt of pain.

"Ain't gonna be no more surprises tonight, John," Sam answered, and cinched the rope tight, cutting into her wrists.

~ * ~

Wakefield's men were ready and eager to hunt at first light. Caitlyn hadn't slept the brief hour before sunup. The rope around her wrists burned into the torn flesh from the previous day and pulsated with pain. For the last half hour, she listened to the night sounds and the men. Boots clicked up to her head, and a shadow draped across her.

"Come on, lady, get up." Wakefield jerked her to her knees and sliced the rope binding her hands and feet. He hauled her to her feet and pushed her in front of him. Holding her arm in a vise-like grip, he motioned to his men.

"Todd, take Jimmy and Hoss and head back into the canyon. See if you can pick up Cabe's trail. Billy, you and Sam follow behind and scour out the canyon walls in case they're hiding. Pete, you and the boy, stay here and guard the horses and supplies. The lady and I are gonna do some talking."

~ * ~

Joshua's soft whimper woke Elizabeth in the early morning hours, and she cuddled him closer. Glancing up, she frowned. Dakota Cabe had already saddled the horse. He pulled the leather cinch tight and jammed his rifle into its sheath. When the horse nickered, he patted her mane and rested both arms on the saddle.

He must live in a foul mood. Well, so be it. None of this was her fault. A fleeting stab of remorse cut into her when she thought of her lie. Now that she was relatively safe, what had happened to Caitlyn? Elizabeth smiled at Joshua's happy face. He didn't seem to mind his mother's absence. She buried her face in his and kissed him.

"Hey, fellow."

She started at Dakota's close presence. She hadn't heard him approach. Bending, he took Joshua from her and tossed him easily into the air, much to Joshua's delight.

"Hungry, boy?" he asked, and Joshua looked back at Elizabeth, then snuggled into his father's embrace.

She watched in amazement. The man was a complete study in dichotomy. Abruptly, he stared down at her.

"You all right?" he asked.

Still, the indifferent, impersonal eyes and gruff voice, but at least, he did possess some concern. "Yes, thank you. However, Joshua and I need some nourishment."

Cabe raised an eyebrow in what appeared to be amusement, and her back bristled. Walking back to his horse, he opened his saddlebag, then removed several pieces of beef jerky and handed one to Joshua.

"Oh no, Mr. Cabe. I don't think that's a suitable substance for Joshua—"

Cabe's emotionless expression stopped her. "Something wrong?"

Rendered speechless again, she stared wide-eyed. Joshua grabbed the jerky from his father's hand and giggled. She watched in horror as the boy gnawed on the beef. Dakota smiled at him, then at her. Still, his eyes maintained a distant darkness. "Some nourishment, Mrs. Cookman?"

Joshua followed his father's gaze to Elizabeth and smiled too.

She pressed her lips together and rose to her feet. "No, thank you, Mr. Cabe, I'll wait."

"For what?"

She glanced at him. "Excuse me?" she asked, forgetting his question.

"I asked you what you were waiting for? As you can see, there doesn't appear to be a restaurant nearby."

Her face burned with anger as Dakota scanned the area around him, Joshua doing the same.

"I thought we might procure something more suitable with your rifle." She shrugged Dakota's coat off her shoulders and brushed debris from her skirt. Her hair hung around her face. With her fingers, she tried to restore order to it, but failed.

"We?" He stopped and cast his gaze to the ground. An expression of contriteness passed over his face. "My apologies, ma'am."

Her angry retort froze on her lips. She closed her mouth and stared at Cabe. An apology? He didn't appear to be a man who'd be sorry for anything. Still, the grimace on his face showed a man partaking in a trip across unfamiliar and hazardous territory.

He glanced around them. "We're in a dangerous situation. We made it this far by pure luck." He paused. "Wakefield's men took the food I brought with me. Beef jerky is all I can offer until we find a homestead.

I would get us something more suitable..." He cringed. "But a gunshot would alert Wakefield and his men as to our whereabouts."

It was the most he had said to her since they met. She was anxious to reciprocate. "Of course, Mr. Cabe, and I appreciate your skillfulness in getting us this far. I'm sure it was more than luck involved."

She tucked her hair behind her ears and smoothed out her skirt in front of her. When she looked up, he appeared distracted or, at least, not interested in what she said.

"Are you worried for Caitlyn?" She surprised herself with the question and soon regretted it.

His eyes frosted over. "We're heading out. If you need to relieve yourself, you best do it now." He turned his back to her and took out another strip of beef jerky for Joshua.

Elizabeth stayed rooted to her spot and fumed. Why had she brought up Caitlyn? They weren't close friends; in fact, they hadn't known one another for long. Joshua brought them together, the child Elizabeth always hoped to have, but didn't. Now, for all immediate purposes, she was his mother. Caitlyn, more likely than not, was dead.

Elizabeth's deceit bothered her. Perhaps she should tell Mr. Cabe the truth. She bit her lip in frustration. No. He would leave and go back for Caitlyn. A man would lay down his life for a woman who bore him a child. She snorted, wanting to scream. It disgusted her, the power a woman had over a man simply by bearing him a child.

She tried to dislodge the fury from her bones. Closing her eyes, she took in several deep breaths, then reopened her eyes and studied Mr. Cabe's profile as he contemplated the territory they had traveled. She couldn't understand her mixed feelings for a stranger.

One minute, she wanted to slap his face, and the next, caress it. Confusion set in. She was educated in the best schools in the East. She should be able to make a mockery of the man, and yet, for the first time in her life, she'd met a man she couldn't make a fool of.

Standing there with the morning sun upon his face, he seemed like a Greek god. His long black hair billowed out behind him, his strong, muscular arms encircling Joshua tightly. She once dreamed of meeting a man like Dakota Cabe, a man of unflinching courage and fearlessness. Nevertheless, she'd exchanged that dream for a life of luxury with Stephen. His family's fortune provided everything she ever wanted or needed. She loved the comforts she had grown dependent on. The truth be told, she'd even forgotten the dream until now.

A twinge of guilt pricked at her conscience, but she batted it away like an annoying mosquito. One thing she'd learned since moving west was to take opportunities when they presented themselves and not a moment later. If one waited for the proper amount of time by Eastern standards, one only trailed another man's dust. Stephen and Caitlyn were dead. She, herself, must be strong for Joshua's sake.

Walking up to Mr. Cabe, she wasn't sure how best to approach him. He seemed unaware of her presence, though she doubted anyone ever came near the man without his knowledge. He seemed so detached, so untouchable she longed to do just that: touch him.

~ * ~

Dakota listened to the woman's timid approach but didn't turn or ask her what she wanted. Because of him, his family was in the midst of a brutal vendetta between Wakefield and himself. The last thing he wanted was to converse with the prim and proper Mrs. Cookman.

He glanced back at the canyon. Something caught his eye a moment ago, but after observing for several minutes, nothing materialized, and he returned to his contemplations. The decision he'd made during the night suffocated him like a wet wool blanket. The rough terrain demanded too much from a woman to travel alone with a small child. He hugged Joshua tighter, pressing him to his chest. If anything happened to the boy, he would never be able to face Caitlyn. He had to get Elizabeth and Joshua safely out of the canyon and to a homestead, then go back for Caitlyn.

No doubt she waited for him in Silverwater, and he was worried about nothing. He nodded with conviction, but the emotion didn't hold. John Wakefield kept coming to mind along with the vision of her torn clothing. He had a score to settle with Wakefield, and he would settle it.

A tug at his sleeve broke his thoughts, and Dakota scowled at Elizabeth with all the hatred he held for the damned soul of John Wakefield.

Her face blanched. "Mr. Cabe, I...you..."

He waited for her to gather her wits. She acted as though she'd seen a grizzly, but that was one threat they didn't need to worry about. He waited a few more moments, but the woman proved incapable of putting her words together, and he didn't have the time to wait.

The sooner he found a haven for Elizabeth and Joshua, the sooner he'd head to Silverwater. He handed Joshua to her and walked to the makeshift basket he had made for Joshua.

Removing a long hunting knife from his boot, he made a small incision in the blanket and tore the material in half. Holding one half of the long blanket, he tapered the two ends. Folding the diamond-shaped blanket in half, he tied the two ends together and then fanned out the center of the fabric to form a large sling.

He cut two holes in the middle of the sling for Joshua's chubby legs, then motioned for Elizabeth. "This ought to make traveling easier."

She dipped her head forward to allow him to put the sling over her head and shoulder. He adjusted it by slipping the knot across her shoulder and fanning out the bottom. She leaned into him.

Lifting Joshua from her arms, Dakota put him into the sling, tugging his sausage-like legs through the slots in the fabric. Joshua giggled and flapped his arms. Elizabeth waited with her arms at her sides. He cut two long strips of the fabric loose on either side of Joshua and used them as ties to secure his lively son to the sling.

"How's that?" he asked.

"A bit heavy on my shoulder."

"Well, unless you want to handle the horse and ride shotgun, it's the best I can do."

Her eyes glinted with anger, and he narrowed his at her quick change of emotions.

"I'll be fine, Mr. Cabe."

Dakota gathered the rest of their gear, including the other half of the torn blanket, and packed it onto the horse. He turned to Elizabeth. She stood at an awkward tilt with Joshua strapped to her.

"I'll give you a hand up."

She lumbered toward him.

Dakota crouched next to the horse, clasped his hands in front of him, and waited. She maneuvered Joshua to one side, placed her foot into his hands, her hand on his shoulder for support, then reached for the saddle horn with the other.

He pushed upward until she could throw her leg across the saddle. Her many petticoats bunched up into a tangled heap beneath her, and she struggled to free them.

Without thought, Dakota jerked her skirts out from underneath her and, in the process, exposed her leg up to her thigh. "You ready?"

When she didn't answer, he turned back around. Her cheeks were flushed, and she stared at him in indignation. He'd apologize, but best he could tell, he didn't do anything wrong. He nodded at his son, who took riding on a horse like he was born on one.

Taking the reins, he grasped the saddle horn, swung up behind her, then prodded the horse forward.

At first, Elizabeth sat as erect as possible in the saddle, but her back soon settled against him.

"Do you know where we're going?" she asked.

"Yup."

Chapter 9

John dragged Caitlyn across the barren ground. She couldn't fight him, not while rage consumed him. She had made him appear inept in front of his men. Her only comfort lay in the fact that his anger wouldn't have lasted this long if his capture of Dakota seemed imminent. She had ruined his carefully laid plan, and if she died this day, she would die knowing that.

Wakefield kept his pace brisk, pulling her along a narrow rocky path that seemed to go nowhere. He had a destination and a purpose, and he seemed confident she would talk.

He stopped without warning, and Caitlyn peered out in front of her. The trail led into a small box canyon with a small waterfall cascading down one wall and emptying into a pool. Undoubtedly the most beautiful spot in the canyon, but a poor choice for a campsite. The walls surrounding the alcove were inaccessible, and the only means of escape remained the way they had entered.

She peeked at Wakefield. A grotesque smile of pure pleasure drifted across his face. She followed his eyes to a lone tree inside the box canyon. Did he plan to hang her? Hardly the method to use if he wanted her to talk. No, he had something else in mind. Beads of fear trickled down her back.

He glanced back at her with triumph. "Now we're gonna get some answers." He shoved her toward the tree.

Turning, she glared at him.

"You're something, aren't you, lady? So proud. So tough. Well, that's all about to change. I'm gonna break you like a wild filly, and when I'm done, I'm going to know your whole life story, including everything you know about Dakota Cabe."

She didn't speak. Escape wasn't possible. She couldn't outrun him, and she couldn't fight him. The best she could do was to take what he dealt out. If he expected her to beg for mercy, it would be a long day for both.

~ * ~

"How much farther do you think it'll be before we find civilization?" Elizabeth leaned forward to adjust Joshua's weight. When Dakota didn't answer, she sighed in displeasure and turned to scowl at him.

His eyes caught hers, then looked beyond her. She stared at him until he drew the horse up short. Twisting back around, she saw what had caught his attention.

Her preoccupation with her discomfort had kept her from noticing the wide-open basin before them. They had made it out of the canyon. Another surge of relief flooded through her. Miles stretched out in front, offering them whatever direction they cared to partake. Nothing but open terrain. She was free from all they'd left behind. She cast a glance back at Dakota and waited for some flicker of his own relief, but he simply stared over her head. Once again, he seemed oblivious to her.

"Well?" She didn't hide the aggravation in her voice.

"Silverwater's southwest on the other side of the canyon, but Jessie Town's northeast from here." Dakota paused. "It's still quite a way from where we are. Without another horse, it would take too long. Our best bet is to head toward Copper Lake. It's a small mining town." He squinted at the sun. "It should be directly north of here, but maybe with luck, we'll find a homestead first."

"Do you think Wakefield and his men found the trail we took?" she asked.

"If they had, they would be here by now. Just dumb luck we found it."

"So, what do we do now?"

"We'll camp here tonight and rest the horse." He motioned toward the basin. "It'll take a full day to get across it, and I don't want to camp out there. We'd be easy targets."

She followed his gaze over the basin before them, pleased that the man didn't intend to travel the entire day and night. She was also thankful that the all-embracing basin need not be tackled tonight, but the thought of being an easy target for John Wakefield when they did, didn't sit well either.

Dakota slid from the horse, freeing his bedroll and blanket. He tossed them to the ground and held up his arms to Elizabeth. "Hand me, Joshua."

She loosened the boy from his carrier and gave him to Dakota. The young child wiggled with anticipation, glad to be free from the confines of the sling. She turned her back to Dakota and carefully dismounted from the horse. His hand on her back surprised her.

Hopeful, she turned to face him, but he wore the same impersonal expression as before, and he let go of her arm. He then gazed down at his son and ran a gloved finger across the youngster's pudgy nose, sending Joshua into a fit of giggles as he tried to catch the elusive glove. Dakota took off his well-worn glove and handed it to him. Fascinated with the garment, Joshua tugged each phantom finger one by one.

Dakota walked a short distance away from the horse and placed Joshua on the ground where he could play safely with the glove. He returned to her and pulled his rifle free from the saddle, then turned the gun over in his hands as if he was examining the weapon for the first time.

She considered the man before her and marveled once more at his complex duality. So calm and collected. Did anything unnerve him? Would a woman like herself unnerve him? The thought intrigued her. She chided herself for giving in to overwrought emotions brought on, no doubt, from the toxicity of her ordeal.

"You need to learn how to shoot a rifle." He handed her the heavy gun.

"Why?" Surprised, she almost dropped the weapon. "You said yourself, John Wakefield hasn't followed us. I believe we're safe enough."

"Because, lady, out here you're never safe enough."

She held the rifle at arm's length as if she held a vile animal.

Dakota sighed in weariness and retrieved the gun from her hands. "I'll show you how it works first."

Words of protest were on her lips, but she stopped herself. She was exhausted, she didn't want to shoot a gun, but she wanted less to argue with the man. For some inane reason, she wanted to please him, and the only way to do that, it appeared, was to learn how to shoot the damn gun. Like horses, she knew nothing about guns. Stephen had owned a valuable assortment of rifles, but he kept them safely stored in his gun cabinet, and as far as she knew, never shot one.

She watched with little interest as Dakota emptied the weapon and reloaded it. He showed her the mechanics of the gun, but the process bored her. Why did she need to bother with handling the gun anyway? That was his job. He was the gunfighter, wasn't he?

Maybe he wasn't the prince in the fairy tales she'd enjoyed as a child, but she'd stayed a princess and always had been. Still, he stirred all the right senses. The warm scent of leather and man caressed her senses. She studied the dark hair draping across his face and shoulder as he bent to see through the gun sight. Her eyes followed his long arm down the weapon's barrel and concentrated on his fingers demonstrating the use of the trigger.

His words were only warm puffs of air between them. Lost in her imaginings, she lacked any comprehension of what he told her. Her senses reeled with delight, and she found herself swept across fanciful ground and make-believe kingdoms.

She tried to think of her departed husband, but his face eluded her. Stephen had been a good man, but he never tantalized her senses as Dakota Cabe did at this very moment. Not once did Stephen make her tingle inside, and his memory hadn't become fonder by his absence. Stephen Cookman was quickly becoming a disappointment next to the brutal masculinity of Dakota Cabe.

"Unless you're going to make an effort, we're wasting time."

Dakota's deep voice snapped her out of her fanciful dreams. He glanced at Joshua, still playing with his gloves.

"I'm sorry, let me try again," she replied, shaking her head to clear it.

"Here, maybe this will help."

Her legs weakened as his arms moved around her, and his strong, capable hands folded over hers, positioning the rifle against her shoulder. If he wanted her to concentrate on shooting the blasted thing, he picked the wrong method of help. His warm, firm body pressed into hers, and she counted each petticoat between them. He spellbound her, and she feared she would do the one thing he surely would despise: faint.

"Put your hands here and keep the gun firm against your shoulder to minimize the impact."

Firm hands repositioned hers. Her blood surged through her, leaving Elizabeth breathless and helpless. Leaning back into the comfort of him, her desire rose to the surface—the proverbial forbidden fruit.

His fingers folded around hers and the trigger as he bent to check the sight. "Brace yourself. The gun has a bit of a kick."

"Kick? What kick?" Passion slurred her speech. She pushed the gun away at the same time his finger pressed down on hers to release the trigger.

The gun slammed into her with the same force as the sound it made, thundering through the quiet evening air. Pain ricocheted from her shoulder to her toes and extinguished all her passion and fanciful notions. Too shocked to move, she stood transfixed at the smoking barrel a brief span from her nose.

"You shouldn't have moved the rifle. I warned you about the kick." His voice, cool and matter-of-fact, broke the shocked silence.

"I could have been killed."

"Not likely." Dakota chuckled. "But you're gonna be pretty damn sore for a couple of days."

Spinning around in his arms, she pushed him away from her. His laughter lit a fuse to her smoldering state of confusion. "Why didn't you warn me? That...that thing's a cannon, not a rifle."

Her anger amused him further.

"What's so damn funny, Mr. Cabe?"

He sobered and said nothing more. She balled up her fists and flashed him a furious glare.

"Nothing, ma'am, nothing at all." With a tight-lipped expression on his face, he walked away from her. He checked on Joshua, who'd only been slightly distracted by the gun blast. He left his son and headed toward the canyon. "Keep an eye on Joshua. I'll be back."

"Where are you going, Mr. Cabe?" She winced. Her fear made her voice sound sharp and demanding.

"To relieve myself, ma'am, unless you'd feel more comfortable in my doing it here."

"No. Of course not, Mr. Cabe. How long before you return?"

"I plan to get some firewood and procure something for our dinner, ma'am, so not long."

"What are we to do until you come back?"

"Setting up a fire would be helpful. There are plenty of small branches to gather."

"How far away will you be?" She assessed the menacing landscape leering at her from every direction.

"Not far." Without a backward glance, he disappeared into the woods with his rifle.

Indignation overrode the fear. She wiggled her hands, trying to release the furious balls of frustration encasing them. Who did the man think he was anyway? So damn cocky, so self-assured. What she'd give to knock him down a peg or two and wipe the all-knowing expression off his face. However exasperated she was by the man, he also intrigued her.

If she were to be angry with anyone, it ought to be with herself for acting like some ingénue. She had been married. She knew what pleased a man. Dakota Cabe was no different from any other man when it came down to the basics. If she wanted him, she could have him.

Her life hadn't turned out the way she'd hoped. Stephen left her well-provided for, but nothing more. She was young and wanted children of her own. She was entitled to have a man of her choosing. One who intrigued and excited her. She'd always received what she wanted, when she wanted it, except for a child, and he was to blame for that. The doctors were wrong. He had been a weak man, his offspring weak as well. Hysterical pregnancies? Only a male doctor could concoct such nonsense, and only Stephen would have the gall to pay one to say it.

That was the past, and this is the present. Despite the hardship, God put her here in this very place so she could claim her rightful family.

She truly felt sorry about Caitlyn—at least, she wanted to be. Nevertheless, she remained realistic. This was life. One didn't wrestle with fate. One embraced it.

Joshua wobbled to his feet and headed in the same direction as Dakota. "Oh no, you don't. You're staying with me." She hurried after him and swept him up into her arms. "Yes, my little one." She surveyed the woods for any sign of movement. "Your papa will find out what a real woman is, and then you'll be my boy forever. I won't ever have to give you up." She hugged him to her. "I'll never give you up."

The horrible ordeal with John Wakefield brought them together as a family. It was the only possible outcome. She'd suffered, but every reward had a price.

"Let's get some firewood, Joshua." She ran her hand through his thick, textured, dark hair.

Extending one pudgy arm, he offered her his prized toy, Dakota's glove.

"What have you got there, sweetie?" She took the glove from him and traced one finger across the sewn edge.

Not a stitch had unraveled despite their well-worn appearance. Elizabeth didn't know much about Dakota Cabe, but she knew about quality. What quality did he want in a woman? Caitlyn came to mind. She wasn't going to compare herself with Caitlyn. They were nothing alike.

Caitlyn, for all her femininity, was capable as any man in the wilderness. A man might find that noteworthy, but to Elizabeth, it chiseled away at a woman's true vocation. A man wanted to protect a woman. Made a man feel like a man. No. Dakota Cabe had never experienced a real woman, a genteel, well-bred lady who knew the finer things of life.

She doubted Caitlyn ever exposed the man to anything of culture. She chuckled to herself. They probably spent their time target shooting.

A twinge of guilt tugged at her again, and she snipped it off like a loose thread. It wasn't her fault if Caitlyn didn't make it. The only reason she didn't tell Dakota the truth was to protect the child. He would be the first to agree with her if she were inclined to tell him, which she wasn't.

Elizabeth hugged Joshua tighter and let her thoughts carry her away to more exciting terrain. Perhaps she was rushing the situation a bit, but then again, she couldn't let some other woman snag him, and no woman would take her son away from her. She laughed. She was only traveling with the man, not sleeping with him. Her face grew hot.

What would he be like? She laughed again, startling Joshua. He patted her cheeks with both hands. She had been so terrified when she first met Dakota and worried he would accost her. Caitlyn drifted back into Elizabeth's thoughts, ruining her musing. What if she had escaped? What then? Caitlyn and Dakota never married, so by omission, he was a free and available man.

Elizabeth chewed her lower lip in aggravation. He hadn't wasted any time coming when Caitlyn needed him, and the woman was resourceful. Sighing in fresh frustration, Elizabeth hoped that all she had to contend with was the memory of Caitlyn and not the woman herself. He felt an obligation to her because of the boy, nothing more.

Elizabeth buried her face against Joshua's neck. "I can't lose you. I won't lose you. You're my boy now," she murmured in his ear.

"Everything all right?"

Startled, her head lifted. Dakota stood a short distance away, his arms full of dead branches and one large log. How long had he been standing there? Hot blood rushed to her face.

"We're fine, but Joshua's getting hungry," she commented, concentrating on the young boy in her arms.

"Then I best start a fire."

She frowned.

"Then I'll cook dinner."

"Were you able to procure something for dinner, Mr. Cabe? I didn't hear your rifle."

"I killed a rattler, if that's what you're asking."

She stared in horror as Dakota tossed a large, grotesque form onto the ground. Joshua wrinkled his nose at the critter but didn't cry.

"You kill rattlers with a knife if you plan on eating them—a bit messy with a rifle."

"Yes, of course." She stared in disbelief at the dead carcass. "You don't intend for us to eat this...this...reptile, do you?"

He eyed her. "Well, ma'am, I didn't risk getting snake-bit for the fun of it."

"I don't believe I can partake of this meal, Mr. Cabe, despite what obstacles you went through to get it." She scooted away from the grotesque critter. "I do, however, appreciate your skillful ability to capture one."

"Suit yourself, ma'am, but you may change your mind."

He cleared an area for their campfire and layered the twigs he'd gathered. He built what appeared to be a pyramid of sticks around and including the base of logs. This she enjoyed watching. Not knowing how to construct a fire, she found the construction of twigs and smaller branches into the shapes of pyramids charming.

Pulling a match from his pocket, he scraped it on a rock, starting a tiny fire, then set it to the dry wood. It piqued her interest when he knelt close to the small flame and gently blew on it. The flame wavered and then grew hungry, grasping at the air to feed itself.

Joshua struggled out of her embrace and waddled to Dakota and the campfire.

"Hey, big fella, where are you off to in such a hurry?" He scooped up the boy in his arms and set him on his bent knee to face the fire.

The fire's warm glow danced upon father and son as they both gazed at the flames. Longing filled Elizabeth's heart.

Chapter 10

Caitlyn stared at the canyon wall, wavering in front of her. Her heart beat madly against her chest as she tried to take herself from the moment. She didn't have any fight left in her. John had tied her hands above her and fastened the other end of the rope to a branch of a lone tree.

She tried to picture Joshua, his smiling face, and his carefree attitude, but the situation proved too ugly to keep his image in mind. Dakota's came easier. The violence of his life was now a part of hers. Her eyes drifted closed, and his face came clearly to mind, so strong and fearless. She could touch his cheek.

The whip cracked, echoing through the box canyon. Her body sprang forward with a life of the whip's making. She trembled with the effort not to cry out. Biting deep into her lip, she tasted blood.

"Tell me about Cabe, lady, and I'll cut you down. Just say the word."

A moment of silence passed, and she didn't respond.

The whip cracked again, and the sound sliced through the box canyon. Her vest wasn't much of a barrier against the whip, and the fabric shredded easily. Her body reverberated from the terrible sting, and her knees buckled, forcing her arms to take all her weight. Tears poured from her eyes, and her head bobbed.

Even as her strength ebbed, she held fast to the reasons why she wouldn't give up. Dakota and Joshua. Straightening her legs, she forced her body upright. There would be no satisfaction in this for John Wakefield. He wouldn't break her. Three more times the whip cracked. Her body jerked, but her mind stayed void.

"Damn. You are one hell of a woman. Cabe sure picked the wrong lady. He—" John's voice stopped mid-sentence.

She strained to hear him, but her ears were ringing. She tried to raise her head, but she didn't have the strength. Her body was drenched with perspiration. Her shoulders were surely torn out of their sockets. Salty tears of desperation seeped from her eyes into her mouth, and she swallowed blood and tears.

A shadow fell across her face. She opened her eyes but couldn't focus. Gradually, John's face came into view. He examined her, scrutinizing every inch of her as if he had never set eyes on her before. Standing to his full height, he walked a few feet away, then raced back to her, his mouth breaking into a broad smile.

His smugness ignited Caitlyn's misery into a rage. It took a painful minute to conjure up enough saliva in her parched mouth before she could transport it to his face. To her amazement, he laughed, wiped his sleeve across his cheek, and kissed her.

"Hell, I'd expect no less from you, girl." Turning toward the box canyon, he removed his hat and smacked it on his knee.

"What a damn fool I've been." He slapped himself on the head with his hat. "Cabe didn't pick the wrong one, I did. You're his woman, aren't you?" He paused in his excitement, then rattled on, "Never mind. Keep your damn mouth shut for all I care. It doesn't matter."

She watched from under hooded eyes as he freed his knife from his gun belt and cut her loose. She dropped to the ground with a hard jolt. With difficulty, she dragged her hands to her face and wiped the sweat from her eyes, realizing with alarm that her faulty vision wasn't due to sweat.

He twirled with glee, oblivious to her plight. "How could I be so stupid? I should have known right away. A woman like you is the perfect match for a man like him. The other woman, hell, she was afraid of her own shadow." He laughed. "Even I couldn't abide her for more than an hour, and I've never been that particular. Once again, all we have to do is wait. Isn't that so, lady? He'll come back for you. That's what you've been so damn tight-lipped about."

He pressed his face close to hers and slid his knife between her hands, cutting the rope binding her wrists. His mouth came down hard on hers with a loud smack. He leaned back to examine her as if she were a toy he always wanted but couldn't afford.

Grabbing her arm, he plucked her up. Pain shot through her, and a small gasp escaped from her lips. He seemed surprised she'd been hurt, but released his grip when he saw the raw, bleeding wounds.

He slid his hand further up her arm and jerked her forward. "Come on, lady, we need to prepare for our guest of honor."

She stumbled alongside him, the effort taking the last of her strength, but she would rather die than have the man carry her.

~ * ~

Elizabeth walked back to the crackling fire where Dakota sat cleaning his guns. The night air was warm. She was safe and protected in what otherwise would have been terrifying surroundings. "Joshua is fast asleep. I think he'll sleep through the night." She studied Dakota's profile, illuminated by the fire.

"Good." He glanced up from his guns. "Did you have enough to eat?"

She thought of the roasted rattlesnake. The reptile turned out to be quite tasty despite her hesitation. "Yes, I'm fine. I appreciate your concern, Mr. Cabe." What would her personal chef at home think if she added rattlesnake to their menu? Not much.

"Tell me how you and Caitlyn met." He continued to clean his gun.

Elizabeth seated herself as ladylike as possible on a large rock a brief distance away. She had been wondering if they would ever have a conversation, and now that they were, it would have to include Caitlyn. He picked up a second rifle, and she watched him prepare to clean the weapon. No doubt, he could do it in his sleep. A complex man, but his words would be simple and to the point. He would expect answers to his questions to be the same. All her feminine ploys and schooling would be of no use on him.

She grew uneasy, realizing her tactics would be transparent to this man. She lacked any front to work behind. Everything was as raw and wide open as the basin before them. The man stripped her of everything she'd learned and left her naked as the day she was born.

"Well?" He stopped his work.

She met his eyes, but his gaze was so dark and penetrating that she became flustered and had to turn away. Her hands were limp in her lap. They were so rough and red from traveling, she wouldn't have recognized them as her own. Turning her wedding ring around on her finger, she wished she had taken the ring off long before. She thrust her hands into the full folds of her skirt and lifted her head.

"I met Caitlyn a couple of days after I arrived in Bisweak. I bought the old McGuire's place in town—a beautiful, stately home. I planned to open a dress shop. Of course, I searched for a couple of skilled women who could sew. That's how I found Caitlyn. A perfect match. I had the means to expand her talent and make a profitable business prospect for her." Elizabeth pleased herself with the last comment. What man could resist a woman who concerned herself with the less endowed? "It's an isolated life for a woman managing alone." She drew a finger across the ground. Her reference pertained to herself since Caitlyn did have her father. Or, at least, she had.

"And as you well know, Mr. Cabe, the West is a hard and brutal place." She paused to study him. Perhaps brutal was too harsh a word. After all, she was talking to a man who coexisted with the land.

He gave her a quick jerk of his head, which she guessed meant for her to continue.

"As soon as I heard of Caitlyn's skills, my driver and I set out in the coach to propose a working contract with her."

With one eyebrow raised in what might be amusement, he asked, "Your driver and coach?"

Was he laughing at her or enjoying the story? She frowned. He was so damned unreadable. "Well, yes, how did you think I got there?"

"Of course. Please, go on. What did Caitlyn think of your coach and driver when you arrived?"

Obviously, frontiersmen didn't appreciate modern conveniences. Stephen was right. The West wouldn't change as soon as they'd hoped.

"She didn't say, but she appeared most gracious. She'd finished her chores and started dinner." Just like a commoner. "She said she could use a break and put a pot of coffee on for us."

Dakota stilled his hands and studied the black basin before them. Elizabeth watched him slip away from their immediate surroundings. The slightest smile touched his lips, and she knew he was no longer in her presence. He had no doubt conjured up a vision of himself and Caitlyn and a pot of coffee between them.

Elizabeth prepared to snap him back to reality, but he seemed to find it on his own. A shake of his head and the deep furrow in his brow confirmed there might have been a dream, but he had given it up. The set of his jaw and the sealed lips suggested it was a decision set in stone.

"I take it the two of you didn't know each other long?"

"No, but I considered her a friend. I absolutely adore Joshua."

"What did the two of you talk about?"

His question surprised her. "Mostly Joshua. She loved him so." She dropped her chin. The air seemed to still.

"You talk as if she's dead."

Even though he sat a good ten feet away, she leaned backward as if to remove herself from harm's way. "No, I didn't mean… I'm sorry. Of course she's not. It's only…" Her words came out wrong, and she stumbled across the hole she had dug to deceive. "She isn't here at the moment. That's all I meant."

He set his guns down, got up, and then walked a few feet away. Turning his back to her, he faced the stars that had begun to fill the vast emptiness above the basin.

"Ma'am, I don't mean to insinuate anything, but you keep speaking of Caitlyn in the past tense. Is there something I need to know that you aren't telling me?" He turned and faced her, a dark scowl on his face.

"There's nothing else to say," she stammered at his hard stare. "I took Joshua and ran."

"What horse did Caitlyn ride out on?"

Elizabeth frowned, befuddled by the sudden change of topics and his questions. "I don't know. Caitlyn told me when I heard a commotion, I needed to take Joshua and run to the back of the canyon, and you would be there."

"That sounds like Caitlyn, but you said you saw the horse she rode out on. Which horse was it? Was it saddled?"

"I don't remember. It all happened so fast." She rubbed her hands together to keep them from shaking.

Dakota stepped closer. "Why didn't Wakefield's men follow you right away?" Standing above her, he stared down at her.

"Caitlyn told me there would be a commotion in the camp, and as soon as it commenced, I was to take Joshua and run." She paused to think and then added, "She said not to stop, nor look back, no matter what."

"But you must have looked back if you saw her ride out on a horse. What type of commotion?"

"Mr. Cabe, it was dark, and nothing was perceivable except that the men were riled and in confusion. I assumed that was the commotion. What else would have created such an upheaval, except Caitlyn riding out? When you get to Silverwater, you can ask her yourself," she snapped.

"When did she tell you she would meet me in Silverwater? And why didn't she make sure you and Joshua escaped?" His eyes drilled into her.

"Mr. Cabe." Elizabeth started to panic. "What are you implying?" She crossed her arms over her chest with an air of hostility. "Perhaps Caitlyn thought you capable of getting us out without her help." She made her implication clear. "I didn't ask to be in this mess, Mr. Cabe. If you would kindly remember, I am the innocent victim, doing what I could to protect your son." Without pause, she aimed another dart. "I did what Caitlyn told me to do. I didn't know I'd be drilled on the details later. The unsavory ordeal lasted only minutes, and I was in a state of pure terror. I thought you would be pleased that I got your son to you. I assumed Caitlyn was capable of taking care of herself.

"As to your question…" She paused, then said, "Caitlyn told me she would head in the opposite direction to split up Wakefield's men. They had horses on both sides of the camp in case of emergencies. I heard one man shout she was getting away. I assumed they meant Caitlyn since they didn't know I'd left yet."

The hardness left Dakota's face. "You're right. You didn't ask to be in this mess. I appreciate your care for Joshua. I had some unanswered questions." He seemed reassured but not convinced. "I'm sure I'll find her in Silverwater. Caitlyn told me about your husband. I'm sorry."

"Thank you, Mr. Cabe." She was relieved at the change of topic. "A tragic episode for myself and others whose husbands died in the mine's collapse. Nevertheless, Stephen left me well provided for, although alone." Hopefully, *the well-provided-for* would raise his melancholy spirit and return his concern to her.

"I'm glad to hear that, ma'am."

"So, Mr. Cabe, how did you and Caitlyn meet?" She didn't care, but it might be the best topic to converse on.

"I met Caitlyn and her father in Bisweak." Walking to the fire, Dakota prodded the glowing logs with a long stick, sending sparks into the night.

She regarded him, trying to decipher the man's inner workings. What attracted her so much to him despite their many differences?

He was a consuming infatuation. It was the first time in Elizabeth's life that she felt alive. She shuddered at the sheer brutality he must be capable of, and yet she'd seen the quiet, gentle side of him that made him even more a man. His duality obsessed her.

There was no comparison between him and Stephen. Where Dakota ran red hot, Stephen had been—at best—lukewarm. Both she and her husband were pampered their entire lives, and both came from wealthy, long-standing families with numerous servants to wait on them. The thought of anyone waiting on Dakota Cabe was pure absurdity. He did everything for himself and needed no one.

With him, there would be great passion. To be the woman to tame him made her blood run as hot as the fire he tended. She hungered for the man like the flames hungered for open air.

"Caitlyn never mentioned her mother to me. Where is she now?" she asked, fanning away her thoughts.

"Dead."

"Oh." Had there been something unseemly about her death? Curiosity stirred her, but she had better manners than to pry. "Did you live in the same town?"

"No, I came to town at the end of a cattle roundup. Our destination was Bisweak."

"Then how did your two paths cross?"

A grin spread across his face. "Caitlyn's not a woman I'd miss."

His reminiscing irritated her.

"And you fell in love, at first sight, I suppose." Her voice had a bitterness she hadn't intended. Softening her tone, she added, "Though I don't blame you. She is beautiful."

"Gutsy too," he added.

Well, if nothing else, at least she learned what he liked in a woman. Beauty and guts. She couldn't help but roll her eyes.

"It was as if I'd known her all my life." His words held a note of finality.

She wished she had asked Caitlyn about him. "Do you love her?"

He stared at the fire as if he were alone. She held her breath waiting for his answer.

"Caitlyn and I have an understanding," he said after a few moments.

An understanding? Now, what in blazes did that mean? Obviously, an understanding known only to the two. Maybe a different approach would work better. "You have a handsome son."

"Yes, I do. You did a fine job taking care of my boy. He doesn't appear to have suffered any ill effects from the ordeal."

"Yes, he seems unaffected. I do love him. I would do anything for him."

He glanced at her, his brows arched.

"I mean, any woman would protect a child at any cost to herself." She touched Joshua's sleeping form and smiled.

"We'd best get some shut-eye. We'll ride out at first light," Dakota said.

Elizabeth eyed the desolate basin. "Do you think we'll find a homestead out there?" She tried to sound anxious for one, but she wasn't. Her guilt concerning Caitlyn had subsided. If anything, she began to hate the woman.

"I hope so. If not, then the mining town I mentioned will be our best bet. Either way, once you and Joshua are safe, I'll head back to Silverwater for Caitlyn."

"Well, I hope we find something soon." Disappointment laced her words.

"You all right?"

"Yes. Tired is all." She rose, dusting off her skirt, then she leaned over to check on Joshua, who was still asleep.

She picked up the blanket Dakota had laid out earlier and contemplated her situation. If they did find a homestead tomorrow, she would only have one day before Dakota left for Silverwater and the truth. That wouldn't do. He wouldn't understand the reason she hadn't told him about Caitlyn's failed escape.

She had to protect her family, but he wouldn't see it as such yet. He was a man of action first, reason second. She must make the right decisions until he could see the new situation himself. One man against the likes of Wakefield and his men? Complete tomfoolery. She would lose Dakota Cabe. Worse, she would lose her perfect family.

Rolling the blanket out next to the small boy, she lay on half and covered herself with the other half. Her eyes burned in desperation. She couldn't lose her precious dream, not this close. She had waited too long for a child of her own and would do whatever she must to keep Dakota from going to Silverwater.

~ * ~

Dakota watched Elizabeth's still form and tried to comprehend her change of mood. She seemed disappointed at the prospect of finding a homestead, and yet throughout their trip, she had done nothing but complain about the lack of one.

Loosening the stiff muscles in his neck, he stared into the fire. The consistent scampering of creatures back and forth in the canyon reassured him that Wakefield hadn't found their path. Dakota inhaled, drinking in the fresh air and studying the open territory beyond them. The basin was dark and formless. He hoped to see a flicker of light, some sign of a homestead, but the only sign of life in the dark abyss of blackness was the twinkling of thousands of stars.

A galaxy of tiny lanterns, Caitlyn once called them. The memory caught him in the middle of his chest like a bullet. That day always came back to him with the same vivid clarity whenever the sky showed this clear and brilliant. He closed his eyes but couldn't stop the bitter ache.

He must have been a sight, fully armed, and sprawled out on his back in the field like a kid. Caitlyn next to him, her delicate hand clasped in his.

The carefree moment had made him more than awkward, yet her laughter and lighthearted charm won him over, and so he let down his guard.

He recalled the moment so well. Caitlyn pointing out the stars to him and insisting he take heed of them. He already knew their names and fabled stories his ma had taught him. Caitlyn wanted him to know them for a completely different reason. If ever we are apart, take note of the stars and know I'm seeing the same ones as you. He closed his eyes, remembering how the stars highlighted her beautiful face.

That night, she told him she not only loved him but also understood him. He bowed his head and thought about the difference. Love had proven unpredictable, unreliable, and easy to buy into in the past. The fact that she understood him and loved him anyway moved him beyond his comprehension.

She was all those things for him, but he had let her down. He had proven to be unpredictable, unreliable, and undependable. He regretted that more than anything else in his life.

Ever since, he'd made it his nightly ritual to connect with the stars, to connect with Caitlyn.

He stared at the stars with a sense of sudden loss. He watched the fire, squinting against the flame's brightness. Coming to his feet, he retrieved another bedroll from his gear, rolled it out, and placed it over Elizabeth and Joshua, then checked on the horse.

The night air cooled by the time Dakota returned to the campfire. He made one final check of the surroundings, then sat on the ground opposite Elizabeth and Joshua. The fire had died, but he chose not to rebuild it. By morning, all traces of smoke would be gone.

Tugging his hair out from under his collar, he settled for the night. His muscles and limbs ached with fatigue. He drew the flaps of his coat across his legs as the campfire's last warm traces faded away.

He would sleep soundly tonight. The constant physical exertion, along with the emotional drain, had depleted him. He slipped away into the dark recesses of his mind. This would be the safest place to let down his guard. His mind raced across the barren ground, searching for memories to carry him far from where he lay, and soon, he found them.

He dreamed of Caitlyn. Her large, innocent eyes warmed him as she crept toward him. Without hesitation, he reached for her. His long fingers wrapped themselves in her silky hair, drawing her closer and closer to him, drinking in the sweetness of her. He was a thirsty man on parched ground, discovering fresh water. The scent of jasmine intoxicated him, leaving him powerless under her control. It had been so long since he had held the reason for his being. Soft, timid hands stroked his long hair away from his face, exposing his warm, slightly parted lips, and his breath caught in his chest.

The heat of her body melted into his as her lips grazed across his. He loosened his fingers from her hair and ran his hand along her cheek and down her neck. The buttons on her blouse gave way to his touch, exposing her delicate skin. He grew weak with longing, but strong with desire. Folding his arms around her, he pulled her hard into his unyielding embrace.

She hesitated. Relaxing his hold on her, he searched Caitlyn's seductive emerald eyes for the reason for her uncertainty, but the emerald eyes were crystal blue.

His body went rigid, and his mind spun back through dark tunnels of confusion searching for clarity. With clarity came reality, and reality found him at the campsite with Elizabeth in his arms.

Abruptly, he dropped hold of her, but her hesitation of a moment ago had fled. Wanton lips sought his. Her fingers popped open the buttons on his shirt, one by one, and he lay too stunned to react.

His senses reeled back into place, and he grasped both her hands in his. "What are you doing?" His voice hoarse and confused. His passion dead.

"I want to be with you, Dakota." Her eyes were wild with lust or madness.

"No, you don't."

Wiggling her hand loose from his, she placed a smooth, slender finger across his lips. "Don't talk."

Her hesitation now gone, she started again with his buttons. However, Dakota was rigid as death, his passion gone like a mirage in the desert. Pulling her lips from his, he tried to form a response.

"You've been through a lot. You don't know what you're doing." He extracted her cool fingers from his bare chest.

"Yes, I do know, and I want this with you."

He studied her in quiet dismay. What was he dealing with?

As if his silence meant consent, she lowered her lips once more to his and slid a slim hand down his chest across his abdomen to the buttons on his Levis.

He grabbed her hand. "This isn't right," he muttered between clenched teeth, his body rigid.

"It's right for me." Elizabeth drew back to study his face.

"Well, it isn't for me." His words were firm but soft, his face a scarce inch from hers. "And it isn't for Caitlyn either."

Anger and humiliation ignited across Elizabeth's face. "Caitlyn? I offer myself to you, and you're thinking of another woman, a dead woman at that." In flight to a full rage, her face took on an ugliness he hadn't seen. "What kind of a man are you?"

Her remark about Caitlyn unnerved and provoked him. Clapping his other hand on the back of Elizabeth's neck, he yanked her away from him like an annoying pup. She landed on her backside next to him. Rising to his feet, he stepped away from her, rubbing the sleeve of his coat against his lips.

A sour taste formed in the pit of his stomach, and he turned to spit. Turning back to Elizabeth, he caught the full force of her hand across his cheek. When she drew back to hit him again, he grabbed her wrist and stared at her in disbelief.

Her eyes held an eerie transparency of deceit.

"What the hell's wrong with you, woman? What did you mean, saving myself for a dead woman?"

"Nothing," she spat, "except that's what Caitlyn will be if she keeps company with you. John Wakefield won't be the last."

He held onto her wrist and watched as the fiery hatred ebbed out of her eyes. "That's not what you meant."

"Well, it's the best answer you're going to get," she snapped.

Maybe her experience with Wakefield had proven too much for her. He needed to be cautious. He could fathom a woman of her breeding breaking under the circumstances, and that could be the case here, but a nagging feeling to the contrary wouldn't leave him.

"You're hurting me."

He released her wrist, and she turned away from him. When he spied her torn dress, a stab of guilt washed over him as if he had been the aggressor. Putting his hands on his hips, he took a deep breath and then released it. His head ached with confusion. The stars above were brilliant in the clear indigo sky, but he found no connection. He was alone.

Joshua whimpered, and Dakota strode over to where the boy lay. The commotion had frightened him awake, and he was soon in full squalor. Morning remained hours away, but there was no hope of pursuing sleep now.

"We'll pack up and head out."

"Whatever you say, Mr. Cabe." Elizabeth's voice was flat and remote.

He felt sorry for the woman. What had Wakefield and his men done to her?

Chapter 11

Caitlyn sat in front of the fire that the boy tended. The cool evening breeze left her sweat-soaked body chilled. She couldn't sit any closer to it without setting herself on fire, but the warmth never reached her. Staring into the flames, she struggled to listen to the men as they gathered. A rider, Todd, approached from the back of the canyon.

"There ain't no sign of him and that woman nowhere. Jimmy went on to Copper Lake and Jessie Town to search there. He said he'd be back the day after tomorrow. Where else you want us to go, John? It don't seem likely they vanished into thin air."

"Hardly, Todd. Cabe's a crafty son-of-a-bitch. He's likely found a crevice leading out. No telling where he's at now. Don't matter anyway."

"What are you saying?" Todd spat out a long stream of tobacco juice and eyed John. "That woman tells you where Cabe's hiding, and now you figure you can cut the rest of us out and collect the bounty yourself? We got a deal, John. You best not forget that." Todd's voice held a warning.

"Sizzle down, Todd. I'm not planning to cut anyone out. You're as stupid as I was."

"What's that supposed to mean?"

"Means we've been hanging on to the wrong bait, 'til now."

A long pause ensued, and she chanced a look. Todd's attention locked full upon her, disbelief and understanding rolling together across his face.

"She's Cabe's woman?" He pointed a long finger at her.

John smiled. "Yup. We've still got the bait."

"Well, it does make more sense, don't it, John?"

Both men nodded.

"What now?" Todd asked.

"Why, we simply wait. Cabe will come back." John gave her a look of appreciation. "I would. In the meantime, we should celebrate our soon to be good fortune and give a toast to our beautiful treasure."

She circled her arms around herself, trying to generate some warmth, but the coldness within her grew, forewarning of worse to come.

The men were quick to break open the liquor and, after an hour, most were feeling no pain. She eyed them across the blazing fire, hoping for a means of escape, but they weren't going to leave her alone. It made little difference. She doubted she could walk, let alone run. Soon, the men were shouting and dancing around the camp like impish boys. The smoke from the campfire changed direction and floated over to her, stinging her eyes, but she didn't attempt to move clear.

Toward midnight, the drunk men settled. She could still hear Todd and John, but she couldn't make out their words. She peered across the fire at their moonlit shapes. John motioned to her with his hand, then walked away alone. Todd rose and walked in a staggered pattern in her direction, a nearly empty bottle of whiskey in his hand.

"Well, hello, darling, it seems you had us all fooled. I reckon you think you're smart, don't 'cha?" Stumbling, he moved closer.

His face had grown more grotesque from the liquor. His scarred lip now relaxed, allowing spittle to run out of his mouth and down his chin. Her stomach churned at the sight of him, and she eyed the ground around her, searching for something to grasp in case she had to defend herself.

"Take it easy, lady. I ain't gonna touch 'cha. Strict orders from the boss man. Any of us lay a hand on you, and they's dead." He glanced over his shoulder, then back at her. "You know what I think, lady?" He loomed precariously above her, trying to keep his balance.

She tried to move out of his way, but his hand clamped down on her shoulder more for balance than for anything else.

"I think ole John's a mite scared of Cabe," he whispered. "Scared of what Cabe'd do if we were to lay a hand on your lily-white skin." Todd took a swig from the bottle. "But me? I ain't afraid of no man, and you know what else?" He bowed over her, placing both hands on her shoulders and spilling liquor down the front of her. "I especially ain't afraid of your Cabe." His eyes trailed after the flow of liquor from the bottle as if it were liquid gold.

"If you had any sense, you would be. Get off me, you pig." She tried to shrug out of his grasp, but his hands dug like claws into her shoulders.

"You're a cold one, ain't ya? Maybe this will warm ya up." Gripping her jaw in one hand, he forced her mouth open and poured whiskey down her throat.

She spat most of it back into his face, then swung her arm wide, catching her palm against the side of his face. The impact made his whiskey-sodden body tumble to the ground, her with him. He floundered to right himself as she pummeled him with her fists, but her actions only brought laughter to his lips.

"You're a spunky one all right. Just the way I like 'em." He drew her across him and then rolled on top of her, his weight crushing the breath from her.

The foul mixture of whiskey and tobacco did nothing to cover his unbearable body stench. Caitlyn's stomach lurched into her throat, and she battled to keep from vomiting.

She managed a short scream before his rough and calloused hand clamped over her mouth. She bit down hard. He jerked his hand free. Reaching, she clawed at his eyes. A trail of blood followed her fingertips.

He knocked her hand aside. "You fool." He sneered. "I was gonna be nice to you, but you want it rough." He drew his hand back to hit her.

Unable to shield herself, she waited for the inevitable blow, but it didn't come. Todd's hand stopped midway, his massive body yanked backward. She took the opportunity to roll to her side and scramble to her feet. In agony, half stumbling, half running, she fled for the canyon.

Footsteps followed close behind her as she searched for a place to hide, but there was nowhere to go. She saw the horses tethered a short distance ahead of her, and self-preservation pushed her wooden legs beyond their usual capacity. Her bare feet were numb to the sharp pebbles beneath them as she sprinted toward the means of her escape. She almost wept with relief when she grasped the first horse's mane and hoisted herself up, but two strong arms grabbed her and jerked her hands loose.

"I've got her," the man yelled, tossing her to the ground, away from the horses.

Pain shot through her, and bitter tears of defeat filled her eyes. The twinkling stars mocked her. "Dakota...please." She pressed the back of her hand against her mouth lest her whispered words turn to sobs.

~ * ~

Dakota and Elizabeth traveled two hours before the first rays of morning greeted them. Neither spoke to the other, and that suited him.

He had offered his help when they mounted, but Elizabeth shrugged off his hand. Now she sat stiff in the saddle, keeping her body from touching his.

Joshua woke with a startled cry, and Elizabeth bent her head to kiss his forehead. Her touch and soft words soothed the boy, and he settled back against her. She was good to his son, that much Dakota knew. The rest he'd have to let pass as simple, overwrought emotions.

At noon, they stopped at a small creek to water the horse. Sliding from the saddle, he took Joshua from Elizabeth. Dakota placed him a short distance from the water, where he soon became fascinated with the shiny, dew-kissed rocks.

Sitting on his heels next to Joshua, he pointed out the different colored rocks and demonstrated how to skip them sideways. Joshua picked up several in delight, but only succeeded in pitching them into the water.

"Mr. Cabe, I..." Elizabeth's voice was soft, and if he could believe his ears, contrite. "I want to apologize for what I said last night. You see, I misread your intentions, and that confused... scared me. Nevertheless, I think it would be best to forget the incident."

He stared at her. Did she accuse him of instigating the sordid episode? Much as he wanted to forget the incident, he wanted more to clear up any misinterpretations she might be entertaining.

Pushing back his hat, he gave her his full puzzled attention, but she failed to comprehend his perplexed scowl or chose to ignore it.

"Mr. Cabe, I furthermore think—"

"Dakota,"

"What?"

"Call me Dakota. You did last night," he said.

She couldn't hold his stare and fidgeted under his scrutiny. "Why are you making this difficult?"

He sighed. "I'm not. I'm trying to understand you. I thought you were Caitlyn's friend."

"I was. I mean, I am. I was terrified when John Wakefield kidnapped Joshua and myself, and I have been terrified ever since. Wakefield and his gang are the most unscrupulous men I've ever had to encounter. I don't know if I'll ever get past the experience or if I'll ever feel safe again." She embraced him, her arms circling his waist. Glancing up at him, shiny plumb tears flowed down her face. "I'm sorry. I don't know what's come over me. Please forgive me."

With reluctance, he gave her a half-hearted embrace. How had the situation gotten so complicated? Her sobs racked her body, and he held her loosely, patting her back as if she were a lost and inconsolable child.

Several minutes passed before she calmed. Dakota watched Joshua over her head, making sure he didn't attempt to crawl into the shallow water, but the boy was still tossing the speckled rocks into the water.

Joshua smiled at them, and Dakota smiled back. What was worse? Having an outlaw for a father or no father at all? He should have stayed. He had protected no one by leaving. How could a decision that once seemed so right now be so wrong?

Elizabeth pushed back from him. "I am sorry. This isn't like me."

"It's all right. You're tired. We're both tired. It's been a rough couple of days. When we get to town, and you rest up, you'll feel like yourself again. We'll forget about last night. No problem."

She stiffened. Anger flashed across her face. "Are those the words you give to all your women the next morning?" Her words held a biting edge to them.

He regarded her without emotion. "I think you forgot...nothing happened." His feelings mixed. One minute, he felt sorry for her, and the next, he wanted to run for cover.

"I guess nothing much matters to a man such as yourself, Mr. Cabe." His calm composure seemed to infuriate her.

"Some things do."

"I suppose you mean Joshua and Caitlyn."

He didn't answer but glanced at where his son sat playing.

Elizabeth followed his gaze. "So, you hold on to them even though you endanger them by being with them," she said, her voice softening. "You know your presence is a death seal on them. The bounty on your head entices unscrupulous men. Or have you forgotten how I got here?"

He returned his focus to her. "Circumstances don't change a man's heart."

"Well, you did the right thing leaving. Caitlyn had a new life and a new beginning."

"I'm not so damn sure what the right thing is anymore," he muttered, mostly to himself, glancing again at his son.

"You forget I met Caitlyn after you left. She was happy, content. She had a good life until John Wakefield stepped into it. What kind of happiness could she or Joshua have with a wanted man? You don't even know if you can keep them alive."

"Caitlyn makes her own decisions."

"Maybe so, but if you love someone, you ought to do what's right for them. There will always be someone like John Wakefield after your bounty. Caitlyn and Joshua will always be pawns in their macabre schemes."

Her words bit into him, scraping too close to the truth. The vision of living as a family in a cabin in the mountains seemed rather absurd in the harsh light of reality. A dream he began to hope for again, but how could he? He hated the fact that the bizarre woman was right.

He backed away. He couldn't deal with this right now, but Elizabeth's hands clasped his leather vest.

"You know I'm right, Dakota Cabe. The best thing you could do for Caitlyn and Joshua is to stay out of their lives forever."

"Like I said, Caitlyn's her own woman. It's her decision to make, not mine, and certainly not yours." Pulling free from her hold, he headed to his horse.

"Then you do love her?" she asked.

"I never said I didn't."

~ * ~

Caitlyn woke at daylight, drenched in sweat, her clothes soaked. Her skin was tender to the touch, and her back throbbed with pain. Tossing the blanket off, she pushed herself into a sitting position. The inside of the tent swirled around her, and she grew nauseous.

"Feeling rough?"

She turned. John sat in the corner watching her.

"I brought you something to eat. Got to keep your strength up so Cabe can see we've been treating you well."

She expected his comment to be a joke, but his eyes held no laughter. Instead, something akin to regret lingered there.

He held out a plate of beans to her, and she reached to take them. The last time she'd eaten was with Dakota, and despite nausea, she was starving. Balancing the plate in her shaky hands, she ate as much as she could.

"Could be any time now, don't you think?"

She eyed her plate, then the man. She had forgotten he still lingered there. She couldn't comprehend his question.

"Your Cabe. He ought to be making an appearance any time. I sure hope the two of you didn't have a lovers' spat before we found you, but I suppose it wouldn't matter. He'd still come for you. I would."

She shot him with a doubtful glare.

"What's wrong?" He broke into laughter. "You don't believe I'd risk my life for a woman like you? Maybe, maybe not, but your kind is a rarity." Leaning forward, he caught a strand of her hair between his fingers and twirled it tight, bringing her closer. "As soon as you've filled your role as bait, I've decided to keep you, for a while anyway. After all, once Cabe's dead, you won't have much use for him, will you?"

"That would depend..." her eyes locked on his, "...on who takes the first bullet, wouldn't it?"

He slapped his knees. "Hell, you've got fire in your blood. I like that, I do. And I'll show you how much I like it." His expression turned serious. "As soon as we've taken care of business. After you've been with me, you'll wonder what you ever saw in Dakota Cabe." He paused, appearing lost in his thoughts. "Since we're soon to be intimate, don't you think it's time I called you by your first name? Found you and your boy, but never found out your name." He waited for her reply.

She said nothing.

"Never mind. I'll find out eventually." He rose. "Even if I have to torture it out of Cabe." He waited for a reaction from her.

She sat like stone.

"Oh well, come on. We need to parade you around outside, in case Cabe is nearby." John yanked her to her feet.

She tried to maintain her balance but couldn't. The space grew dim, and though she struggled to see, nothing but blackness met her eyes. His arms circled her waist. In the deep recesses of her mind, she tumbled down dark and lonely corridors, one after another. She wondered where she was, but it didn't matter. She forgot her thoughts as quickly as they came.

~ * ~

John caught the woman before she hit the ground. He never suspected how ill she was until he touched her and felt the heat radiating from her body.

"Billy," he called, "get me some water."

Minutes later, Billy brought the water. John sponged her hot face, neck, and shoulders.

"She gonna die, John?" Billy squinted at the woman lying on the cot in the tent and then at John.

"Get out," John's command boomed in the cramped quarters.

Billy tripped over a chair as he quickly backed up. "You want anything else?" the kid asked, pushing the tent flap up to leave.

"Just get the hell out," he shouted. As soon as Billy left, John turned to the unconscious woman. "You pushed me too far. You're the bait, nothing more." His anger mounted into frustration. "I planned it all out. The bounty money was mine. It was all so simple." Bending, his face only inches from hers, he asked, "What have you done?"

Chapter 12

Toward dusk, Dakota pointed out a trail of pale blue smoke above the trees. Elizabeth's heart sank. Then they came upon a small cabin nestled in the woods.

Reining in the horse, he scanned the area surrounding the homestead, and so did she, hoping beyond hope no one lived there—a foolish one given the smoke. Split logs lay scattered around a stump with a shiny, well-oiled axe resting on its base, a task still in need of completion. The homesteader was probably inside having his supper. To the side of the house, a well-kept barn and small corral sat, which held three horses. Everything was orderly and well-tended. A hardworking homesteader lived here, one who valued what was his.

On the other side of the house, a full line of clothing for a man, woman, and child, swayed in the evening breeze.

Elizabeth stared at the small but solidly built cabin. Time had run out. Judging from the woman and youngster's clothing, and Dakota's relaxed demeanor, he would likely leave her and Joshua here. It seemed safe enough to her.

Dakota urged the horse to the side of the cabin and approached. She marveled that the man never let down his guard, not even now. A short distance from the cabin, he slid off the horse and freed his rifle.

She started to ask him what she should do, but he silenced her with a finger to his lips. He handed her the reins, then walked to the house. He mounted the three small steps leading up to the cabin's porch. Her heart lurched in her throat.

The sunlit structure silhouetted his broad back. His long hair reached past the collar of his shirt. His sleeves rolled up exposing tanned, well-muscled arms. He was a powerful, intimidating, and dangerous man.

Passing his rifle to his left hand, he knocked twice. When the large wooden door creaked open, he stepped back from the door and off to the side. A large, stocky man filled the doorway. The homesteader stood far beyond six feet tall and had to bow his head to peer out the door. He appeared several years older than Dakota, closer to forty than thirty. Thick, unruly gold hair was clipped close to his collar. His well-trimmed beard had the same hue, with bits of dark red mixed in. His eyes were a shade paler than the noonday sky.

Elizabeth cuddled Joshua closer. The mountain lion of a man scrutinized Dakota, then her. His form relaxed at the sight of her and Joshua. He, too appeared to be a man always on guard.

"What can I do for you, stranger?" The greeting came straight forward with a slight German accent.

"The woman and child need a place to rest for a couple of days. I'm willing to pay whatever you think is fair for your kindness."

Joshua stretched out his limbs and then slipped back to sleep. Riding horseback suited him as much as it did his father.

A blonde-headed woman peeked out from behind the man. A bit smaller than her husband, she had the same pale-blue eyes.

"And you?" The man turned back to Dakota, still blocking the doorway, keeping his wife behind him.

"I have some unfinished business to take care of, then I'll be back, and we'll move on."

"That your woman?" The man nodded in Elizabeth's direction.

"Depends on why you're asking." Shifting his weight, he placed the rifle back into his right hand.

Not a threatening gesture, but the man noticed. "I ain't got no quarrel with you, Mr. Cabe."

Elizabeth's gaze flew to Dakota, but he didn't flinch from his usual stoic expression.

"I'm curious to know if what I heard in town was true or not," the man continued.

Dakota remained silent.

The large German leaned up against the doorframe. "I recognized you from a wanted poster in town. Your reputation intrigued me. Intrigues a lot of people, I reckon." The man paused.

Still, Dakota remained silent.

Elizabeth panicked. Why didn't he do something other than stand there? Couldn't he see they were in danger? The man was out for the bounty on Dakota, like all the rest.

A smile tugged at the corners of the German's mouth. "When in town, hearing all about you, one of John Wakefield's men rode in."

Good Lord, this was a trap, and Dakota was listening as if they were discussing the price of cattle. She wanted to scream at him, to tell him to get them out of this mess, but he seemed ignorant of their peril. Maybe he wasn't as astute as she assumed.

"Seems John Wakefield had quite a scheme going to collect the bounty on your head. Heard he kidnapped your woman to get you out of hiding, but his plans got spoiled because of some other woman you brought with you. 'Mystery Lady,' the man called her."

The homesteader laughed. "Wakefield's man said John was madder than a rabid coon like he had made a generous deal with the devil but lost his soul instead."

Elizabeth focused her concentration on Dakota. Had he flinched? No. He remained ramrod straight.

"So, since there were two women involved," the man nodded in her direction, "I wondered if she was your woman."

"No."

Dakota's answer hit Elizabeth in the pit of her stomach. Why offer information to this stranger? Now the man might be after her, knowing that Dakota had no claim on her. This situation was out of hand. Gripping the reins tightly, she readied herself to command the horse to run. She glanced around her with fear. Where would she go?

The German bowed his head and gave a low whistle before he lifted his gaze, compassion in his eyes. "So that's your unfinished business." A statement, not a question. The sizable man moved toward Dakota and clamped his large hand on his shoulder.

Elizabeth lightly pressed her heels into the horse's side.

"Whatever I can do to help you, Cabe, you name it. Sarah." The man turned toward his wife. "Come and take the child." He turned back to Dakota. "John Wakefield and his men have terrorized every homesteader around here for far too long. He'll steal anything not nailed to the ground, and what he can't steal, he shoots. I can't tell you how damn pleased I was when I heard of Wakefield being bested by a mere woman. He and his men are no damn good. Ain't a shred of human decency amongst them and stealing a man's woman is about as bad as stealing a man's horse." The homesteader's face spread into a wide grin, and he slapped Dakota on the back before offering his hand. "Name's Henry Cooper. Wife here is Sarah."

Dakota tipped his hat to the woman. "Ma'am."

"Pleased to meet you, Mr. Cabe," the woman replied as she hurried past him to where Elizabeth still sat upon the horse.

The sudden turn of events amazed her.

"Come on, Cabe. I'll show you around and try to put you at ease." Henry led Dakota toward the barn. "Show you where we can hide your horse."

Sarah held out her arms to Elizabeth for Joshua. She untied him from the sling and lowered the boy to the woman. Sarah cradled Joshua to her bosom before peering back up at Elizabeth, questioning with her eyes if she needed help dismounting.

"That's all right, I've learned to manage." Tossing a scalding glare in Dakota's direction, she slid to the ground.

Sarah was smaller than her husband but much larger than Elizabeth, and she felt dwarfed in her presence. Sarah appeared to be a strong-minded woman and strong-boned, and she had a warm spirit that set Elizabeth at ease.

"My name is Elizabeth Cookman. Thank you for taking us in."

Sarah patted her shoulder. "Nonsense, child, the pleasure will be all mine. Do you know how long it's been since I had any womenfolk to talk to?"

"A long time, I imagine, living so far from town," Elizabeth commented.

Sarah pondered her own question for a moment. "Good Lord, it's been weeks since I spoke to another woman." She laughed, then tied the reins to a nearby branch before leading Elizabeth toward the house. "Come inside, dear. You are exhausted." Her German accent wasn't as prominent as her husband's. For simple homesteaders, they spoke the English language well.

"Thank you, Mrs. Cooper. I am a bit tired. It's been a challenging experience." As much as she hated to admit it, Dakota couldn't have found a safer place for them to stay.

"Please, call me Sarah. Child, you must have had a horrible time of it." Sarah stared at her, then away. "I'm sorry. I didn't mean to be so blunt." She patted Elizabeth's hand. "Do you need to talk, my dear?" she murmured. "Are you injured in any way?"

On fire with embarrassment and the awkward situation, she put a hand to her cheek. "No." She paused. "I'm...I'm all right." However, the realization of what Wakefield's men could have subjected her to made her legs weak. In her terror of dying, she hadn't considered the alternative. She reached for the porch rail but missed.

"Henry!" Still holding Joshua, Sarah caught Elizabeth by the arm and prevented her from crashing to the ground.

Charging footsteps rushed to Elizabeth's side and swept her up with the swoosh of her petticoats. Sarah opened the door, and Dakota hurried into the cabin.

Inside, a fire burned brightly, illuminating the interior with a soft yellow glow. The private atmosphere was warm and comforting. Sarah pointed out a rugged chair in the corner, and he settled Elizabeth there.

She examined the small cozy cabin, and her mind relaxed. Yes, this was a safe place for Joshua. A sting of bitterness hit her; it was also a safe place for her.

Then an idea came to her, dispelling some of her gloom. Perhaps she could go with Dakota. He shouldn't have any qualms about leaving Joshua here with the Coopers for a short spell. Maybe she could convince him she might be an asset on the trip to Silverwater, then, while in route, she could come up with a convincing explanation as to why Caitlyn might not be there. No, she only deceived herself. He would not see her as an asset in going with him.

"Are you all right, lass?"

She saw Sarah's concerned face. Joshua perched on the older woman's hip, happily devouring a wedge of bread.

"Yes, just dizzy for a moment. I'm exhausted."

"No doubt." Sarah smiled at her, then at the two men standing by the door. She nodded at them, and they exited the cabin.

Two plates rested on the dinner table, the meal only half eaten—a mixture of fresh vegetables surrounded by a large plate of stewed beef. A bowl of whipped potatoes sat in the center of the table. Two cups of coffee sat waiting next to the plates. It smelled delicious, and Elizabeth's stomach growled in hunger.

"I'll fix you a plate in a moment, dear," Sarah half-whispered.

Elizabeth turned away from the feast, ashamed she had been so obvious in her hunger, and concentrated on Sarah's activities. She placed Joshua inside a large wooden crib to finish his wedge of bread. Pushing to her feet, Elizabeth tiptoed to Sarah's side and peered into the crib. Next to Joshua lay a petite girl, who was sound asleep. Joshua offered his bread to the sleeping child, but when she didn't wake, he took it back and chewed it vigorously.

"What's her name?" Elizabeth whispered.

"Sarah Ann. She turned a year old yesterday."

"She's beautiful."

"And the boy?"

Elizabeth hesitated. Sarah knew that Joshua wasn't hers, and the fact irked her. "Joshua. He's fourteen months old."

The front door opened, and both men walked in. Henry seemed out of place in this small, femininely decorated home. Dakota, covered in several days' worth of dust, didn't fit much better. Elizabeth's hand went to her hair. What a sight she must be.

Sarah noticed her distress. "Soon as you've had some dinner, I'll draw you a bath."

Scanning the small interior, Elizabeth wondered where the tub room might be.

"I'm afraid our tub's outside, but our closest neighbor's five miles away, so you'll have complete privacy."

"That's fine, Sarah, thank you." Elizabeth dropped her hand as Dakota turned toward her.

His gaze swept across the room. "Where's Joshua?"

She pointed to the corner where the wooden crib sat. "The Coopers have a daughter, Sarah Ann. She's sharing her crib with Joshua."

"Thank you, ma'am." Dakota nodded toward Sarah.

Henry pulled out a chair for him and gestured for him to sit.

"Come, child, have some dinner." Sarah touched Elizabeth's elbow and urged her to the table.

Moving a chair away from the wall, Dakota slid it to the table, then turned his attention back to Henry. Henry poured himself and Dakota a fresh cup of coffee.

"Ma'am?" Henry held the pot up in the air, staring at Elizabeth.

"No, thank you, Mr. Cooper." She sat, her back ramrod straight as she listened to the conversation.

"You two are lucky that I never learned to cook only for Henry and myself." Sarah tossed over her shoulder. "I come from a large family." She heaped more potatoes into a bowl and placed them on the table.

"Thank you." Dakota nodded at Sarah. "Henry, you said in the barn that you had some information on John Wakefield, but then you changed the subject. Is there something I need to know before I head for Silverwater?" His voice rippled across the small room.

Elizabeth cringed, fearing that Henry knew Caitlyn hadn't escaped.

"First, eat. Don't appear you've had a good meal in days, and I promise you my wife can cook."

Dakota took a forkful of hot meat.

Elizabeth dangled her fork above her plate, waiting for Henry to try his food, but he didn't.

Dakota noticed her unease and glanced back at Henry. "Well?"

"I learned a few things while in town today." He studied his wife. "I thought you knew, but when you mentioned going to Silverwater, I realized you didn't." Henry paused. "Anyway, a hearty meal in your stomach will help you think clearly. A man can make things a hell of a lot worse if he goes off half-starved and half-cocked. And you've got your boy to consider." His voice was morbidly suggestive.

Holding her breath, Elizabeth watched Dakota's reaction. This was it. Not even a chance for them to have a decent meal.

The room grew pale with silence, except for the slight clink of Dakota's fork as he laid it down on his plate. His jaw flinched, and he observed his plate before piercing Henry with storm-filled eyes. "You know something about Caitlyn, I ought to?"

Elizabeth prayed Henry would choose his words with prudent care.

"If that's your woman's name, then yes, Cabe, I do. You won't be finding her in Silverwater."

Elizabeth dropped her fork with a clatter onto her plate. Henry couldn't have sucker-punched Dakota for a greater effect. He pushed away from the table and, in standing, knocked his chair backward. His fingers turned stark white as he gripped the tabletop. She was terrified he might turn the place upside down, or worse, leave.

Leaping to his feet, Henry grasped Dakota's forearms with bear-like hands. "Before you go and turn your boy into an orphan, don't you think it might be helpful to hear what else I know?" He relaxed his hold but didn't let go of Dakota's arms.

Elizabeth didn't dare to intervene or speak. The muscles in Dakota's face and arms relaxed, and Henry let go.

"Sit down and finish your meal, while I tell you everything I know." His voice held a final note of authority.

His burst of anger replaced with an air of despair, Dakota sat. "She never made it out, did she?" His voice was devoid of emotion.

Henry said nothing.

Dropping his gaze to his plate, Dakota gritted his teeth. "Is she dead?"

"No."

His shoulders drooped as Dakota let out his breath. "Then she's with Wakefield?"

"Yes."

"Does he know who she is?"

"Yes."

He ran his hand through his hair. "So he's waiting for me, again."

"Appears so."

"And while I'm sitting here filling my gut, Caitlyn could be…" Dakota started to rise.

Henry gripped his arm. "You of all people ought to know you can't play with what-ifs." He paused, his words very clear as he said, "It makes you ineffective. Besides…" He lowered his voice as if to spare the women from his next words, "If Wakefield wanted to kill her, he would have by now."

He released his hold, and Dakota rose. "Thank you for the meal. I'll be heading out. I'll be back for my son and Elizabeth when I have Caitlyn."

Elizabeth was shocked. If he left now, she would never have a chance. He'd go and take all of her dreams with him: Blast Henry and his damn news.

"So, you intend to go in a second time without a plan? You're exhausted; you believe that'll work on your behalf?" Henry said. "I thought you were smarter than that, but hey, if you want to blow your one chance to get her back, go ahead."

Dakota hesitated. "You got a plan?"

"No, but two heads are better than one, and the way I see it, Wakefield's gonna be a bit more careful the second time around. No doubt he'll be well rested when you show up."

Elizabeth stifled a sigh of relief. She kept her attention on Dakota. The candlelight was unkind. Weary lines of fatigue and despair stretched out across his face, making him appear older.

Resting his chin on the top of his balled-up fists, he gazed at a small, insignificant spot on the table.

Henry grasped his forearm. "I know your heart's telling you to go and go now, but years of experience have got to be telling you to think tactically and without emotion. Am I not right?"

"God damn it, Henry. This isn't some stranger. This is *my* Caitlyn." A heavy stillness filled the room. Minutes passed. "I saw dynamite in your barn. Can I buy it?" His question broke the room's rigid silence.

"Dynamite?" Henry cocked an eye at Dakota with surprise. "What you need dynamite for?"

"I have a plan."

Her appetite lost, Elizabeth studied her plate. Once again, the man had matters under control. When he seemed so defeated, she hoped she might squeeze past his hard shell and plop herself right in the middle of his being.

"I'll draw you a bath now, dear. The men need to talk." Sarah rose and patted Elizabeth on the shoulder. "You must be spent. A nice hot bath will restore your spirits."

She rose to her feet. "May I help you?"

"I should say not. You need rest. I do this all the time, don't I, Henry?"

"Yes, she does. My wife's a strong woman—has to be out here—and you do appear a bit done in, my dear."

Elizabeth sat back down. How bad did she look? "I think I'll have a cup of coffee now, Mr. Cooper. If there's some left."

"There sure is. But please call me Henry. Mr. Cooper makes me feel old." He poured her a cup and scooted it across the table.

Sarah gave her husband a peck on the cheek and went outside.

"Thank you, Mr... uh, Henry."

Dakota came to his feet. "I need to brush down my horse and put her up if that's all right with you, Henry."

"You bet. I'll join you." Henry rose, towering above Elizabeth. "And you, lady, stretch out and rest."

She nodded, sadness seeping into her as Dakota walked out the door without even a glance in her direction.

The door closed behind them. Propping her elbows on the table, she rested her chin in her hands and gazed into her coffee mug. A vague image of herself stared back at her. This is how it will feel tomorrow when he leaves. Her slender finger caressed the rim of her cup as she sat mesmerized.

Hatred for the woman who threatened to ruin all her dreams started to grow inside of her. Caitlyn didn't want the man. If she had, she never would have let him go. For all she knew, she might not even want Joshua. After all, his birth was not sanctioned by the confines of marriage. He may only be an unfortunate product of a night of passion with a man she didn't love enough to keep.

Elizabeth, however, had gone to the extreme to care for the boy, and she wanted the father. It seemed so simple, so uncomplicated to her. She and Dakota could have everything if only Caitlyn had exited the picture...permanently.

The door opened, and Sarah re-entered. Elizabeth jumped in surprise. Embarrassed she had been caught daydreaming, she took a quick sip of her coffee only to find it cool and bitter, much like her thoughts.

Sarah's cool hands rested on her shoulders. "My dear, forgive me for being so forward, but you punish yourself with the impossible."

She raised her chin to assess Sarah's perceptive gaze, not caring that her own eyes glistened with tears of frustration. "You don't understand. Caitlyn doesn't love him as I do." Her voice straining with emotion.

"I understand better than you think. Whoever this Caitlyn is, Dakota Cabe loves her, and no matter what happens, he always will. A man like him has room for only one woman in his heart. Let him go, dear. He can never be yours."

Staring into her cup, Elizabeth wiped her eyes with the back of her hand. A consuming rage rose to the surface. Sarah was nothing more than an uneducated sodbuster. She'd never understand the depth of her relationship with Dakota. The woman didn't even know Caitlyn.

Dakota Cabe wasn't in love with Caitlyn. How ridiculous. He'd left her and never came back.

No. Elizabeth did not intend to let him go, and certainly not Joshua. She would protect her family. If he thought he could leave her with some poor dirt farmers while he went back for some woman who didn't give a hoot about him, he was mistaken.

She rose and turned to address Sarah. "No, I'm afraid you have no idea what you are talking about. I think I'll take my bath now. Excuse me."

Chapter 13

Elizabeth hated the dark as much as she hated the outdoors. Fortunately, a sliver of the moon graced the night, and a gentle breeze whispered through the trees. The warm air was alive with the sound of a thousand crickets.

The clothes, which had hung on the line when she and Dakota first arrived, now circled the tub, providing as much privacy as possible. It was only an act of kindness. The darkness and lack of neighbors rendered it private enough.

Piling her hair up on her head, she allowed Sarah the menial task of unfastening all the hooks running down the back of her dress. She hadn't thought twice about expecting Sarah's assistance. It was easier to relate to her as a servant than a woman who owned her own homestead.

Her dress dropped heavily to the ground. It was soiled and caked with mud along the hem, and the bodice stained beyond repair. Gingerly, Elizabeth sat on the edge of the tub and removed her boots and torn stockings.

"I'll wash these and bring you a clean dress of mine," Sarah said, gathering the soiled clothes. "I have a couple of dresses that might fit you.

I've put on some weight since Sarah Ann, but I'll put a quick tuck in them and raise the hem."

"Thank you, Sarah." Elizabeth studied the older woman with a dismissive air and a slight tilt of the chin. She still wore her camisole and wasn't about to disrobe completely in the woman's company.

"Well then, I'll leave you to your bath. I'll bring you a fresh camisole when I return." Sarah grunted and walked away.

~ * ~

Dakota finished brushing down his horse and led the mare into the barn as Henry finished his evening chores.

He held the lantern high above his head to give Dakota as much light as possible.

Dakota examined the well-organized, but small area. "Are you sure you want her in the barn? She's mighty frisky."

"Yeah, I'm sure." Henry nodded at the mare. "She's a dead giveaway if someone should be scouting these parts for you. She's a handsome one, though. What's her name?"

"Caitie."

The horse nickered.

"She's got me out of more tight spots than I care to remember." Dakota winced, remembering a few.

The horse pranced sideways, keeping a wary eye on Henry. Dakota held the reins firmly in case she decided to nip.

"She's definitely a one-man horse. Reckon she takes a steady hand," Henry commented.

"Most things do," he replied.

"You're not big on conversation, are you?"

He gave a short chuckle. "Guess not. Elizabeth said the same thing."

"She's quite taken with you."

"Who?" he asked, stooping to examine the horse's shoe. He ran an experienced finger inside the hoof, probing for any tenderness. He certainly didn't need a lame horse before he even got started.

"Well, I'm not talking about your horse, and I sure as hell am not talking about my wife, so I reckon it be Elizabeth."

He shrugged. "Sorry. Guess my thoughts were elsewhere. I didn't hear what you said." He bent back to examine another shoe.

"With your woman, I suppose," Henry stated.

Dakota dropped the hoof to the ground, then straightened and eyed Henry more closely, his guard up. He cupped the horse's rump, moving her toward the back of the barn.

Henry held up his hand. "Hey. I know what you're thinking, Cabe, but like I said, I ain't got no quarrel with ya. The bounty on your head is mighty high, but I ain't no bounty hunter, and I ain't no fool. I judge a man by what I see. You're good with me. Hell, so far, I kind of like you."

"Sorry, Henry." Dakota relaxed his shoulders. "I don't mean to be so damn suspicious, especially since you opened your home to us." He held out his hand. "Accept my second, and I hope, last apology?"

Grinning, Henry shook his hand. "I guess if I lived in your boots, I'd be the same way. Better suspicious than chancing a bullet in the back, but you ain't got nothing to fear from me. I can promise you that." He slapped him on the back and headed for the barn door.

"Want me to tie her down for the night?" Dakota motioned back to Caitie, who was chewing on hay in the corner.

"Nah, she seems pretty content. Besides, most women don't like to be confined by a man. I reckon my barn's a lot safer if we give her the space she requires." Henry chuckled.

The men walked out into the warm, starlit night. Henry made his way to the small corral, his boots crunching on the dry ground. Drawing his large form up on the rail, he leaned into the fence and studied a frisky young horse circling the corral.

"Think you can handle her?" Henry asked, an amused expression on his face.

"Haven't run across one I couldn't," Dakota said, sizing up the horse before turning his attention back to Henry.

"Well then, she's all yours."

"Not taking your best horse, Henry."

"Yes. You will. The money and grief Wakefield's caused me the last seven years could have bought that horse ten times over. Call it a small donation to a worthy cause."

He looked back at the young, powerful horse. "I'll pay you for her."

"Don't insult me by offering money, Cabe. This ain't the time to be holding out to good manners. And, like I said, I've got my own grievances with Wakefield."

"She may not come back."

"I know."

Henry pushed off from the fence, causing it to sway before righting itself. His boot scrubbed at the dry earth, his mind seemingly deep in thought as if searching for his next words. The silence gave the air renewed tenseness.

Dakota waited.

"Do you think you can get your woman out?" Henry dug his boot into the parched soil.

Dakota turned to watch the Mustang prance around the corral. "I won't be back without her."

He hadn't meant it to sound dramatic. It was simply the truth. He had to be upfront with Henry since he was leaving his son in his care.

They both watched the young horse dancing around the corral, casting sideways glances at them. The air grew lonely and still. The chorus of crickets became louder as the silence between them grew.

"How'd Elizabeth get involved in all this?" asked Henry.

Dakota let out a deep sigh and explained how she and Caitlyn met, and how Wakefield had mistaken Elizabeth for Caitlyn. He told him, too, how his friend, Judd, had tracked him through the mountains to tell him.

Henry let out a sigh. "Damn, what a mess. How did you meet Caitlyn?"

Dakota's mood lightened thinking about her. He described to Henry their first encounter and subsequent days together. He laughed along with him until Dakota related their reunion in Silverwater and their decision to join forces to find their son.

The jovial mood between them soured as he described the ambush and how Wakefield's men captured Caitlyn. He summed it up with how

Elizabeth and Joshua escaped, and that he'd thought Caitlyn had escaped as well. When he started to tell Henry why he believed she was in Silverwater, he stopped in mid-sentence.

"What?" Henry asked.

"Elizabeth was so damn sure Caitlyn got out."

"Well, maybe she just assumed."

Shaking his head, Dakota tried to remember his conversation with Elizabeth. Fatigue worked against him, and his mind couldn't get beyond the fact that he'd ridden off without Caitlyn. Maybe he wanted to shed the blame on someone else, yet he didn't blame her. He blamed himself for not making sure she escaped. Still, Elizabeth's words of conviction haunted him in their clarity.

"No, Henry. Elizabeth told me she saw Caitlyn ride out on a horse. Elizabeth insisted they were after her, not Caitlyn. Believe me, Henry, if she had managed to get on a horse, she would have made it." Dakota rested his forearms on the fence and rubbed his unshaven chin with his hand. The conclusions he drew were not pretty ones.

"So, what do you think happened?" Henry asked.

Dakota wasn't sure. Something was off with Elizabeth, but would the woman go so far as to leave Caitlyn behind? She was supposed to be Caitlyn's friend. His shoulders dropped. It had all happened so fast. Elizabeth was terrified, half out of her mind. Maybe she wanted to believe Caitlyn was safe.

"I don't know, Henry. I just don't know."

A moment of silence followed.

"This Caitlyn must be one hell of a woman to disarm a man such as yourself."

Henry's words surprised him. He'd never thought of being disarmed by her, but maybe that would account for the knot in his stomach and the emptiness hammering in his chest. Leaning back his head, he examined the stars again. Caitlyn had tried to remember their names, but she couldn't keep them straight.

He closed his eyes at the memory. God's candles. That's what she'd called them. She was his candle, that was for damn sure, but he couldn't say the same for himself. "She's everything I ever wanted but never should have had."

Henry said nothing.

"Reckon I'll go see if the bath water's still warm." Dakota headed to the house and then turned back. "Thanks, Henry."

Henry nodded.

Dakota walked to the cabin and opened the door. The light blinded him, and he waited for his eyes to adjust before entering. Both women focused on him.

Elizabeth sat at the table, freshly bathed with a scent of lavender. Her wet, long blonde hair lay out behind her as Sarah untangled the locks with a large comb. He hadn't noticed Elizabeth's beauty until now.

Her stature was so small and delicate that a deep guilt washed over him for his suspicions. She had taken care of his son in the worst possible scenario, and he had no right to think the worst of her. He hadn't been there for his son, but she had. He owed her.

Walking to the crib, he peeked in at the two sleeping children. Without waking them, he tucked the blanket around the two small bodies, then turned back to the women. "Any more coffee, ma'am?"

Sarah stared for a moment, then responded, "Yes, I put on another pot. It's warming by the fire."

He followed her gaze to a large black kettle resting on top of the wood stove. Striding across the floor in two even steps, he took a mug from a nail on the side of the fireplace. Using the cloth hanging next to the mugs, he picked up the kettle.

He kept his back to the women, but he sensed their gazes following his every move. He poured a steaming cup of coffee, enjoying the rich aroma.

Elizabeth sighed, and he turned around to face her.

"You look refreshed, Mrs. Cookman."

"Yes, I am. The water's still warm if you care to bathe."

"Yup, I think I will." He took another sip of his coffee. "Ladies." He tipped his hat, walked back to the door, picked up his bedroll, and then stepped outside.

"There's a fresh towel on the line, Mr. Cabe," Sarah called after him.

"Thank you, ma'am." He shut the door behind him, leaving the two women in the same position they had been in when he'd entered.

The air had cooled, which made a warm bath more appealing. Standing outside the door, he waited for his eyes to readjust to the darkness and sipped on the rich black coffee.

Henry was right. Dakota needed rest, and he needed a plan. He couldn't let his emotions muddle his senses. He had to be cool-headed, calculating, and most important of all, detached.

Sounds drifted to him from the barn, and he deduced that Henry gave his barn one last check before turning in for the night. This was a good life, natural and right.

He could imagine himself as Henry, giving his own barn a last go over before turning in for the night with his wife. Not only could he envision it, but he hungered for it. With the right woman, it would be all a man could want or need. With Caitlyn, it would be paradise.

A faint light seeped through the cracks in the barn door and cast a silvery finger upon the corral. He could barely make out the horses, but as his eyes adjusted, he picked out Henry's young horse. She was quiet now, watching him as he watched her.

He stepped off the porch, the click of his heels on the wood slats, silencing the wild sounds of nature for a moment. Rounding the corner of the house, he grinned. The tub resembled a fort of surrender with the white sheets and undergarments flapping in the evening breeze. It renewed his spirits to see the bath water still steaming into the cool night air.

The log Sarah used to hang the wash on the high sides of the line, he substituted for a chair. Removing his boots, he wiggled his toes and then stretched out his tired legs. He sat there for several minutes, trying to enjoy the last of his coffee and trying not to think.

Taking one last sip, he rose and undressed. He slid out of his vest, backing away from Sarah's clean laundry before slapping the dust out of it. It rose in a dense cloud, choking him. He placed the vest on the log and unhitched his gun belt, laying it on top. Wearily, he shrugged out of his shirt.

He tensed, his senses ratcheting up. A presence he couldn't define lurked in the air. A touch at his neck set off hard-learned instincts, and he jerked his opponent to the ground.

"Damn." Holding Sarah's dainty petticoat out in front of him, he surveyed the damage. Dirty handprints covered the delicate fabric. Sheepishly, he chuckled and reprimanded himself to relax.

"Be thankful you didn't have an audience, Cabe," he mumbled.

Washing the garment the best he could, he hung it back up. He considered the petticoat for a moment; maybe Sarah would think it fell off the line. The light yet distinctive fingerprints said otherwise. Shrugging, he finished undressing: shirt, bandana, and jeans all tossed to the ground.

He reveled in the darkness. Stretching out his arms and legs, he enjoyed the cool wind rippling against his skin. A sliver of moon dipped in and out of approaching storm clouds.

Scanning his surroundings, something still seemed off, but nothing materialized. He cocked his head, eyed his pistols within easy reach, and stepped into the warm water. His muscles responded to the heat. The effect was dramatic. Days of tension melted from him. He gave in to the relaxation, finding solace in Sarah's old steel tub. The water tugged at the remaining doubt within him. He would get Caitlyn back. It wouldn't be any other way.

He combed his fingers through his hair, and the grittiness of the days traveled broke apart. Sinking into the tub, he let the water cover his head, and he massaged his scalp free of all the grime. It seemed like years of grit broke loose.

Water flowed from his face as he raised his head and searched for the chunk of soap. He discovered it at the side of the tub. The sweet, flowery scent of lavender caused him to hesitate briefly, then he continued. The perfumed soap gave up a rich lather under his rough hands, and he scrubbed his face and neck without mercy. Sandy particles fell into his palms, and he wrung his hands outside the tub to preserve the precious water. Leaning forward, he dropped his head into the water and combed his hair with his fingers until it squeaked.

Hands came down upon his shoulders, and he snapped out of his state of relaxation. Inbred instincts came before thought. He gripped the hands holding him and crossed them as he rose to his feet. He shook his head to free his eyes from the water and wet hair.

"Dakota. You're breaking my arms."

He dropped his hold, and Elizabeth stumbled away from him, rubbing her wrists.

"What in hell's damnation are you doing, woman?" Wiping his hand across his face, he removed the remaining strands of hair from his eyes.

"I need to know what you intend to do tomorrow." She scanned his wet form and stayed rooted below his waist. "You're naked." Her eyes widened as if she had never seen a naked man before.

Dropping back down into the water, he rested his arms on the sides of the tub before staring up at her in exasperation. Tension reclaimed his body and made his head throb. "I'm going back to Devil's Canyon tomorrow. The particulars you don't need to concern yourself with." He put both hands in the cooling water, searching for the soap he dropped.

"What about Joshua and myself? You can't leave us here with strangers."

Resting his head back on the tub's rim, he let out a long sigh and gave up his pursuit of the soap. "Mrs. Cookman, you seem to have forgotten that under the circumstances, we've been lucky. I don't think I could have found a safer place for you and Joshua, even if I had scoured half the countryside." The water grew cool as his agitation grew hotter. "What the hell did you want? The Hotel Paradise?"

She narrowed her eyes when they met his. "There's no need for vulgarities, Mr. Cabe. I believe I have valid concerns."

He bit the side of his mouth. "My apologies, ma'am, but as you can see, I'm indisposed at the moment. For the life of me, I can't imagine any valid concerns you might have. So may I finish my bath?"

"Please, Mr. Cabe. Give me a moment of your time. May I sit?" She motioned to the stump behind him.

He shrugged in defeat, and she settled herself on the log's edge.

A tiny gasp escaped her. No doubt, she noticed the thin white scars zigzagging across his back. He waited for a question as to their existence. No, she was too well-bred to ask. Hopefully, the scars would make her uncomfortable enough to leave.

"May we talk now, Dakota?"

In the darkness, he rolled his eyes. "So, we're back to first names again."

She hesitated and then said, "I want to go with you tomorrow."

"What?" His mouth dropped open.

"I said I want to go with you. I want to help you find Caitlyn."

The laugh shot out of him before he could stop himself. "I'm sorry, but no." He softened his words as he said, "You'd be much safer and more comfortable right here."

"But I can't stay here, and you know that."

"Why, Mrs. Cookman?"

"Because, what if John Wakefield and his men come here? What then?" Her words fairly dripped with fear and dread.

The woman should be on a stage. Maybe she had been. He should have asked. God, she exhausted him. Fatigued, he sighed. "First, Wakefield won't come here. He has what I want, so he doesn't have to waste time searching for me. Secondly, I wouldn't be leaving my son here if it wasn't safe. You're not fending for yourself anyway. Henry is more than capable of protecting you."

"You expect him alone to protect us?" Her tone was incredulous.

"Well, I was all you had for the last couple of days, and you made it this far."

"That's different."

"How's that, ma'am?"

"Because...you're different, that's all."

Dakota laughed. "Ah, I see. You feel safer with a man who has a reputation for being a killer, a man with no morals."

"Of course not," she snapped. "Why do you misconstrue everything I say?"

He turned and shot her with a jaded glare. "Maybe because you're a hard woman to figure out."

"And what, pray tell, is that supposed to imply, Mr. Cabe?"

"So, we're back to formalities now, Mrs. Cookman?" A new weariness made him punchy.

"I'm a young woman. Do I have to point out the obvious? I shudder to think what John Wakefield would do to me if he found me."

The bath water turned to ice. Dakota turned to ice. He stared into the darkness, his heart hammering in his chest.

"Did you hear what I said?" she demanded.

"I heard you."

"Well?"

"Caitlyn's with that man, right now."

"Caitlyn?" Elizabeth flew to her feet.

"Yes, Caitlyn."

"You're impossible." Elizabeth's feet pounded the ground as she made her way back to the cabin.

He rubbed the back of his neck, then ran his hand through his hair. How could he let himself soak in a tub when only God knew what Caitlyn soaked in?

Slipping down under the water, he rinsed the last traces of soap from his back. He stood up in the tub, shook the water from his body, then secured the clean towel around his waist.

Despite Henry's reasoning, Dakota should have left for Devil's Canyon tonight. A lot of good it did staying here for the night, but it was too late to head out now. Disgusted with himself, he rinsed out his dirty clothes and hung them up with Sarah's wash.

The slight moon sliver rose higher in the sky, giving the landscape an eerie effect. He stood in a wide stance, facing the location of Devil's Canyon. The cool evening air rushed over him and took the last drops of water from his skin.

Fearing Elizabeth might storm back upon him, he pulled a fresh pair of Levi's from his bedroll and eased himself into them. Slinging his gun belt over his shoulder, he walked toward the barn and Henry.

Again, he waited for his vision to adjust before entering the tidy barn.

"Well, you look like a new man, not nearly as fearsome as you appeared riding in."

Dakota gave a short laugh. "Mind if I sleep in your barn tonight?"

"I brought you a blanket from the house. Best spot's right there in the corner," Henry pointed to a spot. "I've been resigned there on more than one occasion by the wife."

They both laughed.

"Sarah's fixing up a place near the children for Elizabeth."

"Much obliged for all your hospitality. I won't forget."

"No problem, Cabe. Goodnight." Henry hung the lantern near the door and walked out.

Chapter 14

Caitlyn woke damp and chilled. Pushing herself upright, she fought the nausea assailing her as her sight adjusted to the milky morning light. She ran her hand across her forehead, her fingers outlining the large bruise above her eyebrow. She remembered Wakefield's man tackling her, but nothing else.

She dropped her hand to her chest and fingered the unfamiliar bandage that ran around her upper torso. Over that, she wore an old but clean flannel shirt. Hot anger welled within her. Her memory was shrouded in horrible visions of alternating scenes. What had happened to her?

Men's voices drifted her way, breaking her thoughts and snapping her alert.

"One thing's for sure, if this damn rain keeps up, he'll leave some tracks we'll be able to find."

She couldn't place the voice with any face. Her world was misty and unclear, and she had to fight the urge to sleep. She strained to hear the conversation above the pounding in her head.

"Hell, he's like tracking an Injun. You ever track one of them redskins, Billy?" Todd asked. "You end up tracking yourself. That Cabe may be no Injun, but he's their next of kin, you can be damn sure of that."

"Well, what do you want to do, just sit here and soak up the damn rain?" another man asked.

"I say we string the woman up in plain sight of Cabe and get this thing over and done with. I'm tired of being holed up in this God-for-saken snake-pit."

"No one touches the woman. You hear me, Todd. No one." John's voice was full of venom.

"Don't tell us you've gone sweet on her, John. Could make things messy."

"Hell, no," John said. "I'm using common sense. With his woman right in the middle of things, Cabe's not gonna go blasting away at us. Besides, he pissed enough. There's no point throwing down our last ace."

A brief silence followed.

"You understand me, Todd?"

"Sure, John, just talking. No harm done."

"Now, I want all of you to keep a sharp eye. Cabe's slick as they come, and I don't want any more slip-ups. I figure he took the woman and boy somewhere safe, and he's heading back. If he isn't here already."

"You want us to keep searching for the woman and boy, John?"

"No, Pete. We don't have any use for them now. I want you all to stay here, but spread out. No telling what Cabe's got up his sleeve."

"What about her?" Pete asked.

"She's in bad shape. She won't be running off. Now, mount up and check the canyon. You see any sign of Cabe, you hightail it back here. I don't want any of you trying to take him down alone. Ground's too damn hard to be digging graves."

"All right, John."

Two of the men muttered, shuffling away.

Caitlyn attempted to rise to her feet, but nausea and weakness flooded over her.

John threw open the tent flap and entered. "Trying to kill yourself, lady?"

She swayed sideways, searching the area for his face. "If I don't have to spend another minute with you, then I probably am."

"You always in such a delightful mood when you wake up?" Sitting in a chair, John watched her.

His actions made her leery. "Must be the company I'm keeping." The room spun, and she clutched at the wooden crate serving as a table.

He leaped up and gripped her arm.

"Get your filthy hands off of me." She slapped at his hands. Her eyes stung with fever-laden tears of fury.

He laughed and raised his hands into the air, allowing her to grasp the table. "You didn't object last night when I had to change you out of your wet clothes."

"Unconscious people usually don't." She tossed him a wilted sneer of disgust. As soon as she had her strength, she would kill him. By God, she would.

He twisted away from her, his shoulders stiff. He stretched out his balled-up fists and took several deep breaths, then walked toward his gear stored in the corner. "You never told me your name, so what is it?"

She glared at him and didn't respond.

"All right, I reckon I'll just give you one. Let me see." He gave her a once-over. "How about Spitfire? No? Hmmm. Trouble? No, that won't do either. How about Stormy? Yes, that's it. Like an unanticipated dust storm, which is unpredictable, uncontrollable, and dangerous." Going back to his supplies, he chuckled.

She held her silence, knowing it irritated him.

"Once again, you're not talking, but you sure did last night when you were out." He smirked at her.

She studied his eyes through the thick haze permeating everything around her. Disturbing images trampled through her mind. She tried to disengage from them and focus on what she could have said, and if she had given him any information about Dakota.

As if reading her thoughts, John replied, "Yes. Dakota Cabe." His voice bitter. "Tell me something, Stormy. Doesn't a woman like yourself ever get tired of the same man all the time?" He paused. "Course, I guess he's never around long enough to tire of."

Striding to her, he grabbed a strand of her hair. "Tell me, what is it about Cabe that holds your heart, lady?"

She shifted away from him.

"Don't make much difference, I suppose. How attached can a woman be to a corpse?"

Her stomach rolled like a tumbleweed across the plains. She couldn't maintain her balance much longer. Sweat poured into her eyes, blinding her.

"You'd best sit before you fall. Besides, I need to tend to your back again."

"You touch me, and I'll kill you," she spat out, losing her battle with gravity at a rapid clip.

"With what, my dear?" John chuckled. "If looks could kill, perhaps, but they can't." Laughing, he left the tent.

Her legs went slack, and she crumbled to the ground. Her back was hot and sticky. She waited for her strength to build so she could sit up, unbutton her shirt, then slip it off her shoulder. Instead of her camisole, she found layers of bandages wrapped around her torso. She debated the wisdom of removing the bloody bandage. After she pulled it loose, fresh blood trickled down her back. She lacked the strength to rinse the bandage, so she placed the cloth inside out and retied it. Finishing, she tied the ends into a knot. Sweat poured into her eyes again, her breathing jagged with exhaustion.

Putting the flannel shirt back on, she lay on her side. Silent tears of frustration and pain filled her eyes, and she pressed her palm hard against her face. There wasn't room for emotions, and she'd be damned if she'd let Wakefield get the best of her. She needed rest so she could rebuild her strength and escape. As soon as she closed her eyes, she couldn't open them.

Chapter 15

True to his word, at first light, Dakota had his horse and the mustang ready.

"Sarah packed you plenty of food along with some clothes for Caitlyn. She also put in medical supplies, though I hope you won't need them." Henry entered the barn carrying an armload of supplies.

"I'm much obliged, Henry. I'll repay you for all you've done."

"Take Wakefield out, and your so-called debt will be paid in full."

Clapping Henry on his shoulder in thanks, Dakota led the horses out of the barn.

"You sure you don't want to take a pack horse with you?" Henry asked, nodding at the bulk of supplies both horses carried.

"No." Dakota studied the borrowed horse. "I'll be lucky if I can get her in."

"Good luck, Cabe."

Nodding, Dakota glanced at the cabin. A stiff silhouette of Elizabeth remained at the window, staring out at them. Her ramrod figure spoke of her anger. He studied her for a moment, remembering her late night visit to the barn. She had worn a nightgown of Sarah's and nothing more. Her intentions were quite plain, and he'd made his likewise.

"Keep an eye on my son, would you, Henry?"

"Don't you worry. He'll be safe with Sarah and me."

With a nod, Dakota mounted and rode away.

He traveled for an hour before the rain set in. Not willing to slow his pace, he flipped up his collar to cover his ears and used his duster flaps to protect his legs. Riding at a good clip, he retraced his previous day's steps. Despite the rain, he made good progress.

Toward noon, he stopped to rest the horses and snack on Sarah's goods. He had no appetite, but he needed to keep up his strength. He took the food from his saddlebag. She had packed enough food for two people. He nodded and took a hearty bite of biscuit. Sarah's belief that he'd bring Caitlyn home made the meal more digestible.

In the distance lay Devil's Canyon, a formidable, dark, menacing form. The morning storm hadn't let up. Rainwater ran along the rim of his hat and poured out in a stream behind him. He was thankful he'd taken the time to pack his saddlebags and bedroll extra tight. He couldn't risk the dynamite getting wet, his answer to getting Caitlyn back.

Finishing the dried beef and biscuit, he remounted and urged both horses toward the gloomy horizon.

The constant rain brought back the same ill-omened thoughts he'd hoped to escape. His fears for Caitlyn mingled with a prickling uneasiness about Elizabeth. He tried to shake off the bitter dampness from his shoulders and put aside his dismal thoughts, but they dogged him without mercy.

What happened the day Elizabeth escaped? Was Caitlyn hurt? Had Wakefield or his men touched her? Spurring the horses into a run, he tried to flee his demons, but instead, they kept a steady pace alongside him.

The earth pelted up muddy splats from the grueling beat of the horse's hooves. He didn't slow his pace until the entrance to the canyon surged up in front of him. Reining in, he scanned the rocky walls dancing in brilliant hues before him. Bright, wet reds and yellows accented the moody gray sky hanging above.

He freed his canteen and drank from it as he studied the massive walls of Devil's Canyon. The canyon's interior could be his haven or his enemy. From this side, he couldn't tell which one it would be today.

Pushing on, he located the opening he and Elizabeth had used to escape. He wouldn't have found the passage again if he hadn't already been there. Taking a last glimpse behind him, he urged his horse forward, the mustang close behind.

The canyon's wall sparkled from the fresh rain and brought the damp rock into a brilliant hue of burnt orange. Small trickles of water cascaded down the rock crevices and spilled out into rivulets across his path.

He glanced back at the muddy tracks the horses had created. It didn't matter. No one rode behind him. They were all up ahead waiting.

Removing his glove, he put a finger into the leather bag holding the dynamite. Still dry. He mulled over the canyon's layout. There must be a better plan than the one he'd constructed, but so far, it hadn't come to mind.

He pushed the horses at top speed through the open areas, something he hadn't done with Elizabeth, and Joshua balanced precariously on the same horse. The farther he traveled into the crevice, the narrower the path became and the quicker the darkness settled in. He couldn't risk losing a horse on the rocky ground. With reluctance, he reined in. His emotions churned within him, demanding a physical outlet, but he had to stop for the night.

He slid from the saddle. The rain had ceased, but the air held a murky dampness. His hasty plans ricochet through his mind as he set about making camp.

John Wakefield had positioned his camp to avoid the very thing Dakota planned to do—ambush him. Unloading the gear and feed, he watered the horses for the night, then pulled out the bag of dynamite and carried it back to the fire. The bag felt dry, but he didn't know for sure, and he wasn't going to open the bag in the damp night air to find out. He had to assume it remained as dry as when he'd packed it.

Dakota settled on the ground, the dynamite next to him. He closed his eyes, but sleep evaded him. Timing meant everything for his plan to work, and timing was the one thing he couldn't count on. With these same thoughts, he met the new day, the sun entering the canyon a good half hour after greeting the rest of the world.

Stretching his stiff limbs, he rolled to his feet. The dynamite remained snug within the confines of his discarded coat. He took little heed of how chilled he was as he scanned the rocky walls surrounding him. No need to hurry. He was only a couple of hours from the main canyon, and he'd have to wait there until nightfall before gaining access to Flat Rock, but he couldn't stay idle.

After feeding both horses, he chewed on a biscuit. His mouth tasted like cotton. Saddling the horses, he placed the dynamite back into his saddlebag, mounted, and prodded the two horses across the sometimes muddy, sometimes rocky surface. The closer he got to Wakefield's camp, the warier he became. Keeping a sharp eye peeled, he stopped the horses often to listen to the sounds of the canyon. He scrutinized the treacherous ground before him, mindful of the rocks that could lame a horse if stumbled over. It amazed him that he and Elizabeth had crossed over this rocky terrain in the dark. It was more like a gully wash than a trail.

About an hour before reaching the inner canyon, he stopped and rested until dusk, then started up again, reaching his destination as the sun cast long shadows across the trail. Now that the waiting was over, he was eager to put his plan into action.

Arriving at the canyon's opening, he dismounted and crept into the interior, leaving the two horses behind. The sun's light soon vanished, and a rich, earthy darkness developed, one he used to feel quite at home in.

Making his way into the black abyss, he worked his way back to the old trail that passed through the canyon. The night air was fresh and still. Maybe Wakefield and his men had moved out. Dakota hadn't considered that possibility, and a new fear gripped him. They may have taken Caitlyn away or—God forbid—left her behind in some grisly manner for him to find. The possibility brought an overwhelming fear that chilled him to the bone.

The thunder of galloping horses burst through the night, and he threw his body behind nearby rocks. He pushed back his hat and studied the barrier between himself and the men approaching. He could make out three men on horseback. Two were riding abreast, the third lagging behind.

A crackling laugh echoed out to him. "Well, he ain't out here, and I'm done looking. Cabe's got Indian friends; they'll come from the front canyon and try to overpower us. Waste of time looking back here. Besides, I still say string the woman up and end this waiting game. That way, we call the shots on when Cabe comes instead of waiting for him to get a plan in the mix."

The riders came to a halt a few feet from where he crouched. "Yeah, John says he'll come back for the woman."

"That's exactly what I mean. I say it's time we boys took things into our own hands and get this done. She ain't nothing but trouble." Chewed tobacco splattered across the ground.

A loud laugh bounced off the canyon walls. "Nothing but trouble, huh? I guess a man would say that after getting his eyes clawed out. Hell, I kind of like her spunk. Not too many women ever got the best of you, Todd."

"You wait and see, Pete. She'll get us all killed." Todd chuckled. "Guess it don't matter none. She ain't up to clawing nobody's eyes now. We can have our fun with her and then string her up. Not like she's gonna put up a fight. Once Cabe comes in a fury, we can cash in on him. I say to hell with what John thinks. Cabe bleeds like the rest of us."

"That ain't what I heard."

"You read too many dime novels, Hoss. He's human, believe me."

"Well, if that's true, how come his bounty's so high and how come we ain't caught no sight of him yet. He slips in and gets that woman and kid right out from under our noses. Besides, it don't seem right killing a woman. Funning with her's one thing; killing's another. Maybe John's right. With her in the middle, Cabe ain't gonna risk no wild shooting, but if she's dead, what's gonna stop him?"

"Hell, Hoss, he's one man. You talk as if he's a damn war party. You're more yella than I gave ya credit for."

Again, tobacco splayed out across the ground only a few feet from Dakota.

"So, you want to keep her alive and give Cabe all the time he needs to plan an attack? Hell, did you hear what I said? He's got Indians for friends. You want to give him a chance to round them up? Getting scalped ain't an easy way to go. It's time to end this. I ain't afraid of one lousy bastard. I say kill her. He's bound to lose his head and make a mistake then."

"That's mighty dirty work."

Todd laughed. "Shape she's in, John may have done the dirty work for us."

Dakota pressed himself further into the rock as the men lingered.

"What makes you think he'd lose his head and do something stupid anyway, Todd?"

"You ever been in love with a woman, Pete? Well, I was once, but never again. A woman leaves you wide open. Why do you think John took the woman in the first place?" Todd paused as if telling a favorite story. "'Cause he knew Cabe would come running. You care for a woman, and she'll run you to the ground every time, just like that woman of Cabe's is doing to him. Ain't no one been able to get him out of the mountains, and now here he is. Mark my words, Billy, we string that woman up, Cabe will react like any other man. He'll come a charging, no thought, no plan, but plain old-fashioned rage, and we'll be there to cut him down like a witless rabbit."

"Well, maybe you're right, Todd, but I'm beginning to feel more like the hunted than the hunter. Hell, he could be right here in the canyon with us, and according to you, we wouldn't even know it. Gives me the creeps, it does."

The men remounted.

"Let's head in, boys. Relax, hoss, he ain't around. I'd be feeling it if he was. Only us fools out here, and I'm dead tired. If John wants a lookout, he can do it himself."

"Yeah, I'm with you, Todd. I could go for some more whiskey and shut-eye myself."

Dakota waited until the men were out of sight, then he stepped out and stretched in a wide stance. Resting his hands on his hips, he chewed his lower lip until he tasted blood.

She ain't up to clawing nobody's eyes now. God, what happened? The what-ifs hit him like sucker punches.

We can have our fun with her and then string her up. Swift rage chased the what-ifs from his mind.

"Like hell, you will." With heavy steps, he made his way back to the horses, his rifle in hand. He was more than ready.

The Todd feller was a nasty mix. The disappointment in the man's voice about Caitlyn's condition made it obvious he liked his women to fight. The taste in Dakota's mouth curdled, and he spit.

No man would ever touch her, let alone a pack of them. Not while he was alive. His blood boiled. He shoved his rifle hard into its sheath, startling his horse.

Placing his hand on the horse's flank, he calmed her and then patted her neck in the way of an apology. His emotions were ruling him. He couldn't allow that. "You ready, Caitie?"

The horse nickered.

Checking both pistols was an unnecessary detail; they were both loaded and ready, and he knew that. It was a start over. Inspecting the horses' hooves with his fingers, he fed each horse dried apple slices and contemplated his plan again. There wasn't time for further consideration. The original plan, along with its dubious timetable, remained his only choice.

Hopefully, Wakefield's men would keep their loyalties for one more day.

Would Caitlyn be able to ride? Dakota hoped so, but then he'd hoped for a lot of late. Maybe he should go on foot, but the numerous trips to get all the dynamite to Flat Rock would get him spotted, and he needed both his rifles.

Nope. His horse was sure-footed. She'd have to do her best. Henry's horse he'd leave in Wakefield's corral with the others and come back for her after setting the dynamite in place. Rummaging through both saddlebags, he decided what would stay on each horse. He'd load the non-essentials on Henry's horse, the necessities on his, just in case his plan didn't go the way he hoped. The dynamite, his rifles, extra ammunition, medical supplies, and dainty feminine undergarments rested on Caitie's back. He winced at the sight. Sarah had insisted that a woman always needed a fresh camisole. She even seemed to think it more important than food. Who was he to argue with a woman with that much conviction? He tucked the garments into Caitie's saddlebags.

Finishing his task, Dakota lingered in the dark for several minutes. He was weary with the thoughts he couldn't outrun, but he'd come to peace with one. If he got her out of this mess, he would get out of her life for good. He would turn himself in to the authorities. Damn, impossible to collect bounty on a man already in prison.

His dreams of their cabin evaporated as quickly as the morning dew in the afternoon sun. Caitlyn and Joshua would be free of him, and most important of all, they would be free of men like John Wakefield.

Again, Dakota had to hammer back his emotions. Dropping his hands to his sides, he slapped at his duster, sending a cloud of dust up into the air. Until this very moment, he considered having a family a possibility. He grimaced with disgust. No more realistic than a poor beggar licking his chops over a piece of peppermint candy in the store window.

A man like him didn't deserve a woman like Caitlyn. He was foolish, thinking he might. Mounting, he moved out.

The trail was dark, every bush a possible crouched figure, but he had lived too long on the edge to let his surroundings unnerve him now. His eyes and ears were keener than most, and he could decipher between real and imaginary threats.

The horses plodded along at a moderate pace. Stars dotted the now cloudless cobalt sky, and the air had lost its dampness. Dakota zigzagged the horses, keeping to the hard ground that would leave little evidence of his presence. He needed all the cards stacked in his favor.

Scanning the wall to his left, he searched for the previous path he'd used when he'd descended from Flat Rock, but the dim light from the stars and faint sliver of the moon were not sufficient to mark its location.

The sound of horses alerted him that he was close to Wakefield's makeshift corral. It seemed like another life when he had crouched low in the bushes expecting Caitlyn to make her way to him, but instead Elizabeth had. A black forewarning swept through him, and he steeled his mind against it. He couldn't allow his mind to wander now.

He made his way to Wakefield's horses, doubting the men would notice one more horse in their corral. He half smiled. Wakefield had been short-sighted to keep his horses in the back of the canyon, but then he didn't know about Flat Rock. Wake feared an attack from the front, not from above. After he rigged the dynamite across Flat Rock, he would come back for the mustang and scatter the others. Sliding from his mount, he was careful not to spook the milling horses. He unsaddled Henry's horse and led her into the corral, hiding the saddle and saddlebags in the nearby bushes.

He added a few additional items to Caitie's saddlebags, then stood for a moment to concentrate on the faint sound of men's voices. Leading his horse back down the trail, he traveled more slowly so he wouldn't miss the path again.

The third crevice he examined was the one he sought. He scrutinized the incline where the black shadow of the canyon wall met the cobalt blue sky. It was a long, steep slope, and not a rational venture to take a horse on, but he stuck with his plan. Starting his ascent, he guided Caitie along behind him.

~ * ~

Dakota reached the trail top, half-coaxing, half-pulling his horse. He'd lost track of time in his struggle to get himself, the horse, and most importantly, the dynamite up to Flat Rock.

Gulping in air, he paused and gave his horse a caustic glare. "Hell, am I going to have to carry you the rest of the way?" He leaned forward and placed his hands on his knees to take deeper breaths.

Pulling his bandana free from his neck, he wiped the sweat from his eyes and peered into the darkness. He couldn't see two feet in front of him. He'd have to trust his memory and instincts on this one. Sucking in the night air, his muscles throbbed with pain. His body needed to rest, but there was no time. The sooner he got to Flat Rock, the sooner he could rig up the dynamite, which would take most of the night, and then in the morning he'd trail the fuse line back down to the canyon floor.

Once done, he would light the fuse. He dropped his head and grunted. Timing was everything. Flat Rock needed to explode at the same time he rode into Wakefield's camp. The potential fireworks hopefully would be enough to make Wakefield's men scramble for safety and not get a shot off at him.

Dakota's breathing evened, and he arched his back, rolling his head side-to-side to stretch strained muscles. Damn. His plan sounded ridiculous now that he was exhausted and not feeling so spry. Saddling Henry's horse and scattering the other horses required an amount of time he may have miscalculated.

The vision of himself and Caitlyn riding out of the canyon together, Wakefield and his men dead under a ton of stone, was a might hopeful. Dakota snorted with laughter. The more likely scenario would be that the fuse would die out short of its destination, and he'd be standing in Wakefield's camp with nothing more than a 'howdy-do' on his side.

"Damn, Henry's right. Dealing with what-ifs isn't doing me any good," he muttered.

He searched his pocket for a piece of dried apple and let Caitie munch on it. Gazing up into the dark sky, he made a silent bargain with the one he couldn't see, but still believed in.

~ * ~

John plunked the cloth into the chilly water, rang it out, then laid it across the woman's forehead. His blood curdled each time she mistook him for Cabe, but that would change.

He and Todd had words moments prior. The stupid fool came in drunk with the rest of the crew. His old friend was up to something. John hoped it was the liquor talking, but he couldn't afford any more complications.

The last thing he needed with Cabe in their midst would be an upheaval among his men. Come morning, he'd deal with Todd. Friend or not, this was business.

John gazed down at the woman before him, her skin pale as ice in the muted candlelight. She no longer resembled the fiery woman who wreaked havoc on his plans. He despised the weakness in him for the woman. Soon, Cabe's bounty and his woman would be his. Smiling and feeling victorious, John left the tent. The crisp air was invigorating, making him feel all the more invincible as he anticipated the confrontation with Cabe.

John sighed. His men lay on the ground wasted in drink, resembling discarded scraps of fabric. Even Todd, the night guard, snored unawares.

A chill raced up John's backside, and he did a quick head count. Peering into the dark shadows, his eyes strained to see into the night's unreadable blackness. Scanning the canyon walls, he perceived nothing, but he could feel something amiss, and he could smell the change in the atmosphere.

He grinned. The game was about to begin. He scowled with disgust at the men littering the canyon floor. None of them had the foggiest inkling of what was to transpire, not even Todd, drunken fool that he was.

Chapter 16

The morning's first pink rays of sunshine danced across the canyon walls while Dakota finished rigging the last of the explosives. He stepped away from the rock ledge, his hands on his hips. Stretching his tired back, he assessed his handiwork. The dynamite was well-secured to the large rocks overhanging the canyon, every fuse measured to the next, ensuring that each stick would ignite at the same time. His horse nickered behind him, and he glanced up at her. She stood alert on the ledge above him as if to give him her nod of approval.

Satisfied that he couldn't have done better, he climbed back to his horse. The morning light reached the uppermost walls, while the rest of the canyon sat in murky darkness. The only evidence of Wakefield's camp was the thin traces of smoke. He stared into the charcoal shadows.

Caitlyn was down there and counting on him. An involuntary shudder shot through Dakota. He was cold inside, his bones iced, but not from the chilly canyon air. Something far deeper warned him, though he couldn't put his finger on it. He was like stone. It wasn't exhaustion. God, he knew that sensation all too well, but this sudden darkness in his soul was kin.

A few seconds later, the sun burst out over the trees, sparkling down on Flat Rock. He dipped his chin. A good omen, since he half-expected it to rain. Cocking his head, he listened to a faint sound in the distance. A murmuring of voices filled with anger and discord drifted up from the canyon below.

Dropping back to the ground, he strained to get a better view. His heart locked in a vise when he saw the chaos below. One of Wakefield's men dragged Caitlyn from the tent. She struggled to stand amid the torrent of angry confusion, but couldn't.

For Dakota, the dynamite had detonated. Fury and terror imploded within him like a hot spring capped too late. His dull, wearied senses sprang into fine-tuned action. His essential timetable had run out, and he could smell his own fear.

A heavyset man drew his gun and pointed it directly at John's head. "You wouldn't listen, John. Now I'm taking charge."

"You're a fool, Todd. My men will stop you. You'll never make it out of here alive."

"You're wrong, John. You should have watched your men instead of nursing that woman."

Dakota swung his head back and forth in denial. John's men had begun their own ambush earlier than his. Timing. God damn the timing.

"What do you plan on doing?" John asked.

"Exactly what I said you should have done from the beginning—get rid of her." Todd jerked a thumb at Caitlyn.

"Where's Jimmy?"

"Your brother's dead, John. He wouldn't come around to our way of thinking."

John closed his eyes briefly and set his jaw. "And what do you hope to accomplish by killing her?"

"What you've been pussyfooting around trying to do for the last couple of days. Bring Cabe out in the open. We've waited long enough; we're gonna call the shots now, not Cabe. We'll tell him when to come, not wait until he has a whole band of Injuns rounded up."

Wakefield whirled in disbelief. "Sam, are you in on this?"

"You lost your perspective, John." Sam shuffled his feet and stared at the ground. "There ain't no other way. Todd's right. We've waited too long. Cabe's done got the upper hand while you been wet-nursing the woman. I've heard about Cabe. He ain't one to trifle with."

"And you think killing his woman isn't trifling with him?"

"I ain't much for killing a woman, but we've waited long enough. Like Todd said, we wait any longer, and no telling what he'll bring down on us. This way we call the shots."

"You're all fools. You underestimate Cabe if you think he'll let any of you live."

"Well, thanks for your concern, John, but I'm running things now." Todd spat out a stream of tobacco juice and nodded to the men. "Come on. The sooner we get this done, the sooner we can spend that bounty money."

The rough rope slipped over her head before she could react. She pulled at the rope, but Sam cinched it tight around her neck. "Come on, woman, I ain't gonna carry you."

She fell to the ground, her hands clutching at her neck as Sam dragged her toward the lone tree several yards away. The rest of Wakefield's men followed like wolves after a wounded deer.

Dakota contemplated his options. There wasn't time to get back to Henry's horse as he had planned. Damn. He only had one choice. Sweat poured into his eyes. "Hang on, baby."

Pulling a long hunting knife from his boot, he severed the fuse line a few feet from the main bulk of dynamite and formed it into a straight line.

Despite the rush of blood coursing through his veins, his hands remained steady. He patted his pockets for the matches. Sighing with relief, he struck one against the stone boulders. It ignited, and he brought the lit match to the fuse line. It caught and sizzled in anticipation.

He scrambled up the bank and threw himself into the saddle. He scrutinized the mutiny below and then the burning fuse. He patted his mare's neck. "This is gonna be one hell of a ride, girl."

Tapping his heels into the horse's muscular sides, he plunged off the face of Flat Rock.

~ * ~

The man and horse appeared out of nowhere, descending the canyon wall as if they'd dropped from the clouds above. Caitlyn glanced in surprise at Todd and John, their faces frozen in amazement, their focus riveted on the rider above them. The other men followed their gaze, each stunned motionless as to what was surely a demon from hell sliding down the treacherous wall.

"What the hell?" Todd regained his senses first.

"Cabe." An uneasy grin crossed over John's face.

"What?" He whirled around to face John.

"I said it's Cabe. What's wrong?" He laughed. "Isn't this what you wanted...rash behavior?"

"Damn it." Todd pushed away from John to stare at Cabe, then at the men. "Shoot him. Anyone holding a rifle shoot the damn son-of-a-bitch."

She tried to focus. Dakota had the appearance of the devil himself, a dark foreboding shape against the light, gray-washed walls. To keep from losing its precarious footing, he had leaned back so far in the saddle that he and his mount appeared to be twenty feet tall. She stared transfixed.

The wall exploded into the canyon, ashen rock breaking apart like thin ice as both horse and rider disappeared into a pale gray mist.

"Dakota!" Caitlyn struggled to free herself from the rope.

"Clear out. Cabe plans to kill us all," John shouted.

The two men holding John dropped their grip and scrambled toward the corral, dodging the first rocks rumbling down upon them. Pete dropped the rope holding Caitlyn and ran. Todd moved his large, bulky form at a rabbit's pace.

John pulled the noose from around her neck, grabbed her arm, and then attempted to haul her to safety. She jerked free and threw herself back onto the ground.

"Hell, woman, you're gonna die. Git up." He reached down again.

She sank her teeth into his arm.

"Be damned then. Die with Cabe." John pushed her away and ran after his men.

She placed her bound hands around her raw throat. Taking deep breaths proved impossible; however, slow, steady breaths she could manage. She strained to see into the gray murkiness surrounding her as the canyon wall continued to crumble apart. Despair rushed through her. Dakota couldn't have survived, and neither could she.

Forcing herself to her knees, she stared at a strange wonder materializing out of the mist. Had the gates of hell opened and sent the devil to take her? The horse snorted in defiance, its eyes wild, its chest expanding with effort, then it found its footing and headed straight for her, but she wasn't afraid; Dakota was alive. Scrambling to her feet, she stretched upward.

Slanting sideways in the saddle, he stretched a solid arm out for her. The impact nearly knocked her back to the ground, but she grabbed for the saddle horn and lifted herself across the mare's withers. Dakota scooted back and helped secure her into the saddle.

When the horse stumbled sideways, his steel arm encircled her, keeping her in the seat. She gripped the saddle horn with both hands, and the horse bolted for safety.

Hugging the flanks of the horse with all her strength, she rode into the morning, conscious only of the need to stay on the horse. When the horse slowed its thunderous pace, her eyes grew heavy, and she could no longer maintain her awareness. Canyon walls spun around her, and she slumped back into Dakota.

~ * ~

Dakota pulled up the reins.

"Caitlyn?" Freeing his knife, he sliced the rope binding her hands, then circled his arms around her, hugging her to him. He rested his chin on the top of her head and squinted up into the bright, cloudless sky.

"I'm so sorry, girl. So goddamn sorry." Taking the reins in one hand, he urged the weary horse onward until they reached the place where the ambush occurred.

With care, he dismounted, drawing Caitlyn's limp body with him, and then his bedroll. Carrying her to the dugout, he threw down the bedroll, unrolled it with his boot, and placed her on it.

Shrugging out of his duster, he laid it over her, tucking it underneath her chin. He surveyed the nearby area. Damn, he didn't like leaving her even for a few minutes, but he needed to find a better place than this. The insignificant trail rimming the rocky bank behind the dugout seemed like a good place to start.

Investigating farther back from the ledge, he found a small creek running alongside a wood of pines, and beyond that a small cave hidden from the trail below. It would be an ideal place to camp for the coming night.

Caitlyn's motionless form resembled a fragile porcelain doll more than the independent woman he knew her to be. Gazing at her from the ledge above, he was amazed at the bounty of emotions she never failed to stir in him.

When Bisbe killed his parents, he vowed never again to love anyone that much. Loving meant losing and losing meant pain, but she'd snuck into his heart and now so had the pain.

Hurrying back, he carried her toward his horse. Freeing one hand, he took the reins and coaxed the horse to follow him. He headed toward the gurgling creek, dropping the reins onto a pine branch before lowering Caitlyn to the mossy ground just short of the stream.

Returning to the horse, he removed another blanket from the back of his saddle along with his canteen. He lifted Caitlyn's head and poured a small amount of water into her mouth.

Her shirt gapped open, and he noted the poorly constructed bandage around her chest. Holding her in one arm, he removed her shirt and the dressing and examined her injuries.

Shock and horror shot through him at the sight of the brutal slashes crisscrossing her back. The raw, torn flesh screamed at him. His hand tightened into short spasms of rage as his stomach churned and lurched into his throat. He had seen worse, but never on a woman, and certainly not on his woman. God, what had they done to her? His eyes filled with tears of dread.

Pulling the rest of her garments free from her feverish body, he scooped her naked form into his arms and splashed into the shallow creek. He lowered her into the cool stream and let it flow over her.

As he kept her in the water, the heat slowly ebbed from her body. Looking above, he noted the ominous clouds moving in from the west. The air hung moist and dense.

He removed Caitlyn from the water, tucked her into his blanket, then rubbed her hair and skin dry. Her skin had lost some of its paleness, but it was far from the rosy glow of health he longed to see. Despite the bruises and the drawn expression, her face still possessed the childlike air she strove so hard to conceal from him.

She slept peacefully while he washed her clothes in the creek and prepared camp for the coming night. The cavern was damp and murky until he built a fire. The wood took a while to ignite, but once it did, it swept the dampness away and filled the small area with a comforting, warm glow. In the far corner, he made a bed and lay Caitlyn in it.

Splashing back across the creek, he brought his horse to the mouth of the cave and tied her there, then he unsaddled her and brushed her down. Slinging the saddlebags over his shoulders, he carried them into the cave and laid out the supplies he would need.

Thank God, Sarah had packed whiskey. It would sterilize the wounds.

The fire burned solid, and he glanced from Caitlyn to the flames to the sky outside. Clouds churned across the afternoon sky, staining the blue with gloomy darkness.

Uncorking the bottle of whiskey, he went back to her and knelt next to her. Rotating her onto her stomach, he lifted the blanket. Dousing a clean rag with the whiskey, he washed her abrasions, then rewrapped her with fresh material and dressed her in one of his clean shirts.

It wasn't the first bullet or knife wound he had cleaned. He'd tended plenty, many on himself, but never on a woman. He tossed the garment she had been wearing into the fire and watched it burn, not willing to let his thoughts wander there. He checked her temperature with his lips upon her forehead. The fever was breaking.

Sitting on the ground, he stared at the approaching storm. In the distance, the sky erupted in flashes of bright lightning, illuminating the landscape all around. The mare snorted and stomped her foot as the air grew muggy with moisture.

The first drops of rain splashed into the creek, creating a rhythm that kept him engrossed in his thoughts. He sat for a long time, imprisoned in a world he didn't want, and on the outskirts of the one he did.

The rain continued, separating the outside world from the illuminated cavern. It allowed him, for a short while, to be in the world of his choosing.

He stood and walked back to Caitlyn. Had she stirred? He watched her for several moments. The gentle rise of her chest was the only movement. The next day dawned with a half-hearted attempt at sunshine, with more rain destined to come. Dakota could feel it in his bones. Stretched out across the cave's entrance, he created, he hoped, a single but sufficient barrier between Caitlyn and the world.

He hadn't slept until late in the night. At each unusual sound, he sat up, gun drawn, the fire now only a dim glow in the dark cavern.

Caitlyn still slept. His heart stampeded within him. She had almost died and was now scarred for life because of him. He'd brought this to her. Standing, he walked to the cavern's entrance where his mare waited.

Elizabeth was right. If he stayed, more men like Wakefield would come. If he loved Caitlyn, and he did, he had to turn himself in to the law. No doubt, they'd hang him, but his family would be safe. Life wasn't a curse; he was.

Lifting his arms above his head, he stretched and contemplated the view. All was quiet. The creek had filled out its boundaries and now flowed with a swift current. They would need to cross back on the horse. He patted the mare's neck and rubbed her ears before walking back to Caitlyn.

Her chest rose and fell in gentle harmony with each breath. Kneeling next to her, Dakota placed a hand on her forehead. She was still cool to the touch.

A rustling behind him caught his attention at the cave's entrance, but his horse gazed back at him. Turning back to her, he caught the full force of her fist against his face. The unexpected blow threw him off balance.

She lost little time gaining her feet and stumbling toward the entrance. Dakota jumped to his feet and darted after her. Reaching out with long arms, he caught her as she grasped the mare's mane. He wrapped his arms around her, trying his best not to hurt her.

She moaned. "Let me go. Don't touch me."

His arms held her tight, but she was committed to fighting. She bent her head and bit hard on his arm, but couldn't penetrate his thick leather coat. In a state of desperation, she used her body weight and put it full force on his instep. When he loosened his hold, she spun in his arms and planted her knee hard and fast into his groin.

"Damn, Caitie." Dakota clutched her shirt as he dropped to his knees. Despite the agony radiating from his groin and into the pit of his stomach, he wasn't about to let her go.

She sank to the ground with him and peered at him. "Dakota?" She brushed back his hair, draping it across his face.

"I could be wrong," he said, "but I think you've rendered Joshua an only child. For a small thing, you sure do pack a wallop." He took a deep breath, fighting the nausea.

The tension eased out of her, and she fell back asleep.

Chapter 17

"D akota?"

Her voice was so faint, he thought the wind whispered at him in jest, but then her eyes flickered open.

"Right here, Caitie." He pressed his lips to her cool, dry forehead. Brushing thin tendrils of hair away from her face, Dakota touched her cheek with the back of his hand and then slipped his fingers under the flannel shirt. The fever was gone.

"I waited for you…you know…" She paused to catch her breath, then added, "…to bring the water."

He leaned closer, trying to understand.

"Guess you found a better cup of coffee elsewhere."

"Yeah." He halted and cleared his throat. "I ran into a couple of horse thieves in Mexico. They made a real mean pot. Stayed around for a second cup, or I would have been back sooner."

She gave a small chuckle, then tensed. "Joshua?"

"Joshua is safe, and so is your friend, Elizabeth. They are on the other side of the canyon, about forty miles northeast near a small mining town. When you're well, we'll travel there."

"I'm well now." She started to rise, but her legs were unsteady.

"No, you're not." He laid a hand on her arm. "You need to get your strength back first, and then we'll go. I'm not about to take any chances of losing you."

"But what if John Wakefield gets there first?"

"I'm hoping he's under a ton of rock."

Caitlyn raised an eyebrow. "So, I didn't imagine the whole mountain crumbling down? I thought I dreamed it. I saw you, or what I thought was you, riding toward me while the whole canyon rained down upon us."

"Nope. Just me. I dynamited Flat Rock. Come here." He pulled her across his lap.

"Flat Rock? You made it back there? I'm all right, Dakota," she stated when he lifted the back of her shirt.

"Damn. The wounds have reopened." He gave her a reproving glance and began to repair the damage.

"From what you told me about Flat Rock, you made a few improvements to its original use. Ohhh."

He dapped a whiskey-soaked cloth to the wounds. "A few, but then there weren't a lot of choices."

Silence grew between them as he adjusted the fresh bandages around her.

He finished the dressing, and she turned and locked eyes with him. Her beautiful emerald eyes were a faded shade of green. They no longer sparkled with life. Their eyes held, and she knew he knew, and the hell of it was that he really didn't. Most problems he confronted in life, he could fix. This he couldn't. He shifted away, gauged the rising creek, then glanced back at her.

She lowered her gaze. "How long have I been out?"

"A couple of days." He paused and rubbed the back of his neck. "Caitlyn, I thought you had escaped and were waiting for me in Silverwater. I never would have left if I'd known otherwise."

Pinching the skin at the bridge of his nose, he tried to halt the flood of emotions threatening to break free. His inability to stay his emotions baffled him. He dropped his head, unable to get past the simple fact that he'd left her with Wakefield and his men. "Caitie—"

She reached out to him. "It's over. We're both alive. You saved our son. Nothing else matters."

He glanced at her, then squinted at the creek. Gripping her hand in his larger one, he squeezed it. "Caitie, I have to know. I don't know why. I just do. Did Wakefield or his men..."

Damn, he couldn't even say the words. His throat constricted, and his eyes burned with unshed tears. Had his night of rest cost her the one thing he could never get back for her?

Her gaze darted about the small cave.

"Caitlyn?" He twined his fingers with hers.

She looked up at him then squeezed his fingers in an attempt...to what? Bar any doubt?

"No, Dakota. No, they didn't."

He stared at her in silence, nodding before staring out at the terrain beyond the cavern. He might have believed her if not for the flash of shame and humiliation flooding her eyes, which spoke louder than the lie.

"Good." Stiffly, he rose to his feet and wiped at tired eyes. "I was afraid. You've been through so damn much. I—" He couldn't finish.

Maybe she could forgive him, but he would never forgive himself. He'd failed her in the worst way possible. His hatred for Wakefield took a turn, and he began to hate himself more.

Darkness lay within him as he walked to the cave's entrance and watched the unrelenting rain fill the creek. He struggled to find balance—some kind of bedrock to anchor to—, but none existed.

"I'm gonna check on the horse." Dakota walked out into the storm, grateful for the rain that washed away the tears he couldn't hold back.

~ * ~

The next morning, they decided to head out, or rather, Caitlyn decided. She remained uncompromising in her desire to reunite with her son. Dakota relented.

The previous night was brief as far as sleep went. Where she seemed relieved, Wakefield was dead; he had been around too long to assume the best. Unless he saw Wakefield's dead carcass, he wouldn't rest easy. In fact, a part of him hoped the man wasn't dead, then he would have a chance to release all the hate and guilt that dogged his every step. Nothing but killing Wakefield with his bare hands would help ease his misery.

They rode at a comfortable pace for a couple of hours.

Dakota held the reins in one hand and rested his other on Caitlyn's side. He wondered at her thoughts but didn't ask. When he got her home and her strength returned, they would talk. He'd tell her his plan to turn himself in to the law. Of course, she wouldn't see it as he did, nor would she accept it as being the only thing to do. So for now, he'd hold her as close to him as he could. He would pretend, at least while he could, that circumstances were as he wished them and not as they were.

~ * ~

Two days later, they rode back into Silverwater. Despite Dakota's cautious pace, weariness lined Caitlyn's features. Her bruises shadowed her face, and the ride sapped most of her strength. He couldn't help but frown in frustration. Arguing with her had been to no avail. Once they started, she insisted they keep going.

He thought of hiring a wagon to take them to Henry's. The idea made him smirk. No question what Caitlyn's response would be. She was stubborn, strong-willed, and he smiled—one hell of a woman. If it wasn't for the need for another horse and supplies, he doubted they would even be stopping in Silverwater. Pride filled him as he studied her profile in front of him.

The town was quiet; the shops closed for the day. The only sounds were those from the hotel restaurant and the saloon. Laughter and the clinking of glassware drifted down the street to greet them as they rode to the smithy, where they deposited the horse.

"I'll go to the hotel and get us a room." Caitlyn took note of the lazy stable hand taking his time brushing their mare down for the night.

"No, stay with me, Caitlyn. This won't take long." He held onto her elbow. "Hey, kid." He motioned to the boy. "Where's the owner? I need to buy another horse."

The lad glanced toward the back of the stable, "Fraid Pa's out for the night. I do most of the selling anyways. Horses are out in the corral. Take your pick. I'll be here after you get one chosen." The boy went back to a slow brushing down of the horse.

Caitlyn sighed and glanced at Dakota. "This might take longer than my legs can stand. Like I said, I'll get us a room."

He gauged the weariness in her face. "What about a wagon? I can still—" He stopped at her raised hand.

"No more about the wagon, please. I'm certainly capable of walking to the hotel alone. I'll be fine." She leaned in and kissed him. "I trust your instincts on picking the right horse for me. Although I guess I might need some money to get a room." She smiled and extended her hand.

"Sorry." He pressed several bills into her palm.

Not wanting to have Caitlyn out of his sight longer than necessary, he assessed the horses in the corral and picked the one he liked best. As lazy as the boy was in grooming, he proved to be a sharp bargainer. Dakota gave him an extra coin to close the deal and left the stables for the hotel.

~ * ~

The night air was invigorating, but it didn't revitalize Caitlyn's tired, sore body. She walked with stiff legs down the street, alert to the town's atmosphere. So quiet, the only sign of life was the smoky air drifting down the road from the saloon. Mounting the Rosebud Hotel's three steps, she tugged open the large door.

She sighed with relief to see a different clerk on duty. She didn't want to answer any curious questions. Drawing the bills from her pocket, she asked for a room and then paid the clerk the required amount. Nodding to the clerk, she took the key, stepped back, and ran smack into a large, overbearing man.

When the man chose not to move, she gave him an icy stare and waited. If he persisted, she would ask the clerk for assistance, although the wiry man didn't appear as though he would be of much help. If necessary, she would use the revolver Dakota gave her, but the last thing she wanted was to be the center of attention.

"Shame for a woman to spend the night alone, especially a beautiful-looking woman such as yourself," the man said. The scent of whiskey emanating from his body gave proof of his precarious condition and lack of good sense.

"Kindly allow me to pass, sir." She put out her hand in a gesture of passing.

His enormous, bulky body stayed rooted to the spot in front of her. She could imagine what her disheveled attire might suggest to a man like him.

He stroked her cheek. "My, my, there's a bit of spunk in them there pale cheeks. Oh, lassie, I could change your pale expression into a rose garden. A woman like you shouldn't be alone."

"She ain't alone." The deep voice reverberated off the hotel's walls.

Her gaze skimmed the interior until she spied Dakota inside the double-stained-glass doors.

The man kept his eyes on her as he replied over his shoulder. "You're damn right, friend. Not when Mack O'Brien's around." He smiled a toothless grin at her and raised his hand to catch a strand of her hair between his grubby fingers.

She closed her eyes for a moment, wishing the bear of a man would disappear. She'd been in several hotels, and no one ever propositioned her before. Why, for the love of God, did it have to be now? She hesitated, fearing anything she might say or do would throw the whole situation into an ugly confrontation.

"You best get two things straight, stranger." Dakota's voice boomed deliberately and decisively as he moved closer, then stopped. "You ain't my friend, and the lady is with me. Now, before you make more of an ass out of yourself than you have, move on."

His harsh tone surprised Caitlyn. She glanced around and grimaced at the gathering crowd.

The man's gaze went from her bosom to her eyes. "Boy, you insulted Mack O'Brien, and no one ever insults Mack O'Brien." The older man turned around with a wicked smile on his face, which faded as soon as he eyed Dakota. He seemed taken aback by Dakota's relaxed but determined stance.

She saw him in a different light. He looked mean, and he was no boy. His expression was emotionless and unforgiving with a hint of savagery. His ready stance was a bit too relaxed, as if he spent most of his time in it. O'Brien had indeed bitten off more than he could chew.

O'Brien wavered. His gaze darted about; he apparently wanted to leave, but with the gathering crowd, he wanted less to appear afraid. His hand dropped to his holstered gun, but Dakota's hammer clicking back made him pause.

"You're too drunk and too old to be a fool." Dakota's calm voice was low and steely.

O'Brien raised his hand in an offering of peace. "I meant no offense, mister."

"None taken if you leave now."

The man shuffled out of the hotel, his head low in humiliation.

Dakota replaced his gun and strode through the small crowd.

Caitlyn lowered her eyes, her face burning with embarrassment at being the subject of all the commotion, like an insect pinned onto a board and laid out for all to inspect. Once again, they were the main attraction.

Coming to her side, Dakota glanced at the key in her hand. With his nod, they headed for the stairs.

"Excuse me, sir," the hotel clerk said, having been quiet up to this point.

Nudging her forward, Dakota whispered in her ear, "Go on up to the room. I'll be along in a moment."

She knew better than to argue, so she left him at the base of the stairs and made her way to the room.

~ * ~

Dakota walked back to the clerk and faced him. The wide countertop created a sufficient wall between them, but even so, the young clerk took a step back.

"Is there a problem?" Dakota asked. He'd had enough.

"As a matter of fact, sir, yes." The clerk's willowy form tensed. With false bravado, he pushed his round spectacles high on his nose and adjusted his vest.

"Oh? And what might that be?" Dakota leaned across the counter.

The young man stepped back farther. "Sir, we can't have guns drawn and people threatened in the lobby of our establishment."

Dakota dropped his head, laughed, then stared at the man. "Then I suggest you keep the trash out, and to set the record straight, the lady was threatened. I merely showed the man the error of his ways."

"Sir, must I remind you...you were the one with the gun drawn."

"Yes, I know, and that's why we're both still alive to chat about it." Dakota reached into the pocket of his vest.

The startled young clerk gasped.

Tossing a shiny dollar coin into the air, Dakota added, "If I've offended you—" the coin clattered noisily onto the counter, "perhaps, this will make amends."

The clerk nodded, and Dakota bounded up the stairs to Caitlyn without further comment. Entering the room, he unbuckled his gun belt and laid it across the bedpost. She fell back onto the bed, her eyes fixed on the ceiling.

"You want to go down and get some supper?"

"Thanks, but no. I think the town would be safer if I stayed up here."

"Ah, come on, Cat." Exasperated, he sank onto the bed. "What did you expect me to do?"

"I'm teasing, Dakota." She faced him, a warm smile on her lips. She tugged at his sleeve. "Come here." She patted the bed next to her. "Lay with me and rest."

Feeling a bit foolish, he nevertheless shrugged out of his coat and vest and settled next to her, his gaze on the same spot on the ceiling as hers.

"What are we looking for anyway?" Dakota smiled. If only O'Brien could see me now.

"Shhhh."

"All right," he answered. "What are we listening for?"

"Dakota, you're impossible." She came to her feet and stood before him. "I said, relax. Not ask a hundred questions."

He watched with interest as she knelt in front of him and grasped his left boot. She tugged at it until it came loose, and she toppled backward. Righting herself, she tackled the other boot. "Socks?" A brow raised.

"Yeah. Special occasion."

"Oh? Such as?"

"Rescuing damsels in distress."

Laughing, she pushed his knees apart so she could move between them and unbutton his shirt. "Relax. Inhale deeply and let your whole body unwind." She trailed her fingers down his shirt, flipping each button loose.

"I've got to tell you, Caitlyn. With you between my legs and your fingers traveling down my chest, you're making it damn hard for me to relax."

"Oh, shut up."

"Yes, ma'am. Not much for talk anyway under the circumstances." Grinning up at her, he relinquished his body to her care.

She undid the last button, and his shirt fell open. Without pause, her fingers dropped to his faded jeans, and she tugged at the top button, then the second, and lastly the third.

"Oh Lord, my prayers have been answered." His grin grew.

"Dakota, please." She rolled her eyes in mock exasperation.

"Beg no more, woman." Rising on one elbow, he wrapped his arm around her neck.

Playfully, she placed a hand on his chest in protest, then brought her lips to his.

~ * ~

If Dakota hoped Caitlyn would rest a day or two in town, he was sadly mistaken. His bleary eyes gazed up at her silhouette the following morning.

"Let's go, Dakota."

"Hell, Caitlyn. Go where?" A thousand horses must have trampled him during the night.

"To get my son." She tossed his jeans down to him and kissed him lightly on his lips. "Watch your language, please."

He peered up into her face. Despite her gallant efforts, the paleness beneath her softly tanned skin spoke volumes. "We're not going anywhere, Caitlyn. I want you to see a doctor, make sure you're fit to make the trip."

"A doctor? I don't need a doctor. When have you ever seen a doctor?"

"That's different." He regretted his words as soon as he spoke them. Not wishing to offend her further, he added, "All right, we'll leave, but at an easy pace. First, I need to buy you a gun belt and guns, and we'll need an additional rifle and extra ammunition."

Throwing his legs over the bedside, he ran his fingers through his long, tangled hair, then rubbed his coarse, unshaven chin. A smile curled his lips. If girls were made of sugar and spice, his was pure spice.

~ * ~

True to his word, Dakota kept them at a leisurely pace. Though anxious to see her son, Caitlyn was glad of his insistence after about an hour. He would have stopped if she'd asked, but she couldn't accept the weakness in herself. It made her feel less than adequate.

Before noon, they halted to rest. His gaze settled on her more than once. She was touched by how well he knew her, for when they stopped, he insisted the horses needed a break and that he needed to check their position to make sure they were traveling in the right direction. She chuckled to herself. Dakota Cabe could find his way in a snow blizzard blindfolded.

At dusk, they made camp for the night.

"Be another two days of travel," he said, gazing upward as if reading a map. "Could make it in one," he mused, then must have reconsidered because he said, "but we best keep close to the canyon ridge before branching out into the basin." He glanced at her sitting next to the fire. "We'll be less noticeable that way."

"All right."

He studied her, frowning with surprise, but he didn't comment on it. "I'm gonna check on Caitie and Patches." He knelt and kissed her on the cheek, then rose to leave.

She held him back with her hand. "We've got to talk about that name."

He tossed up his hands. "Hey, she's your horse. Name her whatever you want. I thought Patches fit." He glanced at the Appaloosa he'd purchased.

"I'm talking about Caitie."

"What's wrong with her name?"

"Dakota. You gave her my name."

"Flattered, are you?" He stifled a laugh.

"Hardly. Half the time, I don't know if you're talking to your horse or to me. You talk to Caitie as if she were human."

"Ah ha. You are jealous. Got to say, though, Cat, I didn't think I'd ever see the day."

She took a swing at him. "You're impossible."

"So why do you keep following me around?" he asked, leaping to his feet and dashing away.

She laughed, coming to her feet to chase after him. He let her catch him, then he twirled her around. The campfire lent a mystic sense of enchantment to the full Colorado sky and the brilliant stars twinkling above.

He stopped in mid-twirl and stared intently at her. "You know I love you, don't you, Caitie?"

She gazed up at him in amazement.

When she didn't reply, he added, "I meant you, not my horse."

She smiled.

Chapter 18

The following morning, Caitlyn woke to find Dakota towering above her. "We're staying here for the day."

"What?" Rising, she prepared to do battle. She was much better from the couple of good night's sleep, among other things.

"I'm not arguing with you. We're staying here, and that's all there—" He stopped, searching the area around him, a puzzled frown on his face.

"What?" she whispered.

"Ah, probably nothing. Don't worry," he answered, his brows knitted together in concern.

She studied his face. He might have succeeded with the ruse, but he overplayed his hand. Dakota Cabe never worried. At least, if he did, he never showed it. "Dakota?"

"Shhhh." His hand came up in warning, his face unreadable. Now she wasn't so sure. She surveyed the surroundings.

"I'm going to check around." He gripped his rifle then headed into the trees.

She rose and dressed, checking her gun as a precaution. Glancing around, she waited for Dakota to come back. After a half hour, he returned his face as unreadable as ever.

"Well?" she asked.

"Huh?" He turned in her direction. "Oh yeah, everything's okay. Must be getting edgy, is all. I think I'll do some practice shooting."

"Aren't you afraid you'll draw unwanted attention?" she asked, lifting an eyebrow. This game of his was absurd.

"Nah." He shrugged as he picked up their cans from the meal of the night before. "Like I said, everything seems all right. Want to join me?"

"Do you think it's safe?" she asked, in jest.

He gazed at her with a twinkle in his eyes. "I'm wearing my socks today, so I believe it'll be safe for you to venture out, as long as you don't do any practice shooting, yourself."

She took to her feet, rifle in hand.

He burst into laughter. "Boy, it don't take much to rile you, does it?" He placed his arm around her shoulders.

They walked toward the clearing and a nearby stream. Once there, she relaxed on a large rock and undid several buttons on the blouse he purchased for her in town, thankful for the camisole she wore underneath. She plucked at the thin lace ties at the top. Homemade and well-crafted. The garment eased her mind about Joshua's care and safety. Henry's wife had given thought to a woman she didn't even know. Sighing with relief, Caitlyn leaned back to enjoy the warm mid-day sun.

Dakota lingered several yards away, bare-chested, his jeans tucked haphazardly into his boots. She sat up to study at him. His long nearly black hair flowed over his shoulders, lifting slightly in the afternoon breeze, a faded red bandana tied carelessly around his brawny neck. Never in all her life had she encountered a more striking example of manhood than the one who stood before her. She smiled with satisfaction.

In amusement, she watched while he arranged the empty cans in various positions in the rocky stream. Several times, he rearranged the tins, seeking to make the shot even more difficult to execute. When satisfied, he walked back to his rifle. He loaded it and sighted the first can, his firm, tanned arms flexing with the minor effort.

"You know you're wasting ammunition, don't you?"

He winked at her. "Maybe, but I enjoy impressing the ladies. It tends to make them, ah, well, never mind."

"I'm afraid modesty isn't one of your strong suits, Dakota." She laughed, and then for reasons she didn't understand found herself thinking about Elizabeth.

He never mentioned Elizabeth, nor the time they traveled together. Not unusual. He didn't talk about others, but it seemed strange he hadn't said a word. Discomforted, she realized for the first time in her life, she was indeed jealous. Had Elizabeth seen him like this?

The following two days were more wearing than the first. The sun grew unmerciful, and the dark, threatening skies failed to deliver a single drop of rain.

Dakota watched Caitlyn. The days of travel were taking their toll, but her stubbornness prevailed. She was going to retrieve her son—their son—even if she had to walk the entire distance.

At nightfall on the third day, they arrived at the Cooper's cabin. As he remembered, the homestead remained warm and inviting.

"You did good," she said, pleased.

Sarah was the first one out the door to greet them, followed by Henry.

"Yooo, Cabe," he called, briskly striding up to Dakota's horse.

Sarah scurried to Caitlyn's side.

"Henry." Dakota regarded the older man and smiled, feeling oddly pleased with himself.

Henry nodded in Caitlyn's direction and slapped Dakota on the thigh. "So you pulled it off. You got your woman back. Any problems?"

Dakota thought for a moment. "Not many. I didn't bring your horse back to you, but I will repay you."

"I could see you didn't have her as soon as you rode up. This conversation about paying for her is getting old. Let's put it to rest, all right?" He waited as Dakota dismounted. "God, it's good to have you back in one piece. I don't mind telling you, I thought you were a goner." He retrieved Dakota's gear from his horse.

"Hell, Henry, I think you've grown fond of me. Missed me, did you?"

"Don't let your head swell, boy." He smacked Dakota on his back with his usual gusto. "Is she all right?"

Both men looked to Sarah and Caitlyn. Sarah fussed over Caitlyn as if she were Sarah's own child. Caitlyn glanced at Dakota then shrugged as Sarah brushed away her hands and carried Caitlyn's saddlebags in for her. She trailed along behind. Dakota stared after her.

"She is all right, isn't she?" Henry laid a heavy hand on Dakota's shoulder.

His gaze followed the women to the house where the door burst open, and both children toppled out. Joshua outran Sarah Ann, rushing into his mother's open arms, while Elizabeth waited a few steps behind.

Dakota faced Henry. "He nearly killed her."

"What?" Henry pivoted and stared at Caitlyn.

"The son-of-a-bitch horsewhipped her."

Henry's face blanched as he turned back to Dakota. "Let's get your gear inside. We've got plenty to discuss."

"Like what?" he asked.

Henry ignored him.

"Something happen while I was gone?" Dakota stopped Henry's forward motion with a firm hand on his shoulder.

"Well, in a way. I'm not sure how to bring this up and maybe I shouldn't, it being none of my concern, but then again..."

"Damn, Henry, I hope you're as light on the dance floor as you are at side-stepping questions. Spit it out, man."

"It has to do with Eliza—"

Dakota's eyes locked on Caitlyn. Her whole demeanor had changed; she seemed hesitant and unsure. Leaving Henry's side, he rushed toward her. Taking Joshua from her arms, he watched her expression veil over with simple weariness. Had she become like him, an expert at concealing emotions? But why from him? Holding his son in one arm, he circled his other around Caitlyn and walked her to the door. Elizabeth stood ramrod straight in the doorway not moving.

"Mrs. Cookman." He nodded in greeting. "You and my boy fare all right?"

"Yes, we're fine, Dakota."

He lifted an eyebrow at her familiar tone.

A moment passed before she seemed to regain her thoughts and focused her attention on Caitlyn. "Caitlyn. Thank the Lord. I'm so glad you're all right." She threw her arms around her, squeezing a painful gasp out of Caitlyn.

He broke Elizabeth's embrace. "Caitlyn's injured."

She moved away then examined Caitlyn. "She appears all right to—"

"She will be," he cut her off, "once she's rested." Pushing past Elizabeth, he guided Caitlyn inside.

~ * ~

The next few hours they spent eating and playing with the children before retiring for the night. Joshua hung tight to Caitlyn as if she might disappear. The excitement of their evening arrival wore out both children. Before crankiness set in, faces were scrubbed, hands washed, and stories read. Within thirty minutes, both were fast asleep.

Gazing down at her son, Caitlyn realized how exhausted she was, and a yawn sneaked past her lips. She savored the feel of Dakota's arm around her shoulders and gave him a sleepy smile. At his insistence, she excused herself, relieved to know that they would bed down in the barn rather than the house. She was eager for the privacy she now craved. Sarah offered her a cup of coffee as Caitlyn walked to the door, and she accepted it with a goodnight to all.

Closing the door behind her, she was relieved to be alone with her thoughts. Renewed exhaustion flowed over her body and mind. Her mixed emotions from when they had arrived confused her. No, that wasn't correct. She knew herself quite well. The direct hostility toward her from Elizabeth she hadn't misread. She sipped her coffee and examined the sky. She wouldn't try to figure it out tonight. The night was too beautiful, and she was alive, and so was her family. She reveled in the

simple peacefulness and the pleasurable aroma of the smoke emanating from the chimney.

Dakota had offered to walk with her, but she needed time alone.
Sarah and Henry's cozy home and their dependence on one another
sparked a discarded dream to life. Caitlyn glanced at Sarah's clean
wash hanging on the makeshift line and then at Henry's pile of wood.
Both unique chores, yet she couldn't separate Sarah from the stock
of wood any more than she could separate Henry from the laundry,
each one a part of the other. No beginning or end, an unbreakable
circle of devotion to a life they chose to share.

Standing in silence next to the barn, Caitlyn took another sip
of her coffee. For all her hard-won independence, this was what
she wanted with Dakota. The dream wasn't discarded; it was simply
tucked away. Leaning against the side of the barn, she watched him
through the cabin window. The candlelight encased him like some
mystical dream, and she couldn't believe he wasn't just that—a dream.

Deep in conversation with Henry, he was oblivious to her scrutiny.
His profile clearly outlined in the window, she relished the time she
could study him without his knowledge. His dark, untamed hair covered his shoulders and a portion of his face. Despite the hard, dusty
days of travel, he still maintained a clean, well-groomed appearance.

He glanced in her direction. She pressed herself against the barn
though she knew it was too dark for him to see her. The candlelight
illuminated his face as he searched the darkness. Lines of weary
sadness lay etched across his smooth face; an expression she'd never
seen before on him. An uncanny sense of loss swept over her.

She stepped back toward the house, needing to tell him her heart's
dream. To tell him how much she loved him before it was too late.
She needed to say the words.

Taking two more steps, she stopped. Elizabeth's silhouette filled
the window as she leaned over Dakota and laid a tender hand on his
shoulder refilling his coffee mug. Instead of returning to her chair
next to Sarah, the woman lingered close to him.

Caitlyn's breath caught in her throat. Did her dream now belong to another? Had she lost what she'd never had? Tomorrow, she would ask him. Tonight, she was tired and confused.

Turning, she entered the dark barn. Lighting the lantern hanging by the door, she used it to illuminate her way. She crossed the large central area of the barn to the small corner he described to her. It was very different from his brief description. He had prepared a place in the barn as inviting as the Rosebud Hotel in its glory days. The disconcerting thoughts of Elizabeth fled her mind.

Another lit lantern cast a warm glow upon a makeshift bed of hay, graced by a pretty pillow and Sarah's handmade quilts. Next to the bed sat a table and chair for her convenience. On the table were several items Dakota had laid out for her.

A smile tugged at the corners of Caitlyn's mouth when she saw the bouquet of flowers freshly picked from Sarah's garden. They were too cramped together to be from Sarah's gentle hands. His bedroll lay at the foot of the makeshift bed along with a fresh laundered pair of jeans. She knelt to pick them up. Despite the washing, his rich, masculine scent still lingered with them. Lying down on the soft bed, she thought about her dream. Perhaps it was his dream too.

~ * ~

"Have another cup of coffee, Cabe." Henry leaned across the table to pour the brew.

"Thanks, Henry. Now, what did you want to ask me?" Dakota followed Henry's gaze to the back bedroom. Sarah and Elizabeth had brought in the clothes and taken them to the bedroom to fold. The door remained closed behind them.

"I asked Sarah to keep Elizabeth in the back room. We can talk freely. Well, I won't do any side-stepping as you would call it. I'll jump in feet first. What happened between you and Elizabeth on your way here? To be honest, I don't understand you."

Dakota struggled to keep from spitting out his coffee. He wasn't expecting to hear this. "What in hell are you talking about?"

"I figured you different. Especially after seeing Caitlyn."

"Henry, what are you talking about?"

"You and Elizabeth." He eyed him.

Dakota eyed him back.

"All right, so it's not true." Henry nodded his head. "Makes more sense."

"If what's not true?" Exasperated, Dakota glanced at his cup.

"Elizabeth insinuated to Sarah and me that the two of you got friendly on the trail."

"What?" He slammed his cup onto the table, hot black liquid sloshing over the side.

"Elizabeth made it sound like you and her did more than ride. And..." Henry hesitated, "...kind of like she didn't have a choice."

Dakota glanced at the closed door and gritted his teeth in disgust. "You've got to be kidding."

He lifted both eyebrows and added, "Sorry, man. I should have known better, but she acted so damn convincing...like she didn't want us to know she was ashamed or something."

"Hell no, nothing happened." Dakota ground his teeth not believing what he heard. "Maybe you misunderstood her."

"Maybe," he took a sip. "In fact," he continued, standing to his full height and stretching, "when it comes to women I don't understand much, so you're probably right."

Dakota eyed him again. He didn't believe Henry's words, any more than he did, but maybe she tried to cover her own indiscretion, in case he said something. Staring out the window, Dakota searched for Caitlyn. Had Elizabeth said something to Caitlyn when they first arrived? He scanned the darkness, needing to be with Caitlyn, sensing her absence more acutely.

"More coffee, Dakota?"

He hadn't heard Elizabeth approach until her hand touched his shoulder. It seemed like she had done that more than once this evening. The thought made him frown. "No thanks."

She refilled his cup anyway. He waited for her to step away, and when she didn't, he rose, displacing her hand from his shoulder. "Think I'll go check on Caitlyn."

"I'm sure she's fine, Dakota." Elizabeth remained in his way.

He gave her a cold stare. "I'm sure you're right, but I'll check anyway."

~ * ~

With Dakota's warm body cocooned around her, Caitlyn slept through the night until early the next morning. She untangled herself and laid a gentle kiss on his lips. He stirred but didn't wake.

Quietly, she rose from the bed and slipped outside, tucking his coat around her. She remembered him trying to wake her for a warm tub bath, but she had been more interested in sleeping. However, now a bath sounded wonderful, so she went in search of it.

Sarah's steel bathtub held a glorious bath. Grinning with anticipation, she stripped free from the coat, inhaled deeply and held her breath as she sank into it. The icy water was nothing short of invigorating. She lathered up and scrubbed away every trace of grime and dust. Her hair squeaked clean, and she was renewed. Even her back didn't sting so sharply.

After bathing, she donned Dakota's coat and snuck back to the barn, spotting Henry and Dakota on the other side of the house, Joshua in Dakota's arms.

She dressed in a hurry, but Dakota and Henry were no longer outside. She headed for the house.

"Well, hello there, dear. My, but aren't you refreshed. You even have color in those cheeks of yours." Sarah greeted Caitlyn.

She laughed. "It's amazing what a good night's sleep and a bath will do." Peering around Sarah, she looked for Joshua.

"Dakota has him and he gave me strict instructions that you were to eat a hearty breakfast before you took on the little rascal." Sarah winked at her. "I wish you had let me know. I could have drawn you a fresh hot one."

"Nonsense, Sarah. I wouldn't dream of you doing that. Besides, I think the cool water did me far better than a thousand warm baths."

"Well." She held Caitlyn at arm's length. "You may be right about that. You look so much better than when I first laid eyes on you. Now sit and let me fix you some breakfast." She forced her into a chair.

"No, Sarah, please, I'll make it. There's no need for you to wait on me."

"You most certainly will not. If that man of yours comes in here and sees you a working...well, I shiver to think what he would do to me. Have me drawn and quartered, no doubt."

Caitlyn laughed at Sarah's mocking expression of fright.

"Yes. We wouldn't want that to happen to dear 'ole Sarah, now would we, Caitlyn?"

She hadn't seen Elizabeth sitting in the corner. She reprimanded herself to pay more attention to her surroundings. "Good morning, Elizabeth."

"Same to you, Caitlyn. A bath did you say? A bit chilling on a morning such as this one. Do you think that wise?"

"Well, if it wasn't, it's too late now," Caitlyn stated with a tartness she wasn't prone to using.

"I think it did her a world of good. See those pink cheeks?" Sarah insisted, breaking two eggs into a skillet.

"Yes, you are the picture of health, Caitlyn."

She glanced at Elizabeth. The sneer laced in her voice spoke the opposite of her words.

"You do seem much better," she continued in a warmer tone. "Oh, Joshua is with Dakota and Henry, in case you were wondering."

"Yes, I saw them when I finished my bath. Thank you, Sarah," she murmured as Sarah poured her a steaming cup of coffee.

"Well, I can see you don't need me for anything, so I think I'll go find Dakota. We have things to discuss." Elizabeth tossed the blanket from her lap, tightened her shawl around her then breezed out the door.

Caitlyn stared at the door. The woman she once considered a friend, she barely recognized. She tilted her head and took a sip of coffee under Sarah's watchful eye.

"Are you warm enough, dear?" Sarah's voice was thick with concern.

"Yes, thank you, Sarah. Has something happened to Elizabeth? She seems so changed."

"Don't you worry about her, lass. There's nothing wrong with her that a good swift kick in the fanny wouldn't cure."

Startled, Caitlyn met her gaze.

Sarah laid a gentle hand on her shoulder. "Henry told me what John Wakefield did to you." She glanced down at the table. "I'm so sorry. Is there anything I can do? I've mended Henry a time or two. I'm quite good if I say so myself."

Uncomfortable with the subject, Caitlyn offered a weak smile. "No but thank you. I'm quite on the mend." She grimaced when she thought of what her back must resemble. "What happened to Henry?"

"You mean the time he fell off his horse dead drunk, or the time he shot himself in his foot cleaning his rifle?"

They both burst out laughing and were still laughing when the men entered.

"What's got you so tickled, Sarah?" Henry asked, smiling.

"Oh, nothing dear. Just woman talk."

"I think that means run for cover, Cabe." He winked at Dakota.

"You're like yourself again, Caitie." Dakota came up to her and ran his hands through her hair.

"I took a nice invigorating bath."

"I know." A satisfied smile lingered on his lips.

"One would think she'd have enough sense not to soak in cold water, not to mention in broad daylight." Elizabeth barged through the door behind them.

He eyed the woman wearily. "It wasn't cold when I prepared it for her. She was too exhausted last night to enjoy it." Pausing, he smiled at Caitlyn. "But, unlike some women, she still took pleasure in it this morning, hot or cool, and seems quite refreshed." Running his hand along his chin, he glanced back at Elizabeth. "Maybe you ought to try one. A cold bath that is."

Icy blue eyes met chilled steel gray. "There's something I need to discuss with you, Dakota."

"Fire away, Mrs. Cookman."

"In private, I think would be best." Elizabeth's gaze touched on Henry, Sarah, and then Caitlyn.

Dakota nodded to Henry and Sarah. "There's nothing that can't be discussed in front of them and certainly nothing from Caitlyn."

"Well, perhaps, we could discuss the matter later," Elizabeth said, staring at Caitlyn.

She looked away to greet Joshua and gather him in her arms.

"Then there's nothing to discuss," Dakota said.

~ * ~

Caitlyn helped Sarah with the chores throughout the day. The simple routine of baking bread, washing clothes, and caring for the little ones restored her balance. She could relax and mend from her ordeal with Wakefield, and life began to tilt back into normal. The only dark spot in her day was Elizabeth, who seemed to grow more agitated as the day went on.

Near evening she confronted Caitlyn between the barn and the house.

"You're foolish Caitlyn. And worse, you're embarrassing yourself."

"What's wrong with you, Elizabeth?" Caitlyn asked.

Her straight on approach unnerved Elizabeth. Good. Time to clear the air between them.

"I-I don't want to hurt you, Caitlyn."

"I believe that is your intention, so go on." The air snapped with tension, but Elizabeth was at a disadvantage. Apparently, she didn't like confrontation and kept her gaze averted from Caitlyn's.

Keeping her eyes fastened to the ground, Elizabeth said, "I thought you should know. I couldn't keep it from you once I saw you and Dakota together. You need to know the truth."

"And what is the truth, Mrs. Cookman?"

When Caitlyn turned, she saw Dakota staring fixedly at Elizabeth who cowered at his aggressive tone. "Well?" His harsh tone rattled her stiff composure, and her hands trembled.

She started to leave, but Caitlyn held out her hand to stay her. "Maybe you should go, Dakota." She was irritated and wanted to clear up the matter.

"If the woman has something to say about me, I think I'm entitled to hear it." His angry stare now fell on Caitlyn.

"Intimidation is hardly the way to go about it, Dakota." She glared back at him. "I, for one, would like to clear the air between us." She didn't mean to snap, but the duplicity surrounding her exhausted her. "So, tell me, Elizabeth, what truth do I need to know?"

Elizabeth cast her gaze across the ground in what appeared to be shame. It was difficult enough to read her without Dakota's overpowering presence; he only added to the confusion.

Elizabeth's shoulders hunched into a protective mode. "Please let me go to the house. I shouldn't have said anything." She peeked out at Dakota then ducked back. "Nothing happened between Dakota and I." Sniffing, she trembled slightly. "I'm sorry if I caused any concern on your part, Caitlyn." She shot an insincere look at Caitlyn. "There's nothing to tell you. Please let me go." She held up one tentative, shaky palm.

Caitlyn dropped her hand and sighed with disgust. Tossing a terrified glance at Dakota, Elizabeth scooped her skirts to the side and brushed past them, cowering as best she could away from him.

Caitlyn stared at her retreating form, hating the doubt taking up residence within her. She wanted to question Elizabeth further to find the underlying cause of the sordid ordeal. Her insinuations whirled her mind into confusion, but Caitlyn had to remain sensible and in control of her emotions. Still, might something have happened between Elizabeth and Dakota while on the trail, and she was too naïve to think otherwise? The thought tore at her heart and reminded her of how much she might have lost or perhaps never possessed. Caitlyn loved him, and she needed to trust him, but most of all, she needed the truth.

"Caitlyn." His hand was like an iron vise on her arm. "Hell, can't you see what that woman's doing?"

"Right now, Dakota, I can't see a damn thing." She jerked her arm away with a strength manufactured from pain. She was furious with herself for being so jealous she couldn't think straight. What was wrong with her? There was no reason for her to be jealous. Or, had she fallen into a well-laid trap set for her by a woman she mistook for a friend? Disgusted with the whole situation, she strode away saying, "I need time."

It wasn't until the landscape blurred before her that she realized she was crying. Caitlyn managed the last few steps to the creek then crumbled to her knees.

Cupping cold, clear water in her hands, she pressed her palms to her hot cheeks. She rocked back on her heels until she sat without decorum on the rocks that lined the creek bed.

She ached with the knowledge that she didn't have ties to Dakota. He remained a free man. Unencumbered by the restraints of marriage, he could do anything he damn well pleased. It had never registered to her before, but it did now.

She pressed a palm to her chest to shut down the pain. He'd been gone for two years. What had she expected? Honestly? To be his wife? There. She admitted it. Damn her independence. Pride kept her from ever telling him so, but her stubbornness did little to comfort her now. She was drowning in her own self-sufficiency with her insecurities mocking her.

Time swept by, dried her tears and offered her a fresh perspective. Who had she known longer? Who proved themselves in the past? Not Elizabeth, but Dakota. Marriage certificates consisted of merely words on paper. Meaningless, really. She needed to go with what she knew best, and that was Dakota. Still…

She rubbed her eyes in weariness. Maybe she was naïve. Men like him weren't saints. They never professed to be, and Elizabeth certainly wasn't one either.

The first stars of the evening started to light the night. Leaning back to gaze up at them, Caitlyn searched for the Little Dipper. She wasn't sure of its whereabouts, or when it appeared, but it always delighted her when she spotted it.

"Want some company?"

She hadn't heard Dakota approach. She sighed in resignation. "Sure."

"Cold?"

"A little."

The warmth of his coat was sheer bliss.

She waited as he squatted next to her, his elbows resting easily on his knees. Picking up a small flat stone, he flipped it over in the palm of his large hand. The evening stilled, except for the gentle gurgling creek and chorus of crickets. He bit and released his lower lip, making a soft smacking sound in the dark.

"So, now what?" he asked, skipping the stone across the black water.

"You tell me."

"I remember a time when that wasn't necessary."

"Well…" she tucked his coat tighter around her, watching the flow of the creek, "…times change."

"I reckon they do."

In silence, they both studied the dark water.

"Caitlyn." His voice was subdued, and she strained to hear his words as he said, "I can't tell you I haven't been with other women because I have. I didn't think I'd ever see you again." He took a deep breath then released it. "But, as far as Elizabeth goes, nothing happened. I don't know why she's trying to make you believe otherwise, but that is the truth." He watched her, his face only inches from her in the darkness.

Caitlyn studied his dark, brooding eyes. He held no secrets from her. She gazed back into the water, unsure of her feelings. His words relieved her, and yet, the fact that there were others proved difficult. It wasn't as though she expected otherwise. It was simply until that moment that knowledge was at a safe distance. Now it sat in her lap.

"So, where do I fit in?" she asked. "That is, between Elizabeth and the others."

"I love you, Caitlyn. You don't fit in with any of them."

Moments passed as she mulled over his words. A small shudder rippled through her from the deepening frigid air, and he draped an arm around her.

"You can't see it yet." His gaze followed hers into the sky.

"What?"

"The Little Dipper. You have to wait a couple of hours."

She relaxed into his embrace and laid her head on his shoulder. The other women didn't matter. All that matter was this moment with her man.

Chapter 19

The evening was late when they arrived back at the cabin. Dakota pushed open the heavy door and waited for Caitlyn to enter. He greeted Sarah and Henry as they drank coffee at the table with Elizabeth, who sat prim and proper next to them.

Smiling with warmth at Sarah and Henry, Caitlyn removed Dakota's coat and hung it next to the door.

"A bit chilly out there. No?" Sarah asked.

"Yes, it is. Thank you for watching Joshua. Is he asleep?" Caitlyn asked.

"Oh my, yes. Sound asleep like an angel. The two played till they could play no more." Sarah nodded at the small bed where both children were fast asleep.

Caitlyn walked over and laid a soft hand on her son's cheek then brushed a loose tendril of hair from the girl's face before touching her lightly on her pert, upturned nose. "Yes, angels describe them well."

Dakota approached the table, careful to avoid Elizabeth, least he strangle her in passing, and poured himself a cup of coffee. "Caitlyn?" He raised a cup.

"Yes, please." Walking back to him, she reached for the cup. When he failed to release it, she lifted her gaze to his.

Making sure he had Elizabeth's full attention, he leaned forward and gave Caitlyn a deep kiss.

Elizabeth's cheeks flushed red, giving her a flustered, unbecoming look. Her lips formed into a tight, thin, angry slash.

He sat next to Henry. Placing his arms on the table, he took a short sip of coffee then focused his attention on Henry. "I can't thank you and Sarah enough." He nodded at Sarah.

"Sounds like you're saying goodbye."

"I'm afraid so. Caitlyn has her strength back now."

"We've enjoyed the company. It gets mighty lonely out here, especially for a woman." Henry squeezed Sarah's hand.

"You're like family to me." A tear slipped down Sarah's cheek, and she tilted her head. "I hate to see you go, and Sarah Ann will miss Joshua terribly." Reaching across Henry, she grasped Dakota's hand.

"We'll miss you too. You've become good friends, but it's time we head home." He glanced across the room where Caitlyn rocked gently in Sarah's large rocker.

She nodded.

"When will you leave?" asked Henry.

"Day after tomorrow. Tomorrow, I need to buy some supplies in town, including two horses." He smiled at Henry.

"Nonsense, Cabe. I knew when you left, you might not bring the mare back. Don't want to hear nothing else about it. Save your money for your family." He bobbed his head at Caitlyn then added, "You're welcome to anything we have. You know that."

"You're a generous man, Henry, but I can't accept anything else, and you know that." He grinned at the larger man, surprised and pleased by Henry's obvious disappointment in their leaving.

"Where will you go?"

"First, to Elizabeth's home then to Caitlyn's. We'll try to figure things out from there." Dakota glanced at Caitlyn, sipping lazily on her coffee.

"I know everything will work out for the two of you. You have a beautiful son, and that's reason enough." Sarah beamed at him then at Caitlyn.

He was about to agree with her but stopped when he caught the expression on Elizabeth's face. One of pure hatred. He followed her gaze to Caitlyn. What had brought this about? Nothing hc could figure and that made him all the more uneasy, because it made Elizabeth more unpredictable.

She was oblivious to him watching her for several moments, and when she turned to him, she reacted as though he had reached across the table and backhanded her. He hadn't even batted an eye.

Dashing to her feet, she dropped her coffee cup. "Oh, look what you've made me do." She glanced from him then to Caitlyn with accusation.

Caitlyn raised her eyes and stared at Dakota.

"Mrs. Cookman dropped her cup, that's all." Giving her a reassuring wink, he turned back to the table.

Henry followed Sarah to the kitchen sink where she carried the shattered china cup. Dakota took a rag from the fireplace and mopped up the coffee. He glanced up at Elizabeth, who didn't bother to help.

"I hope you aren't prone to accidents when we leave here, Mrs. Cookman," he said with a smile. "Some injuries are damn near impossible to treat on the trail. Some can even be fatal."

She glared at him with a determined expression.

"I hope I haven't frightened you." His smile faded. "It was just a warning." He narrowed his eyes and gave a quick look at Elizabeth. This woman was going to be real trouble.

~ * ~

Morning came in the midst of an early shower. By mid-morning, it was clear, bringing a bright, fresh day bearing all the markings of a potential scorcher.

Anxious to get to town, to get their supplies and return before the day's heat set in, Dakota woke early, long before sunrise. He gazed at Caitlyn's tranquil face, so peaceful, so content. Maybe it could always be this way.

Maybe he could find another way for them to stay together. He nearly laughed.

Who the hell was he trying to kid? Hadn't he spent the last two years wondering that very thing? And didn't he always ride back over the same old ground?

Now he had a son to consider. How could he ever expect Joshua to respect a wanted outlaw? The most impressive thing he could lay claim to was the bounty on his head. Careful not to wake her, Dakota slipped his arm out from underneath Caitlyn and stole from their bed.

He saddled his horse in minutes. Leaving her with Elizabeth for any length of time didn't sit well but bringing her into town didn't sit any better. They attracted attention wherever they went. He wasn't about to take a chance on Wakefield finding her if the man still lived.

Taking a sip of cold, bitter coffee, Dakota glanced at the sky. Distant thunderheads approached. Another storm, and this one appeared to have gumption.

The house was quiet when he rode off.

~ * ~

Caitlyn rolled to her side and noticed Dakota's absence. A stab of melancholy struck her, but she brushed it aside. He had gone into town. He'd come back.

Dressing in a fresh blouse and skirt, she sorted through their few belongings. His possessions lay mingled in with hers. She had a bandana, a shirt, two pairs of jeans, and a pair of his socks. She sorted them out, deciding which to wash and which to pack. Never in all her imaginings had she thought she'd enjoy washing a man's clothing.

Anxious to see her son and wish him a good morning when he woke, she hurried from the barn to the house. Sarah greeted her as she entered, nodding to the children with a finger to her lips. Both were still asleep.

"Guess they wore themselves out yesterday," Caitlyn whispered.

She nodded, pouring Caitlyn a cup of coffee and handing it to her. "Did Dakota leave for town?"

"Yes, about an hour ago." She sipped the black, steamy coffee.

"He'll be back,"

"I know." Caitlyn smiled. "But it has the same feeling to it."

Sarah patted her hand. "It's different this time."

"How can you know?"

"Because, honey, the man nearly lost the one thing he can't live without. It may take him awhile to put it all in perspective, but, believe me, unless he's an utter fool, he won't make the same mistake twice. And, unless I'm completely snookered, Dakota Cabe ain't no fool."

She laughed at Sarah's uncommon slang. "I hope you're right. It's just—"

"What, honey?" Sarah peered into her eyes.

"I never needed or wanted a man before Dakota. In fact, I prided myself on it." Caitlyn studied her hands, trying to find the accurate words to describe the feeling. "Now, I find myself so incomplete without him, it scares me. What if what I want isn't what he wants?" She glanced around the room, and then at Sarah.

Sarah chuckled. "Child, the man wants the same things you do. It amazes me neither one of you seems to know that." She winked. "He loves you, and nothing in this world will ever change that."

Caitlyn's smile widened, and then she thought of Elizabeth. "Where's Elizabeth?"

"In my room sleeping," Sarah muttered, shaking her head as she peeled potatoes.

"What are you making?"

"Oh, a few things for you to take on your trip, and a potato casserole for tonight."

"Let me help." Caitlyn came alongside her.

"I suppose if I told you to sit and rest, you'd still insist on helping." Sarah wiped her cheek with her sleeve.

She nodded.

"Very well, I could use some good company. Not much of that around here." Sarah tipped her chin in the direction of the bedroom.

Washing her hands, Caitlyn glanced at the closed door, then began to knead the bread dough Sarah had laid out. "What's wrong, Sarah?"

"Not sure, but she tossed and turned all night. Seems she might sleep better if she did some work occasionally."

Caitlyn paused her kneading and studied Sarah.

"Hum?" Sarah didn't meet Caitlyn's eyes.

"There's something you're not telling me."

"That obvious, am I?" Sarah sighed and wiped her hands on her apron. "My dear, I don't believe in worrying about a problem before it presents itself, but a woman needs to protect what rightfully belongs to her."

"What concerns you, Sarah?"

"There's something not right with Elizabeth. I shouldn't say this, but I'm going to anyway. That girl's not your friend. In fact, I'm beginning to think she's more akin to your enemy. That woman's a dangerous breed."

A foreboding encased Caitlyn. She hadn't known Sarah for long, but she knew she wasn't one to gossip about people, nor would she say something she didn't believe.

"In what way do you think she's dangerous?" Caitlyn asked, fearing for Joshua's safety.

"What's so dangerous, ladies?"

Both women whirled to find Elizabeth in the bedroom doorway. Sarah's words were too soft to hear, but not Caitlyn's.

"Good morning, Elizabeth. We were discussing the approaching storm," Sarah said. "Would you like something to eat?"

"No, thank you. I don't have much of an appetite this morning." Elizabeth gave Caitlyn a disregarding glance, then tossed one at Sarah. "Where are the men?"

"Henry's checking to make sure everything's secure before this storm hits, and Dakota's left for town," Sarah said, then returned to her fixings.

"Already? I didn't expect him to leave so soon. I wish he had said something."

Sarah glanced at Caitlyn.

"Well, if you girls don't mind, I think I'll sit a spell. This heat's about to devour me."

"Go ahead, Elizabeth. We'll manage." Sarah set to peeling her potatoes with vigor, and Caitlyn kneaded the bread.

The morning gave way to a sweltering afternoon, without the merest sigh of a breeze to break the monotonous heat. She worked beside Sarah, bringing in the first batch of laundry and washing a second load to hang out to dry. Glancing now and then at Elizabeth, a growing apprehension gnawed at Caitlyn, and the sound of the children busy clanging together the pots and tin cups barely registered.

Once the bread was set aside to rise, they gathered the wash and the children and hurried outside before the storm settled in. Not having brought much with her, Caitlyn soon finished hanging her wash and joined Sarah.

"Run along, child. I can do this."

"It will go much faster if I help."

"No, this time, I insist. You just got your strength back, and you're not to lose it on my account. You have a hard trip ahead of you. You should be resting." She nodded toward the house. "Like Elizabeth does all the time."

"Oh, Sarah."

"Don't, Oh, Sarah, me. She's an odd one, and she bodes trouble. I've warned you, honey. Keep an eye on her. She isn't as she appears." With that, Sarah hurried in the children's direction. "Come on, you two. It's naptime. Hurry up, now." Scooping up the children, she marched inside. At the door, she called out. "Go on, lassie, and rest a spell. The boy's in good hands."

Caitlyn nodded at the closing door and retreated to the barn. It would be impossible to relax with the storm brewing in the distance and Dakota gone. Her uneasiness with Elizabeth's behavior and Sarah's words unnerved her more than she cared to admit. To offset the melancholy building along with the storm, she set about packing. When she finished, she would spend time with Joshua.

Sitting at the table next to the bed with the fresh laundry, Caitlyn glanced around. The lantern in the corner cast a warm, cozy glow on the patch of fresh hay. They'd only been at the Coopers a week, but it was home. She laughed.

"Getting sentimental toward hay is not a good sign, girl." She sighed.

The unfounded nostalgia kept time with the general upheaval of events. Soon they would leave the place where they reunited, where they had become a family. Packing the last items into Dakota's blanket, she rolled it up and secured it with a leather tie. The storm bellowed in the distance announcing its rapid approach. Standing, she retrieved the rest of the laundry.

Elizabeth loitered inside the barn door.

Caitlyn spoke first. "Hello, Elizabeth."

Saying nothing, Elizabeth stared at her.

"Did you need something?"

"Yes." A bemused expression on her face, Elizabeth wandered into the barn.

A warning flashed within Caitlyn. She should have left, but she chose to stay.

Elizabeth twirled around the room like a whimsical child.

"Elizabeth, I have much to do, and Sarah—"

"Don't expect that woman to tell you the truth."

"All right." She fixed Elizabeth with an indifferent stare. "Put your cards on the table. I'm tired of your games."

"My, my, a bit testy, aren't you? And what kind of talk is that, 'put your cards on the table?' Something you picked up in a saloon? No wonder a woman like me has you worried."

"Elizabeth, you aren't making sense."

"About Dakota and me." She smiled with smugness.

"Oh, please. Not this again." Caitlyn groaned and started to bypass Elizabeth.

"I'll tell you the truth." She stepped in front of her.

"Elizabeth, I know the truth. Dakota told me. Nothing happened between the two of you. Why do you want me to believe otherwise?"

Instead of moving, Elizabeth turned to the lantern and adjusted the wick, throwing the barn into shadows.

Apprehension shivered up Caitlyn's spine, but this silly charade needed to stop. The barn door rattled in the fierce wind, and rain pinged hard against the roof.

She grimaced. So much for the laundry. The storm outside began to match the one inside.

"I love Dakota, and he loves me. I want you to quit interfering. He's with me now."

So, that was it. Elizabeth was in love with Dakota. Caitlyn should have guessed. All the signs were there. Like a schoolgirl with her first crush. Her mood softened, and she sought to make her following words gentle. "Dakota doesn't love you, Elizabeth." She reached for the woman's arm.

Elizabeth slapped it away as if she were some repugnant rodent, then focused on Caitlyn with newfound venom. "Oh, yes, he does. Of course, he still holds some misguided sense of obligation toward you, but that's all." Her eyes became glossy with inner rage. "If it weren't for Joshua, he'd feel nothing for you."

The woman's hysteria and hatred shocked her; however, the mention of her son elevated her to battle. "You leave Joshua out of this." Caitlyn's compassion morphed into fury. "This is between you and me."

"No, Caitlyn, you're wrong. It's between Dakota, Joshua, and myself. We could be a family if you would leave the man alone." Elizabeth's voice rose in pitch as she glanced at the makeshift bed. "I suppose you think you can keep him in your bed with your streetwise charm, but when he wants a real lady, he comes to me."

Jerking the bedroll from Caitlyn's arm, Elizabeth fumbled in her pocket. "He only feels pity for you. He loves me!"

Caitlyn's eyes opened wide. The woman was deranged. Reasoning with her in her present state was pointless. Anything she said would be kin to tossing dynamite on an open fire.

"I'm leaving, Elizabeth. We can talk when you have hold of your senses." She caught a glimpse of shiny black steel in the folds of Elizabeth's skirt. "What's in your hand, Elizabeth?" Caitlyn stepped back toward her own revolver hanging near the chair.

"We're settling this now." She grasped Caitlyn's shoulder.

The barn door banged open, and Elizabeth shoved her hand back into her skirt pocket.

Henry marched in. "Everything all right in here?" His eyes darted from Elizabeth to Caitlyn.

"Yes, everything's fine, Henry. Caitlyn and I were discussing our departure tomorrow," Elizabeth said.

"I thought I heard shouting."

"Oh." She laughed wildly. "That was Caitlyn. Storms unnerve her."

He glanced at Caitlyn. "Are you all right?"

She shrugged out of Elizabeth's hold. "What do you have in your side pocket, Elizabeth?"

"Nothing." She glared at Caitlyn and lifted her arms. "Do you want to search me?"

Caitlyn reached for the woman's skirt.

Elizabeth slapped her hand away. "Don't you dare touch me."

"I want you to head to the house, Caitlyn." Henry came between them.

She hesitated. She couldn't leave Henry alone with Elizabeth. She had a gun.

"Go on now. I know what I'm dealing with here. Now go."

"Be careful, Henry." She walked out of the barn and leaned against the side then closed her eyes. Her head pounded with indecision. She had made a costly mistake thinking Elizabeth was a friend.

"I'm not fooled by your antics, lady. And you'll soon find out they won't be tolerated by Cabe either." Henry's authoritative voice boomed through the barn wood, startling Caitlyn.

"Well, I guess that makes you one dandy of a man, Henry."

The rustle of skirts made her stand up straight, readying herself for action.

"I won't have Caitlyn hurt, not while she's under my roof, missy."

"Go to hell, Henry," Elizabeth said in a dismissing tone.

"No doubt I will," he said, "but I won't be alone."

Satisfied that he had the situation under control, Caitlyn pushed off from the barn door and trudged toward the house.

Chapter 20

Sometime past dark, Dakota returned to the cabin. In addition to two horses and extra ammunition, he'd purchased wooden toys for the children, a gift for Sarah, a bottle of whiskey for Henry, and an ornate silver hairbrush for Caitlyn. When the time was right, he would give it to her.

As soon as he entered the cabin, it obviously wouldn't be anytime soon. The air in the cabin was thick with tension. Even the children, usually fast asleep at this hour, were up and contrary.

Removing his wet coat, he set his sack of parcels next to the door and eyed the interior much as he would an unfamiliar saloon. Joshua sat nestled in Caitlyn's lap, his head against her breast as she told him a story. She didn't acknowledge him when he entered and seemed more subdued than the rest. After he waited there for a moment, she lifted her gaze, then sighed in relief. Who else had she been expecting?

Henry and Sarah sat rigidly at the table watching him. Elizabeth was nowhere in sight.

"How about a shot of whiskey, friend, and some company while I mend the window in the barn? It appears it didn't fare well during the storm."

Henry rose from the table and strode to the cabinet. Taking down a bottle of whiskey and two glasses, he filled each to the brim. Handing one glass to Dakota, he waited by the door.

"Sure, Henry." Dakota nodded to Sarah and walked over to Caitlyn. Brushing a warm kiss across her cheek and one on the top of Joshua's sleepy head, he murmured, "I'll be back in a bit. You all right?"

She nodded and patted his hand. He examined her face, noting the additional weariness.

The cabin door sprung open, and Elizabeth breezed through the room, dripping water across the floor and slammed the bedroom door behind her. Joshua jolted and started to cry.

Dakota spun around and gave Henry a questioning stare. He shook his head, lifted his glass then tipped his head toward the door. Picking up his sack of gifts, Dakota followed and closed the door behind him. "What happened, Henry?"

Henry didn't reply until they entered the barn and he lit the lantern. Dakota laid his bag to the side.

"I think you've got a full-fledged dust storm in your backyard, Cabe." Henry took a sip of his whiskey.

"Elizabeth?"

"'Fraid so." Henry crossed the interior of the barn to inspect the broken window. Pulling up the loose frame, he peeked underneath. "Damn. The storm tore the whole frame out. I'll have to rebuild the entire window."

Dakota stepped next to him and examined the window. "What'd she do now?"

"Caitlyn won't say, but I walked into one hell of a storm, and it wasn't the one outside."

"Where were they?"

"Right here." He pointed out an area just past where they stood. "Don't know for sure, but there might have been more than words spoken."

Dakota stared at the spot he indicated then snapped his head around and met Henry's eyes. "What?"

"Elizabeth's sure ain't the sweet thing she tries so hard to appear." He released the torn window frame and glanced back at him. "In fact, I think Elizabeth's downright loco."

Dakota's anger mounted. "I'll put an end to this, right now."

"Whoa there, friend. Not so fast." Henry grabbed his arm.

"You don't expect me to let someone bully Caitlyn? I don't care if it is a damn woman. I won't have it. She's been through enough."

"Aren't you forgetting something?"

"Like what?"

"Caitlyn ain't no wilting prairie flower. She's the kind of woman who takes pride in handling her own affairs. You simply gotta keep an eye on the situation."

"Damn it, Henry, I know that, but all her problems are because of me, and this is one more."

"You can't protect her, Dakota, leastwise, not in all things. Besides, I think Elizabeth's problems run in different territory than what you're used to tackling."

"What the hell is that supposed to mean?"

"Means, I don't think she's storing much in her smokehouse these days."

"That is just great. Not only do I have John Wakefield back on our trail, but we've got a crazy woman in camp?"

"Wait a minute. What's this about Wakefield?"

"I heard some men in town talking. Appears Wakefield's far from dead. He lost most of his men, but he picked up more."

"And?

Dakota spit as if he could rid himself of what he had to say. "Seems this thing with Wakefield has taken a different path." He downed his whiskey. "Appears Wakefield's as interested in Caitlyn as he is in my bounty. Maybe more so."

"Oh, Lord." Henry let out a low whistle. "Trouble sure does trail you. Where's he now?"

"That's the problem. I don't know. I stayed in town longer hoping to find out, but I didn't. Doesn't look good, Henry. I suspect he knows where we are. After all, there aren't many homesteads out here. We need to pack up and leave tonight."

"No way, Cabe. Two guns are better than one."

"No. You've done enough. I don't want you and Sarah involved. You have to think of Sarah Ann like I have to think of Joshua. It's best we go."

"Well, at least, wait 'til sun up. No point waking the boy."

"Seems as though Elizabeth's already done that."

Henry smacked him on the back. "That woman of yours probably has him sound asleep in her arms which is where you ought to be."

"Sounds damn good to me, Henry." Bone-weary, Dakota sighed. "I reckon it wouldn't hurt to wait until morning. What about your window?"

"It can wait. I don't think the two of you will catch cold."

He smiled back at him. "No. Probably not." They ambled out of the barn and back to the house.

There was no sign of Elizabeth when they entered, and Dakota was glad. Despite Henry's warning, he didn't know what his words to her might have entailed.

Caitlyn was in the rocker with Joshua, both sound asleep. Extracting the boy from her arms, he laid him next to Sarah Ann in the small bed. "Caitlyn, let's go to sleep."

She murmured something as he lifted her and walked toward the door, her body cradled in his arms. Nodding good night to Henry and Sarah, he strolled out into the night.

The night air and drops of rain jolted Caitlyn awake. "Dakota, put me down before you hurt yourself." She rubbed sleepy eyes.

"Yeah, you're not kidding, Cat. What you been eating these days anyway?" He puffed in mock exertion.

She punched him in the shoulder. "Very amusing, Mr. Cabe."

"Such formalities when I'm holding you, oh so close." He nipped at her ear.

"Stop it, Dakota." She laughed as they wobbled into the barn.

He stumbled over the bedroll still lying on the floor and nearly tossed her to the bed. "I've never met a woman as ticklish as you, Caitie."

"You tickle that many?" she asked, feigning a shocked expression.

"It's good to hear you laugh." It was good. He walked back to the door and took the hairbrush from his sack. "I purchased this for you when I went into town." He held out the silver hairbrush.

"It's exquisite." She took it from his hand. "Thank you." She flipped it over twice. "It's so beautiful."

"This is how you use it." He took it back and brushed it through her hair.

"Very amusing. Ummm, that feels divine." She closed her eyes.

"So, are you going to tell me what happened today between you and Elizabeth?"

"I figured Henry would enlighten you." She leaned back into him, saying nothing else.

He stopped, his hand halfway through her hair. "That's not much of an answer. What happened? I want to know, Caitie."

"Nothing I can't handle."

"I didn't say you couldn't, but we're in this together."

"I don't want to add to our problems, Dakota. Besides, I'm probably reading more into what happened than I should."

"First off," he rotated her around to face him, "Elizabeth is the one adding to our problems, not you. Secondly, why don't you run it by me? You used to trust my judgment in the past."

"I still do." Taking in a deep breath, she recanted the episode with Elizabeth. "And, there's something else."

"What?"

"I think she had a gun."

He drew her forward to read her face. "What kind of gun? Why didn't you tell Henry?"

"He suspected. I went through her things when she was outside, and I found nothing, but I did see a small revolver of Henry's in his gun case that appeared to be misplaced. I think she took it to scare me."

"To scare you? She could have killed you." His eyes widened in disbelief.

"Wait... I'm not even sure she had a gun. I caught a flash of something like metal, and besides, she couldn't even get a grip on it, if it was a gun."

"Any fool can shoot a gun, Cat."

"Well, it's back in Henry's case. It's enough that the three of us know."

"I'm sorry, Caitlyn."

"You have nothing to be sorry for. Elizabeth fancies herself in love with you. She's obsessed with you."

He brushed her hair back from her face. "I'm sorry if anything I said or did led Elizabeth to believe I was interested in anything more than her welfare. I'll straighten this out once and for all in the morning."

She placed a hand on his arm. "Don't say anything."

"Why not?"

"I can handle this, but not in Henry and Sarah's home. Besides, once Elizabeth's home, she'll be able to right herself again. She's been through a horrible ordeal."

"So have you."

"Please, Dakota."

"If you think that's best, then I won't say anything; although, I'd like to wring her pathetic neck." He let out a long sigh and sat on the bed. "We've got bigger problems anyway."

Her body tensed. "John Wakefield?"

"I'm afraid so. The little snake slithered out from the rockslide." Dakota watched for her reaction. White fear danced across her face. "We need to leave in the morning." He pulled her to him. "Damn, Caitlyn. I wish I'd never gotten you involved with me. I've brought you nothing but heartache."

She ran a cool finger across his lips. "Don't. This is where I want to be. Please don't wish it away." Pushing him down onto their makeshift bed, she covered his lips with hers, her long hair trailing across his cheek. Her shimmering emerald eyes searched his for comfort. "I need you tonight, Dakota."

~ * ~

The night was dark and still. Caitlyn lay in the crook of Dakota's arm, her head nestled on his chest. Her eyes snapped open. His body rigid. His readiness for action pulsed within him. She strained to listen. There were no sounds of the night.

"What is it?" she whispered, searching his face.

His eyes were open and focused on the barn ceiling, a stern expression on his face.

"Trouble. Get dressed." He shoved his shirt into her hands, coiled to his feet, and yanked on his jeans. Fastening his gun belt around his waist, he threw an ammunition belt over his head. Bare-chested, he jogged to the barn door and peered out. Stooping to pull on both boots, he scanned the darkness.

Caitlyn dressed in haste, tucking the oversized shirt into her riding skirt. She strapped on her own gun belt, grabbed her rifle, then darted to the back of the barn to look out.

Dakota snapped his fingers, and she whirled in his direction. He lifted three fingers. She turned back to her window. No, no one on her side. He crept back to her and led her to the broken window. "Stay here."

"Where are you going?" She held onto his arm.

"Outside to warn Henry. If whoever's out there hears a wolf howling in the barn, they might be suspicious." Dakota smiled at her. "If I don't come back in say...ten minutes, get out. You'll be safer out there than if they corner you in the barn."

She nodded.

He heaved himself up and out the window. With a shaky hand, she swept her tousled hair away from her face, crept to the front of the barn, then waited. She squinted through the door cracks and into the night, the only sound, the lonesome howl of a wolf.

There wasn't a moon, and she could barely make out the house. How could he see anyone much less count them? She gripped and regripped the rifle in her hands. Joshua was in the house. Biting her lip in frustration, she agonized. Why did Dakota tell her to stay put when he knew she couldn't? Had ten minutes passed? It seemed like hours. She had to go to the house and make sure her son was all right. Being out here was useless. She tugged at the door.

A steely arm tightened around her chest, and a hand clamped over her mouth. Her heart stopped.

"Remind me to buy you a watch for Christmas."

She spun around in Dakota's arms. "Is it John Wakefield?"

"Has to be, but it's too damn dark out there, and no one's moving."

She peered into the darkness. "What about Henry? Do you think he knows?"

"I saw the bedroom curtain move. We'll have to go on the assumption that I'm the only wolf he's heard around here for a while."

"I'm sure he's never heard one like that before."

"What's that supposed to mean?"

"Nothing," she said, "just the poor thing sounded a bit old and winded."

"Well, you would too if you ran down to the creek and back."

"You certainly go for authenticity, don't you?" Her hands were sweaty with fear. "What about Joshua?"

"For now, he's safer in the house. Henry can hole up until daylight and pick them off one at a time, especially with us outside. Unless, of course, there's an army I can't see. Then we're all in a shit pot."

"That's real encouraging."

"Well." He shrugged. "Figured you'd want it straight up."

"What now?"

"We go for an evening stroll, darling." Tucking his other gun in his waistband, he grasped her hand and led her out the barn door.

In a rush, they circled around the back and headed toward the house. They spotted several dark forms posted in position, waiting. It appeared to her much like an army. She followed Dakota to Sarah's bathtub. Halfway there without warning, he dropped his hand down on her head, and she toppled to the ground. Holding her breath, she strained to hear whatever had alerted him.

A slight rustling ambled past them, and she nearly gasped at Todd's appearance. The scent of stale whiskey and reeking body odor made her shudder. Twisting under Dakota's weight, she locked eyes with him then she heard a hissing from the other side of the house. She concentrated on the sound, but it wasn't until the charred acidic smell reached her nostrils that it became painfully clear to her. Torches.

"Come on," he whispered, yanking her to feet as soon as Todd passed. "They're going to torch the house."

She assumed as much. Joshua. Stumbling behind Dakota, they made their way to Sarah's clothesline and bathtub. Dropping behind it, he grasped Caitlyn's face in his hands. "We've got to draw them away from the house." He peered over the tub at the house and the barn.

Two men exited the barn and pointed to the house.

"Well, it appears they think we're all in the house." He glanced at her then back at the house, his face lined with indecision.

"What, Dakota?"

"Nothing." His usual enigmatic expression covered the momentary flash of indecision. He concentrated on his gun, checking the chamber, making sure it was fully loaded then spun the chamber shut. A stalling tactic since she knew it was, as usual, loaded. He didn't meet her gaze when she laid a hand on his arm and tried to make eye contact with him. Instead, he glanced at the house again.

"We'll move to the other side of the house staying in the tree line then we'll move forward and get behind them. All of Wakefield's men are circling the house. They have no idea we're out here. Shoot to kill, Caitie, and watch out for Henry's fire. He won't be able to tell who's out here."

"That's ridiculous, Dakota."

He refused to meet her eyes, and she knew why.

"We have to split up. I'll go back to the barn and move forward, you—"

"No." His eyes flashed black lightning.

"I'm not going to debate this with you, Dakota, not while Joshua is in the house and we're out here."

His jaw flinched, but he didn't relent.

"I said no, Cat. We go together." He reached for her arm.

"We have to split up." Her voice hard as granite as she said, "You know that. We have to take advantage of the fact there are two of us out here. And—" she couldn't stop the edge her voice held, "I've been known to hold my own a time or two."

"I didn't mean that you couldn't, I—"

"I know what you meant, but we don't have time to argue about it."

He grimaced. "Damn it, all right, but I'll go back to the barn. You stay here. Move forward as quietly as you can. Don't make any noise, or they'll know your position."

"What? You mean I can't go running and screaming to the house? I'd get there quicker."

He closed his eyes for a second. "Sorry. When I'm in position, I'll fire once then we'll both move in toward the house. They'll make easy targets with their torches, but so will we. We'll play it as it comes. No telling what Wakefield will do when he figures out we're not in the house, but instead behind him. All right?"

She nodded.

He pulled her to him and kissed her hard. "Watch your back, Caitie."

"You too." She licked dry lips as he stole out into the night to the barn. After a moment, she crept forward past the side of the house to the front yard.

Two figures were positioned at the front door. She drew back into the tree line and sighted the first man in with her rifle.

A single volley broke the night's stillness.

Caitlyn pulled her own trigger, hitting her target. She dropped lower when the second man rotated in her direction firing. His bullet whizzed without direction past her. She aimed as the man bolted to the right. She fired, catching him in the thigh.

A blur of motion to her left brought her attention there. Scrambling to her feet, she pulled a handgun from her waistband. The man loomed out of the black night. She fired, toppling him to the ground a short distance from her. She glanced at his face without recognition. Men milled out of the darkness like ants. Snatching up her rifle, she darted forward, keeping close to the tree line as it circled around the cabin.

~ * ~

Dakota crouched amidst the wood platforms where Henry split his firewood. The sound of Caitlyn's rifle then her handgun made him want to bolt to her, but he remained in position. Damn it. He swiped at the sweat on his forehead.

A murky shadow slipped through the darkness to his right. He aimed and fired. A second man followed, trying to pinpoint Dakota's position. In an attempt to find shelter inside the barn, the man found Dakota's bullet instead. He grimaced at the multiple black shapes gathering in the dark, scrambling for new positions. He and Caitlyn's element of surprise wouldn't last long.

At last, the blast of Henry's rifle boomed from the cabin, and another man fell. Dakota peered into the darkness, firing at the large objects moving across his line of vision. One by one, they dropped, but there seemed to be no end to the men Wakefield had recruited.

A bullet embedded itself in a log next to him. They had his position. Glancing at the house, he saw the men advancing toward it carrying torches. He had to get Henry, the women, and the children out of the house. Leaping to his feet, he headed to the back of the barn, reloading as he ran.

Dakota opened the back door wide enough to slip through, half expecting to catch the hot scorch of a bullet land in his gut, but the barn appeared to be empty except for the skittish horses. His mare watched him, quite unfazed by the gunfire. Slipping toward her, he led her to the door and peered out into the darkness. He threw himself across Caitie's back and righted himself. A lone figure came into the barn and tried to grab her muzzle, but he slammed the massive horse into the intruder.

"Git." His horse dashed out into the night toward the now well-illuminated house.

Wakefield's men were ready. Drawing out his other gun, Dakota fired on both sides of his horse, bringing down three more of Wakefield's men. The only men with torches were now at the back of the house. Dakota directed the mare on a straight path to the house. In the back of his mind, he counted the shots from Caitlyn's handgun as she laid down cover for him.

With thundering hooves, his horse careened toward the porch then stopped dead in her tracks at the front steps. He rolled from the animal's back onto the porch. Rising to his feet, he took two steps and sailed through the window landing at Henry's feet and the open barrel of his rifle.

"Cabe." He jerked the rifle away and held out his hand.

Dakota struggled to his feet. "Going to have to clear out, Henry. They've torched the back."

"I know, but where?"

"The barn I reckon. It'll buy us some time until they torch that as well. There are too many of them."

"Where's Caitlyn?" Sarah stared past him.

"Out there." He nodded toward the door before glancing at Elizabeth cowering in the corner. "Elizabeth. You take... Elizabeth." He snapped his fingers to break through her shocked trance. "You carry Joshua. Sarah, you carry Sarah Ann, head straight for the barn. I'll go out first. Henry, you bring up the rear."

"All right, Cabe," Henry said, pulling Sarah close. "You run like the devil, honey."

She nodded, clutching Sarah Ann to her chest. He grabbed his second rifle and threw it over his shoulders.

Elizabeth's mouth trembled, and a sob escaped her lips.

"Get your wits about you, woman," Dakota shouted. "Let's go." He picked up Joshua and handed him to her.

The far window cracked from the heat of the fire eating through the cabin's wall. He lifted the wooden bolt from across the door and stepped out, gun drawn. Bullets nicked the wooden walls on either side of him, and he fired back in rapid succession.

"Go," he shouted at the women.

Caitlyn had changed her position, so her bullets volleyed in front of the house, drawing the gunfire away from the fleeing occupants.

"That's my girl." Dakota reloaded and loped alongside the women with Henry close behind.

Gunfire rained down on them. Sarah stayed close behind Dakota then rushed into the barn as soon as he motioned it was safe. Elizabeth stopped short of the barn, frozen in terror, and crumbled to the ground; her arms circled around Joshua.

"Damn." Dakota rushed back to her and yanked her to her feet. "Get in the barn."

Frantically, she glanced around. "No. No. It's too dark. I can't." She crouched lower to the ground.

Tucking his gun in his pants, he swept her off her feet. Henry next to him, firing at the enemy who descended on them. Bursting through the barn doors with Elizabeth and Joshua in his arms, Dakota deposited them safely inside. He turned in time to see Henry sag to the ground only a few feet from the barn's safety, his hand gripping his thigh.

Righting himself, he limped into the barn, and Sarah dashed to her husband's side, ripping her petticoat with her hands. She tore the fabric into long strips and secured his thigh tight above the wound.

Dakota glanced at the wound. It wasn't life-threatening, but it needed tending to. Scanning the surroundings outside the barn, he watched for Caitlyn. Her small form moved along the tree line toward the barn, both guns drawn, the rifle thrown across her back. He nodded. Yes, she had always proven herself more than capable. His gut clenched when he spotted the tall, sinister form moving in behind her. He ran from the barn in her direction, heedless of the gunfire scorching the air around him.

~ * ~

Caitlyn saw Dakota approaching. Her body relaxed until she read the warning on his face. Dropping to the ground, she rolled onto her back and fired into the man behind her.

She lost no time regaining her feet and running to Dakota. Taking her arm in a steel-trap grip, he half carried her to the barn. Once inside, he dropped the wooden latch in place and pulled her to him. Drawing away, he examined her as if she were some exotic jewel.

"You all right?" His voice was rough, anxious.

"I'm good, Dakota." Caitlyn smiled and tweaked his cheek to break the tension.

She glanced at Joshua in Elizabeth's arms, then hurried to the window to take a defensive position. Dakota remained at the front, while Henry posted himself at the rear, sinking to one knee.

"Sarah put the children in the far corner. You and Elizabeth take the other window. We can't let them get close enough to torch the barn," Dakota yelled above the exploding gunfire, crying children, and nervous horses.

Reloading his rifle, he handed it to Elizabeth. "You're gonna have to shoot as best you can. Henry, give Sarah your other rifle." He turned to the door, then turned back to where Elizabeth still hesitated. "Go on, woman."

She nodded and took her position next to Sarah.

"They're coming, Cabe, five on Caitlyn's side," Henry shouted.

"Cat?" Dakota glanced at her.

"I'm ready." The cold steel plate of the rifle pressed into her cheek, and she waited.

"Seven out front," he said.

"Four more, Cabe," Henry called out. "Sarah?"

"Three," Sarah replied, without emotion, wiping sweat from her eyes.

"They're gonna come at one time. Get ready."

The ensuing gunfire drowned out Dakota's voice.

Caitlyn concentrated on the men in front of her. Each one carried a gun and a torch. Her palms were sweaty, but she couldn't take the time to dry them. They were coming and coming fast. The rifle kicked back repeatedly into her shoulder. Three down, two retreating, now one retreating.

The men coming from the rear of the barn came into view, and she reloaded and took aim. "Two down, one coming your way, Cabe."

"I got one." Elizabeth squealed in delight.

Sarah pressed her lips together and continued to fire.

"Caitie, come here," Dakota called to Caitlyn.

Without question, she ran to his side.

"You'll have to cover me. They've torched the woodpile."

She peered around him at the woodpile burning, shooting flames licking at the barn.

"I've got to kick the fire away."

Her throat constricted. She nodded, and he moved past her. Pulling back the lock, he pushed open the door and stepped out, and she laid down cover.

A shot whizzed past her and ripped into him, taking him to the ground.

"Dakota!" Without thought, she rushed to him. She stifled a scream as his blood poured into her hands.

"God Almighty," Henry exclaimed, struggling to his feet.

Caitlyn mentally slapped herself out of her hysteria and clutched Dakota around his waist. Her feet dug into the ground as she struggled to tug his large, limp body back inside. From the corner of her eye, a menacing form approached. Oh, God, no. John Wakefield. She glanced back to where she dropped her gun, but she couldn't reach it.

"Get down, Caitlyn," Henry bellowed.

She bent protectively over Dakota.

Henry aimed his rifle unsteadily and jerked the trigger. The bullet whizzed past Wakefield's ear, and he grinned like a madman. His huge form blocked out the early morning rays of a new day as he stooped over Caitlyn and yanked her to her feet.

She came up fighting. Using all her strength, she kicked at his legs and clawed at his face.

Sarah ran up alongside her husband and aimed at Wakefield.

A deep roar of triumphant laughter filtered through the barn. "Hello, Stormy, that wasn't very sweet of you to run off like you did." Backing out, he pointed his gun at her head, his words directed at Sarah. "I wouldn't try it. If she ain't mine, she ain't nobody's."

Henry kept his rifle on Wakefield, but didn't attempt to bring him down, nor did Sarah.

Wakefield glanced at Dakota and the blood-saturated ground. "Tough luck, Cabe." He grinned. "I ought to finish you off right here, but I'd rather you suffer." He laughed. "Who knows? Maybe you'll be better at holding onto life than you were at holding onto your woman." He signaled to his men and dragged Caitlyn away.

~ * ~

Sarah stared at her husband, her mouth gaping.

"Take care of Cabe," Henry instructed, his rifle aimed at the retreating mob.

She dropped next to Dakota. "Good Lord in heaven, help us."

Henry glanced back at his wife. "How bad is it?"

"It's bad, Henry, I don't know if I...if—"

"Don't think, honey, just tell me what it looks like, and I'll tell you what to do." He grimaced and steadied himself.

Elizabeth hurried to Dakota's side. "Oh, no. No."

"The bullet entered through his back below his shoulder." Sarah bit off sobs and continued, "and exited out the front. It appears to be clean, Henry, but it's bleeding bad."

"Take your petticoat, bunch it up, press it into the wound, and hold it. Hold it tight, girl."

Sarah tore another piece of petticoat free and, with even pressure, pushed the cloth into the open wound. "Elizabeth, take off your petticoat."

Without hesitation, she did as told and helped tie the fabric around Dakota's chest.

When the last of Wakefield's gang rode off, Henry faced Sarah. "I've got to go after them."

Wide-eyed, she nodded.

Chapter 21

Elizabeth made sure her face was the first one Dakota saw when he regained consciousness. He gazed up at her and then around at the unfamiliar surroundings.

"You're at a neighbor's house. Henry and Sarah's house burned." She gauged his questioning expression. "You've been unconscious for a day and a half."

Dipping a cloth into a bowl of hot, soapy water, she wiped his brow.

"Caitlyn?" His hoarse, congested voice was barely recognizable. Yet, his one word was clear enough, and a flash of hatred shot through her.

Elizabeth bowed her head, hoping it conveyed remorse. "She's gone. John Wakefield has her...again." Trying to hide her real feelings, pure glee, from her voice, she lifted her gaze to meet his, grateful for the disingenuous tears that graced her cheek. "I'm sorry, Dakota." She squeezed his large, rough hand. "Henry tried, but with his injured leg, he couldn't keep up, and now the trail's gone."

Gazing out the window, she sighed as if at a loss for any meaningful words at such a tragic time. His intense gaze bore a hole in her, but she didn't trust her shallow facade enough to meet his eyes.

"I want to talk to Henry."

"Later, Dakota. First, you need to rest."

"Tell Henry I want to see him now." He clenched his teeth.

She placed a cool hand against his chest to keep him from sitting up. "There's no point. Not now."

His skin was hot, vibrant to the touch, and she drew back her hand only to replace it.

"Woman. I'm not known for my manners, especially when I've been shot. Now git Henry!" Dakota's ragged voice had lost none of its roughness.

"All right." After all, what did it matter? Caitlyn was gone and gone for good. She had heard enough of what Henry told Sarah to figure out that much.

Henry had tried. She gave him that. He'd nearly bled to death going over the rugged terrain, only to return when he lost the trail. She pursed her lips. She'd never seen a more defeated man.

She glanced back at Dakota. His appearance was too brutal for her tastes now, but a good shave and some tender care would change that. Sweeping her skirts along with her, she headed to the door.

"I'll bring you back some soup for lunch." She stopped in the doorway to tuck a wisp of golden hair back into its bun before she swept out the door.

~ * ~

After releasing a whoosh of air, Dakota dropped back onto the pillows, pain ricocheting through his back and head. Sealing his lips together, he waited.

"This is exactly what I feared." Henry's large frame filled the doorway, appearing to have aged ten years in the last day and a half.

"Oh? And what might that be?" Dakota struggled to prop himself up.

"Trying to kill yourself?" Henry did not attempt to assist him. "So what now, Dakota? Should I saddle up Caitie for you or shoot you myself and save us both the effort?"

"Anybody ever tell you, Henry...you run off at the mouth." Dakota gasped, still trying to right himself.

"A bit testy, I see, but I suppose that means you're healing."

"Where's Caitlyn?" He sat up and glared at Henry.

He glanced away.

"Well? You did do something while I was out cold, didn't you? Or did you sit on your ass and watch me sleep?"

"Being shot sure don't do much for your disposition."

He continued to glare at him. This time, Henry glared back

"I'm painfully aware of my limitations, Henry, so tell me what you know. I ain't going anywhere...yet."

"He's in a place called Back Gap, about a day's ride from here. I followed him to the gap, but I ain't no tracker." Henry cast his gaze to the floor. "Sorry, Cabe."

Dakota's jaw muscle flinched. "How many men he got with him?"

"None. They've all cut out."

"Why?" Dakota raised one eyebrow as he reached for the bowl Elizabeth brought. When she attempted to help feed him, he brushed away her hand. He took a shaky spoonful of the warm potato broth.

"Because, instead of dragging you out and collecting the bounty, he high-tailed it out with Caitlyn. Like you said, I don't reckon he cares much about the money anymore."

At Henry's words, a fresh wave of nausea swept over Dakota, and he lowered the bowl in disgust. Caitlyn was with the bastard. He closed his eyes. He needed to regain his strength.

"Could I have more?" He held out the bowl to Henry.

Their eyes met, and a mutual understanding passed between them.

"I'll be going with you, Cabe."

"Figured you would, Henry. Thanks." No point arguing. Henry need-ed to go, and Dakota understood why.

The following day, he pulled himself out of bed and met the owner of the house they were staying at. They were a pleasant couple, young, but intimidated by him.

Susan Peters, a young homemaker, was the most unsettled. Every time he spoke, she jumped. He kept his voice as soft as he could, but his presence seemed to unnerve her. Tom Peters chose to stay away from him unless his wife was nearby; then he watched his every move.

"The Peters are good people, Cabe," Henry said. "It's only that they're not used to a man of your caliber. They've had their own problems with Wakefield, and the fact that you're about to go after the man makes them nervous."

"I'm sorry I've brought this into their home. It's bad enough I brought it into yours. When I get Caitlyn back, I'll help you rebuild."

"You might not get a chance. Folks around here come in a hurry when their neighbor has troubles. They already started. It will probably be livable by the time we get back."

"That's good to hear. Does Sarah know you're coming with me?"

"She knows."

"You've got a good woman."

"So do you, Cabe." Henry locked eyes with him. "We'll get her back; don't you doubt it." He thumped on Dakota's shoulder, and he winced.

~ * ~

Caitlyn informed Wakefield he would have to drag her wherever they went, and she meant it. She would fight him every step of the way to Back Gap. She watched with satisfaction as he backtracked—repeatedly, to destroy little clues she left behind for any pursuers to follow.

Wakefield was exhausted. A brief one-day trip had manifested into a horrendous two-day ordeal, and she couldn't be more pleased.

"You know Cabe's dead."

"Maybe, maybe not," she said, trying to convince herself.

Even with her hands bound, she sought ways to leave clues behind. Wakefield was furious to find several and finally had her ride in front of him on the horse.

By evening, they came to a trapper's vacated cabin and stayed the night. After tying her up, he soon fell asleep.

Her hatred and disgust for the man kept her fear under control. No doubt, this wasn't going to end well for her, but her mind was set. It wasn't going to end well for John Wakefield either.

The next morning, she began a new day of badgering him. "Tell me, Mr. Wakefield, are you truly that afraid of Dakota?" She had caught him for the third time, peering out the cabin's window.

"Don't push me, my dear. I don't have anything else to lose."

"Well, you do have a point. It must be quite embarrassing to have your men run out on you like that."

Before she could defend herself, he backhanded her.

"You do have your own special way with women, don't you?" She touched her stinging cheek.

"I'm sorry." He stared at her. "Woman, you would try the patience of a saint. Why do you push me? Don't you know I'm all you have now? You best warm up to that fact. Cabe's gone."

"Is he?"

He studied her for a moment, and she smiled as if privy to a secret he should know about. "You were there, lady. You saw him take that bullet. I don't know where it came from, but it don't matter. He's dead."

Her hands trembled at his words, but she struggled to keep her face unreadable. Where had the bullet come from? Could Dakota have survived? "I wouldn't be so sure if I were you." She made her words light and carefree. Dakota had survived; she couldn't maintain this combative fortitude if he hadn't.

Grabbing her by the arm, Wakefield peered out the window again. "We're leaving." He draped his coat over her shoulders as they exited the cabin, but she shrugged it off.

"So." She paused in the doorway. "You are afraid of him."

"You sure have a lot of faith in him."

"It pays to have faith in one who delivers."

"You might be in for a surprise then, lady, 'cuz I think Cabe's done delivering."

~ * ~

Henry and Dakota kept a steady pace. Twice, Henry urged Dakota to slow down, but he refused. Blood seeped through his bandages, staining his outer shirt, and his eyes were dry, gritty, and bleared. His head buzzed like an angry hive of hornets had gone to war in his mind. He forced himself to focus.

Reining in the horse, he swung down to inspect the ground. Henry followed suit. "Well?"

Dakota gave a short grunt.

Henry placed a firm hand on his shoulder. "Well?" he repeated.

"Caitlyn left a trail a child could follow."

"You sure? Wakefield can't be that stupid."

"Oh, but he is. He's too busy covering one trail to see the other." Dakota gave another chuckle. "Oh, Cat, you're one hell of a woman."

Henry knelt next to him and inspected the ground. "I don't see anything."

Dakota glanced up at him, his vision clearing. "Trust me, Henry."

They traveled over the rough terrain, making steady progress into Back Gap. At nightfall, they came upon a deserted cabin.

"Damn," Henry exclaimed, sounding disappointed. "We'll never catch up to them."

"He'd be a fool to stop now." Dakota inspected the cabin, then stooped next to the fireplace and laid his hand on the rocks. "Must have left this morning. If we keep on, we should find them by daybreak."

"Don't you think you ought to rest?" Henry knelt next to him, placing his own hand on the cold stone.

"Nope. I'm not taking a chance of losing them." Dakota ran his hand through his coarse dark whiskers. "Why don't you stay here, Henry? I can manage."

"No way, Cabe. I'm seeing this through to the end."

"You don't have to."

"Yes, I do. Hell, with those shaky hands of yours, you might miss then where would you be?"

He laughed half-heartedly. "With your aim, Henry, if I miss, we're all in the shit pot."

"Well, you're full of talk now. We'll see what you have to say when I drag you home strapped across your horse." Henry nodded at Dakota's side then frowned.

He glanced at his wound. "Doubt I'll be saying much, my friend."

Henry was silent.

They mounted back up. The night air became frosty enough to transform their breath into white puffy clouds. The sky was clear, and a thousand stars lit their way. Glancing upward, Dakota nodded at the stars. "That's a good omen."

Henry stared skyward. "I sure hope so."

Dakota kept his gaze glued to the ground, riding over the same ground twice. Henry stopped his horse and waited.

"What now?" he asked when Dakota reined in.

"Boy, he's good. I give him that. Even with Caitlyn's help, he's a hard one to track. Must have been born in these hills."

"You lost him then?" Henry's voice was filled with disappointment.

Dakota gave a grim smile. "He's not that good." Directing his horse, he backtracked several yards and started again.

Caitlyn stared at the forest as John Wakefield loosened the ties on her wrists. Little sunlight reached this remote spot.

"Eat your breakfast, then the ties go back on."

"Do I make you that nervous?" She chuckled with repugnance.

"Let's just say I don't plan on getting a knife in my back. Not after all the trouble I've been through to get this far."

"What's the point of keeping me if you're afraid of me?"

Wakefield whirled on her. "I ain't afraid of no woman." Immediately, he calmed. "I see your game, trying to provoke me. It won't work." He smiled at her. "You'll come around. Where we're going, you'll have to depend on me."

"Don't count on it." She took another bite of the stale biscuit he'd given her.

He stared at her for a long time. "If I have to, I'll kill you. Don't think otherwise. You might as well forget about Cabe as you can see, he ain't coming." He spun around in grandiose fashion.

Wakefield's words unnerved her. Leaving a trail for Dakota had been optimistic. Fatigue fractured her will, but she refused to believe a low-life like Wakefield had taken the love of her life. She wouldn't give up what kept her alive—her hope and faith in Dakota Cabe.

Her eyes stung with tears. Taking in a deep breath, she assessed her situation. She couldn't let Wakefield take her any further into these woods. She had watched as they traveled, but even so, it would be difficult to find her way back out. He knew these woods well, but she didn't. They could kill her as quickly as he could. Her options were limited. He kept her hands bound during the day and her feet at night. He slept with his guns, with his knife tucked into his waistband.

Dakota. If he could have come, he would have. The thought burned into her like a red-hot poker. She couldn't imagine life without him or Joshua.

Joshua. If she went any deeper into this wilderness, she'd never get back to her son. Blinking back the tears, Caitlyn forced her voice to remain steady and unemotional. "Well, perhaps you're right. Maybe Dakota isn't coming, but then again, it's hard to tell. He's always been unpredictable."

Her words were light and had the desired effect on Wakefield. He canvassed the woods surrounding them. The dim morning light was favorable, but an expression of apprehension flashed across his face. Wakefield knew Dakota well enough to know he could be unpredictable. Good.

She shivered with expectation. Good heavens. Was she so worn out that she believed in her own desperate hopes?

Wakefield rose and walked the camp's perimeter, sipping his coffee, his gun at the ready. Turning, he walked back to the small fire where the coffeepot sat perched on a rock.

"Nope." He shoved his gun back into its holster. "I don't believe we'll be having any company out here."

Caitlyn dropped her head into her hands, wanting to cry, but instead, she pinched her cheeks so hard she winced. She needed to accept what might be and do her best. Dakota would expect no less of her.

"May I have some coffee, please?" She stared at Wakefield and forced a smile to her lips. A better opportunity wasn't likely to come. Her hands would be tied again after breakfast.

He refilled his cup and handed it to her.

"Why don't you join me, Mr. Wakefield?" She allowed a note of defeat to taint her words.

Eyeing her with wariness, he hesitated and then sat next to her.

"So, have you been doing this very long?"

"What?"

"Capturing and carting off women against their will. I wouldn't ask, but I was curious if you had any prior experience, or if you were going on gut intuition."

He gave her a sharp glare.

Sipping on her coffee, she gazed up at him. "Obviously, bounty-hunting wasn't your forte since you bungled that so badly." She paused in thought. "I wondered if you would be any better at this or if this would be another disaster."

"I don't think it's in your best interest to push me, my dear. I have little left in the way of patience."

"Or other things it appears." Glancing at his chest, then down to his crotch, she smirked. One thing she had discovered in life was that a quick lit, uncontrolled temper never served any man well. It made them careless and stupid.

Furious, he jumped to his feet and yanked her up, knocking the cup of coffee from her hand. She winced when he wrapped his hand in her hair and jerked her to him. Savagely, he bit her lips, and she screamed in pain.

"You've never been with a man until you've been with John Wakefield." He fumbled with the buttons of her blouse.

Caitlyn laughed. "You call yourself a man? You're nothing but a dim-witted old has-been."

His eyes flared with fury, his mouth an ugly slash of venom. Shoving her to the ground, he loosened his gun belt and dropped it. She leaped to her feet and came at him. He seemed dazed by her actions. No doubt, he expected her to run so he could give chase. He hadn't expected her to throw herself into his arms.

Without hesitation, she wrenched the knife from his waistband. He snatched at her hand, but she jumped out of reach.

"I'll kill you." She pointed the knife at him.

He dropped his head and held his palms to his sides. "My dear, you threaten a man who has nothing left to lose."

"You're a fool. No one wants to die." She backed up as he took a step towards her. Licking her lips, she waited for the inevitable.

Laughing, he lunged at her, but she gripped the knife with both hands and held it with all of her strength. The blade wavered a second before cutting into him. Unfortunately, it was not a life-threatening wound, only enough to momentarily stun him.

The air rushed out of him, and his eyes flickered with evil intent. He grasped her arms in a vice hold. She wiggled to free herself, but he only smiled and squeezed her arms tighter, sliding one hand down her arm to the knife.

"I told you, Stormy; I have nothing to lose—except for you, and you're too much trouble."

The knife slid out of him, his strength greater than hers. The blade pricked her chin.

"Now who's the fool, my dear?"

The knife quivered at her chin then danced into the air. A sudden impact knocked them both to the ground. Her cheek hit the ground with enough force she saw flickering lights. Then a chaotic tangle of leather and men ensnared her.

Large, rough hands jerked her upward and shoved her to the side. Tumbling over and over she then staggered to her feet.

Dakota.

Wakefield and Dakota rolled across the ground. Blood was everywhere. Dakota's mare stood several yards away; his rifle still tucked in its saddle sheath. Dashing to his horse, she jerked it free, barely acknowledging Henry's presence as he lumbered off his mount, freeing his own rifle.

Gripping Dakota's Winchester in her hands, she approached the two struggling men. Pulling back the hammer, she readied the weapon and aimed, but she couldn't distinguish where one man ended, and the other began. They were a blur of pestilent motion.

Dakota flipped on top of Wakefield and pinned him to the ground, and she gasped at Dakota's pale complexion. The face of death. She aimed carefully, dropping the sight of the gun down to Wakefield's head. Her finger pulsed on the trigger, but the men's constant motion kept her from being sure of her target.

Wakefield jerked the knife up between them, and Dakota threw himself to the side. Wakefield took advantage, leaping to his feet and throwing his body onto Dakota. The two men were locked tight together, leather against leather. All she could do was watch and wait.

He gripped Wakefield by the hair, rotating his face upward and sinking a hard fist into his mouth. Blood spurted from his lip, and Wakefield rocked his head back and forth. Using Dakota's weakened condition, he threw a well-aimed punch into Dakota's wounded shoulder, bringing a fresh stream of blood. Dakota grunted, pitched to his side, struggling to draw air into his lungs. With unconcealed glee, Wakefield picked up his gun, cocked it, then pointed it at Dakota's face.

The sound was deafening as it echoed through the mountain pass. Wakefield's gun slipped from his fingers, and he brought wide, disbelieving eyes in her direction, then slumped to the ground.

A thin ribbon of smoke rose from the end of Dakota's rifle and trailed up into the brisk morning air.

~ * ~

Days later, when Dakota could ride, they made their way back to the Peters' homestead. They spoke little on the way through the pass. As far as Caitlyn was concerned, no words were necessary. He was alive.

Henry's gaze fell on them more than once, and she shifted in her saddle to check on him. "Henry, are you all right?"

He grunted. "Yeah, just wondering."

"Watch it, Caitie. When he starts a conversation like that, he's about to launch into something deep." Dakota chuckled.

"Watch your mouth, boy. Just wondering how the two of you, who fit so perfectly together, managed to live separate lives for the last two years. Pure foolishness."

"I heard you, Henry." Dakota gave Caitlyn a crooked smile. "He tends to get long-winded when he's trying to make a point."

She smiled at Dakota. The last two years had been rough. Rougher than she would admit.

The reception they received upon returning to the Peters' home was grand. Caitlyn asked Dakota and Henry not to mention her part in the shooting of John Wakefield, so they didn't.

The Peters warmed to Dakota, now that Wakefield was no longer a concern. They even asked him a few questions, going so far as to thank him for pursuing Wakefield and ending his reign of terror.

"You have Henry to thank for that," Dakota said, winking at the older man.

Less than a week later, they left the Peters and headed to the Coopers' new homestead.

Sarah sat next to Henry on the borrowed buckboard. Dakota, Caitlyn, Elizabeth, and the two children rode in the back. After bidding farewell to the Peters, Henry gave his wife an affectionate peck on the cheek, then gathered the reins and prodded the horses forward. The wagon wheels creaked and moaned as it rolled down the road.

"I still don't think they were sorry to see me go." Dakota draped his arm around Caitlyn's shoulders.

"They didn't have enough time to get to know you, that's all." She smiled and patted his leg. "Once you get past your rifles, pistols, gutting knives, and extra belt of ammunition, you're just like the average townsman."

"Thanks, Caitie."

"People like that are frightened of the world in general, Dakota. I wouldn't take it personally," Elizabeth muttered.

It was the most she had said in days. An awkward silence sat amongst them.

"There she be." Henry pointed at the new structure in the distance.

"She's looking mighty fine, Henry. Are you sure you didn't help burn the old one down?"

He chuckled. "It is an improvement. Hard to believe I have Wakefield to thank for it." He squeezed his wife. "You and Caitlyn will have a room in the house now."

"Thanks, Henry, but I'm kind of partial to the barn. Besides, it's time we moved on."

"Careful what you say, friend. Last time you said that all hell broke loose."

"Don't worry. Wakefield was the last bounty hunter. I promise you." Dakota kissed the side of Caitlyn's head, but his gaze stayed locked on something far in the distance. A rush of fear shot through her, and her heart jammed in her throat. She pushed the feeling as far away as she could. He would stay. No reason for him to leave. John Wakefield had proven the folly of that idea.

Henry and Sarah entered their new home, greeted by the neighbor's homecoming gifts: a beautiful oak table, matching chairs, two pie safes, and other essential living items.

The new home was indeed grander than its predecessor. The cabin now had five rooms instead of three, and the kitchen was more substantial with an extra working area. Caitlyn marveled at it and hugged Sarah. "It's beautiful, Sarah."

"Yup, and time to think about a brother or sister for Sarah Ann." Henry's eyes twinkled at his wife.

Sarah laughed and shot her husband a mock glare. "Don't get any ideas, old man."

Dakota stepped inside and surveyed the new furnishings. "You do have kind neighbors."

"It's perfect." Caitlyn walked into the main room and peeked into the two new rooms. Beautiful quilts graced each bed.

"Yes, lovely, isn't it?" Elizabeth said. A disdainful expression crossed her face.

The children entered last, oblivious to the new decorations. All that concerned them were the hand-carved toys in the corner.

After dinner, as the sun sank home, Caitlyn and Dakota headed to the creek. The evening grew warm, the air clean and fresh. She felt young and carefree, and none of Elizabeth's unpredictable moods could dampen her spirits. She was with the man she loved. Life held all types of possibilities.

"What's got you so full of sunshine, Caitie? I do believe you're actually glowing." Dakota chuckled affectionately.

"You."

"What? Me?"

"Yes, you. Don't act so shocked. I love you. You've made my life good."

"How's that?"

She squeezed his arm, careful to avoid his shoulder. "Because we've been through so much, and yet the best remains. You gave me a son, but even more, you gave me your love."

He glanced down. "I think I gave you mostly heartache."

The seriousness of his tone brought her up short. She took both his hands in hers.

"You can't have one without the other, just like you can't have mountains without the valleys." Stepping closer, she hoped to make him understand when she said, "Love fades, like a vivid sunset. So full of color, so beautiful it can't sustain itself." She slipped her arms around his waist. "But my love for you, Dakota, is greater, more beautiful than when we first met."

Cupping her face in his hands, he kissed her. "I do love you, Cat." He paused. "But I remember a certain look of defiance when we first met. I sure didn't read anything friendly."

"Oh? What did you read?"

"Something akin to calling me out."

"A famous outlaw like yourself? I wouldn't have dared."

"Oh, you were quite safe. Your beauty completely blinded me." He draped his good arm around her and squeezed.

"Dakota Cabe, you're a rogue." She giggled as he backed her up against a tree.

Removing her jacket, he started on the buttons of her blouse.

"Dakota, watch your shoulder, you'll reopen—"

"I'm not interested in my shoulder at the moment, my love."

"But you're not fully recovered."

"I'm well enough for the things that count. Now shhh—"

~ * ~

They stayed with the Coopers for several more days, falling into a routine Caitlyn was sorry to break.

On the morning of departure, she sat at the small table in the barn, staring at her reflection. Something kept gnawing at her. Ever since the evening by the creek, she had sensed or imagined an aloofness in Dakota. Everything was coming together for them, so why did she feel the need to draw up a wall of defense? And defense against what?

She hadn't anticipated how difficult it would be to say goodbye to the people she had grown to respect and love. The situation worsened after leaving with Elizabeth, a woman she once considered a friend who now seemed more like an enemy.

Thankfully, Dakota had insisted on an early departure, and the good-byes were kept to a minimum. Caitlyn never liked goodbyes. Though she wished she could say goodbye to Elizabeth. Things were far from over between them. When she said goodbye to Sarah and Henry, Caitlyn feared she was saying hello to a whole new kind of hell.

Chapter 22

"It's getting late, Elizabeth, and you're too far from the fire. I thought you disliked the dark," Caitlyn said.

"No, not anymore because of Dakota. I don't believe I'll ever fear the dark again." Elizabeth's eyes took on a dreamy effect.

Caitlyn rolled her eyes in exasperation. Oh, please, not another innuendo. "Well, don't wander any farther from the fire. There are too many wild animals out here."

"Worry about yourself, Caitlyn," Elizabeth snapped.

She considered the woman for a moment. Why had she concerned herself about the woman, anyway? "Suit yourself." Pressing down the creases of her riding skirt, Caitlyn stepped backward, reluctant to leave her back to the woman. "I'm going back to the fire."

The crackling campfire illuminated Dakota and their son in a warm, vibrant light.

"Everything all right?" he asked.

"I guess." Caitlyn shrugged.

"We'll be at her house by noon tomorrow."

She nodded and knelt to take Joshua into her arms. "I'm going to put this rascal to bed." She smiled at her yawning son.

It didn't take him long to fall asleep, and she soon rejoined Dakota by the fireside. "She's been gone a long time, Dakota."

"I know." When she said nothing further, he asked, "Do you want me to go get her?"

No, she didn't, since Elizabeth probably intended that. Yet... Caitlyn bit her lower lip. The dangers out here were real, and the foolish woman had no idea what could befall her. "I guess you'd better."

Letting out a long sigh, he came to his feet, then stretched his back and rolled his shoulders before picking up his rifle.

"I'll be right back." He walked away, then looked back. "I'll be glad when tomorrow afternoon comes."

"Me too."

Melancholy washed over her. She was apprehensive about the next day. Every time she thought of it, her old defense mechanisms kicked in. Dakota hadn't said anything, but a disconnection lay between them.

~ * ~

"Elizabeth?" Dakota studied the woman's form in the dark.

She didn't move.

"Elizabeth. It's time to get back to the fire. It's not a good idea for you to stay out here alone."

She turned and faced him, eyes a puffy red, her cheeks shiny patches in the starlight.

He hesitated. "Are you all right?"

She brought her hand up to her cheek, and a sob broke free. "No."

He waited, not approaching her. "Then come back to the fire. Perhaps Caitlyn can offer some assistance."

"Only you can help me, Dakota. Not Caitlyn. She wouldn't understand."

"She understands more than you think. She's a good listener."

Taking a step towards him, she held out her hand to him. "Do you think she would understand if I told her I love you?"

He took a deep breath, held it briefly, and then let it out. "Let's go back to the fire. It's been an exhausting ride today. Get a good night's rest, and you'll feel better in the morning."

"No, I won't. You said that once before, and I didn't feel better then. I won't tomorrow. I love you."

Dakota sighed in weariness. "No, you don't. You don't even know me."

"I do know you. I know what you need, and I can provide it."

He thought of Caitlyn and his dream. Caitlyn, whom he wanted, who he needed, and yet, he couldn't have her. "No, you don't, and you can't."

Closing the distance between them, she put her hand on his cheek. "I do love you, Dakota, and I want you. I know you want me. You love me. I know you do."

He pulled away from her hand. "I don't love you, Elizabeth." To make it as straightforward as possible to her, he added, "I love Caitlyn. I always have, and I always will." He took a few steps back from her.

"If only I'd killed her," Elizabeth sneered. "If only that bullet hadn't—" She clamped her mouth shut.

But it was too late, her confession lit a fury in Dakota he couldn't nor wanted to contain.

"So, you were the one who shot me. I never could make sense of where that bullet came from. You were aiming for Caitlyn and shot me in the back?" He roughly grabbed her chin. His words hissed through clenched teeth with all the venom of a rattler preparing to strike. "I've never threatened a woman in my life, but then I've never met a woman like you. I have coddled you. I've made excuses for you, and I've given you the benefit of the doubt when I obviously shouldn't have."

"Please stop, you're hurting me."

He didn't release his steel grip.

"I don't give a damn," he continued. "You ought to be glad I don't do a hell of a lot more. I don't know what your problem is, lady, but I'm gonna fix it. If you ever mention Caitlyn's name again, I guarantee you, it will be the last word you ever utter. You stay away from her. You stay away from Joshua. You understand me?" He shook her chin then dropped his hand, repulsed at the touch of her. He headed back to the campfire. "Stay out here all damn night if you want."

"How dare you threaten me?" Elizabeth ran after him and grasped a handful of leather in each hand; she yanked him around to face her. She drew back her fist.

His hand caught hers inches from his cheek. "I've never struck a lady before, but you sure as hell are no lady." He shrugged out of her grip and stomped back to the campfire.

"What happened, Dakota?" Caitlyn rose as he approached, grasping his arm. "What's wrong?" She glanced over his shoulder.

Dakota rolled his shoulders twice, trying to dislodge the unspent anger and disgust he held for Elizabeth Cookman. Draping an arm around Caitlyn's shoulders, he pulled her to him. What could he tell her? He didn't understand it himself. "I want you to stay away from Elizabeth and keep Joshua away from her, too."

"Why? What happened out there?" Caitlyn drew away from him and scanned the darkness, then brought her attention back to him.

He refused to meet her eyes. She shifted, and he released her. It was better this way. As much as he longed to hold her, it was better for the space between them.

He'd have that much less distance to go when he left. "Elizabeth's not your friend. Maybe she never was."

Caitlyn frowned at him. "Whatever you say, Dakota."

Raw pain and disbelief filled her face, and she was too tired to hide it. He hesitated. Again, he had brought her heartache. He wanted to promise he would always be there for her and Joshua, and she could depend on him, but it would be an empty promise.

The best thing would be to get her home, then protect her and Joshua by turning himself in to the authorities. No bounty, no bounty hunters. Simple as that. He twisted away from her as if he hadn't a care in the world, and walked in the opposite direction from Elizabeth. He needed the dark, the solitude, but he wouldn't let Caitie or Joshua out of his sight.

Dakota was doing the right thing. He dropped his head in defeat. But hell—just as the sun set in the west, Caitlyn would disagree. Worse, she would feel betrayed because he hadn't told her his intentions. He could console himself by saying he hadn't had the opportunity, but that would be a lie. The reality was he was too much of a coward to tell her, and that rattled him more than the open end of a gun ever had. He was doing the right thing, but he had done it all wrong.

~ * ~

Morning came and relieved Caitlyn of the ominous task of staring into the darkness. The growing ache in her chest hadn't subsided. Where was the defensive wall she'd built so long ago and now needed? Rubbing her brow, she tried to dislodge her thoughts, but they remained. She glanced around searching for Dakota, but he was nowhere in sight, though he wouldn't be far.

Elizabeth lay on the outside of camp. Sometime during the night, she had returned.

When Joshua roused for the morning, Caitlyn went about the daily ritual she had adopted for his sake—a breakfast of soft biscuit and cereal, mixed with a bit of water from her canteen. The simple chore of caring for her son brought back the equilibrium she needed.

Eventually, Elizabeth woke up and walked a short distance away from the camp. After several minutes, she came back, sat down next to the fire, and poured herself a cup of coffee. Neither spoke. Even Joshua kept close to his mother and didn't venture out.

"Since everyone's up, we might as well head out." Dakota's tone was light, but his gaze darkened when he glanced at Elizabeth.

"We're ready," Caitlyn replied for herself and Joshua.

"Mrs. Cookman?"

"I have what I need. The rest I'd rather leave here in this God-for-saken place."

"Suit yourself." He picked up the two bedrolls Caitlyn packed. "You got everything in here?"

She nodded. "The one on the right is yours." Her own words startled her. She had packed Joshua's and her things in one blanket and Dakota's in the other. Had her own soul betrayed her?

Unaware of her inner turmoil, he tied them to their horses, not bothering to assist Elizabeth. She and Dakota rode side by side, Elizabeth tagging along behind.

Around noon, they arrived at Elizabeth's home. A houseful of servants flooded out the door to greet her. Dismounting, she meandered up the front walk as if she had been on a social call. A groom hurried to her horse, leading it away as her personal maid fussed over her and helped her onto the porch. She twirled and gazed back at Dakota.

He maneuvered his horse and moved alongside Caitlyn. "Let's go."

Caitlyn glanced at him, then at Elizabeth.

"Please come to tea on Sunday, Caitlyn. I'll have tea cakes made for Joshua." Elizabeth's face was a mask of propriety.

Without replying, Caitlyn stared at the woman she thought she once knew.

"Come on, Cat." Dakota blocked her view with his horse. "There's nothing you can do. She'll come around."

~ * ~

Caitlyn's home was the way she had left it, the windows broken, the chairs upside down, and the table on its side. Her gaze trailed to the wall where Wakefield had stuck his note. The gouged mark was clearly visible, and she remembered how she felt when she pulled the knife free and read the brief message. A bit as she did now.

Dakota stepped in behind her, holding Joshua. Heaving the large oak dining table upright, he pushed the chairs underneath it, then placed his rifle on the table and shrugged out of his coat. "I'll repair the window and whatever else needs fixing."

"Thanks, Dakota."

"Anything for you, my love."

Was that an avowal of his love or a thoughtless endearment? A smile lay upon his lips, drawing her inexpressibly to him. She wanted to kiss him, to taste the warmth that would be there, but something warned her not to.

"Feels like a long time ago, doesn't it?" She surveyed the room, the absence of her father another cruel reminder of what she had lost.

"Yeah, it does, but you're home now. Everything will right itself." Dakota closed his eyes and took a step away from her.

"What would you like for dinner?" she asked, sitting Joshua on a chair and cleaning the area around him.

"Why don't you let me worry about that? I'll surprise you." Picking up his rifle, he headed for the door.

She laughed. "No rabbits, all right?"

"How about bear?" His eyes twinkled at her.

"A bit over-confident, aren't you?"

"Just trying to impress you, ma'am." He strode back to her and covered her lips with his. Caressing her cheek with his thumb, he drew back and gazed down at her. He closed his eyes and took a deep breath. "I won't be gone long."

~ * ~

By the time Dakota returned, the house gleamed spotless, and Caitlyn had built a fire. The coffee was hot, and the vegetables roasted. She had bathed and refreshed herself.

He stared at her as he came through the door. She wore a deep coral dress that highlighted the copper tones in her hair. She resembled a mythical being of purity as she bent to tuck Joshua into his bed, his body relaxed in sleep and peace. Dakota's senses reeled, and his heart hammered in his chest.

Tonight was all they had left. She didn't know that, but he did. Guilt washed over him. He should tell her his plans. He should give her a chance to ask him to leave now...tonight, before he complicated the situation more, but what he should do and what he could do were complete opposites.

"Caitie?"

Turning, she answered the question he hadn't realized he had asked.

His hands were rough with a yearning he couldn't stay. He grasped her face and kissed her with a need he couldn't control.

He was home, at least for the night.

~ * ~

Morning was still an hour away when Caitlyn woke. The fire's light danced upon the walls. Shifting her head to the side, she listened to Dakota's soft breathing. His arm lay heavy but comfortably across her chest. His hair draped across her face, the scent of him warm and heady.

His eyes opened, and his smile greeted hers. Lifting onto one elbow, he pushed her hair from her face and traced a warm line down her nose to her lips, where his gaze lingered for a moment. "Are you still hungry?"

"Ravenous."

"Help me drag the bear in, and we can eat." He twirled a lock of her hair around his finger.

She laughed. "You do like to flatter yourself, don't you?"

"What?" Mock disbelief shone in his eyes. "You don't believe I brought home a bear?"

"Not really. A bear around here?"

"Uh-oh. You aren't missing a large, cumbersome neighbor, are you?"

She laughed and punched him lightly on his shoulder.

He leaned over her. "You and Josh are my life. You'll remember that, won't you?"

Her heart beat harder, and she frowned. "And you mine. We're going to have a good life together. We'll be a family now."

He faced away and sat on the edge of the bed.

"What is it?" When he didn't answer, she reached out for him. "Dakota? Answer me."

"What it has always been, Caitlyn." Despair and pain laced his words.

She released her hold, and he rose. The air chilled around her, and she gathered the covers about her for protection.

"I'll make us breakfast. Joshua will be up soon." Pulling on his jeans, he fastened his gun belt around his hips.

"I'm not hungry," she said.

He was about to say something, but changed his mind and walked out of the room. Joshua woke and started crying.

She sat on the bed, frozen with fear. Her life was unraveling, and she had no idea where it had started and, worse, how to stop it. Throwing back the covers, she dressed and then ran into the small room where Joshua slept. She covered him with a blanket and patted his back.

"Momma will be right back, sweetie." She handed him a small wooden toy Henry had given him and hurried out into the main room.

Dakota was nowhere in sight. She raced to the window. Outside, he stood next to the small corral, saddle in hand.

Her heart slammed in her chest. Total disbelief rolled through her, then she noticed the rider coming in from the east at a gallop. She rushed to the door.

"Stay in the house." Dakota grabbed the rifle leaning against the corral fence, cocked it, then waited for the rider to approach.

Running back to the bedside table, she removed the handgun she kept there and stepped out onto the porch.

The man on horseback hardly appeared menacing. If anything, he seemed as though he might topple from his mount. Abruptly, he drew in his horse as if he had been asleep at the reins and came to a complete halt.

Dakota uncocked his rifle.

"Dakota Cabe?" The man's horse stepped sideways in exhaustion.

"Who wants to know?"

"Got a message for him from Judd Williams. Mr. Williams told me not to stop until I delivered it to Mr. Cabe. So, I'm hoping you're him."

Stepping closer to the man, Dakota grabbed the horse's bit. "I am."

The rider reached into his vest pocket and retrieved a folded pack of papers. "Then these are for you."

Caitlyn stepped off the porch and headed toward the reason for her life's undoing. If possible, she would stop it in its tracks. She grasped Dakota's sleeve. "What does he want?"

He scanned the message, folded it, then placed it in his pocket before facing her. "It's all right. It's what I hoped for." Yet his expression told a different story. "We've got to talk, Caitie."

She refrained from asking any questions in front of the stranger. Instead, she went into the house and prepared something for the man to eat while Dakota cared for the lathered horse. Already the color was draining from her world, and there wasn't a damn thing she could do about it.

After a brief meal, the messenger remounted. "Thank you for your hospitality, Mrs. Cabe." The man nodded his hat in her direction.

Mrs. Cabe. An unintentional mistake, but still salt to an open wound.

"You're welcome to stay the night and rest," Dakota offered.

"No. I can't, but thanks."

Her stomach had been rolling back and forth ever since she saw the rider, so she was relieved when the man nudged his horse and rode off. "All right, Dakota, talk."

"Where's Joshua?"

"He's taking a nap. The trip wore him out. Quit stalling and talk."

Leading her to the porch steps, he motioned for her to sit. "Caitlyn, I need you to understand why I'm doing this."

Caitlyn sat and clutched the wood railing. Whatever he told her had already been mulled over and decided. She was simply to be informed. "What are you doing?"

"When we were at Henry's, the day I went into town, I sent a telegraph to Judd Williams, an attorney I knew long ago. I asked him if there was any way to clear my name."

"Dakota, you've been down this route."

"Hear me out, Cat. There are things you don't know."

She grew sick with trepidation.

"Judd said he'd find out and get back to me. He did." Dakota removed the papers from his shirt pocket. "I think it would make more sense if you read these."

He held out the papers. She didn't want to touch them, let alone read them. A sense of stagnating loss overwhelmed her, and this letter was the reason.

"Please, Caitlyn." He pushed the papers toward her.

She took them and read.

Dakota, I have what I hope will be good news. I sent a proposal to the government to procure amnesty for you. As lawlessness in the West escalates each day, the government is willing to consider my proposal. They have agreed to offer you full amnesty under the following criteria:

1. You become part of a government task force committed to restoring order in the West for one year.

2. You sign a document stating your full committed intention and devoted cooperation to the government in these activities. And you agree to forsake any and all acquaintances you may have among the outlaws the government is sworn to apprehend.

3. If you should abandon your duties to or commit any affront to the government, and/or its specialized teams, you will be subjected to the same law and punishment you now face.

4. At the end of your year of deployment, you will be given the option to act as sheriff in a select number of towns now seeking a law official.

Dakota, since you have ridden with the worst outlaws now residing on the western frontier, your knowledge of their habits and local hangouts is indispensable to the government. The very fact that you were able to get into Devil's Canyon and outwit John Wakefield was an excellent incentive for the authorities to agree to this.

I have convinced the Governor that your expertise would be of more value to the territory than hanging you or the additional expense of housing you in prison.

That said, this is a dangerous proposition. I wish it were less risky, but there isn't a better man suited for this type of work.

It would give you clemency and a new start. Either tell my man your decision or send me a telegraph as soon as possible.

Best regards, Judd

Caitlyn stared at the paper long after she finished reading it. The rider was gone, so, "Are you going to telegraph him?"

"No." Dakota rolled to his feet and walked to his horse.

Well, he told the rider his decision. Spellbound, she watched him gather his saddle from the fence and heave it onto Caitie's back.

"Dakota." Caitlyn rubbed the ache from her eyebrows. "You're not thinking of leaving."

"I don't want to but—"

"Stay. We'll move on. We'll change our names, whatever, don't do this." The fact she begged him didn't bother her as much as the thought of his leaving did.

"Caitie, I've made up my mind. I'm going. I love you and Joshua, but I can't stay, knowing I endanger both of you. I have to make things right."

"You tried that, Dakota. It didn't work."

"This time it will. It's a far better gamble than just turning myself in to hang. If I do this, Caitlyn, there will be no bounty on my head. No bounty hunters coming after you or Joshua." He tightened the saddle cinch.

"Please. I'm asking you not to go."

"The sooner I leave, the sooner I'll be back."

"This is too dangerous, even for you, Dakota. What do you hope to accomplish?"

"To get clemency and to be in a position to provide for my family." He bowed his head. "Caitlyn, you have to know that not doing anything would be a bigger mistake. I'm not that kind of man."

"And just what kind of man will you be when you are dead? You talk about providing for us, yet—"

"I'm sorry, Caitlyn. The decision's made. Please don't make this harder than it has to be."

Anger rose through the pain. "What about Joshua? He needs his father."

"No. Joshua needs a man he can respect, not a wanted outlaw."

She grasped his sleeve and tried to make him face her. Roughly, he jerked his arm free. His action astounded her as if he had struck her with the full force of his hand. Speechless, she stepped away from him.

Dakota threw himself into the saddle, and the familiarity of the scene paralyzed her. She relived the horror of two years past with no escape. Her mind no longer functioned. The tears ceased, and her heart crystallized into ice.

He stared down at her. "I plan on coming back, Caitlyn. This isn't like the last time. I will be back." Bringing the reins up to keep his horse steady, his steel gray eyes bore into hers. "I love you. Have faith in me."

He kicked his horse into a run, and they bolted out into the morning air—bitter pain draped over her like a well-worn slicker.

Chapter 23

T he months slipped away with brutal slowness as if time itself was ending. Caitlyn and Joshua settled into a routine that suited both of them. Eventually, her son stopped asking when that man would come back. She hadn't told him that man was his father. It seemed easier not to, and in the end, proved to be the right choice.

Cool weather seeped in at the end of October, so she gave up her nightly watch from the front porch. Winter marched in, and she closed the window of her bedroom. She no longer hoped or longed for the sound of an approaching horse.

When Christmas drew near, she invested each evening in the creation of dresses that the more gallant townswomen ordered from her. Her needlework was indeed flawless, but Elizabeth's constant gossip soon morphed into scandalous tales and took its toll. Few proper women wanted to associate with a woman with the reputation Elizabeth had created for her. Caitlyn sighed. She didn't care, but it would soon affect Joshua.

That night when the clock struck midnight, she put aside her work and brought out the quilt she had started the day Dakota left. A project of her heart, it was meticulous work. Her best work yet. She had cursed it and even threatened to burn it a time or two, but she wouldn't. It partially filled the space within which nothing else could.

When the candle burned out, she rose and lit another one. Pieces of Dakota's old shirt lay tousled about her feet, a painful reminder of the man who hadn't come back.

Sighing, she glanced at her bedroom. Joshua slept despite the storm brewing outside the door. She turned, sat back down, and examined the quilt once more. The wedding circle of Indian paintbrushes around the brilliant blue stars resting in each corner had been difficult but worth the effort.

At the top, among all the other stars, she placed The Little Dipper. She'd laughed with sadness when the thought occurred to her to put it where she would always find it. At the quilt's bottom, underneath the stars, she stitched the forget-me-nots, which seemed to say it all. A single solitary tear trickled down her cheek, and she let it be.

Weary, she dropped the quilt to the floor and leaned her head back against the rocker. She eased the chair into a smooth, steady gait as the whistling wind outside her door mounted in intensity. It swirled around her small cabin, and she was thankful she and Joshua had a warm place to nestle down on such a night.

In time, she and Joshua would have to move on, away from Elizabeth and the gossip the woman fueled. However, tonight they were safe and content. The fire across the room snapped and hissed in defiance against the bitter, impersonal world that roared around them. She closed her eyes, and in comfort, she slept.

~ * ~

A breath of icy air swept light across her cheek, and her eyes snapped open. The candle had burned out and, except for the fire's fading glow, she sat in darkness. How long had she slept? Long enough for the fire to die out. A sigh of irritation slipped through her lips.

Complete silence, and not even the wind howled. Her heart raced. Something was amiss. Fear crawled up her spine and burned a hot swatch of fire to her neck. She squinted through the poorly lit room, seeking the cause of her alarm. A slight chill remained in the room as if a window or door had been opened.

She hadn't left a window open, yet an escalating foreboding told her she wasn't alone. Her rifle and revolver by the door, she lowered her hand to the wicker basket beside her, her fingers brushed aside needles and thread as she sought the small pistol she always kept there. Icy steel rolled up into her palm. She withdrew her hand and pressed the gun into the folds of her skirt to muffle the sound as she drew back the hammer.

Why had Dakota insisted on leaving them? Her thoughts careened through her mind in reckless patterns. Fear tumbled into a rage and became the final blow to the last fifteen months of agony. She wanted to hate him, to blame him for this moment, but she suffered the same constant longing for him that always tore at her heart. She loved him; she always would.

Damn him to Hades and back.

Another lonesome tear emerged, and she squeezed it off. Infuriated at herself and whoever else was in the room, she pushed to her feet, spun around, then leveled the gun at what she hoped was her intruder. It was.

The shadowy silhouette in the corner of the room was so still, she could have mistaken him for a piece of furniture. Her gaze burned through the darkness at the man who had been watching her for some time. Tall, broad-shouldered, and heavily armed. Her small derringer insignificant even at this close range. Another bounty hunter seeking money? She wasn't surprised. She knew they would come.

"He isn't here." Her voice faltered, raspy and unsure. Damn you, Caitlyn, don't let your fear show. "And he's not coming back, so move on and go back to whatever hole you crawled out of."

The man's confident stance shifted. "I'd appreciate it if you didn't shoot me until I've said what I've come to say." His words were low, uncertain, and cautious as if he expected her to shoot him anyway.

She didn't move. She couldn't. Blinking twice, she hoped to wake from what could only be another nightmare. Her mouth was dry, her hand shaky.

"I see," the man said when she failed to lower her gun. "You do know I can draw and shoot before you can even pull the trigger." In slow motion, his hand dropped to his gun belt.

"You don't intimidate me." Her words were steady, merely a statement of fact.

"I never did." He dropped his belt on the chair beside him.

"Why are you here, Dakota? I thought you'd moved on when I didn't hear from you." Her gun stayed level with his chest.

"I couldn't contact you, Caitie. They thought I'd skip and run once I had my amnesty papers. I had to prove my loyalty by going up against a gang of outlaws. They stuck me in the middle to see which side I'd choose—the ones with better guns and more experience or the law." Dropping his coat onto her rocker, he waited. "I'm still alive. I came back as soon as I could."

No word from him or Judd? No explanation for his long disappearance until now? "So...you're just here to rest your horse and stock up?"

"I deserved that." He wrestled in his vest pocket for papers. "This explains why I couldn't contact you until now."

When she still didn't move, he took the derringer from her hand and replaced it with the papers. "Please, Caitlyn, give me a chance."

Dakota moved to the table, lit a candle, and brought it closer.

She unrolled the papers but kept staring at him.

Shifting from one foot to the other, he regarded the room as if searching for the right words, the necessary words. "Cat, I'm sorry. I didn't know how else to protect you and Joshua."

She glanced down at the papers and then back to him. His gaze held hers.

"If you would forgive me, I'd like to spend the rest of my life making it up to you. There's no more bounty. I'm a free man."

She shuffled through the papers. The words amnesty, government, secret service, official pardon, and work for hire were written on several pages.

"What does all this mean?" It was too much information to take in at one time.

"It means we can try again. We can start over."

Caitlyn stared at the pages, then at Dakota. No, she couldn't be hurt again. She didn't have it in her to go that route again. "No."

"Caitlyn, I'm doing this poorly." Grunting, he mumbled, "You'd think traveling non-stop for the last two days, I would have ridden across the right words to say to you, but I haven't."

He closed his eyes and took a deep breath. "Let me try again. When I'm finished, if you still want me gone, I'll give you back your gun, and you can shoot me. And that will be the end of it." He rolled his head in disgust. "Hell, if I screw this up anymore, I'll shoot myself and save you the ammunition."

Caitlyn sighed. "You make it hard for a girl to resist you, Dakota," she said, her words glib but soft.

As if realizing he was still wearing his hat, he jerked it off and held it in his hands.

"Now that I am an honest man, I want to make an honest woman out of you." He gritted his teeth. "Shit, I didn't mean that the way it sounded." He paused. "I want to ask you if you would marry me. If you'd have me—you know—in wedlock." He winced. "Wedlock sounds brutal. That's not the right word either. Ah, matrimony-like." He paused again, then muttered a soft damn under his breath.

She started to laugh, but the moment was wrong. Could this be Dakota Cabe proposing marriage and sounding like a schoolboy? He was right.

He was doing it poorly. "So, what's in it for me, Dakota? I have a son to consider."

Her short response seemed to startle him. "Never took you for a bargaining woman, Caitlyn, but what I have is yours." His lips thinned for a moment, then he added, "I guess I don't have much except a few guns, a good horse, and well...myself."

The last words spoken were like a weak bargaining tool, and perhaps better not mentioned.

"All that, huh? Damn, Dakota, you make it downright impossible to refuse you."

He waited, and she saw the pain of a man who had lost more than he had ever possessed.

"I'll take the latter."

Puzzled, he studied her.

"I already have a good horse and my own guns, but a good man is damn hard to find." With that, she stepped forward and kissed the man of her dreams.

Acknowledgments

To Mike for always being my hero. Thank you for running up and down the stairs with edits in hand.

Jes and Dakota, who show me daily what faith and determination actually mean.

My big bro, Bruce, whose creativity inspired my own.

Suzanne Purvis for her endless energy, constant encouragement, and candid advice.

Rosalind Cesen for her faith in my writing from the very first draft, years ago, to this one.

And Shannon for walking my backyard.

About the Author

Caren Gallimore, despite being born 133 years too late, lives in the beautiful Blue Ridge Mountains.

Her love for the Wild West began during a Girl Scout camp at an old Pony Express station in Utah. Her characters tend to write their own stories, and Caren is grateful to be asked to record them. She would prefer to do this during the day, with a cup of coffee in hand, rather than in the middle of the night or while in the shower. But her characters follow their own timetable. Caren doesn't always agree with her characters' decisions, but it all works out in the end.

Her passions beyond her family are writing fiction and non-fiction, screen printing, long walks in the woods with her pup, and illustrating life as she sees it.

Twice a year, she travels south to the ocean and communicates with the mermaids who have their own stories to tell.

~ * ~

We hope you enjoyed *Wanted*. If you did, please write a review, tell your friends, or check out the other offerings from Caren at CarenGallimore .com.